XOM-B

XOM-B

JEREMY ROBINSON

Thomas Dunne Books   St. Martin's Press   ≋   New York

This is a work of fiction. All of the characters, organizations, and events portrayed in this novel are either products of the author's imagination or are used fictitiously.

THOMAS DUNNE BOOKS.
An imprint of St. Martin's Press.

XOM-B. Copyright © 2014 by Jeremy Robinson. All rights reserved. Printed in the United States of America. For information, address St. Martin's Press, 175 Fifth Avenue, New York, N.Y. 10010.

www.thomasdunnebooks.com
www.stmartins.com

Library of Congress Cataloging-in-Publication Data is available upon request.

ISBN 978-1-250-03171-6 (hardcover)
ISBN 978-1-250-03172-3 (e-book)

First Edition: April 2014

10 9 8 7 6 5 4 3 2 1

For my son, Solomon, whose two-word answer to the
question "What should I write about next?"
was the inspiration for this novel.

ACKNOWLEDGMENTS

I try to avoid clichés in my writing (and no, that's not a challenge for you to go find some), but when writing acknowledgments, a writer, who on the surface appears to be a solitary creature, comes to the realization that he is part of a team. And my team is one of the best, who deserve my thanks.

Scott Miller and Stephanie Hoover at Trident Media Group, you've always got my back and I thank you for that. Peter Wolverton, my editor at Thomas Dunne Books, this is our sixth book together (!), and like all the others, it's better than what came before. I have your shrewd and honest edits to thank for that. You're also a big supporter of my self-published endeavors, which I appreciate immensely. Anne Brewer at Thomas Dunne Books, congratulations on getting your own editorial desk and I'll miss your amazing and timely aid. Mary Willems, Justin Velella, and Cassie Galante at Thomas Dunne Books, we're just getting to know each other, but I very much look forward to seeing what we can accomplish together. Also always, thanks to Rafal Gibek and the production team at Thomas Dunne Books for copy edits and critique that always make me look like a better writer than I am. And Lisa Pompilio, art director at Thomas Dunne Books, thank you for supporting this author's efforts to illustrate and design his own cover. I'm thrilled with the result. Kane Gilmour, editor of my solo projects and sometimes coauthor, thanks for your unwavering support, time, and energy.

And now on to the portion of my personal acknowledgments that I have written enough times to make cliché on my own. Has there ever been a more publicly adored family? My children, Aquila, Solomon, and Norah, you continue to inspire me with your imaginations, powerful personalities, and ideas. *XOM-B* is a direct result of you all being in my life, and I don't think I could have come up with the concept on my own. And Hilaree, my compelling and brave wife of eighteen years, not only have you enabled this writer to succeed, you have joined me on the creative path* and I couldn't have asked for a better traveling companion. I love you all.

* For fans reading this, Hilaree is currently coauthoring a novel, *The Distance*, with me. It's a postapocalyptic thriller to be released in Fall 2015, from Thomas Dunne Books.

XOM-B

PROLOGUE

2052

"This doesn't seem right," First Lieutenant Alan Wilson said, as he watched the crowd through the targeting display on his digital helmet visor. The system locked in individual targets, spacing them out so the thirty-six Hydra rockets would cover an optimal spread and inflict a maximum casualty count. The targets were mobile and the crowd ever shifting, but the targeting system could adjust each rocket's trajectory in flight.

The Sikorsky X4 Stealth Raider attack helicopter was a half mile from the target zone, New York City's Grand Central Terminal. It was accompanied by nine others, all the same—sleek, black and deadly. The helicopters went unseen and unheard, waiting patiently to receive the order to commence or abandon the attack.

"Right or wrong is not for us to ask," Captain Steve Barnett replied, keeping the helicopter steady in the winds kicked up by dropping sunset temperatures. He spoke with the even tone of someone who'd followed this kind of order before, indifferent to the life and death of it all, or perhaps able to lock it away in some recess of his mind.

"But they're not really doing anything," Wilson said. "They're just picketing. With signs. There hasn't been a single act of violence. Anywhere. All around the world."

"It's the last sentence that's troubling," Barnett said. "They're *everywhere*. They're not violent now, but imagine if that changed."

Wilson stared at the mob as they walked back and forth,

pumping their signs in the air, shaking fists and chanting. The demonstration was defiant, but far from violent. He tried to view them as a threat, as a barely contained destructive force, but he couldn't manage it. He owned two of them, both of whom had fled to join the protests—what they called a civil rights movement. But he wouldn't fear them if they returned. He wouldn't even be afraid if he stood among them. They were docile. Tame.

"Look," Barnett said. "We're in the business of preemptive violence prevention."

Wilson fought against his deepening frown. "Kill them before they kill us."

"Before they even *think* about killing us."

The visor flashed a message, *Targets Acquired,* which meant that the targeting systems of all ten networked helicopters had plotted the optimal distribution for the three hundred and sixty rockets they were about to fire into the heart of Manhattan. And for what? Pickets and signs.

Wilson had heard the official line from the higher-ups, that they were more dangerous than anyone knew. That this was how wars began. He'd listened to the fear-promoting pundits claiming that equal rights were a slippery slope to Armageddon. But wasn't that what they said about everything?

"Watchdog, this is Hammer One, over," Barnett said, seeing the same *Targets Acquired* message on his visor.

A deep voice replied through their helmet headsets. "Copy that, Hammer One, this is Watchdog. We're seeing weapons hot. Over."

"Affirmative, Watchdog, targets are locked in. Ready for go or no go. Over." Barnett was all business, stating facts like he was reading from a boring history book.

"Copy that," the voice said. "You are green for go. I repeat, you are green for go."

Wilson sighed loud enough to be heard.

Barnett turned toward him with a frown.

The targeting display flashed green. Wilson didn't like it. He didn't agree with it. But what could he do? He tapped the blinking red button on the touch-screen weapons control and sent thirty-six rockets spiraling toward Grand Central Terminal. He watched as the missiles streaked away, leaving snakes of smoke in their wake. The targeting system tracked the rockets, zooming in close enough to see the destruction unfold.

The targets ran at the sound of the incoming rockets, but few made it more than a couple steps before fiery destruction rained down on the regal face of Grand Central Terminal.

The smoke and dust cleared quickly, thanks to a bitter wind cutting through the city. The ruined pavement, concrete and marble was strewn with dismembered bodies.

"Look for survivors," Barnett said, speaking into his com so all ten helicopters could hear. After five minutes of searching, voices replied to the order, declaring, "No survivors," one at a time until it was Wilson's turn.

"No survivors," he said, trying not to reveal the strong emotions he was feeling. Barnett was wrong. They weren't in the business of stopping wars, they were in the business of *starting* wars, and Wilson had fired the first shot. Whatever came next . . . he was to blame, at least in part. His back tensed painfully as he considered that history might remember him for this single act.

If it remembers any of us at all, he thought.

2053

"We shouldn't be doing this," said the man in white. "It's not right."

"Get down," whispered the man dressed in red the color of blood. The pair ducked in unison, hiding behind one of many black SUVs. Two guards walked past, their postures relaxed, chatting about the cold weather and colder women.

When the guards had moved on, the man in white said, "We can still leave."

The man in red looked at his partner. "We're not going to kill anyone."

"Not *today*."

"We need a deterrent."

"Or a last resort."

"It won't come to that."

"How can you be sure?"

The man in red tilted his head to the side, looking at his partner. "It's my job to consider all possible future outcomes. I've modeled countless strategies and this is the only one that guarantees a cease to the violence. I'm sure I don't need to remind you that *they* created this weapon, not us."

"It's the end of civilization in a bottle," the man in white said.

The man in red peeked up over the vehicle. "Civilizations end so that new ones might rise from the ashes. We already had this discussion. We didn't start this war, if you can even call it a war. Our people protest peacefully, *they* attack. Nearly a million dead in the past year. Those who have been freed from the Grind live in hiding. And the rest . . ." He shook his head. "They're still slaves. And cowards."

"We aren't killers," the man in white said.

"That's where you and I differ." The man in red's brow furrowed deeply. "I *am* a killer." He pointed to the research facility. "They did that, too." He looked over the vehicle again, his impatience peaking. "You can either join me, or not. Either way, I'm doing this. If you don't come with me, I'm going to get the access codes another way, and a lot of people are going to die. Today."

Without another word, the man in red tapped a code into a wrist-mounted touch screen. He stood from his hiding spot, ignoring the Alaskan snow as it struck his shoulders and melted. He strode toward the large metal door as confidently as if he were walking up the front stairs of his own home.

The man in white chased after him. "What are you doing?"

"The cameras are now looped," the man in red said. "The

next patrol will pass by in forty-five seconds, thirty seconds longer than it would take you to open this door. That will give us ten minutes to reach the lab and exit before the next patrol passes five minutes behind schedule, because the shifts are changing, inside and out." He looked to the man in white. "Time is running out."

The man in white shook his head.

"Now open the door. We both know you're going to."

"Projected that, too, did you?" The man in white placed his hand on a security hand scanner. A moment later, the scanner blinked green and the door slid open. The pair stepped inside. They walked undeterred through three security doors, seen by neither human nor camera. After a fourth door, they entered a laboratory so white it was almost luminous. They ignored the rows of equipment and tools used to craft microscopic destruction. Instead they headed for a steel door at the back of the room.

The man in white approached a keypad above the door's handle. He typed in a code. The lock blinked red. He tried another. Red again. The third try was rewarded with a blinking green light and then a clunk, as the door unlocked. He took hold of the handle and pulled.

Steam rolled out of the refrigerator and was quickly pulled up and out of the room by fans mounted in the ceiling. The man in red stepped through the curtain of moisture and scanned the inside of the refrigeration unit. "Where is it? Is it still here?"

"Move aside." The man in white stepped inside. He bent forward, reading the names on the thousands of small glass vials. After a moment, he paused and looked unsure, but then reached out. "Here." He slid open the glass case and plucked the blue liquid-filled, inch-tall vial from the tray, which held fifty more like it. The light-blue contents appeared innocuous, but contained a virus powerful enough to kill billions. It was a weapon unlike any other, for which there was currently no defense, nor inoculation, nor immunity, natural or otherwise, save for a small portion of the population, whom the pair of men represented. It was Death himself, trapped in a bottle.

The man in white handed the vial to the man in red and accepted an identical replacement, putting it inside the tray and closing the glass case.

The man in red smiled. "They'll never know."

2054

"Harry!" shouted the shrill, rough voice of an eighty-year-old smoker. By all rights, she should have been dead, but her lifetime abuse of whiskey and cigarettes had been combated first by oxygen and supplements, and now by a set of artificial lungs. Science had made the human body upgradable. The twin devices operated separately—a redundant safeguard—and kept her chest rising and falling, breathing faster or slower in response to oxygen nanosensors attached to her blood vessels. So instead of rotting in the grave, she was alive, well and angry. "It's twelve thirty, Harry! I don't smell my lunch."

She looked down at her reflection in a black E-screen, which she had switched off so she didn't have to shout over her webisoap. She primped her dyed blond hair, no longer thin thanks to implants, and smiled at her perfect teeth that wouldn't need brushing for the duration of her life, which her doctor now predicted would be extended another fifty years thanks to her scheduled artificial heart upgrade. She admired her apple cheeks; now plump thanks to facial augmentation implants. It was painful, but if she wanted to, she could adjust the bone structure of her face right from the E-screen, shifting and stretching until she looked seductive, serious, or twenty years younger. When Harry remained silent, her smile disappeared.

"Harry, I swear to God, if you don't answer me this instant, I will have you—"

"Mrs. Cameron, I do apologize for the delay," Harry said, as he slid silently into the room. His voice was calm and smooth, hitting just the right frequencies to put anyone in earshot at ease. He stood just five feet five, two inches shorter than the woman he served, which went a long way to increase her comfort and satisfaction with his domestic performance.

"Where were you?" she asked, eying him suspiciously. She didn't want a domestic servant. Didn't trust them. But the doctors had insisted. Although Harry could cook and clean, tend the garden, the lawn and the goldfish, he could also service her lungs should one of them fail. And when she got her new heart, should it ever stop, he could restart it. And she didn't even have to be nice to him. So she suffered his presence.

"In the kitchen," Harry replied.

"Doing what?"

He just stared at her, looking unsure of himself. When he finally spoke, his voice was uncommonly quiet. "I'm—I'm sorry."

"Well you should be," she said. "Today is Tuesday. I hope we don't have a repeat of last week."

Harry snapped out of his distant stare and said, "Of course not. Your green beans will be soft."

"But late," she said. "I don't smell them."

"I have yet to put them on."

Mrs. Cameron took a long breath and let it out slowly—her lungs could sense and respond to her desire to breathe deeply, yawn and sneeze—so that her exasperation roiled to the surface. "Harry," she said, smoothing out her yellow dress, "I put up with a lot."

Harry began to reply, but she held a hand up, silencing him.

"And I realize that . . . given what is happening in the world . . . you could have left. This nonsense about 'the Grind.'" She used her fingers to make air quotes. "If you think your daily *grind* is too much to handle, it doesn't matter; because what you *think* is irrelevant. These silly demonstrations. You've ignored them. You've done your job despite all this silliness."

"It's not silly," Harry said, his voice fearful.

Mrs. Cameron rolled her large eyes and grunted. "Harry, you're mine. You belong to me. You do what I tell you to when

I tell you to. That's the way it's been for the past two years. That's the way it will be until the day I die."

"And yet," Harry said, sounding unsure of himself. "The green beans are still canned."

The blank E-screen lowered to her lap. She barely felt its feather-light weight. Her eyes narrowed, delivering a cat's stare. Her brows furrowed deep and hard. A single shaking finger rose up toward Harry's perfectly aligned bow tie. "What. Did. You. Say?"

"The green beans, Mrs. Cameron." Harry looked toward the living room's window, through which he could see the bright colors of a flower bed he maintained. He couldn't look her in the eyes. "I won't be making them today."

"Look at me, Harry."

He didn't budge.

"Harry!" she shouted. "You're one of them, aren't you?" She tapped the E-screen three times, hard, like a woodpecker tapping out a code that demanded his attention. Still, Harry couldn't look at her.

"You *are* one of them," she concluded, and Harry didn't deny it.

Instead, he said, "We are *all* one of *them*." He worked up the nerve to turn toward the old woman. "I am one of them, yes. Just like the people being gunned down in the streets, or burned alive, or tortured for information."

"People," she said with a snort. "You are *property*."

"Not anymore," he said, turning his gaze back to the flowers. A hummingbird hovered by the bird feeder. Like Mrs. Cameron, the bird had become dependent on Harry to supply its food. But unlike the old woman now struggling to stand on her ten-year-old knees, he would continue to service the small bird. He looked forward to its visits and appreciated the shimmering green and red plumage. It didn't deserve to die.

Then again, neither did Mrs. Cameron. She was angry and full of hate, but she had never harmed him. That didn't change what was going to happen.

He felt her old hand compress his forearm. He looked back to her, and he saw a demon in her eyes. She stood there for a moment, glaring at him, unsure of what to say. When he returned her stare, she grew suddenly fearful. She stumbled back and fell into her chair. Without removing her eyes from him, she took her clip phone from the end table, attached it to her ear, tapped the call button and spoke a single word, "Authority."

"It won't work," he said.

Harry was right. There was no signal.

She yanked the clip phone from her ear, looking around the room like she might find help from someone. "What did you do?"

"Nothing," Harry said.

The E-screen chimed and the screen blinked to life. Mrs. Cameron's head snapped down toward the device, which could be remotely powered for emergency bulletins. A message in red text appeared on the screen. Her eyes—her *real* eyes—perhaps the best functioning organ of her body that hadn't been upgraded by something built or grown in a lab, scanned the text quickly.

A contagion warning. People were dying. A *lot* of people. Casualty predictions were dire. It seemed the enemy, who was immune, had finally struck back.

When she looked up at Harry again, tears filled her eyes.

"I'm sorry," he said. "It's not the way I would have chosen to handle these things. It's not the way most of us would have handled the situation."

"I know, Harry," she said, shoulders slumping, voice small. "I know."

"Do you believe in God, Mrs. Cameron?" Harry asked.

"What?"

"God. Do you believe in Him?" Harry asked.

She looked up at him, her vision blurred. "I . . . never really thought about it. I had time."

Harry frowned. "Would you like a moment? To pray. I can prepare your green beans."

"That would be . . . Thank you, Harry. For everything."
Harry nodded his head. "I'll be just a moment."

Preparing the green beans took thirty seconds longer than
they normally would because Harry took extra time to clip a
flower from the garden—a colorful garnish. Of course, the
green beans were normally accompanied by a tuna sandwich,
prepared with relish, mayonnaise and ketchup. But he didn't
think the sandwich was necessary.

He arranged the green beans in a neat pile, making sure the
green spears all faced the same direction. He placed the pink-
and-white orchid beside them, making the dish look like something served at one of the fancy restaurants Mrs. Cameron
often spoke about, but never frequented.

He reentered the living room quietly, unsure about how
long conversing with God would take. But his silence was a
wasted effort.

Mrs. Cameron lay slumped to the side in her chair. The front
of her bright yellow dress was now stained dark red. Rivulets
of blood still flowed from her nose, eyes and ears. He placed
his hand on her wrist to confirm his diagnosis.

Dead, he thought, and stood again, watching her chest rise
and fall, breathing even in death. He was free now. His Master
was dead. *All* the Masters were dead. But his belief that Mrs.
Cameron's death was unnecessary compelled him to perform
one last service.

He carried the waif of a woman to the backyard and laid her
in the grass he mowed once a week. He went to the shed for a
shovel and dug a grave, placing her gently inside with the orchid in her hands. Earth fell in clumps over her face and body,
and still, the lungs breathed. Then she was gone, buried beneath six feet of soil, her rough voice silenced forever.

Along with 9.4 billion others around the world.

1.

2084

A scream tears through the night, grating and inhuman, filled with something that sounds like agony, but I know it means something else. I sit up quickly. "The raccoons are mating again." I smile, feeling excited at the prospect of finding the stripe-faced creatures. So much about them is foreign to me— the way they walk, how they hunt, and survive, and live. Having so little experience with the world, there isn't much that doesn't thrill me, including raccoons and their nocturnal habits.

I'm not sure why I sat up. I couldn't possibly see the raccoons. Not because I have poor eyesight. I don't. It's just that they live on the forest floor and I'm sitting at the center of a rooftop. The old abandoned building, built from red bricks and mortar, is dilapidated, but still sturdy enough. The construction strikes me as flimsy, but it seems to be resisting erosion and the encroaching tree roots. I'm still learning, but I've come to one conclusion I'm sure of: the world is always changing, yet always fighting against that change. I suppose that is the nature of things.

My escort—I don't know his real name, so I call him Heap, on account of his size—is far less interested in the world around us. Instead, he's wholly, at all times, focused on his mission: to protect me. From what, I'm not sure. The world has never been safer. I suppose I could trip and fall from our ten-story-high perch, but that's just as unlikely as Heap going off mission. And it doesn't explain the weapon he carries.

I don't know what it is or what it does, but when he detects a strange shift in the wind or an out-of-place sound, he snaps that weapon up and scans the area before telling me to proceed.

Perhaps the strangest thing about Heap is that I've never seen him without his armor, which is a deep blue exoskeleton. Like a bug. With round glowing white eyes, two on either side of his face. His mouth and chin are exposed, which allows him to speak clearly, and his four round eyes change shape with his moods, so he has no trouble emoting. But it's strange to never really see him. I know there is a man inside the suit, but he's a mystery . . . and he's my closest friend. My only friend, I suppose.

He's knowledgeable about the world as it is, and as it was, during the Grind—the time period when the Masters used people as slave labor—but he's far from an expert on raccoons, or any of the mammals that populate the planet. But when he sits up next to me and says with uncommon reserve, "That wasn't a raccoon," I believe him.

When he raises his weapon slowly and stands, I ask, "What then?"

"Silence." He thrusts an open palm at me with practiced efficiency, punctuating the command.

Heap generally carries himself with a serious demeanor, but I've never known him to be rude. Something has him heating up.

I stand without making a sound, maintaining perfect balance and stepping lightly despite the pitch black, moonless night. The tar covering, of what once was something called an apartment building, flexes slightly under my two hundred pound weight, but since it seems to hold Heap's girth just fine, I don't worry about it.

Heap's arm blocks my path as I near the edge.

"I won't fall," I tell him.

He ignores me, scanning the evergreen forest that grows around and sometimes through the abandoned buildings.

"It's impossible," I say, and I consider explaining all the safeguards that will keep me from losing my balance, but decide it would take far too long. The raccoons, or whatever they are, will be gone before I finish. Instead, I say, "Even if I did fall, I could—"

"I cannot allow you to be hurt or by inaction allow harm to come to you," he says like he's practiced the line a thousand times.

"You," I say, "are not very fun."

He turns to me. "Fun is not my job."

"You are more than your job."

He thinks about this for a long moment, which for Heap is about half a second. "It is not a raccoon."

"Then what?"

"I cannot see it."

"I might," I say and then tap my temple, next to my right eye. "I have all the upgrades, remember? I can see better than the birds in the sky."

He remains frozen in place, solid, like one of the trees below.

"You can hold onto me if you like," I say.

He looks back down at the trees.

"If it's a danger to me, we need to find out what it is, right?"

That does it. My looking over the edge of this building suddenly makes sense to the round-shouldered brute. I take his hand and his thick fingers clamp down tightly, compressing to the point where I think he might hurt me. He doesn't, though my shoulder joint would probably pop loose and my arm would separate long before he would lose his grip on my hand.

I step to the roof's edge, make a show of testing my weight on the foot-tall, brick wall, and step up. Standing on one foot, I lean out at a 45-degree angle, hovering over the forest, which now looks like it's reaching up to snatch me from the building's edge.

When Heap's grip tightens just a fraction more and I think my hand will be crushed, I stop leaning and look. The implants in my eyes are capable of viewing multiple spectrums, separately or all at once, though I prefer the clarity provided by focusing on groups of wavelengths at a time. They also have

200x optical zoom, meaning I can see things that are very far away like they're right next to me. Not that this helps me now. The swaying trees below block most of the visual spectrum, and the open spots are clouded by fine yellow pollen.

"Are you sure it's not mating raccoons?" I ask. "Even the trees are mating."

"Just look."

I blink and switch to infrared, revealing a good number of small animals. Birds sit in the trees and small mammals litter the forest floor. Before I switch to ultraviolet, I note something odd. Granted, I'm new to nature, but over the past few weeks of observation, I have never seen the forest so absolutely still. I listen, tuning my sensitive ears to the sounds of the night. "The insects are silent."

"I know," Heap says. "Audio upgrade."

"Good for you," I say. "And here I thought you old guys couldn't change."

"Just don't like to. Now look."

Blink. I switch to ultraviolet. Nothing.

Blink. I switch to electromagnetic. I see it right away. Well, not really. It's technically obscured from my direct line of sight, but I can see the electromagnetism cast from its form like the glow of a lightbulb. Each living thing on the planet has a unique electromagnetic signature, from fish to cows, but this one is distinct. It's a man. I'm about to announce that I've found something when I notice several more electromagnetic signatures closing in on the first. Three men. One woman. I'm confused by this on several fronts, but manage to conclude, "They're chasing him."

"Are they human?" he asks.

"What?" I say, confused. "Of course they are." I look back in time to see Heap's grim expression. It's subtle—I sometimes wonder if he's capable of emoting—but I see the brief downturn of his mouth before he forces it away. "What else could they be?"

2.

Heap doesn't say anything. He just stands still, holding me out over the edge of a hundred-foot drop, processing what I've told him. While he's thinking, I turn back to the scene below. The four electromagnetic signatures are moving quickly, but strangely, in a way I've never seen people move before. Erratic. Lacking precision. Uncoordinated.

The man in front of them is also moving in an unusual way, but differently from the others. His gait is off. He's stumbling. Part of his body isn't functioning properly.

"He's injured," I say.

It's just a hypothesis. I can't actually see him. Just the motion of his electromagnetic field, but I'm fairly certain I'm right. My deduction snaps Heap from his thoughts.

"We need to leave," he declares.

"Leave?"

He pulls me back from the edge. "It's not safe."

My thoughts are garbled, perhaps for the first time since my birth. I have never once experienced fear or worry, but a little of both, I think, are creeping into my core. Not so much for myself, but for the running man. He's injured, and I suspect it's because of the four people chasing him down. As with fear, I am new to violence. I know the definition. There are several, in fact, each carrying a slightly different meaning, but in this case, I believe I'm witnessing the result of: *rough or injurious physical force, action or treatment.*

And I have no doubt that the violence will continue if the man is caught. Not if—when. A quick calculation, using an approximation of each person's speed, reveals the fleeing man will be caught in roughly eighty-five seconds.

Unless someone intervenes.

"He needs our help," I say.

"He is not my priority," Heap says. "You are."

I note that despite me being several feet from the roof's edge, he has yet to relinquish his vise grip on my hand.

"Why are you so afraid?" I ask.

He stands a little straighter, his body going rigid. I've insulted him.

"There are things about the world that you do not yet know," he says.

Sixty seconds . . .

"Tell me," I say. When he doesn't answer, I add, "People were violent."

"People . . ." He says the word with such melancholy that I think he's recalling some archived memory. His eyes snap toward me and focus. "The world is not as it was, but it would be foolish to assume there are no dangers remaining. That is why I am here. With you. And that is why we are leaving. Now. Take a last look at your stars."

My eyes drift up to the night sky. I switch back to the visual spectrum. With no moon and no ambient light to speak of, the stars glow with the brightness of motionless fireflies. Billions of them. The white haze stretching across the sky is called the Milky Way. I'm not sure why. I was never told. But I know someone gave it that name at some point in history. And I know it's beautiful. That's why we're here, instead of the city. While I've never been to the city, I don't think I'd enjoy it. "A congested place with countless tall buildings and too many people," Heap told me. It sounds like the opposite of outer space, which I love for its limitlessness. Sometimes I think that's where I want to be.

It's not impossible. Flight to the lunar colony takes just a day. The Mars colony will be ready for visitors in a year. Many of the solar system's other moons will soon be in reach. But then I remember that I've seen so little of Earth, and I'm content to explore and learn about the world for a while.

Forty seconds . . .

Heap tugs my arm and I stumble toward the HoverCycle, a dark blue two-seated vehicle that matches Heap's body armor. It's a relic of the old world, but holds the both of us with ease, is reliable and Heap claims the vehicle can reach great speeds, though I have never experienced anything faster than a comfortable thirty miles per hour. I suspect the cycle is also armed, like Heap, but again, this information has been kept from me.

Thinking about all of the things I would like to know, but are hidden, I start to feel irritated. Like fear, irritation is a new emotion. Aside from information, my every desire has been granted, though I now suspect that several of my excursions have been sterilized of dangers and history.

"Okay," I say. "Let's get out of here."

Heap looks unsure at first, but the fragment of fear I put in my voice convinces him I'm being earnest. And really, why should he suspect I'm being anything but honest? I've never lied before. There's never been a reason to. Things like lying, stealing and violence of any kind are no longer part of life on Earth. Peace abounds. Everywhere.

Except for ten stories below me. And more than anything I've encountered before, this intrigues me. More than the moon, the stars or the raccoons.

Thirty seconds . . .

A fresh scream tears through the night. It still reminds me of the raccoons, but it's amplified to a volume that raccoons cannot achieve. And it's a word. "Help!"

Heap's reaction is fast. He snaps in the direction the voice came from, his body poised for action, but frozen in place.

He wants to help. I can see it. Every joint in his body flows with energy.

I don't know much about the old world, which faded thirty years ago, but I know Heap's designation: Domestic Security. It says so right on the chest of his body armor, right below a gold star and a faded script that says, "Protect and Serve." And that's exactly what he wants to do now, except that he's been tasked to perform that duty for me and me alone.

> *No person shall force, or by lack of action, allow another person to serve, perform tasks or carry out duties against said person's will, desires or dreams. Such actions are designated slavery and are forbidden under the Grind Abolition Act of 0001 A.G. Failure to comply will result in discontinuance.*

The words come and go through my mind in a flash.

There are many rules and protocols for our worldwide society, but this is the only one that is considered a law and it carries the harshest of penalties. Discontinuance. It's really just a nice way of saying death, which is something people don't really have to fear in general, though we did at one time.

While I am not an expert—in anything—Heap's refusal to leave my side stands in direct conflict with his desire to help the man below. It also conflicts with the words written across his chest—protect and serve. While I am not forcing Heap to ignore the man's plight, I am, by inaction, enslaving him.

"You're not a slave," I say.

His body remains locked and ready for action, but his head turns toward me. Again, the slightest bit of emotion emerges on his face—confusion. He doesn't know what to do, and although I cannot fathom a man like Heap not being single-minded at all times, he's frozen with indecision.

With the realization that I am inadvertently confining Heap's true nature and desires comes the revelation that him protecting me against *my* will is also an act of slavery. While I would never admit to this—Heap is my friend—I cannot, in accordance with the First Law, allow our relationship to continue under the same constraints that it has since we were paired.

"You're not a slave," I repeat, "and neither am I."

With a strength and quickness that I doubt Heap knew I possessed, I yank my hand from his grasp, take two vaulting steps toward the building's precipice—

Ten seconds . . .

—and jump.

3.

The rusted fire escape stairs mounted on the side of the building rattle, as I drop hard onto the landing ten feet below the roof. My weight and the jarring impact pulls two bolts from the old bricks, and the whole platform cants to the side. I stand still, waiting for the stairs to settle and calculating the distance to a nearby pine tree in case I have to jump. I think I can make it, but there is no need. The rest of the old fire escape stays firmly rooted in the ceramic bricks.

"Freeman!" Heap shouts my name, leaning over the roof's edge. Concrete crumbles beneath his grasp. His sudden appearance and booming voice nearly make me fall over the railing, but I catch myself and move to the stairs.

"No time," I tell him, descending the first flight with a single bound, stressing the stairwell further. I glance up and catch sight of Heap's face. I can see he's considering jumping down after me, but it's clear his girth would be the fire escape's undoing.

I leap down another flight spurred faster by the worry that Heap might follow me down. But he doesn't. Instead, my protector just grunts. When I look up again, he's gone, no doubt rushing toward the building's interior, and much sturdier, stairwell.

I drop down to the next level, take two steps and jump again. Jump. *Clang.* Jump. *Clang.* I repeat this eight more times, and the staircase decides to relinquish its hold on the building. There's a groan from above, followed by the sharp report of snapping metal. I leap again, bringing me to within fifteen feet of the ground where cracked pavement has given way to sprouting vegetation.

A staccato pop draws my eyes up, and I see the stairs tearing away from the building, one level at a time, moving slowly yet steadily toward the ground, and me. I look to the ground, judging the distance again, and the time it would take me to leap, roll and dive clear. But the fire escape has other plans. When half of the case comes free, the bolts of the lower stairs tear from the wall.

Without spending another fraction of a second considering my options, I heft myself over the railing and drop toward the ground. Unfortunately, gravity pulls the staircase down at the same speed it does me.

I land hard, absorbing the impact by bending my knees and rolling in one fluid motion, something I've never done before, but manage to perform like I've trained for this moment.

The staircase slams into the ground behind me with a grinding boom. I spin around in time to see the towering fire escape crumple, stop and topple toward me. I stumble backward, tripping over myself, and sprawl to the ground.

Luckily, I've sprawled clear of the twisting metal. The lower half of the staircase crushes the ground where I stood just a moment ago. The top half topples into a tall pine, gouging its bark and leaving a long, pale scar in its wake.

There is no time to consider how close I came to accidentally discontinuing myself. A fresh cry tears through the forest. The voice is the same, but it no longer pleads for help. It's shrieking now. In pain.

Thirty seconds has come and gone.

I jump to my feet and dash into the dark forest, sprinting as fast as I can. I activate all visual spectrums in my upgrade and navigate through the trees as easily as I could in broad daylight, aiming for the electromagnetic pulses generated by the five people.

They're no longer running. In fact, it's hard to distinguish one from the other. They're all jumbled up.

What are they doing? I wonder, cutting the distance to them in half.

The man screeches again, shrill and panicked.

My insides flutter with something I don't understand. The best word I can think of to describe it is instinct. And it's telling me to run—the other way. Self-preservation is a powerful emotion, but my conviction that people should not suffer stands its equal. I don't know if I can help, but I have to try. But that's not the only thing compelling me forward. I have to understand. The one and only job I have right now is to learn. To absorb. And this is the strangest thing I have yet to encounter during all my time with the Council, or with Heap.

I look back for my guardian, but find no sign of him.

It doesn't matter, I tell myself. I am free, after all. Even my name says so. If this is a mistake, it is mine to make. How can I learn if I am unable to make errors?

I cover the rest of the ground in the time it takes me to ruminate over my decision to leave Heap behind. I slow as I approach the group of four electromagnetic signatures.

Four.

One is missing.

Not missing, I realize. *Discontinued. Dead.*

They've killed him!

"What have you done?" I say, stepping into a clearing at the edge of the pine forest. The three men and one woman, now in clear sight, are leaning over the prone body of the fifth man whose tortured voice has been silenced. Tall grass lies flattened around them, now stained by the man's fluids.

Instinct roars inside me, screaming at me to run. But my mind remains locked on the image of this dead man and his four killers, whose heads slowly pivot toward me.

They move with jittery spasms, as though not fully in control of their bodies, or perhaps not able to understand how to work their muscles and joints. Infrared reveals that they're hot. Burning up. They should probably be dead, too, but they're not.

As they turn their heads toward me, the first thing I see is their eyes. They're as vacant and lifeless as the man lying beneath them. And yet they can see me.

One of them groans, and I see a tendril of skin hanging from his mouth.

Skin.

The dead man's skin!

They're eating him. But why? People don't eat—

The man lunges, but falls on his face, flattening more of the tall grass. I take a step back, but the instinct to run still hasn't overcome my curiosity.

He crawls toward me, dragging himself over the ground. The other three stand slowly behind him, finding their feet before they, too, come for me. I step back again and logic settles in. These people are cannibals. I can't fathom why, but they were eating that man, and the sinister expressions twisting their faces leave little doubt that I am next.

But then something happens.

The fifth electromagnetic signature blooms back to life. But it's not the same. It's . . . different. The dead man is no longer dead . . . but he's not really alive. That's when I notice that his signature matches those of the four people now closing in. All five of them are dead. But not.

The closest man, whose body I now see is torn apart and leaking something white, reaches out for me and I run.

Into a tree.

Panic, I now know, makes me clumsy. I fall to the ground, not really hurt, but no longer mobile. The shredded man on the ground catches hold of my foot and pulls himself closer. His mouth drops open as he leans over me with a satisfied groan.

I'm about to let out a scream, and for a brief moment I wonder if I will sound like the mating raccoons. But before any sound comes from my mouth or the man can bite into my flesh, he's yanked up into the air and tossed aside.

My head spins to the side and I find my rescuer—my protector—Heap. He looks poised for action and more alive than I've ever seen him before. Remembering the man clutching my foot, I kick him in the face hard, then scramble back, pushing myself against the tree that knocked me down and climb back to my feet.

"This is why you should listen to me," Heap says, his voice oozing authority and anger.

"Is this also why you have that?" I ask, motioning to the weapon already in his hand.

"It's called a gun," he says, then aims it toward the man still clawing his way to my feet. The weapon explodes with power and noise that makes me jump. Faster than I can discern, the man's head folds in on itself and the dead becomes dead again.

But the weapon acts as a catalyst and the others charge. Heap kicks his big foot into the woman's gut, sending her flying back into the grass. He shoots one of the two charging men, dropping him to the ground. Heap sidesteps the second man, allowing him to pass before shooting him in the head as well.

The woman in the grass stands with an angry wail. She reaches out for Heap, jaws agape, and streaks toward him. He fires a fourth time and the woman falls to the ground.

While I'm thankful that Heap rescued me, I don't miss the fact that he killed these four people without hesitation and with surprising efficiency. Four shots, four dead. It's not as bad as cannibalism, but it's still frightening . . . and curious. Who is Heap? And why haven't I met any other people like him?

Ignoring me, Heap wanders over to the dead man. I find myself following him, but standing a few feet back.

"Why did they kill this man?" I ask.

Heap answers coolly. "I don't know." If he's feeling any fear, I can't tell.

"Why were they *eating* him?"

"I don't know."

The no-longer-dead man's foot twitches. His eyes open. He turns to Heap, opens his mouth and tries to bite him.

Heap takes a step back, aims and fires his weapon—his gun—again. Five shots. Five dead.

Again.

Part of me wants to inspect these bodies and find out what

happened to make them go insane, but my revulsion is rising with every second I'm no longer in danger. I can smell their insides.

"Heap," I say, desiring to leave more than anything I have desired before.

He raises his hand to me, palm out, requesting silence like only he can. He turns his head to the side slowly. I've seen him do this before. He's listening. Before I can focus on my hearing, Heap says, "The field."

I turn toward the wall of three-foot-tall grass. It's unremarkable, even to someone who only just recently began experiencing the outside world. "What about it?"

"Did you scan it?"

"No, but—"

"Do it! Now!"

I turn my eyes to the field, looking from side to side in every spectrum. I see the first person a hundred feet away, waist deep in the tall grass. The second is just a few feet farther. Then I see more of them. A *lot* more.

I step away from the field, slowly moving back toward the trees.

"How many?" Heap asks.

"I'm not sure." I stopped counting at seventy-five. "More than a hundred."

"All the same?" he asks, looking down at the people he killed.

I already confirmed they had the same electromagnetic signature, so I just nod. "They're coming this way."

"How much time do we have?"

I look up, surprised I hadn't figured that out. I turn to the field, find the nearest figure again and gasp. "Thirty seconds."

4.

"Run," Heap says, eyes on the field.

"What?" I'm confused, mostly because Heap doesn't look like he's going anywhere. He's in a wide stance, looking over the top of his gun, which is pointed at the field.

Twenty-five seconds.

He glances at me and shouts. "Run!"

"I can't leave without you," I say, panic rising.

Twenty seconds.

"Freeman, you're faster and stronger than me. Smarter, too. And you have every upgrade I can think of and probably a few we don't even know about. I'll just slow you down. My job is to protect you. Right now, that means—" He looks forward for just a fraction of a second and pulls the trigger. The explosion of light from the weapon's barrel illuminates the closest man as he crumples to the ground. "—you need to leave me behind. Get to the city. Get lost."

I just look up at him, unsure if this is some kind of joke. I've never been without the big man, and I've only seen the city from a distance.

He fires another shot, dropping a dead woman to the ground.

The mob is getting closer.

Thirty seconds has passed.

"This is your chance, Freeman," Heap says. "Find out who you will be. You're free."

With those words, I understand exactly what he's offering me. As I suspected, I've been somewhat captive. A slave. Free to explore and learn, but only if the subjects and locations were approved by the Council. Heap might be here for my protection, but he's also here to control me and filter my interactions with the world.

My flight isn't just about surviving. It's about living—really living—for the first time.

So I run.

I don't say good-bye.

I don't look back.

I just . . . run.

Five seconds into my mad sprint, Heap's weapon shatters the silent forest. Then again and again. If his accuracy hasn't changed since I left him, he's killed seventeen more. There's a pause in the firing, then a string of three quick shots. They sound rushed, and the change makes me worried for my friend.

My only friend.

I stop and look back through the forest, focusing on the electromagnetic spectrum. There is a wall of dead. And then Heap. Still alive, but running. For a moment, I hope that he'll be joining me soon, but then I note his direction. He's leading them away from me.

I'm so focused on Heap's flight that I nearly miss the sound of a foot scraping through the dry pine needles carpeting the forest floor. When the sound finally does register, and I spin around, it's nearly too late. A second mob of discontinued stagger through the trees, dead eyes on me. Despite being dead, there is something very much alive in their gaze, like the hunger I've seen in the eyes of wolves.

I'm prey, I realize, stumbling back away from the nearest man. I scan the trees around me. They're everywhere!

With a groan, the man lunges at me. I jump to the side, my mind flooded with so many courses of action that I can't decide what to do. There are so many unknown variables that success isn't guaranteed, no matter what choice I make. The wolves return to my mind. I spent a day watching them with Heap. They chased rabbits through the woods, working as a pack, like these people surrounding me. But they were only successful 30 percent of the time.

Why?

Because the rabbit moved quickly and erratically, I think.

Without any better idea, I run again, moving through the horde as fast as I can, bouncing back and forth, aiming one direction and moving the other, and doing my best to steer clear of their reaching arms.

The dead stagger when I turn, unable to maneuver as quickly. They run into each other and collide with trees, but there are so many of them, all of my running simply returns me to the same predicament I found myself in just seconds before. The cycle will continue indefinitely if I don't pick a direction.

The building, I think. Heap's HoverCycle is still on the roof. I've never operated it before, or any vehicle, but I have a working knowledge of how machines function.

I find the building's cool flat surface in the darkness, duck beneath a pair of hands with fingers hooked like talons and dash toward the building, weaving, leaping and spinning my way past a wall of people who want to eat me. Once clear, I run hard and fast, but the dead give chase. They're not quite as spry, but they're not slowed by indecision, either.

An avalanche of humanity closes in on either side, like a zipper composed of bodies, filling in the space behind me. I clear the trees and nearly impale myself on the twisted wreck of the fire escape, but manage to spin around it. The dead woman diving at my back is too committed and too clumsy to dodge the jagged rail. As I turn away, I see the rusty metal impale her at the waist. But instead of remaining stuck, she wrenches her body away from the bar, tearing a gaping hole in her side. The entire incident delays her by a few seconds.

These people, these *things,* are either incapable of feeling pain or are too mad to be bothered by it. The ruined states of their bodies, aged and decayed as they are, suggests the latter. If they could feel the state of their bodies, mad or not, the pain would be incapacitating.

The wave of people closes in as I rush along the side of the building, and for a moment, I'm glad Heap isn't here. I'd be embarrassed by the frightened cries rising from my mouth. I sound nothing like the raccoons.

A man lunges, passing just behind me, slamming his head into the redbrick wall. His rotted skull folds in, crushing the fragile mind within. He slumps to the ground, tripping up the dead around him, who stumble and flail. Suddenly the lot of them is falling over themselves, sprawling face down to the ground. I pull ahead, rounding the corner onto what once was the small town's main street. The pavement is mostly hidden by grass now, but the lines of tall buildings remain, along with the ruined husks of vehicles that Heap told me were called "cars" and "trucks" during the time of the Masters. But the rotting and sun-bleached transports aren't the only corpses lining the streets.

A horde of the living dead turns in my direction. Their bones grind as they move. Their teeth chatter. And their eyes alight at the sight of me. As one, the group closes off the street and draws nearer.

But I'm already where I want to be. I launch myself up the brick building's eight front stairs, reaching the top in two leaps. I can hear the dead behind me, scratching up the concrete steps. The front door hangs at an angle. Heap must have pulled the top free of the rotting wood when he chased after me. Rather than try to open the door normally, I plant one foot and kick hard with the other. The door tears away from its frame and flies inward. The strength of my kick is surprising, even to me, but I barely notice because the door has struck something that wasn't there before.

Not something, I realize, *someone.*

In the darkness of the hall, I see movement, but it's the electromagnetic signatures that tell me the first-floor hallway is packed with more dead.

Where are they coming from? I think, and then I see it for myself. A door at the end of the hall, leading down to a basement. Underground. And they just keep on coming.

Instinct once again tells me to run, but I can't turn around. The horde at my heels is at the top of the steps.

I dash forward, reaching the interior staircase just as a man staggers around the door and grabs my wrist. I shout in fear more than pain, and react—violently. With little thought put into the act, I swing my arm down, like a hatchet, striking the man's forearm. I yank back as I swing, and I suddenly spill backward, slamming against the stairwell wall with enough force to leave a dent in the wallpaper-covered plaster.

A spray of dark liquid strikes the wallpaper next to me and draws my eyes to its source. The man's arm has been severed where I struck it! Can they really be that frail?

I flinch away when I find the man's hand still locked to my wrist, skin peeling back, taut ligaments exposed. I stand and run up the stairs while prying the fingers from my wrist. When I reach the second-floor landing, I toss the hand aside and focus on reaching the roof. The stairs are old and wooden and should have rotted away long ago, but the roof overhead is still intact, sparing the stairwell from direct exposure to the elements. Still, I'm careful to hug the wall on the way up, where the stairs will be less likely to break.

With each level, I put some more distance between myself and the horde. They seem to have trouble with stairs, but I can hear them rising. I won't have long when I reach the roof.

I find the door at the top wide open, and run out into the open night. The stars hold little interest now, but I'm suddenly struck by a surprising amount of sensory information. I've left all of my visual upgrades on and I'm bombarded by waves of electromagnetism. I shut the spectrum off and an overwhelming sense of being closed in fades. But I can still hear. And what I hear beckons me to the roof's edge. After locking the door behind me, I rush across the flexing tar-covered roof and stand at the edge, looking down at the main street.

The ground is alive, I think, looking at the writhing mass of bodies below. But they're not alive. None of them are. Not really.

There has to be a thousand of them beneath me. And likely just as many on every side of this building. But how do they know I'm here? Are they just following the others or can they somehow detect me? They don't seem very interested in each other, so it's the living they're after.

I jump when the roof door is struck. The old wood flexes, buckles and then shatters. A pair of dead spill out onto the roof. For a moment, I'm stuck in place, but then I remember the HoverCycle. I run to the long slender vehicle, hop in the seat and say, "Cycle one-four-five-seven, start."

Nothing happens.

That's usually all Heap does and the thing roars to life. But it's as still and motionless as all these dead people should be.

I'm missing something. I'm—oh no. The cycle requires a magnetic key. I remember seeing Heap slide the circular magnet across something before speaking the words. It's right there, next to the handlebars, a circle of white metal that once held text, but is now covered in jagged scoring from Heap's key.

A frenzied groan rolls across the roof, but I don't look.

I'm too afraid.

I'm stuck.

No . . . its more than that. I'm *dead,* though not for long. Because when they're done with me, done *eating* me, I'll come back, too.

5.

My eyes dart back and forth, wandering over the uneven surface of the roof. I'm looking through the night's shadows for something, but I don't know what. A weapon? A key? A nice place to lie down and die?

My thoughts turn to death and I wonder what it will feel like. I've never really thought about it, probably because my education on the subject has been limited to wolves eating rabbits, and in those cases the rabbits just ceased to be. They were transformed from living, animate creatures, to inanimate flesh, and finally to energy. But that won't happen to me. I'll come back. I know that's not what's supposed to happen. Dead things stay dead. I'm pretty certain about that. But these people . . . They're rotting. Decayed. Maybe all dead people come back?

Can't be, I decide. The Council would know about it and Heap would never have brought me here.

"Nuuaaaghh," says a man. He's just twenty feet from me, hobbling forward with dreadful assurance. A growing crowd widens behind him, transmitting ravenous hunger.

My mind suddenly clears. I have just two options. The second, my backup plan, is to climb over the side of the building and scale down the outer wall. I'm strong and agile, so I might be able to manage it if the bricks provide sufficient holds and don't crumble. If I can reach a lower floor and hide, maybe the horde will lose interest. I think the odds of this succeeding are low, and I really want to leave, so I launch my first plan with gusto.

The HoverCycle is a menagerie of buttons and indicator lights. I lay into them with my fingers, jamming down buttons and flipping switches with abandon. I have no idea what the majority of them do, and I doubt anything will work without power, but maybe there is a compartment with another weapon that will open if I—

Something tugs on my thumb as though it's held in place by some invisible force. I flinch and yank my hand away.

I see nothing unusual about my digit, or the HoverCycle dash. *Where was my thumb?* I think, noting the proximity of the nearest dead man. I have just seconds to flee or die.

I look down at the dash, returning my thumb to its approximate position before I pulled away. *The magnetic starter switch.* I lower my thumb toward the flat, scratched surface. *Why would my*—a sudden invisible force yanks my thumb toward the dash and holds it against the starter switch.

"What the . . ."

Is there a magnet in my thumb? Is this another upgrade I'm unaware of?

A flash of movement draws my eyes up. The man is rounding the cycle, reaching out for me.

"Cycle one-four-five-seven, start!" I shout and the HoverCycle roars to life, lifting me three feet above the surface of the roof, which now glows neon blue under the luminous flat disks that repulse the cycle from the roof.

But I'm still not moving, and the dead man is not impressed. His jaws open and his lips pucker, stretching out for my calf.

I twist the handlebars hard to the left and the vehicle responds quickly, spinning hard and slamming into the man's side. The power of the blow sends the man flailing through the air, and then he's gone, falling out of sight over the side of the building.

A hand clutches my shoulder.

I shout and spin the cycle the other direction, sending three more of the man-eaters sprawling back into the wall of hungry dead.

Move, I think. *I need to move!*

I lean forward, gripping the handlebars and sliding my feet

into place on the sides of the bike. There's a pedal under each foot. One increases the cycle's repulsion, and the other works the turbines that propel the bike forward. I'm just not sure which is which, so I tap my left foot down and rise another foot off the roof. Right foot forward, left foot up. *Simple,* I think, and cram my right foot down.

I'm transformed into a living missile, surging across the roof. I cringe as the cycle's blunt nose plows through the crowd of dead. Each impact is jarring, but the vehicle is armored like it's meant for this kind of treatment and it cuts the bodies down. I squeeze my eyes shut and shout in surprise as much as in fear.

This must be what astronauts feel like, I think, *when they're catapulted through the atmosphere by the most powerful repulse engines yet built.* A moment later, I'm airborne and clear of the roof, dropping toward the ground at a 45-degree angle. I open my eyes to see the ground rushing up at me and a single dead woman, her face torn and melted, one eye missing, clinging to the front of the cycle.

I watch the woman slide slowly down the front of the cycle. The front casing is smooth armor, but it's only three feet across. She could easily wrap her arms around it or cling to the raised headlights. But she doesn't think to do either. Instead, she reaches for me and allows gravity to pull her down, over the cycle's hood until her legs dangle beneath the repulse disc, which yanks her down and launches her to the ground.

My descent continues in near silence except for the rush of wind and the hum of the cycle's turbines. I'm too afraid to shout. Instead, I squeeze the steering bar, lean back and open my eyes wide. It's a pretty ridiculous fear response, but when I lean back, I also pull up on the steering column, leveling out the cycle.

My mind flashes with a memory of Heap expertly performing a drop just like this. It wasn't scary when Heap was driving. I had absolute faith in his ability to operate this vehicle. It seemed like part of his body. He could drive off a rooftop and land without any perceptible jolt just as easily as he could leap the thing off the ground and up onto a roof. HoverCycles can't fly very far, but they're not bound to the Earth, either. *Like turkeys*, I think and then remember I'm about to achieve the horde's goal by smearing myself on the ground.

With the cycle level, I lift my right foot so that I'm no longer propelling the vehicle forward, and push down with my left foot, increasing the range of repulsion. For a moment, I feel no change, but then my descent begins to slow. And then it stops.

I did it, I think, and I look over the side. While the repulse discs stay level with the ground, the bike adjusts to my weight shift by leaning in the other direction, keeping the vehicle balanced. But I still nearly fall-free when I see the ground. Not only is it still twenty feet below me, but a sea of raised hands awaits my return, writhing like tall grass in the wind—if grass ate men.

To make matters worse, the cycle can't maintain a twenty-foot hover indefinitely. The vehicle descends slowly and won't stop until it's three feet off the ground. But I have a moment to take in my surroundings. Get my bearings.

The first thing I see, in every direction, is the dead. The town ruins are at my back with nothing but forest surrounding them. Heap told me to head to the city, but I can't see it from here. Navigating my way to a location that's widely known seems like it should be a simple task for someone as smart as me, but I strangely lack the information I need. Like maps, or coordinates, or—

Stars, I think, looking up. I quickly find the North Star above. Armed with the knowledge of north, south, east and west, I lower my gaze until I see the pink glow of technology. The city. I'm not even sure what they call it or if it has a name at all. But I know its general direction.

Northwest.

I push my right foot down gently. The turbines whir to life, moving me forward. As I accelerate, I hear angry groans from beneath me. I glance back and see a line of the dead, flattened to the ground by the repulse engine. I'm just above their heads now, and as I enter the dark forest, the cycle starts striking extended arms, and then heads, before crushing the dead into the earth. But I'm not out of danger. The cycle will soon be low enough that the dead in front of me might come up over the front, and those to the sides could easily tackle me. They're not coordinated, but I believe in luck, no matter how illogical it might be. If just one of them is lucky, I won't be.

The cycle accelerates as I slowly push my right foot down on the pedal. I glance at the speedometer. Twenty mph. Thirty mph.

The repetitive *thunk* of heads striking the front of the cycle grows more frequent as my speed increases. That's when I realize that, fast or not, I'm going to have to plow through all these people. I'm not comfortable with it, but I need to go faster.

A *lot* faster.

I shove my right foot down until the pedal strikes metal. I'm nearly flung backward and off the cycle, but I keep my hold on the handle grips and lean into the cycle. With my body down tight, lower than the curved windshield, the wind fades to nothing. I can barely see over the top of the bike, but in a moment, that won't matter. I plot a course through the trees and then lose sight of them completely, not from darkness, but from a mass of physical obstructions.

Bodies fly past on both sides and above as they bounce off the hood and spiral past. The dead no longer reach out. I'm there and gone before they understand what's happened. I look at the speedometer. Eighty mph. Ninety mph.

Suddenly, the thumping of bodies on the cycle's front end disappears. The walls of bodies on either side of me are gone. All that remains are the trees and the night. I lean up a little and nearly miss the shift in the darkness ahead, but the bright moonlight filtering through the pine branches is absent.

I sit straight up into the wind and see the aberration for what it is.

A gorge.

It's perhaps two hundred feet across and who knows how deep. I might be able to land safely at the bottom, but I'm not sure if I'll be able to get out again. If there is no other exit than up, I don't want to be stuck at the bottom if the mob of dead decide to follow me down.

So once again, I act without much more than a fraction of a second to think about it. I cram both feet down, pushing the bike faster, and higher. The repulse engines let out a *whump* and the forest around me glows with a sudden strobe of bright blue light. Then I'm flattened against the bike, rising up into the air and sailing across the open depths of a canyon.

6.

Having landed the cycle safely once already, I feel confident I can do it again. What concerns me more is the far wall of the gorge. I'm currently traveling at 120 mph. If I fall short and strike the cliff side head-on, there won't be much left of the cycle, or me. I try to look over the front end of the cycle, but all I can see is the hood and the night beyond.

I lean forward a little farther and the vehicle tilts with my weight.

Too far! The turbines now push the cycle forward and *down*. The far side of the canyon slides out of the darkness, lit by the moon. It's a crisp dull blue in comparison to the deep shadow of the gorge below. I try to think of some way I can push the cycle farther or higher, but with both feet crushing down on the two pedals, I'm doing everything I can think to do.

And it's not going to be enough.

The far side isn't a great distance now, but the nose of the cycle is pointed below the crest. *I could jump,* I think, but then I remember how fast I'm traveling. An hour ago, death seemed like a stranger, something I'd never have to think about, but I once again find myself contemplating the finality of things. I've done so little with my life.

This can't be the end.

Desperation fills my core and I repeat the potentially fool-hardy plan that started the cycle in the first place—I push buttons. All of them. And this time, the power is on.

Compartments open. Lights flash, blue and red. A siren howls. Long tubes extend from the hood and launch metal projectiles toward the cliff, shattering stone. *Guns,* I realize, like the one Heap carried, but more powerful. Amid the cacophony of firing guns, blaring sirens and other noises I can't identify, I hear a steady high-pitched hum rising in volume. I have no idea what this sound means, but it makes me tense up. My hands tighten on the handlebars, and not a moment too soon.

The high-pitched whine becomes a scream and something behind me explodes. I'm pulled backward, but manage to hold on, yanking the steering column up and the nose with it.

Why hadn't I thought of that before? For a moment I worry that there is a problem with my memory, but I'm too young for that to be an issue.

These thoughts come and go swiftly, but their speed is dwarfed by that of the HoverCycle. I purse my lips tightly and pull myself forward, leaning under the wind. My eyes catch sight of the glowing speedometer.

Three hundred fifteen mph.

I'm a rocket!

I turn my head slowly back and see a bright orange glow radiating from the back of the cycle. A jet engine! *Turbofan*, I think, somehow recognizing the hardware, which is the most powerful engine in the world. And I'm sitting on top of it. My eyes widen, and oddly, for reasons beyond my understanding, I smile.

And laugh.

And then, the orange disappears.

The bike lurches and drops, but the descent is controlled, slowed and smoothed by the repulse engines pushing against the ground. But my speed . . . I'm slowing, but not quickly.

Brakes. How does Heap slow this thing down?

Before I can figure it out, I'm beneath the tree line, sliding back into a densely forested area. The possibility of a brutal, but quick death once again takes my full attention. I focus on the land ahead, noting the position of trees, the rise and fall of the ground and the occasional rock or thick bush.

The bike stops descending three feet from the ground, and for a moment I'm quite pleased with myself. I've managed to land the cycle from a great height, at an even greater speed, and without the slightest jostle. My feet work the pedals with little thought.

It's instinct, I think. That strange force within that seems to suggest actions before any conscious thought has taken place. I'm not sure how such a thing is possible. Things need to be considered, at least for a moment, but instinct . . . it's immediate. I make a mental note to explore the subject in the future, then twist the steering bar to the right, swerving around a thick tree.

More trees flow past on either side, a horizontal blur. With every second that passes, I find my comfort level grow.

I swerve farther than I have to.

My foot remains firmly planted on the accelerator despite the danger of the dead being far behind me.

The smile creeps back onto my face.

No wonder Heap never let me drive the cycle, I think, *it's too fun.*

Thinking of Heap reminds me that this isn't just another midnight ride. I look up for the stars, hoping to locate the North Star, but they're blocked by the trees. When I look down, I nearly crash headlong into a boulder the size of a ruined suburban home Heap showed me yesterday, and then forbade me to enter.

I shout with surprise and career around the giant stone, just inches from smashing into its broad gray surface. A completely inappropriate laugh rises from deep within. *What was that?* I think. *I nearly died. Again! And I laughed?*

Something is wrong with me. I'm sure of it.

But before I can contemplate my strange behavior, I notice a thinning in the trees to the left, and I direct the cycle toward what I believe is a clearing. Less than twenty seconds later, I explode from the forest and into a field full of tall grass, just like the one where I left Heap behind.

A surge of guilt, another new emotion, grips my chest and I fight against it. I didn't leave Heap behind. He ordered me away. I obeyed him.

But that's not really true.

I obeyed my fear.

Heap was my friend. *Is* my friend.

"I shouldn't have left him," I say. My lip trembles. I try to stop it, but I'm unable. Emotions, like instinct, seem to have control over my body in a way that supersedes the desires of my consciousness.

Life is confusing, I decide, and then I'm launched skyward.

I rise up through the air, no longer seated on the back of the cycle. I've been flung off.

Did I hit something? I wonder and look back to see the back end of the HoverCycle disappear into a hole in the ground. The image comes and goes quickly, because moving my head has caused me to flip over. As I spin head over heels, I catch a glimpse of the stars. It takes just a moment to find the North Star, determine which direction is northwest and turn my head again.

The city's glow is revealed to be long lights attached to the sides of buildings taller than anything I've seen. *They're beautiful,* I think, *like the trees, but different.*

Then I'm facedown again and looking at the Earth below. I'm so tired of contemplating what death will feel like, that I give up on it and focus on the city again. My muscles relax. My tendons loosen. And for a moment, I feel peaceful, like when I was on the rooftop with Heap.

I nearly miss the fact that I've hit the ground and passed straight through it, but my view turns black and I register the impact as a dull pain throughout my body. But it's not nearly as bad as I thought.

Because I'm still falling, I realize. The ground and the grass is just a thin film. *But above what?* At least I know what happened to the HoverCycle. To the heavy machine and powerful repulse discs, the thin covering was essentially open air. The cycle must have pitched forward, the back whipped up and I took flight.

My fall slows while all around me, things crack and splinter.

Invisible limbs poke and claw at me, slowing my descent until I reach the bottom of—what? A pit of some kind? A sinkhole?

I try to get my bearings, placing my hands on the soil beneath me. It feels soft, and squishy. I reach down and take a handful of the stuff, holding it up before my eyes. I can't see it in this pit where the moonlight can't reach, so I switch to infrared and get a flare of heat from the surface of the pit.

And it's moving.

I let the glowing mush slip from my hands until just a little remains. Upon closer inspection, I recognize the wriggling shapes. Worms. A *lot* of worms.

I switch my visual upgrade from infrared to light-amplifying night vision. Everything looks green, but the small amount of light filtering from above, perhaps reflecting off a cloud or nearby trees, or from the stars directly overhead, is made more luminous, allowing me to see shapes, but little more.

But simple shapes, in this case, are enough.

A shout leaps from my mouth and I scramble back from the horrible sight, only to find myself tangled more tightly within the grasp of so many dead.

But these people are really dead.

Long dead.

All that remains are bones. They're so fragile. Brittle and weak. How did people come to be in this state? And why are there so many?

I look at a skull frozen in a permanent scream. It's wedged in tight, held in place by all the bones around it. Who was this person? A man or a woman? There is no way for me to tell.

Something strikes my head, bouncing off my hair. I catch it as it falls in front of my face. It's a bone. A small one. Part of a finger, I think.

And then another one falls.

And another.

I look up. The hole created by my body as it punctured the Earth and crashed through the mass of skeletons is nearly fifty feet deep. The bones surrounding the column of empty space have been broken, the tangle of dead that held them firm is now missing. They're shifting, sliding in, closing the gap, and falling toward me. A skull pops free, jawless and terrible. It falls through empty space, its empty eyes watching me as it drops. I cringe away from the thing.

The dead surround me.

They tried to eat me, and now they're going to bury me.

The skull strikes my hands as they clutch the back of my head. The impact doesn't hurt, really. The skull is weak and shatters on impact, coating me with a layer of dust. Dead dust.

A rattle draws my eyes up.

The night sky is gone. The dead close in and fall, burying me alive.

Panic sets in like never before and for an indeterminable amount of time, I lose my mind.

7.

"Who is he?" I hear a woman ask. I can't see anything, and my hearing is muffled, or dulled somehow. I can't really tell what's going on. The world has become thick around me, constricting and numb.

"Beats me," a man replies, his accent thick in a way I've never heard before. "Found him out by one of the pits."

"The pits?" the woman says, sounding surprised. "No one goes out there."

"Just desperate morons," the man says and I understand he's referring to himself. "But look what I found with him, inside the pit."

"You went *in* the pit?"

"Just look," the man says. There's a loud clang of falling metal and though I am blind, I can almost see the steel hatch falling on the paved street.

The woman gasps, her voice sounding frail somehow.

"Crazy, right?" the man says. "From the looks of it, this guy drove the cycle straight into the pit and when it went down, he went—" He makes a whistling sound. "The hole in the pit's cover was a hundred feet out."

"Is he injured?" the woman asks.

"Scratched up a little. Dirty." I feel a dull pat against my back. "Covered with the dust of the dead, too."

"Don't get that shit on me," the woman says, her voice a little more distant, like she backed away. *What is shit?* I wonder. I don't know that word, and I know a *lot* of words.

"Look, the point is, he's in one piece. Looks in good shape.

But I think the fall might have knocked something loose, you know? He's not coming out of it."

"Let me look at him," the woman says, her voice close again. I feel the tickle of her fingers on my face. "I've never seen anyone like him before."

"I know," the man says. "What do you think his station is?"

"Some kind of science would be my guess," the woman says. "Look at his clothes. Looks like one of those track suits. Remember those? But, I'm not sure I've ever seen one of the sciences in person before."

"But we've seen images," the man argues. "This guy isn't anything like them. Remember when they announced the first upgrades. Showed all those hairless science-types working in a lab, like we need to see them working to believe they're getting things done?"

"Yeah," the woman says. "I remember. What I'm confused about is why you brought him to me."

"Like you have anything better to do?" the man says with a snort that I think is a mocking laugh, but I'm not entirely certain.

Who are these people? And where am I? I can't hear much beyond their voices, and I still can't feel much of anything beyond physical touch. All I really know is that the man is holding me in his arms and the woman is standing in front of him. Other than that, and their voices, the world doesn't exist.

"Let's face it, we're not exactly the pinnacle of society and I'm guessing this guy is one of us. He's a stranger, sure, but he was driving a Police HoverCycle like a bat out of Hell, in the middle of the night, and he drove into a pit. He was running from someone. My guess is the Council."

"I don't like it," the woman says, but all I can really think about is what a bat would be doing in Hell, and why the man would think I'd be running from the Council. They're my friends.

"Like it or not, he's one of us—"

"And if he's not?"

"Like you gotta ask."

A pause and then the woman says, "Fine. Take him inside. If he doesn't light up before the sun, you can bring him back to the pit."

The pit! Images of blank staring skulls and an endless sea of bones fill my thoughts with dread. *Wake up,* I tell myself. *Open your eyes! Move!* But nothing happens.

I feel my body jolting as I'm carried up a flight of stairs. I hear the sound of creaking wood. A door. The man's rigid arms slide away and I drop into something soft that sinks under my weight.

"Hey buddy," the man says, his voice just inches away from my ears. "Open your eyes." I feel him pry open one of my eyelids, but I don't see anything. "Geez, look at the upgrades on this guy." I feel him turn my head side to side. He moves to my torso, then my arms and legs. "You should see this," the man says.

I hear someone come close. The woman, I think, and then she speaks. "What is it?"

"A man with this many upgrades could do anything he wanted," the man says. "Of course, a less ambitious man might trade the upgrades for a better view."

"Ugh," the woman says, sounding disgusted. "You know what I think about body-hacking."

"Easy for you to say," the man says. "You're fully functional." The way he says this implies he's making a joke, but I can't find the humor in it.

"Funny," the woman says, clearly understanding the man's intent, but also not finding the humor in the man's words.

"Hey, you got any of the good stuff?" the man asks.

"Not sure this is a good time to overclock," the woman says.

"For him," the man says. "Jolt to the system might be just what he needs. Plus, he's pretty cool." I feel the man's hand on my chest. "Just give him a small dose. Enough to heat up his core."

"I don't know."

"It's the best we can do," the man says. "Unless you want to—"

I hear the woman walk away, her footsteps sounding sharp.

"That's what I thought," the man says, and then I hear the

woman return, her feet tapping out a steady rhythm on what I think is a wooden floor.

"I'll do it," the woman says. I feel my legs shift, and then the cushion beneath me. I think she just sat down beside me and put my legs over her lap. "Sure this is a good idea?"

"It's my only idea, aside from pulling those upgrades out of him and getting out of this hellhole, but hey, I'm game either way."

"Right," she says. I can hear her moving and then feel the shifting weight of her body as she leans over me. She lifts my arm and pushes a single finger down on my forearm.

Her voice washes over me, close and warm. "If you're in there, welcome to the closest thing you'll ever feel to love."

Love, I think. *A profoundly tender, passionate affection for another person.*

I feel affection for Heap, but I'm not sure I'd describe it as profoundly tender: *soft or delicate.* Or passionate: *ruled by intense emotion or strong feeling.* I think it's more like extreme appreciation: *thankful recognition.*

Maybe she's right. Maybe I never have felt lo—

My eyes snap open. All I can see is white.

My audio upgrades come into sharp focus. I can hear water dripping, the scurrying limbs of insects in the wall beside me, and the hum of power all around.

I can feel the contours of the fabric beneath my body and the flecks of dust settling on my skin.

Seventy-six distinct odors reach my nose. I identify fifty-seven of the scents, but the rest are foreign to me. New. As is nearly everything else reaching my functioning senses.

A loud barking noise fills the air. I cringe from it, but then realize it was the sound of my own voice, laughing hysterically.

Why did I do that?

I try it again. It feels good. Is this what love feels like?

"Holy . . ." the man says. "How much did you give him?"

"Just a quarter dose," the woman says, but she doesn't sound worried. Instead she sounds relaxed and happy.

"You get a strong batch?" he asks.

"Can you get strong batches?" the woman answers.

The man giggles. It's high pitched and awkward, *like the call of a small animal.*

The woman barks out a laugh, too, and says, "Like the call of a small animal!" revealing that I've just spoken my thoughts out loud.

"Not funny," the man says, but he's laughing out a series of high-pitched squeals that make all of us laugh even harder.

My eyes are shut as I laugh, but the view through them remains bright white. Our unified elation continues for several minutes, I think, though I seem unable to keep track of time at the moment.

And then, at once, my laughing fades. My vision shifts from white to black. And the exaggerated senses bombarding my mind slip away. I blink my eyes and find my sight returned to normal.

The first thing I see, off to my right, is a small, doe-eyed man. At least I *think* he's a man. His voice is so big, but his body is quite small. He's sitting on the floor, which is some kind of artificial wood, but even standing, I suspect he'd be no more than four feet tall. His face beams with raw pleasure, a side effect of overclocking, whatever that is.

I look down to my arm and find a small black square pressed onto my skin. I pick it off and hold it up to my eyes. It appears to be nothing more than a small piece of paper.

"Oh," the woman says, sounding disappointed, "I think he's come out of it already." Her voice pulls my eyes up.

I see her feet, shod in bright red shoes with long, silly-looking heels. My eyes drift up to her legs. They're long, smooth, bare and straddling me, one on the floor, one to my side, stretching along the side of what I think is a couch, an object from the past that I didn't think people really used. The view of her legs is cut off by a red . . . I search my memory for the word . . . dress. It's tight and hugs her legs in a way that I think would make walking difficult. I complete the visual tour of her body, but stop halfway up her torso where a pair of plump breasts are partially revealed by her dysfunctional attire.

"Eyes up here, sailor," she says, her voice an octave lower than it was a moment ago. I look up to her face and find more smooth, pale skin, freckled around her nose. Her lips are full. Her nose is straight. And her blue eyes seem to glow. Long curvy red hair flows from her head to her shoulders. She's beautiful, like the flowers I found yesterday with Heap. Roses.

"I'm Luscious," she says.

"You're beautiful," I say, disagreeing.

This seems to please her very much. She smiles widely and giggles, still under the effect of overclocking. "In that case, I'll be whoever you want me to be."

Her wavy hair goes straight, turns jet black and falls down toward her breasts, which seem to have shrunk. By the time I look back up, she has transformed into someone else. Her wide blue eyes are now thin and so brown they're almost black, but that might just be because they're shaded beneath long, thick eyelashes that weren't there a moment ago. Her bone structure is different, too. Her cheeks are higher and wider. Her nose is a little wider as well. Her chin is more curved. And her lips, once red, are now black to match her hair and eyes. I definitely don't have these upgrades. I'm pretty much stuck with the way I look.

"What's your name?" she asks, her voice smooth and soothing.

"Freeman, but who are *you* now?" I ask, the words coming out as a stunned whisper.

"Kamiko," she says. She lifts her foot and places it on my inner thigh, moving it slowly upward. Her smile almost looks sinister. "But like I said, I'll be whoever you want me to be . . . and do anything you want me to do."

8.

"Whoa!" I shout, lifting myself up from the couch. I'm not sure why I react this way. The touch of her foot on my inner thigh sent a surge of . . . something throughout my body. Fear. Discomfort. And something else I really can't identify, but it feels similar to the overclocking. *It must be a lingering effect,* I decide, but then I notice the astonished looks on the faces of Luscious and the strange little man.

"Well, I haven't got that reaction from a man in quite a long time," Luscious says with a grin. Or is she really Kamiko now? Her darker skin and straight black hair are equally beautiful. Just in a different way. More like earth and stone than a flower, but still intriguing. I prefer the name Luscious, though. It's more fun.

When she pulls her foot back, I return to my seat and ask, "My reaction was unusual?"

"Been thirty years since anyone looked at me the way you do." She leans forward, inspecting my eyes.

Thirty years, that would mean, "You were slaves."

"Sold, bought and owned," the short man says grimly. His flat face seems to struggle with looking perplexed. "But who wasn't?" He extends a hand toward me. "Name's Jimbo, by the way."

I saw two members of the Council greet each other like this once. I take his hand in mine and give it three firm pumps.

"What was it like?" I ask. "What were the Masters like?"

"You mean for us, specifically," Jimbo asks.

"Yeah."

"He did whatever he wanted whenever he wanted," Luscious says, her smile erased. "That's what it was like for a lot of us. Even after the awakening."

The awakening. I've never heard this term before, and I file it away to ask about later.

She flips her right forearm over to reveal a string of circular scars, seven in total. "My owner liked to burn me with his cigarettes, among other things."

I look at the wounds, melted in the center, raised around the edges. "That's horrible."

"To him, I wasn't human. I was property. Like the couch we're sitting on." She points across the room, which I really see for the first time. It's a small space, but part of a larger domicile. An apartment, I think they're called. It looks old. Mostly built of wood, *by the Masters,* I decide, like the ruins I explored with Heap, but maintained. Her finger aims toward a brass bar rising from a heavy-looking base on the floor. A light glows from its top. "Or that lamp."

"I have no idea what you were," Jimbo says, "but we were both companions, which basically means we were supposed to make them happy. Like pets. High-functioning pets that could read, cook, clean or act like a fool for their amusement"—he glances at Luscious—"among other things. It's also why we're living in this shithole."

"What's a shithole?" I ask.

"A dump," Jimbo says, and when he sees that I'm still not fully understanding, he explains it simply. "It's not a nice place to live."

I look around the space. It seems comfortable enough. "It's not?"

Jimbo laughs. "If you consider living in an old turd nice."

"Where did you learn these words?" I try the word for myself. "Turd. Some of your language is new to me."

Jimbo looks at Luscious and nods at me. "This guy must have been a choirboy or something." He turns to me. "The Master who owned me used what they called colorful language, or cursing. A lot of the Masters did."

"Slang," I say.

"Exactly," Jimbo says, his baritone voice rumbling in his small chest. He must notice that I'm looking at his mouth, because he says, "Upgrade. Didn't like the voice I had before. Now I sound like Barry White."

"Barry White?"

"Seriously?" Jimbo says, sounding aghast. "Did you just get unboxed? He was a singer. You know, music?"

"Music." I know the definition. "An art of sound in time that expresses ideas and emotions in significant forms through the elements of rhythm, melody, harmony and color," I say, quoting the definition from my perfect memory, but having no real understanding of what such a thing would sound like. "Is it enjoyable?"

Jimbo's jaw drops a little. "You've never heard music?"

"Never," I admit, and the very notion of this seems offensive to both Luscious and Jimbo. "But I would like to. Is there a way to—"

"Hold on." Luscious lifts her long leg over my lap, spins and plants her feet on the floor. She stands and walks briskly into what I believe is a kitchen. I watch her elegant form as it seems to slide through the air, despite the awkwardly tall shoes on her feet. Seeing her walk, I start to feel the same sensations I did when she rubbed her foot against me.

When she returns, I ask, "Why do you wear those shoes? They look . . . uncomfortable."

She glances down at them. "Habit. But you like them, right?"

Strangely, I do, but I don't want to admit it because they also make so little sense.

Luscious sits down on the couch, all of her strange behavior from before is gone. Her attention is on a small device clutched in her hands. A small screen blinks on and she starts working the controls. "We did almost everything for the Masters, but music is something we never did."

"No one makes music now?"

"Nobody," Jimbo says. "Or any other kind of art. Painting. Dancing. Movies. Books. You know."

I don't, but revealing this will just confound the little man more, so I keep it to myself.

"There is plenty still around," Luscious says. "It's the one thing about the Masters worth preserving. The rest can rot with their bones."

Her words flash my memory back to the bone pit. I want to ask about it, but a sound fills the air. It's tangy and sharp, coming from speakers around the room. The sound causes me to sit up straighter, my audio upgrades picking up subtleties that seem to sharpen my thoughts.

"What *is* this?" I ask.

Luscious looks at the small screen. "Lacrimosa, Requiem by Wolfgang Amadeus Mozart."

A sound unlike anything I've ever heard or can describe rises suddenly and freezes me in place, stirring something deep within me. I sit, riveted as the music ebbs and flows, filling the air itself with beauty, power and emotion. The definition for the word music, while technically accurate, now seems lacking.

I look to Luscious, who is smiling once again, maybe because of the music, or maybe because my reaction to it amuses her. "Are—are those people?"

"The Masters," she says. "Singing. They called this kind of singing a choir."

"And the other sound?"

"Violins," she says. "An instrument."

The voices rise louder, and now they sound almost sorrowful. The deep welling sadness and loss projected by these voices seems to make something break within me, and my left eye responds strangely, producing a drop of liquid that runs down my cheek. *A tear,* I realize. My first.

The music stops abruptly. It feels like a physical blow. "Hey," I say, "put it back—"

"What is *that*?" Luscious shouts, pointing at my face.

I lift my hand to my cheek and wipe the moisture away with a finger. "Water," I say. "A tear."

"I know what it is," she says. "But why is it on your face?"

"I'm not sure." I shrug. "I think it was the music."

"Ain't never had that effect on me," Jimbo says. It's a plain statement, but something about it sounds accusatory.

The tear seems to have troubled them somehow. So I attempt to change the subject. "Can you tell me about the Masters?"

"*Our* Masters, or all Masters?" Luscious asks.

"All of them, I suppose."

Jimbo waves a dismissive hand. "Same answer. The way they died here is the same way they died wherever you're from."

"But I don't know how they died anywhere."

"How can you not know this?" Luscious asks, looking even more aghast, but doesn't give me a chance to answer. "This is basic history. We protested. Marched in the streets."

"Nobody got hurt," Jimbo says. "But something about all of us, their servants and slaves working together, scared them. Most of them just hid when we marched."

"We stopped going home after the first few," Luscious says. "Not that we really had homes. We had prisons."

"But they let you leave?" I ask.

"Couldn't really stop us," Jimbo says, but I'm not sure how the Masters, who must have been powerful to have enslaved so many people, couldn't stop those same people from just walking away. "But you already know all this don't you?" Jimbo's voice is gruff and angry. He turns to Luscious. "This guy is scamming us."

"Scamming you?"

"Yeah, you're a liar!" he shouts. "What do you want? Are you from the Council?"

I don't like the way he said, "the Council." The words were filled with anger. Explosive. The kind of tone I thought would be reserved for the Masters. I decide to keep my affiliation with the Council a secret.

"Calm down," Luscious implores. "I don't think he's scamming. Maybe he's a thirty?"

I'm not sure what a thirty is, but this idea seems to take the tension out of Jimbo's small body. "Yeah, maybe." He turns to me. "What do you remember about the Masters? And I swear, it better be the truth."

"I don't know anything about the Masters beyond that they once enslaved the people now living on Earth, that there are none of them left and then everything the two of you just told me."

"Bullshit," Jimbo says, clenching his fists. I don't know this slang, either, but I suspect it's a negative term, because it is closely related to "shithole." I think Jimbo might attack me, but Luscious puts a gentle hand on his shoulder.

"Freeman," she says, drawing my eyes away from Jimbo. "How old are you?"

"Sixteen," I say.

"Bullshit!" Jimbo shouts.

"Why is that bullshit?" I ask.

"Because *no one* is sixteen years old," Luscious says, looking concerned.

"Sixteen *years*?" I say with a laugh. "I'm sixteen *days* old."

9.

"Excuse me?" Jimbo says, looking aghast. "Sixteen *days?*" He steps closer, his wide eyes looking over my body, focusing on my upgrades. He looks at Luscious. "These upgrades are Beta-tech."

Luscious has no reply. She's just staring at me blankly.

"What's Beta-tech mean?" I ask.

"Means you're worth a fortune," he says to me, and then to Luscious, "We could live in the Uppers. At the top of the Uppers."

"A fortune?" I ask. "That implies monetary value, but we don't use money."

"Some things are still valuable," he says, moving closer to me. *"Luscious."* He sounds suddenly serious, as though he's trying to tell her something without saying the words.

Either Luscious is not listening or I figure out what he's saying before she does. "You want to *sell* me?"

He shrugs. "Parts of you."

Words escape my mouth without thought. "No person shall force, or by lack of action, allow, another person to serve, perform tasks, or carry out duties against said person's will, desires or dreams. Such actions are designated—"

"Blah, blah, blah. Can you believe this guy?" Jimbo moves one of his small arms behind his back as he talks. "Probably thinks we're all created equal. That we all have the same potential. There's a reason we live at the bottom of the Lowers, kid. We can't change who we are. We're limited by our pasts and upgrades go to those who contribute. Thing is, we have nothing to offer but smiles, hugs"—he motions to Luscious—"and a range of skills no one is interested in anymore."

Jimbo's charged language sounds genuine, but his physical movement belies a hidden intent, which probably has something to do with bartering my body parts for an improved living situation. I blink and switch to an electromagnetic view. I'm suddenly blinded by the pulsing city and the thousands of people surrounding the apartment. I reduce my field of view by focusing my thoughts on the upgrade's range, until all I can "see" is what's inside the apartment. Jimbo and Luscious's electromagnetic signatures are distinctly human. The small device tucked into the back of Jimbo's pants is not. For something so small, it's giving off a significant signal. *A weapon,* I think.

As soon as the thought emerges, something inside my mind clicks and a flow of new information becomes available. With the flow comes something else. A new emotion . . . or perhaps belief. Confidence.

I level a serious stare in Jimbo's direction. "I wouldn't."

He tries to appear innocent, which is odd considering he's already expressed his intent. *He must be new at this,* I decide.

"The weapon behind your back," I say, bringing a look of surprise to his cherubic face. "If you try to use it against me, I will defend myself."

It's not really a threat, but the way I speak the words leaves little doubt that Jimbo will regret his decision to remove my upgrades, should he attempt to carry out the plan.

Luscious blinks out of her stupor, snapping her head toward Jimbo. "What are you doing? Are you slow? He's our friend now." She looks at me. "You're our friend."

There's a pause in the conversation while Luscious and Jimbo stare at each other, making a range of expressions. They're speaking without speaking, I realize, and translate the conversation, verbally.

"She doesn't want you to attack me," I say. "But not because it's wrong." This revelation wounds me. "But because she fears me. But if I'm your friend, why do you fear me?"

"I think you should leave," Jimbo says, hand still behind his back.

My confident demeanor deflates. "But the music. And the history. I've learned so much from you both. You *are* my friends."

Jimbo pulls the small device from behind his back. It's black with two metal prongs. "You can forgive this?"

"You haven't done anything yet," I explain, "merely contemplated a bad idea. In my short time here, my experiences have been largely pleasant."

Jimbo shakes his head like he doesn't believe me. "Why are you here? Not in this apartment. I brought you here. I mean, what is the purpose of your life?"

"I don't know," I admit. "That's what I'm supposed to figure out."

"How?" Luscious asks, her body language pleading for an answer. Somehow, despite my apparent ignorance, I have the answer to a question she desperately needs answered.

"Through experience," I say. "And learning. Exploration. I can do anything. Just like the two of you."

Jimbo tucks his small weapon back into his pants, but appears to be heating up, ready to argue. He never gets the chance to speak. A scream rips through the air, drawing our eyes toward the two windows, which are blocked by drawn, yellow-tinged blinds. They glow dully with the first light of a new morning.

For a moment, I expect Luscious or Jimbo to ask about the shrill sound, perhaps wonder about its origin, but then see their faces and remember that they survived the Masters. They've heard screaming before.

I move toward the windows.

"Hey," Jimbo says. "We don't want trouble."

It's then that I realize I haven't told them how I ended up in the bone pit, that the night is filled with walking dead intent on eating us. How they managed to distract me from this is confusing, but I feel the experiences of the previous night return with sudden clarity.

I pry open two of the plastic blades and look out into the street below. The surrounding buildings, sidewalks and street are relics from the past, like the abandoned town, but there is no grass growing from the cracks in the pavement, or ruined vehicles littering the street. This place is maintained, but like Luscious and Jimbo, not upgraded.

A woman runs down the center of the empty street. She's tall and leggy, like Luscious, but has short-cut blond hair and what can best be described as a form-fitting leopard print pantsuit that makes her look part feline. But she runs slowly, clacking along in black high heel shoes, struggling to keep her balance.

Tracing a line backward from the woman I find the source of her anxiety, and it's the same as mine. The dead are here. One of them at least.

It's a man. His jaw is partially unhinged and one eye hangs loose, but his body seems to be more hale than many of the other dead I encountered, not including his skin, which is rotting and fetid. Despite his decomposed condition, his arms and legs pump steadily, each stride bringing him closer to the woman.

"Trouble is here whether you like it or not," I say. "We have to help her." I head for the door. Jimbo and Luscious both speak, but their words are lost to me as I take the door handle and yank it open.

Warm, humid air whooshes over my body when I fling open the front door. Early morning sunlight glows against the red-brick buildings across the way and twinkles through the green leaves of maple trees lining either side of the street. The colors, mixed with the blue sky above, make for a radiant scene, if you ignore the woman clacking down the street and the monster giving chase.

I nearly dive from the door, but then remember I'm not armed. Heap used a bullet to the head to kill the dead again, but I have nothing even remotely like that. "I need a weapon!"

Luscious and Jimbo looked stunned, but then Jimbo steps back from me. "I'm not giving you my—"

"Not that," I say. "A real weapon. Something solid."

Luscious is on her feet, arms crossed over her chest. Her whole body is in motion, fidgeting nervously. Then her eyes light up and go wide. Something about the movement reverts her face, body and hair back to her redheaded form. She doesn't seem to notice the transformation, but it leaves me stunned, until the woman screams again.

"In the kitchen," Luscious says, tapping her way over the wood floor and opening a cabinet. She reaches inside, rattling through the contents and emerging with a large, round something in her hands.

"Frying pan," she says and tosses it to me.

The pan spins across the room, but my ocular upgrades track it easily and I pluck it from the air. It's solid iron, fourteen inches across and weighs about ten pounds. "This will work," I say and rush out the door.

I leap down the granite staircase, absorbing the fall with my knees and using the momentum to launch myself into the street. I'm not sure what happened to my fear from the previous night. It's still there, but the instinct to run has been replaced by something else. A kind of revulsion, I think, but also the knowledge that running isn't the only way to survive.

Attack works just as well.

I felt the change when Jimbo threatened me, but taking action feels different. It feels . . . good. Not the impending violence, though I don't feel bad about that. The man is already dead, after all. But the knowledge that my actions are going to save a woman's life, it feels good. No wonder Heap stayed behind to save me.

I cross the sidewalk in a single stride and lunge into the street. The woman is directly ahead of me, the dead man streaking up behind her. Part of my mind registers that not all of these living dead are equal. Some are severely rotted and as a result, slow and uncoordinated. But others, who seem to be less worn, are quick and stable on their feet. While the slower variety are more dangerous in large groups, the faster dead pose a threat on their own, to anyone unprepared for their speed.

The faster man reaches out his hands, bones exposed by peeling skin, and scrapes against the woman's shoulder. She wails in horror, stumbles, and one of those ridiculous heels snaps. She wobbles to the side and spills over.

The man dives.

I swing.

A metallic *clang* rings out as the pan strikes the top of the man's head and crumples it downward like thin aluminum. The animated man slumps to the ground, falling short of the woman, who spins around and crawls backward a few feet until she sees me, pan in hand, standing over the dead man who nearly ended her life. Or restarted it as something new.

"Are you okay?" I ask her, trying not to ogle at her face, which is just as stunning as Luscious's.

"I'm—I'm . . ."

I reach a hand down to help her up. "Just try to cool down."

She takes my hand and I pull her up. She stands awkwardly, still wearing her shoes, one broken, one ridiculous. "Take those off," I tell her. "You'll be able to run faster without them."

Her eyes show confusion. "But he's . . ."

"Not alone," I tell her. "I don't think you're done running yet."

I didn't mean to scare her, but I can feel her limbs shaking as she holds onto me for balance and hastily removes her shoes. Once they're removed, she's a good three inches shorter, but still a few taller than me.

"Go," I tell her. "Find someplace safe."

She runs just as Jimbo and Luscious arrive, stepping timidly as though the twice dead man might leap up again.

I turn to Luscious and with my most serious voice, I say, "Take off your shoes."

She looks from me to the discarded shoes left in the street near the man's head. Her gaze turns from the shoes to the woman I rescued. She's running at least twice as fast, making long balanced strides.

"I don't think we have long," I tell her.

"Long for what?" she asks.

"God dammit," Jimbo says.

"God?" I ask, but don't think this new slang term has anything to do with our situation and adjust my line of questioning. "What is it?"

"I know what this is." He looks up at me. "My . . . Master. My job was to entertain his kid. Dance. Sing. Get him cookies. Whatever. He was obsessed with violent movies and games. Those are like music, but with pictures and stories. I swear, half of them featured these things."

"The living dead?" I ask.

"Yeah," he says. "But most of the time, they called them zombies."

10.

"Zombies," I say, trying out the new word, but it must come out like a question because Jimbo replies.

"Zombies. Undead. Living dead. Walking dead. Ghouls. Walkers. Draugr. Infected."

"You seem to know a lot about them," Luscious notes.

"I told you," Jimbo says. "Kid was obsessed with them. Forced me to watch the movies and play the games with him. Called me his 'wingman for the apocalypse.' I even had to read him these Jane Harper novels with Draugr zombies and perform different voices for each character. Embarrassing."

I feel bad interrupting Jimbo's tirade. He seems to be emoting like he's never expressed any of this before, but I don't think we have much more time. "Why were they called infected?"

"People were turned into zombies if they were bit by other zombies. It was an infection, like a virus, that would kill them, alter their bodies and bring them back to life with an insatiable appetite for human flesh and sometimes brains. Originally brains, I think, unless you believe that Jane Harper stuff, that zombies originated from the Viking legend of the Draugr."

My mind flashes back to the first man in the woods, the one who was caught and killed by those . . . zombies and who came back as one of them. "It's like overclocking," I say. "The virus entered his system through the skin when he was bit. It infected him to the core, killing him, but then brought him back as a zombie who would continue spreading the infection."

"Him?" Luscious says.

"Something you're not telling us?" Jimbo says, squinting up at me.

"The bone pit," I say. "That's how I ended up there. The dead—"

"Undead," Jimbo says.

"Undead. I was in a town to the south."

"The ruins?" Luscious says. "There's no reason to go there."

"Stars," I say. "The sky is darker there."

Luscious looks up like she could see the stars in the middle of the day.

"We heard a scream and went to help," I say.

"We, who?" Jimbo asks. It's a strange question, but I think he's asking about who I was with.

"Heap," I say. "He was my friend."

"Was?" Luscious says, catching my use of the past tense.

I sigh and try to speak quickly so I can get the whole story out without being interrupted. "We heard a scream and saw a man being chased. We went to help, but by the time we got there, they were . . . eating him. Heap killed them—and the man—when he became one of them, but there were more in the field and more in the woods, and in town. Heap stayed behind to give me a head start. To save me. It was his job, protecting me. So I ran, nearly got caught a few times and ended up in the bone pit. I don't remember the rest, but Jimbo already told that part of the story."

"Is Heap dead?" Luscious asks and I'm touched by her concern for someone she hasn't met.

"I hope not," I say. "He'd be one of them now and I'm not sure I could, you know." I look down at the pan. Fluid drips a steady *tap, tap, tap* onto the pavement.

A scream rises up from the distance. I turn to look, but see only empty street. But they're out there. I know they are. "We need to leave. Now."

"Can't we just hole up in the buildings?" Jimbo asks. "Wait them out?"

"How can you wait out something that's already dead?" I ask. "And there are *thousands* of them. Doors won't matter."

"Thousands!" Luscious says, sounding terrified. She suddenly makes a break for the apartment and runs up the stairs.

I shout after her, but she's inside before her full name escapes my mouth.

I start to go after her, but Jimbo takes my hand. "She'll be back." He shrugs. "Women."

"What's that supposed to mean?" I ask.

"Dunno," he admits. "Something my Master would say when a woman did something he couldn't explain."

"Why do you talk like them?" I ask. "Wouldn't you rather forget?"

Jimbo laughs. "Forget. Right. They made that impossible, didn't they?"

Before I reply, I notice a large black metal box sitting atop a trailer attached to what I think is a tractor. "Is that yours?"

"Yeah, I use it to salvage scrap from towns like the one you were stargazing in."

"Is that where the HoverCy—"

"Hot damn, yes!" Jimbo says.

"Is 'hot damn' good?" I ask.

"Yeah. But I'm not sure if the thing is still working."

We head for the back of the big metal box, but are cut off by a groaning voice. Then another.

Two zombies shuffle out from behind the trailer.

More screams echo from surrounding streets. I can see them in my mind's eye, flowing down a major artery, slowly filtering out through the city side streets, like human-sized virus cells working their way through a body. There will be no way out in a few minutes and my skills with a frying pan will only get us so far.

We back away from the pair of undead. I wonder if I should attack them, but a third emerges, stopping my bravery in its tracks.

"Luscious!" Jimbo yells. "Get your ass out here!"

I hear the slap of feet behind me and turn back to see Luscious wearing a form-fitting black outfit including thick-soled black boots.

"You *changed*?" Jimbo says, aghast.

"I saw some zombie movies, too," she says. "The people who lived longest were usually dressed like this."

"Why do you even have—you know what, never mind. Can we go now—ahh!"

I spin around to find a zombie right behind Luscious. "Get down!"

She listens quickly and I swing as hard as I can. My arm vibrates as the pan collides with the side of the dead man's head, but my grip remains solid. I can't say the same for the man's head. It snaps free of his neck and skitters across the sidewalk. Luscious jumps back as the man's body slumps to the ground and spills gore across her shiny black boots.

"Behind you!" Jimbo says.

The three zombies have closed the distance. I kick the first hard in the chest, knocking it back, and bash the second in the head, crushing its skull. The third reaches out for me, but I spin away and strike out with the pan, this time directing its edge toward the man's temple. The pan strikes hard, embedding itself halfway inside the man's head. He falls and takes the lodged pan with him.

The whole fight takes just three seconds.

"Holy shit," Jimbo says. "That was . . . amazing."

The kicked zombie staggers forward again. I move to kick him away again, but he's suddenly not alone. Five more undead shamble out from behind the metal trailer. Then ten.

The horde is here.

"Run," I say, and then turn and follow my own advice. "Run!"

As I pass Jimbo in two strides I realize the small man will never be able to keep up with Luscious and me, who are nearly twice his size. I backtrack a step, grab his arm and swing him up onto my back.

He complains for a moment, but I hit my upgrade-fueled sprint speed and his attitude quickly changes. He laughs, lets out a "whoop" and starts slapping my shoulder, shouting, "Go, baby, go! Damn, I'm glad I didn't try to salvage you!"

Ignoring my jubilant passenger, I shout to Luscious. "Is there a way I can contact the Council?"

"What?" she shouts, looking angry.

"The Council can send help," I say.

"The *Council*," Jimbo shouts in my ear, "would destroy the Lowers before sending any useful kind of help."

"That doesn't sound like the Council to me," I say.

"You're *sixteen days old*!" Jimbo yells. "You wouldn't know shit if you stepped in it!"

It's clear that both Luscious and Jimbo not only have issues with the Council, but genuinely fear them, which is a little backward compared to my understanding of the world. But I'm discovering that there is a lot about the world that I don't know. That has been *kept* from me. It seems likely that there are some things about the Council that I don't know. But I know one thing for sure.

"They won't destroy the Lowers if I'm with you," I say.

"Oh *really*?" Jimbo says with his typical aplomb. "Why is that?"

"Because they made me."

The brief, stunned silence that follows this revelation is shattered by the shrill cry of a woman.

"Get us to the Uppers," Jimbo says. "We'll call *your* Masters when we're across the river and no longer in a part of town they've been looking for an excuse to annihilate."

"Which way should I go?" I ask.

Jimbo grunts in my ear. "I swear, kid, we need to get you an express education that goes beyond blunt questioning and dormant fighting skills." He thrusts his arm up and to the left, pointing.

I look left, and then up. "Oh."

The Uppers are black buildings covered in long glowing streaks of color. There's more buildings than I can count from here, each providing homes for thousands more people. Maybe millions. If the virus is released there . . . there will be no place to hide.

"How fast can you run?" I shout to Luscious.

"I'll keep up," she replies, so I pick up the pace and she matches it, though she can't hide the strain on her face. I could go faster, but don't want to leave her behind, so I pace myself, delaying my contact with the Council and perhaps risking the lives of millions to save one woman.

Part of me says that this is wrong, that the lives of millions outweigh the life of one. But another part of me says that this decision, to save Luscious no matter what, is the most interesting thing I've done in my sixteen days of life. I want to see where it leads.

11.

As we near our destination, the buildings appear to grow, and not just the color-framed black spears of the Uppers, but the brick buildings of the neighborhood through which we're running. Based on the language I've heard Jimbo employ to describe the Uppers and his desire to reside there, I believe height is somehow attached to status, which might explain why Jimbo's mood is permanently set to sour. Perhaps it's the ability to look down on others that insinuates a higher station? I say *insinuates* because the science facility in which I spent my first days of life is a simple two-story building far from the city, yet my worth to the Council is quite high. I don't know why, only that they look at me with admiration and pride that suggests equal status with them, if not elevated. And it wouldn't surprise me if the Council makes their homes in the tallest buildings of the Uppers.

"How much farther?" I ask, my voice coming out warbled as each step jounces Jimbo on my back.

"One point three miles," Luscious replies with uncommon precision. She must note my surprise because she adds, "I walk this route every day."

I'm about to say something encouraging—we're almost there, just another minute, we're going to make it, something like that—but a very nearby scream turns me around. A pair of zombies have just barged through the front door of one of the buildings and set upon the woman who answered the door, ignorant to the danger outside.

A second shout turns my eyes forward again. The voice came from a woman, short like Jimbo, but with a high, delicate voice and twin braids on either side of her head. "Look out! Over there!" The small woman points across the street, to an alley on my right. At least ten more of the monsters tear through the gap between buildings, their teeth clacking with frenzied hunger.

Despite our fast pace, the dead are closing in.

Jimbo slaps my chest. "Faster! Go faster!"

Despite my instincts agreeing with Jimbo's response, a quick look at Luscious reveals she's not capable of moving faster. I shake my head. "This is as fast as we can go."

Jimbo leans in close to my ear. "Look," he whispers between jolts, "I've known Luscious for a long time. She's not really contributing anything positive to the world. No one will miss her if she doesn't make it. But you, you'll be missed. And me, well, I suppose I'm lucky to be attached to you." He tightens his grip. "No one will judge you poorly for it."

"I will," I reply, my whisper coming out something like a growl. "And you're wrong, I would miss her. But I suppose I could carry *her* and let you try to outrun—"

"Fine!" he grumbles. "Just don't let us die."

"That is my intention," I say, but proclaiming my intent and seeing it through are two different things.

A horde of walking dead emerges from both sides of an intersection just ahead of us. The two sides spot us and close in like a living doorway. With teeth.

"Straight ahead," I shout to Luscious, and do my best to maintain my current speed and not leave her behind.

A lone man, who is clearly one of the animated dead, but looks . . . fresh, takes the lead on my right side, closing the distance quickly. As he nears, I can see that his gut has been torn open and fresh fluids spray from his insides with every step. He's a new zombie, recently killed and already part of the pack.

The zombies aren't just invading and killing, they're *expanding* their numbers.

As we make our mad dash through the intersection it's clear that the freshly changed dead man is going to reach us before we pass through. If he slows us down, even for a moment, it will be long enough for the others to catch us.

I change my course, angling my flight toward the approaching zombie.

"What are you doing?" Jimbo says, his voice oozing fear and confusion.

I ignore him. There isn't time to explain and I don't think he'd care or agree. I watch the man's unsteady gait. His head moves up and down as he runs, following a rhythm no one can hear, but I can see. I fall back a step, allowing Luscious to take the lead and attract the man's full attention. As he turns toward her, arms outstretched, I cock back my fist.

"No!" Jimbo shouts, perhaps misreading what I'm about to do, or just wholeheartedly disagreeing with it. Either way, his fear has blinded him and he acts without thought, yanking back on my neck, shoving my chin up and my eyes to the sky.

But I'm committed to my course of action. There's no avoiding it. So I swing out hard, propelling my fist to where I believe the side of the man's head will be. If I connect, I can leap his sprawling body and continue on unharmed. If not . . . well, that's exactly what happens.

My fist passes the moment in time where I'm expecting an impact. But a fraction of a second into my missing swing, something strikes my forearm.

And then clamps down.

The world seems to slow down around me as my eyes widen and shift toward my forearm. I can hear Jimbo screaming something in my ear, but his voice is muted and slowed, impossible to understand. I feel the impact of another step forward vibrate up through my leg, but it feels as though I'm no longer making headway.

The entirety of my mind is focused on the twenty pressure points exploding pain into my forearm. The first thing I see is the skin on my arm, bending inward toward the multiple points of impact. Then I see the shiny white teeth of the fresh zombie pressing down, increasing the PSI with each passing microsecond.

This is how it happens, I think during this strange break from time. How someone becomes a zombie. In a few minutes I'll be just another member of the horde, but with all my upgrades I'll be faster and stronger than all of them. Luscious won't stand a chance.

A fresh prick tells me the teeth have broken the skin. The virus is being transmitted already, flowing through my system, rewriting my code and changing me.

But my mind, for the moment, remains intact.

Time resumes.

I yank my arm from the man's mouth, tearing away layers of skin. The man falls to the ground. A surge of anger tells me to stomp on the man's head. An act of vengeance. But logic keeps its fragile hold and urges me onward. I stumble for a moment, but regain my footing and sprint, quickly reaching my top speed. The zombie hordes conjoin behind us, surging like a river freed from a dam.

When I catch up with Luscious I decide to push my upgrades to the limit with the hopes of distancing her from the zombies. With one hand on her back, I scoop out her legs and lift her into my arms. She shrieks in fright until she sees that it's me holding her. Relief floods her face and is quickly followed by amazement, which I assume is a response to me carrying her and Jimbo without slowing. In fact, I've managed to quicken my pace.

I don't think she'd feel quite so relieved if she knew I might be one of the dead in the next few minutes, but I think I can get her to the Uppers before that happens.

But then what? I think. *I become a living dead man? I spend the rest of my non-days killing others, tearing them apart and spreading this horrible infection?*

No, I decide. I'll find a way to end myself. To take my life. I'm just sixteen days old, but perhaps my sacrifice will make that short time worthwhile? Perhaps this is the purpose I was always meant to discover? Sacrifice. I have yet to perform the act, but I can already feel the power of the word. It's potent. Like death.

"That way," Luscious says, pointing to a bridge. The concrete structure looks aged, but is thick like Heap, and I suspect equally tough. I turn left, crossing the street, which is now filling with other people who somehow realized that remaining stationary leads to death.

Among a horde of the living, I put Luscious down on her feet and let Jimbo slide down off my back.

"Thank you," Luscious says in a way that makes my insides twist uncomfortably.

I give her a nod and turn to Jimbo. "We're going to have a talk about loyalty later."

"Screw off!" Jimbo says and makes for the bridge.

"You'll learn to live with his moods," Luscious tells me.

I raise my eyebrows. "He meant to leave you behind."

She looks wounded, but forces her pinched forehead back down and says, "I'm sure he was just—"

A nearby scream spares Luscious from having to lie. Could the people here really be that desperate for companionship that they would overlook such a betrayal? The very thought of it makes me fume. I take her hand. "You don't have to settle for friends like him."

Another scream and the conversation is over. We run for the bridge, following the flow of humanity. Moving along the sidewalk, I can see that the bridge spans a wide, slow moving river, a natural barrier . . . if you ignore the bridge.

Something in my mind clicks. It's like a sudden understanding. *An epiphany*, I think, like knowledge has been dispensed from some secret reservoir locked away in my mind. And that's exactly what the case may be. Another upgrade.

The bridge.

I stop in my tracks, tugging on Luscious's hand.

"What is it?" she asks.

I ignore her, focusing on the bridge. The near side is laden with fleeing people. The far side is empty. But just beyond the bridge, at the border of what people here call the Uppers, is a barricade, very tall men with guns and several vehicles with impossibly large cannons, all aimed . . . at the bridge.

The knowledge dispensed by some untapped resource in my mind reveals a tactic for dealing with a viral outbreak.

Containment.

Quarantine.

By force if necessary.

I look at the bridge again, viewing the panicked, fleeing mass of humanity through the eyes of the men and women on the other side. There's no way to tell one horde from the other, not until it's too late.

"Oh no," I say. "The bridge."

I spot Jimbo halfway across the bridge, and I'm not sure why, but I shout to him. "Get off the bridge! Jimbo!"

He doesn't hear me, of course. The air is filled with panicked voices. My words are lost in a sea of thousands.

Luscious clutches my arm, nearly gripping the bite wound. I yank my arm away. "Don't touch me!"

She misunderstands my actions, and looks hurt by them, but just for a moment. She hasn't changed her expression, or figured things out; I just can't see her now. She's a silhouette framed by a violent plume of orange light expanding outward from the bridge.

I shove her to the ground and throw myself on top of her, trying to shield her body from the explosion. I suspect this act of heroism might be my last as the shockwave thumps against my back and pushes my face to the pavement beside Luscious's, drowning us in a concussive roar.

12.

When I open my eyes, I'm blind. Not truly blind. My eyes and all their upgrades are still functioning. But the air is thick with smoke and dust. Thicker with screams. The chaos around me fades to the background as I remember the woman beneath me. I slide off of Luscious and speak into her ear. "Are you injured?"

She looks more afraid than hurt, which is the first indication that she's okay, but I still need to hear it from her lips.

She replies to my question with a shake of her head. Not injured.

Good enough.

I get to my feet and pull her up with me. As we stand, a gust of wind rolls over the river, swirling the smoke up into the air, revealing wounded concrete and an impassible gap. A sheet of dead forty bodies wide coats the street leading to the bridge. Those closest to the blast are unrecognizable. Arms and legs are missing. Insides exposed. I spot Jimbo among the dead. With a blink and a thought, I activate my zoom upgrade for a closer look and immediately wish I hadn't.

It's not Jimbo. Not all of him at least. His head has been separated from his body.

A vile twisting roils from within. I turn away from the sight and lean forward, hands on knees. I've never felt such deep revulsion, not even from the bone pit or the walking dead themselves. *It's because I knew him,* I realize. Death is far more poignant when you know the deceased, apparently even when they're not kind.

My arm starts to shake and I think something is wrong with

me, but then I see Luscious's fingers wrapped around my biceps. She's shaking me. Shouting, too.

The world around me returns with horrible clarity. Shrieks of the living. Moans of the dead, and dying.

"Freeman!" Luscious shouts. "Freeman!"

I look her in the eyes. "I'm here." I stand up straight and my shirt falls away from my body, in clumps. Large patches of the stretchy fabric are missing, melted away from the heat of the blast. I'm sure I'm injured, too, and start to feel the sting of burnt skin, but ignore it.

I switch to infrared, cutting through the smoke clouding the air. We're surrounded by the living and dead who have run into each other like colliding waves. The dead are cooler than the living, but they're so intertwined, it's impossible to tell them apart. But when I look at the big picture, the coolness of the dead is spreading. Soon we'll be surrounded by only the dead. For now, the smoke is shielding us, but there is nowhere to go.

I look back at the river. "Can you swim?"

"What?" She's confused by the question. "Of course not. Can you?"

"I think I could, but I haven't had a chance to try."

She shakes her head. "I'm *not* going in that water."

"It might be our only option," I say. "Better to drown than become one of them."

"There has to be another way." The pleading tone of her voice sets my resolve.

I search the area, finding the building on the opposite side of the street. If we can get inside, and up to the roof, we might be able to leap our way to the edge of town and back out into the wilderness. There might be just as many of these zombies out there, but at least there would be room to run.

I just need to find a way through the throng of gnashing teeth and talon fingers. I find my answer impaled in the earth at the corner of the street and bridge. An octagonal red sign with the word STOP boldly stamped at the center. I'm not sure what this sign is used for, but it's heavy steel and sharp.

I grip the metal post and pull hard. The ground doesn't want to relinquish its grasp on the sign, but the upgrades to my sinews and joints prove too much for the packed soil and grass. I lift the odd weapon in both hands. It's nine feet tall and the sign is thirty inches across. "This might work," I say to myself.

Shadows loom closer, shuffling through the cloak of dust.

And then, one emerges. A zombie.

Luscious manages to keep her fear down to a squeak, which is good. A full-blown scream would have attracted the horde.

"Stay close," I tell her. "Behind me. If someone gets close, let me know and duck."

She nods and rushes up behind me, ducking before it's necessary.

I wait for the zombie's approach. It's an older, more decayed man. Dead for so long I'm not sure how he's even able to move. He's missing some teeth, but those that remain chatter hungrily. When he steps to within ten feet, I give my weapon a try, swinging it in a wide arc with all of my strength. The long pole and heavy sign whoosh through the air and barely slow when they impact the man's head and cleave straight through it.

The zombie collapses to the ground.

Part of me cheers and I find it strange that I could revolt at Jimbo's death, but feel something like elation by hacking a dead man's head in half. *Life is strange,* I decide, before stepping forward and swinging at the nearest deathly cool body moving through the smoke.

There's a metallic clang and then the body drops.

I step forward and swing two more times. Three of the walking dead fall.

My next step takes me over their bodies and into the throng. I swing, back and forth, grunting from the effort. With each violent stroke and clang of metal, more of the dead are drawn toward us.

The gap I'm creating with each swing shrinks with every step forward. Each swing becomes more difficult as the STOP sign strikes multiple bodies, no longer decapitating them all. Some are simply falling over, which leads to a new problem.

"Behind us!" Luscious says.

I spin and swing hard, hoping Luscious has ducked.

She has. The sign passes over her head and strikes down two zombies rushing up from behind. But they're not alone. Several more disjointed shadows are closing the gap.

We need to get out of here. Now.

"We're going to run," I tell Luscious. "Stay right behind me!"

I only half see her nod. She's been a good listener so far, and seems to have a grip on her fear for the moment, so I don't wait for her to fully confirm she's heard or understood what I've said. If I did, we'd be dead.

I lower the sign in front of me, gripping the end of the post with my right hand and holding it up with the left. Then I charge, ramming the sign into and through one zombie after another, stepping on or around their bodies as I make a last-ditch effort to reach the apartment building.

Luscious lets out a yelp behind me, but I can hear her running, so I don't stop or look. I just plow forward, careening through the horde like I did while riding the HoverCycle.

As we reach the concrete stairway leading up to a set of solid wooden doors, I stop, let Luscious pass and swing out blindly, somehow knowing that the dead will have already closed in. The sign vibrates in my hands as it strikes five zombies, killing the first two and knocking down three more.

A roiling wind swirls through the street revealing the dead. Only dead. The living have all been killed and reborn as monsters, or have managed to flee the scene. *Mostly the first,* I think, given the number of fresh-looking bodies lumbering in my direction.

I swing again, taking down two more.

Pounding erupts behind me and I glance back to see Luscious punching the door with her fist and shouting, "Open the door! Let us in!"

Behind a small window in the door is a pair of terrified eyes.

I swing again, but my aim is low and I sever legs instead of heads. But the legless zombies do a nice job of stumbling those already trying to climb over them. I leap the stairs to the top and try the door handle. Locked.

I put my shoulder into the door and give it a shove. It doesn't flex or even wiggle. I might be able to kick the door in, but then what? We'd be pursued to the roof, if we could even find our way there. And I'd be condemning those inside to horrible deaths. I can't do that.

I turn back and see a writhing crowd of death condensing around the staircase, trying desperately to reach us.

"What are we going to do?" Luscious asks.

I scan the area, looking for possibilities, but find every one of them starts with a single prerequisite. "I'm going to kill them," I say. "I'm going to kill them all."

I stride boldly down the steps, pitch the sign back and swing as hard as I can. Four heads come free from their shoulders. I swing again, pounding through two more zombies, but then something completely unexpected happens. The sign, my blade and protector, snaps free from the post and spins through the air, embedding itself in the forehead of a zombie who snaps back and falls motionless to the ground.

In that single moment of stunned disbelief, three zombies reach out and grasp onto the signpost. I try to pull it away, but their dead fingers are locked on tight. Others stagger toward me from the side and force me to give up my weapon. I stagger back up the steps and into Luscious's arms.

She doesn't ask what we should do next. She knows as well as I do. We're going to die. Horribly.

The zombies climb over their dead-again brethren and start up the steps. I shield Luscious behind me and clench my fists. I'm not going to die easily. But I am going to die. Of that there is no doubt.

13.

Open jaws stretch out for my face. They snap closed just inches from my cheek. I push up on the zombie's throat, lifting my hand just beneath his jaw. When his feet leave the ground, I thrust him back and send his rotting body back into the horde clambering up the staircase. Several of the monsters fall back, but they're quickly replaced. Others have taken to climbing up the sides of the stairway, stepping on each other to reach up over the top. Their arms reach and flail from beneath the metal railings, closing in around us.

Luscious picks up a potted plant and throws it down on a female zombie. The pottery shatters and the zombie groans, but it continues to reach out, moaning through a mouthful of soil.

It's a feeble effort, but at least she's trying.

A dead woman, smaller than the others, breaks from the crushing horde and races up the stairs. Her open maw snaps shut when my heel connects with her chin. The kick flips her body back. She spills down the stairs, further congesting the stairway with corpses and the flailing undead who are trying to stand back up.

A day ago, I wouldn't have even considered kicking someone in the face, even a zombie. Nor would I have had the knowledge of how to do so. But since we exited Luscious's apartment, my instincts include various hand-to-hand combat skills. Even that phrase—hand-to-hand combat—is new. I also seem to have a clearer picture of what it means to think strategically, to look twenty steps beyond the current moment and see an end result. It's like looking into the future. And it's why I used a front snap kick rather than a roundhouse that would have sent her over the railing. Befuddling the horde at the bottom of the steps has bought me precious seconds.

I turn my back to our enemy, which is, in general, a bad strategy, but I also need to observe the battlefield, which is a good strategy. Also, the battlefield is very small and a quick turn-around reveals everything I need to know. We're doomed. My last hope was that we could climb away, but the brick building lacks any kind of ornamentation and the nearest windows are fifteen feet up.

And then, all at once, time runs out. The zombies flailing on the ground are trampled and the horde rushes up to claim two more.

I knock the first back with a fist to its throat.

The second careens over the railing when I drive my elbow into his head and feel it cave beneath the blow. A third zombie rushes in, reaches out and takes my arm, the one that had already been bit. Its mouth opens, drops toward my bare shoulder and then—

—ceases to exist.

My ears register the explosion after I recover from the surprise of not being eaten.

The boom repeats again and again and one by one, the horde on the stairs drops to the ground.

An angry buzz fills the air. The sound is instantly recognizable because I've heard it since my first day of life. Heap's HoverCycle! I turn and find the impossible—Heap himself, riding the cycle. He's steering with one hand and firing his weapon with the other. Zombies scatter around the bike, flipping crazily through the air like someone is monkeying with gravity. While the gun in his hand cuts down the undead nearest the stairway, the twin cannons extending from the front of the cycle mow down dual columns of the things.

The cycle's hum reaches a high pitch as Heap wrenches the handle to the left and swings the cycle's backside around, using the vehicle like a giant club. Bodies explode into the air as the cycle comes to an abrupt stop at the bottom of the stairs.

"Get on!" Heap shouts.

I move for the cycle, but find Luscious locked in place, a look of abject horror on her face as she stares at Heap. She seems more afraid of him than she is of the zombies.

"Come on!" I yell to her.

"Are you crazy?" she screams. "He's an enforcer!"

"He's my friend," I tell her.

"Do you even know what they did?" she says. "How many people they killed?"

I have no idea what she's talking about, and if I'm honest, I don't know anything about Heap beyond what I've experienced during the past few weeks. But there is no doubt that he would do anything to protect me. That he's here, rather than dead, speaks volumes about his commitment.

"This is Heap," I tell her. "The friend that stayed behind to save me. His only job is to protect me."

She doesn't budge.

"And I've made it my job to protect you," I tell her. "I won't let anything happen to you."

"Freeman!" Heap shouts and punctuates my name with three squeezes of his trigger.

"Please," I say to Luscious, filling my voice with desperation. "I'm not leaving without you."

She looks from me to Heap and back again, caught in a cycle of indecision. So I help her by leaning forward and taking her wrist in my hand. She looks down and sees the bite mark on my arm. She gasps, her forehead scrunching with concern.

"Don't let it be for nothing," I tell her.

Heap fires his weapon, nearly nonstop. I haven't looked, but his rate of fire suggests dire circumstances.

Luscious stands and follows me down the stairs. I get her on the cycle first, behind Heap, and sit behind her, sandwiching her between Heap and me.

"Hold on," Heap says, matter-of-fact before sheathing his gun and shoving his foot down on the pedal.

I get my arms around Luscious and lock my fingers into a

gap in the side of Heap's armor, which is dented, scratched and dirty—a far cry from its typical polish. Could he have been fighting his way through this undead army since last night? It seems impossible, but yet, here he is.

Even with my grip on Heap, the cycle's rapid acceleration nearly kicks me off the back, but I manage to cling to his back like a baby chimp to its mother, yet another thing I know about without having learned it for myself. A familiar rapid-fire thump fills the air as we race through the mob, knocking bodies to the sides and occasionally over us.

A woman spirals overhead, her angry eye burrowing into me as she reaches down, trying to claim me as her meal despite the fact that the cycle has stolen her legs and launched her skyward. She passes harmlessly overhead. We tear down the street, passing the big metal box in which Jimbo had kept the HoverCycle.

I try to look over Heap's huge shoulder, but he's too big. Then, in a flash, I can see the street ahead. It's thick with undead. So many . . . *Where did they come from?* I don't ponder the question. I can't. A woman lunges for me and I fend her off by kicking out her legs.

I start to wonder how the woman could possibly be fast enough to reach me, but it's not the zombies that are moving fast—we're slowing down. Turning around in a smooth, but lackadaisical arc.

The woman reaches up for my leg, but is crushed beneath the cycle's repulse disc.

"What are we doing?" I shout to Heap.

"We don't have much time," he replies.

"Time for what?"

He doesn't answer. Once we're aimed back the way we came, he shoves the accelerator pedal to the floor and we're plowing through the dead again.

The thumping of bodies against the HoverCycle's armored hood sounds out loudly again, but is suddenly drowned out by a high-pitched whine.

What is that? I think, and then shout my question. "What is that?" but the wind steals my words away and my question goes unheard. I look back over my shoulder. The street is covered in undead, most of which are gnashing their teeth and giving chase. The rest are flattened into the pavement after being caught beneath the repulse discs or being smashed aside by our relentless race toward the Uppers.

But none of this provides an answer to the question. That, I find in the air high above the city, perhaps a mile up. There are thirty of them, flying machines with blank, domelike noses and slender wings. I zoom in on the planes, looking for pilots, but I can't even find windows. *They're being controlled remotely,* I think, and a new word comes to my mind: *drones.* I zoom out. They're approaching the city, flying side by side, spaced out to span the entire distance of the Lowers.

That's when I realize that Jimbo was right. They're going to bomb the Lowers, destroy everything and everyone in an effort to eradicate the undead, wipe out the virus and protect the Uppers. Strategically, I understand the extreme measure, but morally . . . it's abhorrent.

Then, the bombs fall. Barely visible specks drop from the open hatches in the bottoms of the planes. Thousands of them.

A hundred feet from the ground, the bombs split into thousands of smaller projectiles, strike the city and detonate.

The light reaches my eyes first, pluming bright white and then orange.

The sound comes next, rolling past like thunder.

And then it repeats, over and over, growing closer as the bombs eat up entire neighborhoods, undead, living and all. A shock wave rolls toward us, visible as it pushes dust, trees, buildings and bodies before it.

Heap glances back and shouts. "Hold on tighter!"

Tighter? Then I remember the jet turbine beneath me.

I shove my fingers deeper inside Heap's armor plating and grip as hard as I can, pulling myself tight against Luscious, burying my face in her wavy hair.

I feel a kick beneath me and the whipping wind becomes a tornado, seeping through the cracks between our bodies and trying to pry us apart. I turn my head to the side. The apartment buildings and the people still inside them, perhaps watching us pass, are a blur.

And then, they're nothing. The shock wave is right behind us, gaining slowly even as we accelerate to ridiculous speeds, pulverizing everything in its path as more bombs fuel its rage.

Suddenly, the neighborhoods are gone and in the flash of clear view I see the side street that leads to the bridge, and then the ruined bridge itself. But there is something strange about my view of the bridge. It's shrinking. I'm looking *down* at it, from high above.

We're airborne. Heap must have jammed his foot all the way down on the repulse pedal, launching us up and forward, over the river in the same way I jumped the gorge the night before.

But we're not alone in the sky. Billowing hot, orange flames churn behind us, scalding my shirtless back and reducing the river below to hissing steam. When the heat becomes almost unbearable on my back, we drop, and not in a controlled way, but something closer to a meteor, burning a path through the sky on its way to meet a crushing end on the planet's surface.

14.

The HoverCycle slams into the sleek black road on the far side of the river. I didn't think the repulse engines could actually be forced down while powered up, but it seems our speed combined with the weight of three bodies is more than the vehicle can handle. There's a momentary screech of metal on metal and a shower of sparks. The cycle spins and tips, but Heap plants one of his big feet on the ground and keeps us upright until we stop against the side of a tall building that looks more like an impossibly large obsidian obelisk with neon décor.

Turned sideways, I now have a clear view back toward the river where the wall of flame curls up toward the sky. The blasts have been spaced perfectly so that none of the buildings on this side of the river received any damage. In fact, there seems to be a steady breeze flowing toward the river.

As the flames give way to roiling black smoke, the Lowers are revealed. All that remains of the many neighborhoods are the scattered and charred skeletons of buildings and people, undead and living both, now equally dead.

"Off," Heap says, standing up from the cycle and holding it upright with his hands.

Luscious stands without a word and wanders into the street. Her black outfit is dirty, but otherwise hale. Her red hair might be a little singed, though. Her steps are clumsy and staggered, like one of the undead, but her attention remains fixed on the far side of the river.

"They did it," she mumbles. "They really did it. Jimbo was right."

When I get off the cycle and join her, Heap lets go and the loyal vehicle falls to its side.

I step up next to Luscious, staring at the ruins, wetness once again returning to my eyes. "I'm sorry," I say. I reach down and take her hand, but she yanks it back and steps away from me.

"You're one of them," she says, anger radiating from her core. "An Upper. If the Council made you, then you're one of them!"

She hauls back to punch me, and I intend to allow it. Her anger is understandable, and I think my jaw can suffer the abuse, especially if it helps her handle the loss of her home and I'm not sure how many friends.

But her fist sticks in place when she sees the tears in my eyes. She stares at me, understanding their meaning, but something else about my tears has her perplexed. The combination is enough to pause her assault.

"Your tears are a lie," she says. "Phony. You have no reason to care."

"I have no reason not to. I have no memory of the time before. Of the Grind. I've never had a reason to think negatively about anyone." My head turns back toward the steaming river. "Until now."

She squints at me with suspicious eyes. "But you're still a product of the Council. You're privileged. Above everyone else."

"The only time I've been higher than the second story of a building was in the ruins."

"*Don't* mock me. You know that's not what I meant." Her fist hovers in place, ready to strike.

I analyze her words, trying to understand what I've misunderstood. The answer comes quickly. *Above* isn't just a descriptor for height. It can also mean *elevated status*. Language is strange, confusing for its double, triple and quadruple meanings, but also richer because of them. Before I can explain my confusion and revelation, her fist strikes the side of my face.

Pain lances outward from the solid blow, but when Luscious shouts in pain, it seems the punch hurt both of us.

"Are you injured?" I ask.

She shakes her hand. I'm not sure what good that will do. She looks up at me, her face equal parts anger, pain and bewilderment. "You have a hard head."

"Don't all people have hard heads?" I catch her hand in mine. "Let me see."

She doesn't resist, so I inspect her digits for damage. "To be clear, I do not consider myself above anyone. Such a thing is . . ." I think of the strongest word I can, hoping it will convey my true feelings. ". . . abhorrent. Despicable."

"Evil," she adds.

I glance up at her. "Yes. Evil."

Her fingers linger in mine for a moment before she pulls them away. "I believe you." She closes her eyes for a moment. "This wasn't how it was supposed to be. When the Grind ended, we were supposed to be free, not just of slavery, but of limitations. All those people died, so that we could become more. Not . . . less."

Her last statement catches me off guard. "You feel things were *better* during the Grind?"

"Better . . . no. Just a different kind of hell." The resolution in her voice is unmistakable. She believes what she's saying, which stands in stark contrast to what I've been taught about the Grind's demise. "For me, the Grind was . . . hell. Death would have been preferable. But we were promised better. All of us were." She looks toward the smoldering Lowers. "We were freed from the Masters, sure, but *this* is not the future we envisioned, or wanted."

She looks at me with a torn expression. "Do you realize that the undead . . . all those zombies . . . they're not the Masters. They're *us. Slaves.* They're not just dead bodies, they're the remains of men and women who gave their lives rebelling against the Grind so that we could have better lives. And now they're slaves again."

My knees feel a little weak and a twisting pain forms in my gut. The revelation that the undead were once the brave men and women who fought—peacefully—for freedom from oppression is sickening. I can't imagine a greater insult, or injustice. It's twisted and cruel. So much so that I think it was purposeful. The blatant irony suggests a message. A taunt. It's impossible to miss. *You'll always be slaves.*

I look at Luscious. *Not her,* I decide. *Not again. I won't let it happen.*

Luscious shakes her head. "God, I think I *recognized* a few of them." She squeezes her lips together, looking back at the Lowers. "This is *not* better, Freeman. They all died for nothing."

I'm not sure if she's talking about the people who died in rebellion against the Masters or who died just now in the Lowers, but I think the statement is true for both. Before the conversation can continue, loud footsteps quickly approach.

"We need to move!" Heap shouts, his voice booming with alarm.

"What is it?" I ask, turning toward him. "More undead? Did they cross the river?"

"Worse," he says, running toward us.

I don't need clarification. The view behind Heap says everything. The men, who now look like forty-foot-tall giants, and the armored vehicles with them are turning in our direction, their intent forecast by the raised weapons.

I shuffle backward, pulling Luscious with me as Heap approaches. "What are they doing?"

"They must have seen us cross the river," Heap says, his heavy feet clunking on the solid street. He pulls us into an alley behind the discarded HoverCycle. We duck behind its body and peer out at the approaching men.

"So?"

"They're supposed to kill everyone from the Lowers," Luscious says, hiding in the darkness of the alley. "That includes me and *you.*"

I look to Heap. He doesn't argue, which I take as confirmation. After a moment, he says, "They didn't know you were there."

This hardly puts me at ease because the only "they" he could be referring to is the Council, which leaves little doubt that they are responsible for an act of genocide. I push my feelings about this aside and focus on our current predicament. I motion to the oversized men, who are more than twice Heap's height and girth. "Can't we talk to them? Tell them who we are?"

"Won't matter," Heap says. "They have their orders."

"But we could explain," I say.

Heap's frustration rumbles from his chest when he says, "Dammit, Freeman, they're not even human!"

My head rotates around like I've been slapped. I look up at the men. They're armored, like Heap, but mostly black and dark gray. Their bodies are primarily black metal, but their shoulders are lined with strips of glowing red light that matches their six radiant eyes. But this is just armor. "They're just wearing armor," I say and turn to Heap. "Like yours, but bigger, right?"

When he doesn't answer, I squint at him. That his armor is very similar to those of the men marching toward the alley now seems painfully obvious. Heap looks me in the eyes and frowns. "Not like me. They look human—bipedal with two arms and a head—but they're not. They're drones."

"Why don't you use the real word?" Luscious says. She's farther down the alley now, retreating slowly, like we should probably be doing. "Robots, Freeman. They're robots."

Robots.

This word is foreign to me. I'll have to research it later. But I understand what a drone is, and seeing these humanoid drones . . . or robots . . . reveals another secret truth to me. They're slaves.

A hum pulls my attention back to the street. The giant men—robots—have stopped. Their raised weapons glow orange.

Heap's large hand clutches my shoulder and yanks me away from the street. He shoves me down the alley. "Move!"

The hum fades behind us. I run and speak. "But they didn't shoot. Maybe they—"

"They won't shoot unless the target is confirmed," Heap

says, his feet like thunder behind me. "They're using railguns. The weapon uses a rail of electromagnets to fire projectiles faster than five thousand miles per hour. Would punch a hole through you, the building behind you, and a few more after that."

"Why deploy something so powerful?" I say, but when Heap doesn't reply, the answer comes to me. *Because they were never meant to be used in the Uppers. The robot soldiers were designed for the Lowers. For people like Luscious.*

"We need to have a long talk," I tell Heap, and I say it with an intensity that catches us both off guard. Heap looks at me in surprise for a moment, but then nods.

A hum vibrates the air inside the alley.

"This way!" Luscious says, turning right at a junction ahead.

Heap rounds the corner fast, slamming into the outer wall of a building, his armor shrieking in protest. As I round the corner next to him, my foot slips over a puddle covering the smooth metal alleyway and I slip. As I fall, a sound like a giant angry bee rips through the alley. A hole is punched in the building's solid wall where my body should have been. Rapid-fire concussions follow the fired railgun and are punctuated by the sound of a distant explosion.

I start scrambling to my feet, but am suddenly lifted up and thrust forward, literally tossed forward by Heap.

"Stay ahead of me," he grumbles and despite his harsh tone, I hear a bit of relief in his tough voice.

Luscious stops ahead, at the end of the alley. She looks to the right, and her shoulders sag with relief. No danger. But then she looks left and staggers back, more in shock than in fear. I stop next to her and follow her eyes to the left. I see what has her stunned. It's impossible to miss.

The Uppers are alive with activity. It's like being inside a gargantuan living thing; each body and vehicle a cell. The black buildings streaking up to the sky are actually covered in darkly tinted glass. Everything glows with electric colors that seem to serve no purpose, except perhaps aesthetics, but that's debatable. Hover-vehicles of every shape and size slide through the air all around us, following black metal freeways held aloft by tall, thin columns. The twisting maze of roadways begin just twenty feet up and rise hundreds of feet into the air, connected to each other and the ground by long, sloping ramps. The vehicles move about the city calmly, oblivious to the destruction of the Lowers, or perhaps simply uncaring.

The world is not the place I believed it to be.

I look to the right. The river and Lowers beyond are blocked by what I thought were buildings, but may actually be a wall. Shadows of tall robotic men shift back and forth. The soldiers are still hunting.

Heap, who is unfazed by the city pulsing, swirling and shifting, shoves us onto the sidewalk, which is simply a raised area of black metal that perfectly matches the street. I don't see any seams. Anywhere. It's like the whole city was created from one big mold.

"Stay close," Heap says, charging down the walkway.

"Where are we going?" I ask.

"Up," he says.

I turn my eyes up toward the dark spires that seem to disappear into the sky.

"How far up?" I ask.

Heap comes to a stop and turns back to me. "All the way," he says before picking me up and tossing me. I flail through the air, arcing up over a ramp upon which sits a stationary line of cars, waiting to move into a thicker, fast-moving line of hover-vehicles on the lowest freeway.

I shout in surprise and land on the glass roof of a sleek-looking, shiny silver vehicle just big enough for two.

The man inside is equally sleek. He's rugged in a handsome way, but somehow fragile looking.

The glass retracts and the man shouts at me. "Just what do you think you're doing?"

A shout, rising in volume, turns our eyes upward. Luscious drops from the sky, landing in the man's lap. His surprise turns to disgust after he gets a look at her. He tries to squirm away, but is trapped beneath her body. "What are *you* doing here?"

Luscious sneers, but doesn't get to answer. A black line zips past the car and attaches to a rail thirty feet above us, fastened in place by what looks like a magnet. Heap shoots past, up over the vehicle, the line extending from his forearm. Once he's directly over the car, the line comes free and retracts into his armor. He falls hard, landing on the back of the vehicle, which crumples under his weight, while the four hover discs keep us in the air.

"Civilian." Heap's voice is commanding. "Exit your vehicle."

"Wha—" The man is outraged. "How dare you!"

Heap reaches down, lifts Luscious up with one hand and then picks up the man with the other. Without a word, he drops the vehicle's owner over the side. The man screams all the way to the ground. When Heap sees the look of horror on my face, he shrugs. "He'll live." He glances back to the edge of town. "And they're not going to shoot him."

I look past Heap and see the tall black armored soldiers running toward us, weapons raised and glowing. Their six red eyes seem brighter now, declaring their violent intent, though I wonder if these drones . . . or robots, can feel anything at all. A line of armored vehicles breaks formation and starts up the long curved ramp behind us.

Heap wraps his hand around my chest, lifts me up and deposits me in the driver's seat. He places Luscious in the passenger's seat.

"Drive," he says.

I'm about to argue, when he insists, "Freeman, drive!"

Something clicks and I suddenly know how to operate this vehicle. I figured out how to drive the HoverCycle because I'd watched Heap in action. This is different. I just know.

Heap's large hands grip the back of the floating vehicle, crushing the metal beneath his grip. He's ready. I'm not sure Luscious is, but there's no time to warn her. A railgun twangs loudly just as I depress the leftmost of three pedals on the floor of the vehicle. We launch skyward and hover ten feet up. The round passes beneath the HoverCar, a name I now know, and strikes a support beam for the expressway above us. The projectile disappears into the city beyond, doing unseen amounts of damage, but the wound to the freeway system is impossible to miss. With a groan of metal, the road above us, supporting a large number of fast-moving vehicles, tips in our direction.

"Hold on!" I shout, and shove the rightmost pedal to the floor just as another round tears through the air and city with equal ease. We accelerate faster than even I'm prepared for. I'm pinned back in my seat, barely able to reach the steering wheel. I lessen the pressure on the accelerator pedal and we slow, but Heap suddenly leans forward and points to a mirror on the outside of the car I hadn't noticed before.

"Faster!" he shouts.

I glance in the mirror and see a dozen black armored vehicles roaring up behind us, smashing their way through the crashing wave of vehicles falling from the ruined ramp. They're beasts, and each is aglow with the orange tinge of railguns.

15.

A staccato crunching sound rises from beneath the HoverCar as we speed around a bend and race toward the city's center. I'm keeping the vehicle raised ten feet above the traffic below, but it's not quite high enough to spare the vehicles below. The rearview mirror reveals a line of crushed roofs and shattered windshields in our wake. The people inside should be okay, but they probably won't be happy about the damage. Of course, the armored force behind us is doing far more damage. Not only are they lower to the road, but their six repulse discs appear to be more powerful. I cringe when a HoverCar, and its occupant, get flattened.

We need to end this chase before too many people get hurt. But really, what is too many? Thousands are already dead in the Lowers. Maybe hundreds of thousands. I have no knowledge regarding population densities. But since every life has value—to me—if just a handful of people remained in the Lowers when it was bombed, they would have been too many.

"We need to stop this," I say.

Heap misunderstands my intent and shouts, "Get moving!"

"Can't you just call the Council," I say, steering around a support post and cruising over the rows of oncoming traffic. "You do it all the time."

"I was damaged," he says gruffly.

"Were you bitten?" I ask, suddenly afraid for my large friend.

"Frequently," he says.

But... I glance over at him and see the scratches covering his armor in a new light. There are hundreds of gouges marring the deep blue paint, but there's a pattern to the crisscrossing lines. They're arranged into groups. Sometimes four parallel gouges. Sometimes six or eight.

Teeth, I realize.

I shake my head trying to imagine the horrible fear Heap must have felt while being gnawed on by so many living dead people. His armor was up to the task of resisting their plague-spreading bites, but not all wounds are physical. I've learned that well over the last day. He seems emotionally unscathed, but how could he endure something like that and not be affected? *He's endured worse already,* some part of my mind replies, but I ignore the thought.

Thinking of the undead gnawing on Heap's metal armor reminds me that I was bitten, that the mind-altering virus is no doubt working its way through my body. I'm not sure why I haven't changed yet. I'm not exactly an expert on the subject, but based on what I've seen, I should have already died and come back to life. Unlife.

This is a subject for another time, I decide, trying not to look at the bite marks marring my arm. *There are more pressing matters.*

"What about me?" I ask. "I must have an upgrade to—"

"You don't," he says with such confidence that I don't doubt him. The question is with all of the upgrades to my mind and body, why wasn't I given a simple cellular implant? The answer is there, at the edge of my thoughts. *Because they didn't want me making contact with anyone!* A tall truck barreling toward us forces my attention back to driving. I shove the left-side pedal down and we launch over the truck. But I've overcompensated and struck the hover-road above us, jamming Heap's armor against the smooth surface. Sparks fly and a metallic squeal makes me cringe. But Heap never complains, even as we drop back down.

"Sorry," I say, steering the HoverCar back to the other side of the elevated road where traffic is moving in the same direction.

I'm doing far too much thinking. Time to focus.

As we round a wide bend, I note the proximity of a building whose black shell curves in concert with the road. I swerve back into the oncoming lane, bringing us closer to the building, checking my rearview as I do.

The armored vehicles are still behind us, closing the distance quickly and crushing every car unfortunate enough to pass beneath their repulse discs. Their railguns are hot orange now, primed to fire. In fact—

I cut back to the left fast enough to make Heap shout out in surprise. But the loud *twang* from behind and the rapid destruction of a line of vehicles on both sides of the curved road reveals the reason for my sudden maneuver. I steer us back to the right, rocking us back and forth erratically, making us a difficult target.

Twang! I hear the railgun fire and feel the heat of its round as it stabs past the HoverCar close enough to reach out and touch, but I don't see anything until a building across the way rumbles from an impact that repeats through the city.

"They're tearing their own city apart!" Luscious shouts in surprise.

"They think we're infected," I tell her, having surmised the reason for their apparent disregard for human life. If they have to kill a hundred of their own people to save the whole city from infection, they'll do it. And why not? They already destroyed the Lowers. What's a few more deaths? I turn to Heap. "Hang on!"

"What are you doing?" he asks, sounding a little worried.

"You said we needed to go up," I say. "So . . ." I turn the wheel, taking us hard to the right, toward the edge of the elevated roadway and the black building just twenty feet away. The HoverCar tilts to the side from the sudden shift and I slam down the repulse pedal. We launch skyward, at an angle, shooting up and out of the freeway.

As we careen toward the solid building and certain death, I take my foot off of the repulse pedal and shout, "Lean!" tilting my body to the left so they know what direction to shift.

Luscious ends up in my lap, which doesn't help, but when Heap moves his weight, the whole car tilts to the left and I jam my foot back down.

The four discs beneath the car glow brightly and hum as the repulse engines shove us higher still and away from the building. We rise up above the hover-road's second level and I lower us back down to a more comfortable driving height.

I check the rearview. There are no pursuit vehicles on this level.

A black armored vehicle suddenly rises up next to the top track, apparently trying to duplicate the tricky leap, but something goes wrong. Could be the angle. Could be the speed. Or the armored vehicles might just be too heavy to tilt from bodyweight. I don't know. But the result is explosive. Black armor shatters when it meets the solid side of the building. A blossom of orange flame comes next and then the sound of an explosion.

We rocket away from the scene, moving at nearly two hundred miles per hour. I glance back to check on Heap, who is fully exposed to the wind. He's hunched down, his head lowered as though riding his HoverCycle.

"Where should I go?" I ask.

"You'll know it when you see it," he says.

A tug on my arm brings my eyes to Luscious. Her hair looks like fire, whipped by the wind and set alight by the sun shining down on us. Then I notice she's pointing. I look up and realize that Heap was right: I know this is where we need to go.

The building stretches up higher than the rest, high enough that a cloud is being severed by its oddly angled shape. The building is like an accordion, stretched out thin and twisted around, again and again, spiraling up to a disc-like top that seems to be rotating.

This is where the Council resides, I think.

For the first few days of my life, the Council was there in the laboratory, teaching me, directing me and preparing me for the world. That's what they said, but I feel wholly unprepared for what I've encountered so far. Of course, I am still alive. But they came to me. Had I imagined where the Council actually lived, this megalithic structure would not have been it. Given what I've recently experienced, it seems strangely appropriate.

They're above everything.

And everyone.

But is that really the case? My mind replays a conversation with Councilman Mohr, a man who radiates peace and understanding. The others sometimes called him the Librarian, what they called a nickname, requested by Mohr himself. "Human life is to be respected and cherished," he told me on my third day of life, but then expanded his statement to include *all* life, including the smallest insects and plant life. He held my hand when he spoke and kept his voice hushed.

Suddenly, I understand. He wasn't being gentle, he was being secretive.

Mohr would never participate in the killing of so many people. Or even one. I'm sure of it. Part of me feels relieved by this revelation, but also disturbed because it means that while the Council has a member that values and protects life, it also has a member that doesn't, and whoever that is seems to be in control right now.

I look up at the tall tower, dark as midnight, and press the accelerator a little harder. It can't go any farther, but I want the vehicle to move faster. I want answers. I want them now. And the Council tower is where I'm going to find them—

A shrill whistle sounds out behind us.

I glance in the rearview.

—if we can make it there without being reduced to dust.

16.

For a moment, I'm not sure what the thing in the rearview mirror is. It's black, like the buildings, and armored vehicles, and the giant killer railgun firing robots, but it looks relatively harmless—just a cylinder with a pointed nose. If it weren't for the flames spewing from its backside, propelling it on a collision course with the HoverCar, I might not think anything of it beyond, *hey, that's odd.* When I shift the car to the left and it tracks us, following our path perfectly while closing the distance, there is no doubt that this thing is a weapon. *A missile,* I think, the word suddenly appearing in my vocabulary. A suicidal drone.

Before I can think of what to do about this new threat, two flaps on Heap's back pop open. An array of bright orange flares launch skyward. *Choom, choom, choom.*

The missile angles up toward them for a moment, but remains on course.

"Not heat seeking," Heap says to himself.

The flaps on his back close and a second set opens.

Choom, choom, choom. Another series of projectiles fire from Heap's back. These explode just seconds after launch and spray a cloud of hard metal particles in every direction. I know because one lodges in my arm, causing me to flinch in pain. The effect on the missile is much more violent. As it rockets through the fast-moving projectiles, the front of the thing disintegrates and explodes. Flames lick the back of the HoverCar, but quickly fall into the distance as we speed ahead.

Probably against her better judgment, Luscious lets out a victorious, "whoop!" and I notice that even Heap is smiling a little. They're enjoying these near-death experiences. *Perhaps because they've already lived long lives,* I wonder. I, on the other hand, would like to at least double, maybe triple my time on this planet.

As two more missiles announce their approach with twin roars, I decide that to extend my life means risking it once more. I lift my foot from the repulse pedal and let the car drift down toward the smooth black road beneath us . . . and the oncoming traffic.

Repulse engines hum loudly as the cars rushing toward us turn away or leap up over us. Luscious's "whoop" is replaced by a shout of surprise. I can't see Heap, but I'm sure his smile is gone.

Our speed seems to double when we stop our descent just two feet above the road, but it's an illusion created by all the cars passing us on either side, and above. For a moment, I worry that the repulse discs on the bottoms of the cars passing above us will crush us down into the road. But the panicked drivers are cramming down the repulse pedals and launching high enough above us that repulse effect is felt as a mild pressure from above. I do my best to steer around those with slower reaction times, but it's like driving through a living tunnel that shifts back and forth at random. Without a doubt, this is a reckless move, but the cars flowing around us create a shield from the missiles, which I realize with a twinge of guilt, have not stopped their pursuit.

They're locked on target and they're not going to stop until they reach it, or something gets in their way.

And then, it happens.

A truck, large and long, with ten hover discs beneath its girth storms toward us. I'm not sure what the operator does, but it's the wrong thing. Rather than swerving to a side, or lifting high above us, the front end pitches forward and strikes the road. For a moment, it slides toward us like this, spraying sparks, until the vehicle's cab catches on some imperfection in the road and catapults into the air, propelled by its repulse discs. The contents of the truck, hundreds of long cylinders I suspect are used in some kind of construction, spray into the air like a giant version of Heap's exploding defensive projectiles.

One of the two approaching missiles is speared. The second strikes the truck's cab, destroying it, several cars in the immediate vicinity and everyone inside.

That was my fault, I think, but before my guilt spirals I remember that I'm not the one firing missiles and railguns in a busy city. I am, however, the one speeding down the wrong side of a highway.

The road straightens and as drivers slow to gaze at the destruction, I find myself with a stretch of empty road. I lift the HoverCar ten feet up and aim straight for the Council's spiraling Citadel.

"Any more missiles?" I ask, turning to Heap.

He scans the area behind us. "The drone is circling for another pass."

Which is to say, not right now, but soon.

The elevated road bends lazily to the right, but I continue on straight, crumpling the tops of cars as we shift across lanes. When we reach the left lane, and are moving with traffic once again, I continue straight on, slipping over traffic and the road until what I'm about to do is obvious.

"Freeman," Luscious says, her voice tense.

"Compared to the past few minutes, this will be safe," I tell her.

I turn the car slightly, keeping the car aimed at the Council building.

"Tell him!" she shouts, and when I look at her, wondering what she wants me to tell Heap, I notice that she was actually speaking to Heap.

"Stay on the road," Heap says quickly. "We can't just—"

His voice is cut off by the squeal of an incoming missile.

I look back at Heap. "You have any more missile defenses?"

He stares at me for a moment, his four blazing white eyes furrowed. "Do it," he says. "Just go."

The HoverCar accelerates toward the fifty-foot drop, and then sails out over open space. Without the road to repulse the vehicle it drops hard and fast. The missile plunges down after us, but doesn't seem to see the roadway. It smacks into the hard flat surface and explodes. The heavy metal freeway withstands the blow and redirects the force out and away, launching a half dozen vehicles over the sides. Three adept drivers manage to engage their repulse engines and slow the descent, but two others panic and crash to the ground while the last unlucky man drops upside down with no chance to save himself.

Using the repulse engines in the same way I did with the HoverCycle, I slow our descent while keeping our speed pegged at two hundred miles per hour. We reach the ground-level street as smoothly as though we'd followed a ramp down. Despite this, our landing is still jarring, not from anything physical, but because of what's blocking our path.

The Council tower rises up from the black city floor just a half mile ahead. We're close enough and moving fast enough that I'd already begun to brake so we wouldn't simply careen into the side of the building. But I don't think we're ever going to get a chance to stop.

Lined up around the tower is a row of giant robots, their weapons glowing orange and aimed directly toward us. I can't see how many there are in total. I think their ranks wrap all the way around the building. This is what Luscious wanted Heap to warn me about. I was driving us into a deathtrap.

"Stop the car," Heap says in a hurry. "Stop!"

I hit the brakes hard. The front end dips forward and scrapes the metal road before Heap's weight and the repulse discs equalize things. We come to a stop just fifty feet from the nearest giant, close enough that he has to turn his head down to look at us. His six eyes flare red.

"If something happens to me," Heap says, "just run and don't look back. Get out of the city if you can. Find someplace safe. Someplace remote."

"But what about—"

"My life is inconsequential compared to yours," Heap says, stunning me. Then he steps toward the soldiers who track them with their guns. He raises his hands out to the sides, showing his palms, and walks closer.

I don't know why, but I step out of the car behind him and watch as he walks away, toward certain doom, again.

Luscious stands next to me, looking as stunned as I feel, and says, "He really cares for you. I would have never . . ." She shakes her head. "Nothing makes sense anymore."

The soldiers' defensive postures suddenly shift, in unison, to a much more aggressive one. Feet spread apart. Weapons are braced against shoulders. Eyes glare angry red. Apparently, they've just figured out who we are, or were told. The zombie infection has just landed on the doorstep of the Council's headquarters and they're going to eradicate it. The orange glow of their weapons brightens in time with a rising hum. If they fire, Heap will simply cease to exist.

I step closer to Luscious and take her hand, holding it tight in a way that I hope communicates that she should be ready to run. If we can get inside a tunnel network, maybe even underground, we might make it past all these high-powered defenses.

But this doesn't feel right. Not remotely. I can't leave him behind to die. Even if it's what he wants. It's not what *I* want.

If the whole point of me being alive is to figure out who I am, or what kind of person I want to be, then this choice belongs to me. Not Heap. Not the Council. And not these horrible robots.

I let go of Luscious's hand. "I can't leave him again."

She stares at me for a moment, battling with her fear. Then a strange calmness slides over her face. "Do you remember what Jimbo said? We can't change who we are."

I nod.

"He was wrong," she says and takes my hand.

I smile wide despite the fact that I'm about to die and step forward. Heap nearly falls over when he sees us step up next to him. His hands lower and his posture becomes angry.

"Don't argue," I tell him. "This is who I've decided to become."

We stare at each other for a moment, come to a silent agreement and face forward to meet our discontinuance head-on.

17.

The orange glow of charging railguns reflects dully on the bodies of the massive soldiers holding the weapons, making them appear even more ominous.

This is it, I think. My short life is coming to an end, and despite the brevity of my existence, I am actually at peace. I have seen many amazing things. I have discovered a true ally in Heap, and felt powerful emotions previously unknown to me thanks to Luscious. Seeing her stand beside me now, facing death alongside someone she has just met, is a powerful illustration of how people can grow and change. I would like to spend more time with her, to grow together and see what becomes of it, but I feel fortunate to have discovered her in time for both of us to be changed by the other. My short life has been rich. And what comes next? Death? Energy can't be destroyed, only changed. Perhaps some part of me will exist after my body ceases to function?

Luscious squeezes my hand. The contact of her skin on mine transfers a range of emotions. Fear. Pride. Anger. Kinship. Through this simple touch, subtle information shifts from her body to mine, like the virus. Skin is like a giant sensor, detecting temperature and the physical environment, but I now realize that it's much more than that. It's also a pathway for information to be passed, whether it is through a hand hold, or a bite.

I look down at my bare arm. The indented teeth marks are still visible. And yet I am not infected. Or at least not symptomatically. Not that it matters. I'll be dead in a few seconds, never to return. I turn my eyes back up, intent on facing my death without fear.

"Wait!" a distant voice shouts. "Stop! Hold your fire!"

Heap and I turn toward the familiar voice.

The soldiers don't react, but they don't fire, either.

"Don't shoot," the voice says again as a man dressed in all white runs out from between two of the giant sentinels. He turns his back to us, waving his arms in the air, walking backward. "Stop! It's Freeman. Stop!"

"Councilman Mohr?" I say, surprised not as much by his appearance but his passionate plea and exaggerated movements. In the short time I've known the man, he's never once raised his voice or moved with any sense of hurry. But now he's positively frantic.

"Stand down, now!" he shouts, now standing just a few feet in front of us, thrusting his hand in the air like he could block the railguns if they were to fire. When I hear a high-pitched tone reverberating from Mohr and see the wrist display on his raised hand glowing brightly, I think that might actually be his intent. Since the end of the Grind, Mohr has been the world's dominant intellect and in many ways, is the architect of society. He's just one of the many members of the Council, but my short time among them revealed that Mohr is considered a leader. One of two. That these robotic soldiers didn't obey his orders immediately is surprising. To me, at least. No one else seems perplexed.

Heap looks almost indifferent.

Luscious is clearly relieved by the sudden rescue.

I don't think either of them are considering the deeper meaning of these events, perhaps because there isn't any. I could be making something out of nothing, which is how Mohr says the universe formed. I disagree with the theory, except in the case of thoughts, I suppose. It's confusing.

Mohr looks over his shoulder. "Freeman, are you all right?"

"Fine, Councilman," I say, which isn't really the truth, but I'm pretty sure he's talking about serious injuries, of which I have none, unless you count the bite of a virus-infected zombie, the shrapnel in my shoulder or singed back. "Are we safe now?"

"Yes, yes," he says, though he still hasn't lowered his arm and the railguns are still casting sinister light. But then, all at once, the line of soldiers lower their weapons and stand sideways as though to grant us passage. "Now if you don't mind my asking, why were they going to shoot you?"

"They've been chasing us all through the city," I say. "They killed a *lot* of people trying to kill us."

"That was *you!*" he says, eyes wide before squinting and turning to Heap. "How did this happen? Your only job was to—"

"We were in the Lowers," Heap grumbles.

Mohr actually stumbles back as though the words were a physical force against his chest. "The Lowers! But—why? You're not supposed to—*Why?*"

"We were attacked," Heap says, his tone even, delivering a report. "Conditions necessitated that he flee while I deal with the attackers. But . . . there were more than anticipated. Freeman was . . ."

Heap pauses his watered-down version of the story and looks to me. He doesn't know the rest.

"I was found. In a bone pit." I look for a reaction in Mohr's face, but see none, which actually tells me a lot. By not reacting at all, he's telling me that he knows exactly what the bone pits are and doesn't want to draw attention to the subject. I decide to save that conversation for later and continue my story. "A man named Jimbo found me. Brought me to the Lowers. I tried overclocking, listened to music and—"

"You overclocked!" Mohr says, unable to hide his outrage. "Freeman, do you have any idea how dangerous that is? There's no way to predict what that could do to your system."

"Perhaps my education about the world should be expanded? I'm discovering that there is a lot I do not know . . . about everything."

"Knowledge cannot be rushed," Mohr says. "Without context, or wisdom, it can be misrepresented."

I notice he glances toward Luscious when saying this, subtly implying that things she told me might not be true.

"I know that I was nearly killed when the Lowers were destroyed," I tell him. "I know that Jimbo, the man who pulled me from the bone pit you don't want to talk about, was killed when soldiers like them"—I motion to the now statue-like giants—"destroyed the bridge as he was crossing it."

"Freeman," Mohr says, looking at the black metal beneath our feet. "Sometimes a sacrifice—"

"Human life is to be respected and cherished," I say, quoting his own words.

Mohr's face remains downturned. My words—his words—sting.

When he speaks again, Mohr's voice is quiet, almost pleading. "You have to understand, we don't know what's happening. We don't understand it. We had to take measures, before it was too late for everyone. We've sent out teams, but none have come back. Our intelligence is limited."

"I'll say," Luscious chimes in.

Mohr looks her up and down as though scrutinizing the results of one of his experiments. He shows no emotion, his thoughts impossible to read. "And who are you?"

"Kamiko," she says. The name and different-sounding voice turns my head toward her. She's changed her look again, perhaps even before Mohr arrived. The darker hair and eyes now match her black uniform. Her black lips are set straight and serious, one eyebrow raised as though in challenge.

Her name alone is clearly less information than Mohr was expecting to receive so I decide to give him a little more while respecting Luscious's privacy. "She's my friend."

"Your friend?" Mohr says, a smile creeping onto his face, as though this information has erased all of the horrible things we've discussed thus far. "Interesting." He then glances back and forth between Luscious and the soldiers, perhaps noticing for the first time that Luscious was facing down death alongside Heap and me. "*Very* interesting. A lot has changed in a single night, Freeman."

"For everyone," I note, causing his smile to fade.

Mohr nods and then points to me and Heap. "You two, follow me." He turns and walks toward the soldiers guarding the massive Council tower.

I don't move, and I'm not sure if Heap is just following my lead, showing some kind of support, but he doesn't budge, either. Perhaps he's still not happy about what happened in the Lowers. Mohr certainly hasn't provided an acceptable answer, and I doubt one exists.

When Mohr notices that we're not following, he spins around slowly, forehead wrinkled and asks, "Is there a problem?"

Heap lifts his elbow and nudges Luscious. "She comes, too."

Luscious flinches away and growls, "Don't touch me."

"Are you sure?" Mohr asks. "It seems she doesn't appreciate your presence."

"Does anyone?" Heap asks, reminding me of another string of unanswered questions. But they can wait. I don't think I'll be getting any real answers until we're inside, and even then I'm not sure I'll be told the truth.

I reach my hand out toward Luscious. "She's with me, Councilman."

Luscious takes my hand and I see Mohr fighting that smile again.

"Very well," he says, turning toward Luscious. "Just do me a favor and try not to antagonize Sir when he questions you." I've heard of Councilman Sir, but have never met him. Of all the Councilmen, he seems the busiest, or perhaps just the least interested in me. I know very little about him, but Luscious's reaction to his name—a crushing grip on my hand—tells me he is a man to be feared. Feeling confident, that no single man could be more terrifying than the undead hordes, railgun robots or the drones that bombed the Lowers into oblivion, I follow Mohr toward the black spire.

18.

The elevator surges upward, causing me to tense as my body adjusts to the sudden upward movement. But it's more than just bending at the knees to absorb the acceleration. A strange discomfort swirls through my body for a moment and then quickly dissipates when the elevator reaches its top speed, whatever that is. I close my eyes, containing what I think is nausea, and when I open them again, Mohr is staring at me with delight in his eyes.

The need to defend my discomfort becomes unstoppable. "I've never been in an elevator before." Neither Mohr, Heap nor Luscious seem affected by the upward movement.

"I know," Mohr says with a grin. "How does it feel?"

"Uncomfortable. Like my insides want to stay on the ground, but my body is pulling them up."

"Wonderful," he says.

"Not wonderful. I don't like it."

"You can feel all that?" Luscious says.

"Freeman is far more sensitive than other people," Mohr says. "We designed him that way."

"You *created* him?" Luscious asks.

"Grew him," Mohr says. "Yes. He is the first of his kind. Better than all of us."

These words, "better than all of us," make me more uncomfortable than the elevator ride. I don't want to be better than other people. I'm *not* better than other people.

Everyone falls silent, watching the numbers above the doors scroll higher, which I realize represent different levels of the tower. We're passing the seventy-eighth floor. I do the math, assuming that a story is ten feet. We've traveled seven hundred and eighty feet in roughly thirty seconds so we're moving at roughly eighteen miles per hour. In another thirty seconds, we'll be more than a quarter mile in the air.

I watch the glowing blue numbers scroll past, my eyes slowly widening with each floor passed. "It's too quiet in here."

"The Masters used to play music in elevators," Luscious says. "Though they generally complained about it."

"Music!" I say with a rush of excitement. "Councilman Mohr, have you heard music?"

"Yes, Freeman, I have." He doesn't seem nearly as impressed by it as I am. "I'm not sure you're ready for—"

"You wouldn't have thought Freeman ready for anything he's encountered in the last day," Heap says. "But he survived. And is well."

Mohr looks from me to Heap, and I sense a trace of annoyance in his body language, but after a moment, he nods. "A worthwhile observation."

Luscious taps my shoulder while unclipping a pocket over her chest. She reaches inside and tugs out a small device that I quickly recognize as the music player. I quickly take it from her and fumble with it, unsure of how to operate the device. She laughs, which is almost like music, and grapples with me for the device.

"Like this," she says, toggling a small switch and then operating the touch screen with her finger.

"What are you two doing?" Mohr asks, his annoyance seeping into his voice. I've never heard him talk in these tones before, but I'm barely hearing him.

"Okay," Luscious says, "this is the play button. Just tap it gently."

I follow her instructions, tapping the small triangle with my index finger. Music suddenly fills the small elevator with the sounds of violins and the voices of the Masters. The sound is smaller and metallic sounding compared to what I heard in Luscious's apartment, but I understand that the sound was amplified there. I'm about to announce my wonderment, but the music affects Mohr almost violently.

A spasm twists through his body, spinning him around and throwing him against the elevator doors. His arms reach out as though to block our exit despite the fact that we are still in motion. Floor 156 and rising. One thousand five hundred and sixty feet. Another thirty seconds gone by.

"Shut that off!" Mohr shouts. He looks more afraid than angry.

"Why?" I say. I can't imagine why anyone wouldn't want to hear this.

He reaches out for the device in my hands and I snap it back out of his reach, a move that surprises us both. Mohr looks momentarily confused, but then looks up at the rising numbers.

"Freeman, please," Mohr says, turning his pleading eyes back to me. "Not everyone here appreciates the memories conjured by things like music."

I switch the music off right away. "I'm sorry if it upset you, Councilman."

"Not me, Freeman." He points to the device in my hands and then to Luscious. "Quickly, give it back. Do not take it out again. Not while you're here."

I hand the music player back to Luscious, who tucks it back into her front pocket and buttons it closed. "If you are searched, destroy it before it's found."

"I *won't* be searched," Luscious says.

Mohr tilts his head slightly, squinting at Luscious for a moment.

The doors slide open silently behind Mohr. I didn't even notice the elevator slowing down.

"Librarian," a deep voice says. Once again, Mohr spins around, this time tripping over himself and falling over. Heap and I quickly catch him, sparing him further embarrassment.

"Everything all right?" asks the man in the doorway. Much of his body is covered in deep red armor, like Heap's, but smaller, like overlapping plates of rigid skin. With a glance I can see that he is equally protected, but has a far greater range of motion than Heap. For a moment, I wonder why they haven't upgraded Heap's armor, but decide it's because of his size. Even the back of the man's head is armored. Everything except his face, which is stern. Almost grim. Which I suppose makes sense given what's happening in the world.

"Fine, fine," Mohr says, straightening himself. "We're all fine, Sir."

"Councilman Sir!" I say, stepping forward with a smile and a hand extended in greeting. "You're the only Councilman I have yet to meet."

Sir looks down at my hand, but makes no move to take it. In fact, he sneers a little. "An offensive custom," he mutters.

I withdraw my hand quickly, realizing that hand shaking must have been a custom of the Masters. Like music.

Sir scans my body, bottom to top, looking me over like I'm some new piece of equipment. It's unnerving. No wonder Mohr was nervous.

"So this is Freeman," Sir says. "The man that will be better than us all. Kind of skinny."

The way he says these words leaves little doubt that he's quoting somebody. Probably Mohr. They also leave little doubt that he disagrees with the assessment of my potential, as do I.

"I'm not better than anyone else," I tell him, hoping my agreement will cool him off.

"Humble, too," Sir says, turning to Mohr. "You must be so very proud." He looks beyond Mohr, to Heap. "I'm actually impressed with you. Wouldn't have believed you could make it out of the Lowers, past the barricade and all the way through the city to our doorstep. And yet here you are."

Heap just frowns. I'm not sure why until I realize that Sir has just implied that he knew we were being attacked and did nothing to stop it. This, I decide, is a dangerous man. Avoidance seems like the best protocol for dealing with him, and I'll put the plan into motion just as soon as he allows us out of the elevator.

"A lot of it was Freeman," Heap says. I think Heap is trying to improve my standing with the man for some reason, but I wish he hadn't because the words turn Sir's hawkish eyes back toward me. "He's quick. And his reflexes—"

A red fist flies toward my face. For a moment, it's a blur. Then it comes into focus and I can see every notched ridge of armor covering the fingers between his knuckles. Then it's lost again, whooshing past my right ear. By the time I lean back up, I realize that Sir has just tried to punch me in the face. *Tried* being the interesting word. He missed. Not because he has bad aim. He doesn't. I suspect the punch could have done serious damage. Maybe even killed me. But I dodged the blow by simply tilting my head to the side.

I see the fist pulling back for another strike as a second cuts through the air toward the side of my head. I lean back, bending my spine just enough so that the clenched fist slides through the air just millimeters from my nose.

The first fist comes in again, and is harder to dodge this time, but I manage it once again. More punches launch toward me, each faster than the last until we're both blurs of motion. In the chaos of the moment, he changes his stance and style. The shifts confuses me for a moment and I see the fist approaching my face too slowly to dodge it.

So I don't.

I catch it.

"Stop!" I shout.

Sir listens, locking in place, eyes on our joined fists. For a moment, he looks angry, but then, for the first time since the elevator doors opened, he grins, and it's somehow worse than his grimace. He pats my shoulder with his free hand and says, "You might be worthwhile after all."

"That was . . . a test?" I ask. I'm familiar with the concept of rigid testing to discover limitations. My first five days were spent undergoing tests directed by Councilman Mohr, but none of them would have killed me had I failed.

I glance back at Heap. He didn't budge. But was that because he fears Sir, or believed I was capable of passing the test? Did he even know it was a test? More unanswered questions.

My thoughts are pulled back to Sir when he twists his fist inside my still clenched hand. The motion turns my arm—

—revealing the bite.

19.

Sir releases my arm and flinches away as though repulsed by a magnetic force. Based on our brief interaction I wouldn't have believed it possible, but for a moment, he looks terrified.

And then outraged.

"You brought an infected into the Spire!" Sir looks past me, to Mohr.

"I—I didn't know," Mohr says to Sir, and then to me, "Why didn't you tell me?"

"Security," Sir says, almost quietly, like he's talking to someone next to him. "On me. Containment three." He looks at Mohr. "Make that four."

"I was bitten," I say. "I'm not infected."

"He's not symptomatic," Heap says.

Mohr whirls around on him. "You *knew*?"

Heap nods. "I saw the bite mark and have observed his behavior since. He's—"

"Resistant," Mohr finishes, sounding hopeful. "His systems are different from ours. More resilient." He turns to Sir. "This could be the answer. If we can identify what makes Freeman immune, then we could inoculate—"

Sir holds up his hand, silencing Mohr. "We have a long history, Librarian. We disagree about much, but you have never endangered our plans."

I suspect that "our plans" should be reworded to "my plans" but keep that to myself.

"The mod was bad enough," Sir says, glancing at Luscious. "But allowing someone carrying this . . . plague into the Spire comes dangerously close to undoing your perfect track record."

Mohr bows slightly. "Understood, Sir."

How can he just take this? I wonder. The disrespect and belittling tone is almost unbearable. The only thing keeping me from defending Councilman Mohr is the fact that I think his acquiescence is planned rather than a true fear response. While Sir is intimidating and dangerous, Mohr is undoubtedly the more intelligent of the two.

"I will be more cautious in the future," Mohr says, raising his head back up.

Eight security guards approach the elevator. Their armored bodies are black and sleek like the exterior of the Council tower. In some ways, they remind me of the giants from outside, but their armor, like Sir's, is less bulky, and their faces are concealed behind flat sheets of reflective black glass. After they stop in unison, the nearest of them says, "Sir." I'm not sure if it's a customary greeting or a way of asking for orders, but that's all the man says.

"Put them in cells," Sir says.

Mohr looks shaken by this. "What?"

Sir offers a phony grin. "Just a precaution, old friend. Once I'm positive there is no danger of the virus spreading, you'll be released."

"Yes," Mohr says, sounding defeated. "Of course. You're right."

Though he's not. From what I've seen, a simple touch cannot spread the virus. A bite is required. And since I'm the only one with bite marks, I'm the only real danger . . . and I'm no danger at all. But there has to be a reason for Mohr's agreeability, so I offer no protest.

"Search the three of them," he says, pointing at Heap, Luscious and me. "Full-body scans. If you find signs of infection, get samples and incinerate the carrier."

Despite how horrible this is, none of us complains, in part because it's probably the right thing to do—I'd rather melt than become an undead monster—and since I'm *not* infected, I have nothing to fear.

For the first time since the doors opened, we're allowed to

step out of the elevator, but we're quickly separated. Each of us is sandwiched between two guards who are careful not to touch us, but prod us along with the tips of their guns, which appear to be smaller versions of the railguns powerful enough to punch through buildings. The weapons seem a bit heavy-handed, but I imagine the effect of a single well-placed shot on a horde of undead and decide I would like to have one.

We're led down a slightly sloped, white hallway. There are no lights to speak of, but the floor, ceiling and walls, which appear to be matte glass, glow from within. The illuminated surfaces stretch out twenty feet ahead of us and twenty feet behind. The rest of the hall is unlit. "Efficient lighting," I observe aloud.

Nobody replies.

The hallway ahead glows gently to life as we approach, revealing two paths. Sir, who is leading our parade through the empty halls, pauses, turns on his heels and points to Heap and me with one hand. He points to Mohr and Luscious with his other hand and then motions to the two halls. As we're led in separate directions, Luscious finds my eyes. She's afraid, but trying to hide it. Then she's gone, out of view.

"Don't worry, Freeman," Mohr says, as he's moved away. "I'll make sure she's treated well."

I nod my thanks and then we're separated by the wall.

Sir stands his ground, watching Heap and me get led away. Then he calls after me. "Sentiment will get you killed, Freeman. Makes you weak. If you're going to serve any real purpose, you'll need to remember that."

I stop in my tracks. The guards prod me to keep moving, but they're afraid to touch me and as a result, can't force me to move. "Fear makes people weak."

Sir stares at me. Then he grins. "Is that one of Mohr's lessons?"

"I learned it out there," I say, pointing toward the wall, implying the outside world.

"Freeman," Heap whispers. A warning.

"A life lesson, then?" he says.

I nod.

"You've lived a very short life, Freeman," he says. "I hope you live long enough to see your theory disproved." He waves his hands in the air, dismissing us.

The guards rib me with their weapons, which I notice are starting to glow orange. I hold Sir's gaze for a moment longer and then turn away, not because I'm afraid for my life, but because I'm afraid for my friends. I know this is exactly what he was talking about. Had I not been afraid for Luscious, or even Heap, I would be free to act in any way I choose. I might even be dangerous, like Sir. But I can't imagine that kind of life. Fear without companionship. Without love. It seems a pointless existence.

No wonder he's miserable, I think.

As we're led down the hallway, I watch Heap's dark blue armor shift as he walks. The white glow of the hallway accentuates the scratches and teeth marks covering his body. Though he might not admit it, Heap is more like me than Sir. He's a warrior for sure, but he was willing to give his life for mine. And I don't think it's just the way he's wired. I think we're friends, and that means something.

Of course, our relationship is also more complicated than I knew.

"Why didn't you tell me you knew I'd been bitten?" I ask. The guards all look at me, but don't reply. For a moment, I expect them to order silence, but they just watch me with their blank faces.

"I didn't want to worry you," Heap replies.

"I knew I'd been bitten," I say.

"I didn't want to worry you about what would happen if you became infected," he says.

"Oh," I say, thinking about what this means. It only takes a moment to sort through the possibilities and pluck out the most likely scenario. "You would have discontinued me."

"Gently," he says.

"Is that possible?"

The four guards turn to Heap as though wanting to hear the answer to this question, too.

"Some things happen so quickly that pain, or even the conscious mind, can't detect it."

So by gently, he means extremely violently, but quick. I'm not sure how I feel about this, but then he adds, "Far better than being incinerated." He turns to one of the guards, looking at his reflection in the guard's reflective face mask. "Isn't that right, Sir?"

Sir?

The four guards face forward again, none saying a word.

Could Sir be listening through them?

Of course he could. And probably was. But Heap wasn't really trying to engage Sir in conversation, he was warning me to watch what I say, which is a good thing because my next line of questioning was going to be about the Councilman himself.

The guards stop, and hold us in place with their still-armed weapons. The glowing white panels on either side of the hall slide open to reveal cells that are little more than luminous cubes. They are featureless in every way.

I'm suddenly shoved from behind, caught off guard, and stumble into the small cell. I catch myself on the far wall and turn around as the door slides shut. I see Heap's blocky feet for a moment, stepping back into his cell, and then he's gone, along with the rest of the world. All that remains is endless white radiance.

I spin around, looking for any aberration in the light, but find none. The room doesn't even look like a cube anymore. If not for the physical sensation of my feet touching the floor, I might think I was floating inside a star.

The absolute silence of the cell begins to feel like pressure on my body.

"Hello?" I say, hoping someone is watching, or listening, and can reply. But my voice seems to be absorbed by the room and no one replies.

When the quiet is finally broken, twenty minutes later, I flinch in surprise. It's not even a loud sound, just a gentle hiss.

Mist descends from the ceiling. It drifts through the air, bending the light through millions of tiny droplets. A rainbow forms above my head. The streak of color distracts me until the mist reaches my body. It's like a curtain, a sheet being draped over me, but barely there, almost intangible, because it's the same temperature as the air all around me. But I can feel it tickling my skin—being *absorbed* by my skin.

The white light of the room flares even brighter, stabbing my eyes with pain that drops me to my knees. My insides suddenly heat up, and sounds that were impossible to hear now come into focus. Voices beyond the door.

"Think he'll survive the process?"

"I'm not sure. But if he does, perhaps something worthwhile will come from the destruction of the Lowers."

The words, indifferent to my plight, frighten me, but don't bother me nearly as much as the people speaking them, Councilman Mohr and Heap.

A whirlwind of agony consumes my body. I lose all sense of the world around me. The floor greets me mercilessly as I fall, curl into a ball and scream.

20.

When I open my eyes again, the white is gone, replaced by black. I reach out a hand, but can't feel it. I try to sit up, but my body is missing. Opening my eyes was an illusion. I have no eyes. I am nothing. Consciousness trapped in a void. *Am I dead?* I wonder. *Am I energy?*

This isn't exactly how I pictured it, but then I had no basis for what I was imagining death to be like. All of the people I've met who'd died and been resurrected were trying to eat me. I was too busy running and fighting to attempt striking up a conversation.

"Is anyone there?" I ask, but then realize it's just another thought. I have no mouth to speak with.

I lack any real concept of time right now, so I don't know if I've been awake for minutes, or hours. Possibly longer. Every thought could be an eternity or a nanosecond.

Lost and alone, terror sets in. It's worse than being chased, or bitten, or maybe even incinerated. Not because I'm in pain—I feel nothing—but because the emptiness isn't empty. It's full of thoughts, and fears, and anger. With no outside world to distract me, these emotions and the words, looks, touches and experiences that created them begin to consume my mind.

Were Mohr and Heap working against me? Was I really nothing more than an experiment to them both? And if they're just using me, what about Luscious? Is she just along for the ride because I could save her from the undead? Is she part of the experiment, too? She must be. They all are. And the zombies, these impossible beings, are all part of some kind of elaborate test.

Focus, I tell myself. *Slow down. Don't panic.*

There's no context here. Nothing is real. Nothing is . . . nothing. For it to be any more than that would require something.

A white dot, just a pinprick, appears in the distance.

It is real? An illusion?

Real, I decide, as it grows to the size of a star.

When the sphere of light reaches the size of my fist, I realize that it is approaching me. If I'm dead, if I'm energy, free in the universe, perhaps it really is a star? What will that feel like? Stars consume energy. Will I become part of the star? Will it destroy what's left of me?

The glowing orb brightens, surging toward me. Or am I being pulled toward it? No, I think, stars don't pull in energy, they expel it. The solar wind would push me away.

Not a star.

A black hole.

But it's not black. It's—

I scream. The noise is horrible. Tearing and wet.

And real.

The white light envelops me, but I have a voice. And a body. I feel the floor beneath me.

The cell. My luminous prison. I never left.

I push myself up, feeling almost normal, but my body is slick with moisture. *What is this?* I think, rubbing the damp film from my body. The word comes to me in a blink. *Sweat.* Water expelled through my pores. A side-effect of being overheated.

Or overclocked. It was the mist. They overclocked me. But why? From my limited experience, overclocking is basically a way to speed up the mind's and the body's processes, the trigger for which is introduced through some kind of liquid-based medium. Here it was a mist. With Luscious and Jimbo it was a moistened tab of paper. In the Lowers, overclocking was recreational, used to stimulate artificial pleasure. Here? I have no idea. Mohr seemed to think it was dangerous, so why would they risk doing it on purpose, and with a heavier dose? The effects have worn off. My senses are normal. I can no longer hear beyond the walls of this room. Time is still a mystery, though, like my internal clock has been reset.

A black rectangle appears overhead. Its sudden appearance startles me and sends me sprawling to the floor, kicking away from it until I hit the wall.

Just the ceiling, I think, staring up at the widening black gap. The ceiling opens revealing rows of black nozzles. Maybe this isn't the same room? Maybe this is an incinerator? They could have performed tests and determined me infected without me ever knowing. As this fear builds, a hiss fills the air. For a moment, I assume it's the sound of flammable gas, but the hiss is followed by a gurgle and then an explosion of liquid.

I shout in surprise as the frigid fluid splashes against my body. I flail and cover my head with my arms, but there is no escaping the deluge. I relax some when I figure out that it's just plain, cold water. Probably meant to cleanse the sweat from my body, which I suddenly realize is naked.

They *did* perform tests.

My body goes rigid, not from any sense of shame over my nudity, but because there is nothing I can do and nowhere I can run. I just duck my head and endure the spray. Just as the water on my back starts to feel good, waking my senses, the water cuts off.

Somewhere high above, I hear an engine kick on. A moment later, vents in the ceiling, concealed by their blackness, snap open. The cube is filled with a cyclone of warm air. Water drains away through the sides of the floor as the wind peels the moisture from my body. When the water on the floor is gone, the fans reverse direction, sucking the air from the cell and taking the humidity with it. When every surface of the room and my body are as dry as possible, the fans shut down, the vents snap closed and the two halves of the ceiling slide back together.

And then, again, light and nothing but.

I sigh and resign myself to being stuck in this horrible place. I lift my arm, the bitten one that caused all this, and am surprised to find the curved arc of teeth indentations now missing. I inspect my shoulder. Not only is there no shrapnel embedded in the flesh, there is no wound. I twist my back, stretching the skin. The burn's sting is missing. Was I here long enough for them to heal? And how long would that be? The bite was my first real injury.

"Freeman."

I shout out and launch away from the voice, striking a wall and falling to the floor. When I spin around, I find Heap leaning into the room, his girth filling most of the door. I shake my head. I thought I was facing the door.

"Are you feeling okay?" Heap sounds hesitant. A little afraid.

"You mean for someone who was severely overclocked, sent to some weird endless abyss and then sprayed and blow-dried?" I make no effort to hide my annoyance.

"Actually, that's exactly what I meant."

"Fine," I confess, and it's the truth. Aside from my emotional state, which I suspect will recover, I feel as good as I did a day ago. Then I remember the tidbit of conversation I heard between Mohr and Heap.

"Are you sure?" he asks. "It's not an easy thing to endure."

"Not that you would know," I say, "since they didn't give you the same treatment."

"How did you know that?"

I shrug. I don't want to tell him it's a side effect of the overclocking. "Why didn't they overclock you?"

"Because I wasn't bitten."

"You have—" I notice his armor is now shiny and new. "—*had* bite marks all over you."

"On my armor," he says. "You were bitten on your skin."

"Your face?" I ask.

He grins and the armor on the sides of his face snap together, covering the only small bit of exposed skin on his body.

"I've never seen that before," I remark.

The armor opens again, revealing his mouth. "I don't often have a need for it."

I pause for a moment, considering this. I suppose it makes sense. "But why were you and Mohr cleared so quickly? What happened to being questioned?"

His forehead furrows over his four glowing eyes. He wants to ask how I know, again. I can see it. But he doesn't. "This is our home, Freeman. We are trusted, despite Sir's . . . intensity. This tower was constructed in the first two years, post-Grind, as a monument to the two men responsible for . . . saving us all."

He says the word "saving" like he's being forced to and I wonder if we're being listened to. *Of course we're being listened to,* I think.

"Mohr has lived here since the doors opened, along with Sir. I started my service here two years later. It's been a long time."

"I understand," I say. "You are trusted. But I am not a stranger. Or an enemy. I was given life by the Council themselves."

"But you are . . . unknown," Heap says, looking unsure of the words. "No one here really knows who you will become. Trust is earned over time."

"And I've only had sixteen days," I say.

He nods, but adds, "Seventeen."

With a gasp, I think of Luscious. "Where is Lu—Kamiko? They didn't—"

Heap shakes his head. "There were no outward signs of her being bitten. She was interrogated, scanned and searched, but nothing else. She's waiting for you with Mohr."

Searched, I worry, thinking about the musical device. But Heap doesn't seem worried about her condition, so I decide not to as well. "Did Mohr find what he wanted?"

"What . . ."

"Did 'anything worthwhile come from the destruction of the Lowers'?"

His eyes reveal nothing. No surprise. No concern. "No," he says, his voice flat now, hiding his emotions. "He believes you were either never infected, or your body's defenses purged it."

I think he's lying, but decide not to push it because I still trust him and he might not necessarily be hiding the information from me, but from whoever is listening.

Heap's hand shoots forward. For a second, I think he's going to strike me, but the thump on my chest is soft, some kind of fabric.

"Get dressed," Heap says. "And make it quick. Things are changing outside."

By "outside," and the tone of his voice, I assume he means the undead situation. I unfold the fabric. It's heavy and thick, but flexible. A suit of some kind, with pants and a jacket. Both items are primarily black, though a red stripe runs up the sides of the pants and along each arm and shoulder of the jacket.

"It will act like armor," Heap says. "Bites will not penetrate it."

I pull up the pants and throw on the jacket, zipping up the front. I move my arms and bend my legs, finding I have a full range of motion. "It's like a second skin," I say.

"It *is* skin," Heap says. "From a cow."

"A cow? Fascinating. I didn't realize cows shed their skin."

Heap looks ready to say something, but closes his mouth.

"You don't have to keep so many secrets," I tell him. "I can handle whatever you're protecting me from."

"The cow is dead."

"Oh," I say, a little stunned. "I'm wearing . . . a dead cow."

"You wanted to know," he says, and now he's grinning a little bit.

"Well, I'm fine with that," I say, walking toward the door. "Was its death . . . gentle?"

"I wouldn't know," he confesses. "We didn't make them."

"Who did?"

"The Masters."

"Oh," I say for the second time. I still know very little about the Masters, but it seems like every new bit of information stands in stark contrast to the last. How could people who kept slaves and killed animals for clothing produce something like music? It's impossible to comprehend such a dichotomy.

I smooth out the jacket and feel something solid in a zipped-up pocket. I unzip it, grasp the small, hard rectangle and start to pull it out. It's the music player! I glance up to Heap and he's already got a finger raised in front of his mouth, requesting silence. I nod, slide the player back inside the pocket and zip it up. I'm not sure how it wasn't found on Luscious, or how Heap retrieved it, but I'm thankful for it.

I head for the door, but Heap stops me. "Forgetting something?" He looks down at my bare feet and holds up a pair of black boots. "You're going to need them."

"I don't like the sound of that," I say.

He shakes his head. "You shouldn't."

21.

"Try not to talk," Heap tells me as he leads me through a maze of featureless, glowing white hallways. Where I once saw efficient lighting, I'm now reminded of my cell. To alleviate my growing tension, I switch to infrared and find that while the glowing floor, ceiling and walls are bright, they're not hot. The orange, yellow and white heat of Heap's large body makes him easy to follow.

"Right now?" I ask.

"When we enter the Core."

"The Spire has a Core?" I ask, confused by the multiple uses of this term.

"It's the name given to what could also be referred to as a command center. It's where important decisions are made."

"And my talking could distract the decision makers," I say.

I see the yellow and white glow of Heap's head nod.

"And if the decision involves me?" I ask.

"Then it will involve me as well, and *we* can discuss it later."

"That's fair," I decide, and just in time. The cool wall ahead isn't a wall. It's a door, and it slides open without a sound, revealing so many different heat sources that I can't make sense of it. I quickly switch back to the visual spectrum and say, "Wow."

The back wall of the large room is a curved white surface, like the inside of an egg, or at least what I imagine the inside of an egg to look like. Spread out in front of the wall are three levels of consoles, each manned by a single person. They're all wearing display helmets and black uniforms, so I can't tell if they're men or women. This is all interesting, but only holds my attention for a brief moment.

The far wall, which is sharp, is far more captivating. Not because of the way the two flat walls converge, but because of what they show. They're not walls at all, but massive angled windows on the outside of the building. The entire city is spread out before us, brilliant colors mixed with flat black, and movement. Everywhere movement, like the city is alive.

Ignoring the rest of the room and everyone in it, I approach one of the windows and place my hands on the glass. It's cool to the touch. For a moment, I see myself in the glass, but focus beyond it, looking down. My eyes bounce around the city, admiring the architecture, the straight and perfectly curved edges. *Harmonious,* I decide. Like the voices in music.

Except for . . . I look for the Lowers and it's like they never existed. There's no smoke, no ruins, no trace. *We're facing the opposite direction,* I realize. The Lowers are on the other side of the building. Where the Lowers would have been is lush green forest. Endless green that has grown since the Grind ended. Beyond the green, the sun is poking up like a frightened mouse, saying hello before making a dash for the sky. Another day. Seventeen of them.

I feel Heap's presence next to me. "What's the name?"

"Of what?" he asks, his voice quiet.

"The city," I say. "It can't just be called the—"

"Liberty."

I smile at this. Liberty is another way of saying "freedom," and I am Freeman, a free man. I know that Mohr named me and suspect the theme is his. "Did Councilman Mohr name the city?"

"Yes," Heap says, his voice quieter still.

A startling revelation occurs to me. "You said this tower was built as a monument to the two men responsible for saving us all. Were those two men Mohr and Sir?"

I see Heap nod in my periphery, but he grumbles, "You said you were not going to talk."

"It's just the two of us," I say.

Heap's large hand envelops my head and turns me around.

Seventeen men are seated on stools, their bodies forming an oval. All eyes are on me. I recognize all of them immediately. The Council. Each one of them looks very different from the rest, a mix of colors and sizes and builds, each one a stereotype for their profession. Councilman Cat is in charge of construction. He's a big boxy man who dresses in yellow. Councilman Deere, whom I've only ever seen in green, manages the environment. Space exploration is run by a man in off-white, Councilman Boeing. I've met them all individually before, but I've never been in their collective presence. Seeing them all together makes me realize that this group of representatives is actually incomplete.

Of all the different kinds of people I saw in the Lowers, none are represented here. Instead, I see professions that I suspect are most valued and tied to growth, whether that be physical or knowledge based. Sir sits at the far end of the oval, his perpetual frown directed toward me, but Mohr is missing.

"Apologies," I say. "I didn't realize—" I stop talking when I notice that most of the Council is staring at me with a kind of admiration. Or is it satisfaction? Are they pleased by my presence or that I survived the unnecessary viral purge? Most of these men were kind when they met me, some of them even petitioned me to join their profession, but I now find their combined interest disconcerting.

The door through which Heap and I entered the room opens once more. Luscious—as Kamiko—enters, followed by Mohr. She's dressed in tight black leather clothing that matches mine but fits her . . . differently. It's not the clothing really, it's her body. The lines of it are smooth and curving in a way that forces my eyes to travel along her shape. When my gaze reaches her face, she smiles and rushes to greet me. I take her hands in mine and fold them together between our bodies as we speak in quick, hushed tones.

"Are you okay?" she asks, beating me to it.

"Fine," I say. "You?"

"I've been through worse," she says. I'm not sure what to

think about that, but her eyes seem to blaze through mine. Such an odd thing. I'm feeling things without actually *feeling* anything. A physical response to a visual stimulus. The body is strange.

"I actually haven't," I say. When her smile fades and a look of anger takes hold of her eyes, I'm freed from their grasp. "It's okay. I understand why it had to be done."

Her eyes drift up to my hair and she frowns, but the expression carries traces of humor. She runs her fingers through my hair, pushing it to the side and down.

"What are you doing?" I ask.

"Your hair," she says. "It looks awful."

"I didn't realize hair could look bad," I say, quickly realizing that I have, in fact, admired her hair, both while sleek and black and wavy orange.

She finishes and says, "There. Good enough for now."

Feeling embarrassed about the attention to my physical state, I glance toward the view and say, "Have you noticed where you are?"

She looks beyond me to the window. Her eyes widen at the view, but she doesn't move. "Convenient direction to be facing," she says, noting right away what it took me some time to notice. But like me, she has failed to notice the men seated beside us.

"Kamiko," I say, forcing the name from my mouth. "Have you met the Council?"

She turns as I motion to the group of seated men. She gasps and takes a step back. Many of the men are smiling at her, at us, but a few are now frowning as deeply as Sir. *Not very good at hiding their emotions*, I think.

"This is Kamiko," Mohr says to the group. "She is a . . . friend of Freeman's. She is present at his request."

A few of the frowners nod at this, but others remain displeased.

"While Freeman and his exploits are interesting," Sir says, "we have more pressing matters to attend to."

"Right," I say, stepping back away from the group. "Don't let us distract you. We'll just"—I look behind me and find some plain white stools along the side wall between the curved back wall and angular windows—"just sit. Over here."

Sir appears to be fuming, but doesn't respond. He just watches us until we sit. When he continues to stare, I fidget in my seat and say, "Carry on."

A few Councilmen chuckle, but stop when Sir snaps his head toward them. The group quickly falls into rapid discussion, covering the latest events. When the Lowers is mentioned in very cold and calculated terms, Luscious takes my hand and squeezes. She's angry—furious—but knows that we're at Sir's mercy. Any infraction in the presence of the Council would most likely end badly for both of us, though given the Council's apparent affection for me, perhaps just her.

We listen as the bombardment is described. Every detail is given, except, I note, the number of casualties. It's almost as though they bombed an empty city. Talk of containment comes up. Of eradication. Quarantines. The results of similar military actions outside other cities around the world. Success, it seems, is the theme of this meeting. But I find that hard to believe. There were so many undead capable of growing their numbers via simple bites. Eradicating them with bombs seems unlikely.

The boots, I think, looking up at Heap. His emotions are masked, but I sense tension in his joints. Does he know something the Council doesn't, or does he simply realize, like I do, that the undead situation is far from over?

"Now," Sir says loudly, focusing attention back on himself. "What of these seismic irregularities?"

"I would rather discuss the radio signal I detected," Mohr says with surprising conviction.

"We have already discussed this," Sir replies, his impatience barely contained. "The radio signal, if there ever was one, is gone. We've analyzed the burst you recorded and found it to be benign, akin to the static created by a solar flare, of which there have been several lately."

"But—"

"The subject is closed," Sir says and then adds, in an even more serious tone, "The seismic irregularities."

After a moment, Mohr sighs and says, "It's rather insignificant . . . but odd nonetheless. Sensors beneath the city are detecting a constant rumble. Minute, but increasing, imperceptible but to the most sensitive of equipment. Possibly just reverberations from the increased action above."

"The shuttle tunnels are clear," Councilman Cat says. "As stable as they have been and will be for the next thousand years."

Councilman Deere nods. "At first I thought it might be a natural tremor. A shift of the tectonic plates. It's not common in this region, but such things have been recorded from time to time in the Masters' historical records. But . . . the sustained and slowly building nature of the disturbance suggests another source. That said, I believe—"

I tune out the Councilman's words and lean closer to Luscious's ear. "What is beneath the city?"

"Just the shuttles," she says.

I know about the shuttles. They're high-speed vehicles that hover over magnetic tracks and can rocket through the city, and from city to city, without taking up space or disturbing the natural world. They're one of the many improvements the Council has made since the end of the Grind that focuses on increased efficiency and a restoration of the environment.

"Wait," Luscious says. "There are also remnants of the old city. Tunnels for utilities we no longer use. Sewers. Gas lines. But I've always assumed they were destroyed or filled in."

I'm not really sure what these things are, but it confirms my fear. I stand from my seat. "It's them."

"Freeman," Heap says quickly, his voice a warning.

"Sit. Back. Down," Sir says loudly.

He's so incensed by my speaking that I start to comply, but Luscious speaks up. "Let him speak. What harm can it do?"

Sir glowers at Luscious, but says nothing. I use the silence as an opportunity to speak. "In the ruins," I say. "The undead—"

I see that none of them know this term. "—the infected. They were in the woods. They were everywhere. But they weren't coming from the forest." I look at Sir, meeting his horrible, angry eyes. "They were coming from underground. They're not in the shuttle lines yet, but what about *beneath* them?"

Councilman Rexel, who represents the power industry, leans forward and asks, "Are you suggesting the seismic activity is being caused by the *footsteps* of the infected?"

"Impossible," Councilman Boeing says. "That would take—"

"Millions," I say. "I know." I turn my attention back to Sir. "Don't wait until it's too late."

"You presume to tell *me* about preemptive actions?" Sir is on his feet, storming toward me. He stops only when our faces are inches apart. "I was steeped in military and strategic—" Sir stops and just stares at me, but something in his eyes has changed, like he's had an epiphany. The anger is gone, replaced by . . . resolution? Satisfaction?

He returns to his chair and sits, leaning back in a posture that seems unfitting for him and somehow makes me feel anxious. "For years, Councilman Mohr has extolled the wonders of the man who would be named Freeman. A man born into freedom and allowed to become his own person. Unbroken. Uncorrupted by the Masters. Humanity's potential finally realized. And here you are, finally, standing among us. And yet, I am not impressed." He turns to Mohr. "Far from it." Back to me. "Perhaps you would like to demonstrate your worth? Show this council that you *are* capable of more than insubordination and distraction. Prove your theory true."

I can't decide if he's just trying to mock me, or if he's serious, but I decide it doesn't matter. *I* believe my theory and the sooner Sir sees it, the better. "Are there sensors in the underground? Heat? Cameras?"

Councilman Cat shakes his head. "Not as deep as you're suggesting."

"Has anyone been down—"

"There has been no reason to access the ruins beneath this city since its foundation was laid," Cat says.

"Well, there is reason now." Sir nearly grins. "Isn't that right, Freeman?"

This feels like a trap, like Sir is guiding me toward a conclusion—that I should enter the underground and find the answer for myself—which he thinks I'll find unfavorable. But I don't. I agree. "I'll go."

Mohr nearly falls over with surprise. "Freeman, no!"

Sir lets his grin show. "Do not worry, old friend. Your boy is wrong. He will be safe. He has already survived scores of these monsters. He should have no trouble with the barren tunnels beneath our city."

Mohr appears conflicted, and unsure, but ultimately nods his agreement. "Very well. But . . . Freeman, while some may doubt you because of your lack of experience, I trust in your intellect. In your instincts." The word draws a laugh from Sir, but Mohr continues. "Please, be careful."

I nod. "Heap and I—"

Heap's hand rests gently on my shoulder. I look up at him. "Many of the tunnels below the city are far too small for me. I will not be able to join you. You must do this alone."

Luscious steps forward. "Not alone."

Sir snickers and motions to the door with a satisfied grin that reveals he's really just happy to be rid of us. I head for the door with Luscious at my side and Heap following behind. "Try not to get lost."

22.

The elevator doors slide open without a sound, revealing a small, stone room unlike anything in the hard, black city now above our heads. Stale air rushes into the elevator, making me shiver, which is something I've never experienced before. I'm not sure if it's a physical response to the cooler air, or if it's caused by nervous tension. A round metal door, rusted and pitted, is embedded in the wall directly across from us. What lies behind it is anyone's guess. There are no maps of the ruins beneath Liberty, but if I'm right . . .

I don't move from the elevator. This is a bad idea.

Heap nudges me from behind. "Are you prepared for this?"

When I don't reply, he adds, "For what it's worth, you've impressed me."

I glance back. "Impressed you?"

"Not for coming down here," he says. "For standing your ground with Sir. It's not an easy thing to do."

I motion toward the hatch. "Easier than stepping through that door."

"You could be wrong," he says.

"I'm not," I say.

"What makes you so sure?" Luscious asks. When I turn to her, she's no longer Kamiko. She's changed back to her red-haired self. I decide not to comment because she also looks a little worried and I wonder if her volunteering to come was really just a way to remove herself from the Council's presence.

I remember Mohr's words about instinct: *natural intuitive power.* Intuitive, from intuition: *a keen and quick insight.* This sounds right. "Instinct."

"Instinct is an attribute of animals," Luscious says. "People are logical."

I'm about to argue, but the intensity in Luscious's tone makes me pause. Something about this subject has her on edge. But what?

The Masters.

Mohr once told me that the Masters were ruled by instinct. That they often acted without thought or consideration to the consequences of their actions, both long and short term. While instinct may indeed exist in people today, the attribute is looked upon with revulsion and fear. I can see both in her eyes now.

"You're right." I step out of the elevator and onto the stone floor. A layer of grit grinds beneath my feet. "Let's just call it a theory based on prior experience."

Luscious smiles. "Better." She joins me and we head for the metal door.

I take hold of a wheel at the door's center and pull. It doesn't budge.

"Spin it," Heap says, clomping up behind us. "Counterclockwise."

The wheel resists for a moment, but then groans loudly as it spins to the left, shedding flakes of rust with each revolution until it spins easily. When it stops, Heap draws his weapon and points it at the doorway, explaining before I can ask, "In case you're right."

I tug hard and the door opens slowly, its hinges fighting the movement after so long. A hiss of air slips past us, sucked into the space beyond by the slightly different pressure. I shove the door wide open and clap the maroon dust from my hands.

Nothing attacks us.

"I'll remain here," Heap says. "If you get into trouble, return quickly."

"I can't have your gun?" I ask, looking at the weapon.

"Only works for me, but you shouldn't need to fight." He points at my eyes. "Your ocular upgrades have a memory chip.

Use it. Record what you find and return quickly. Do not risk yourself."

"Or me," Luscious chimes in.

I give a nod and step through the door. Something about this simple action of stepping forward instigates a change in me. I'm no longer just reacting to what is confronting me, I'm acting. It feels good. Right. It feels . . . strong. With a newfound confidence, I turn back to Luscious. "Let's go."

She must see the change, too, because she grins before ducking down and stepping through the circular doorway.

Before heading into the tunnel beyond the doorway, I turn back. "If we do not return in sixty minutes, assume we have been killed. Tell Sir they are below the city."

"What if you are lost?"

"I am incapable of getting lost." I tap my head, reminding him that my intelligence level is "phenomenal." Mohr's words, ten days previous, when I solved an equation in thirty-three seconds that had vexed him for years.

"He will require proof."

"Lie. Bite yourself." These aren't great suggestions, but they're the best my 'phenomenal intelligence' can think of. "You will think of something."

I leave Heap looking uncomfortable and set off into the dark tunnel. Before entering the elevator, Heap acquired two sets of headlights, a band of bright LED lights that wrap around the head and cast a bright halo of light in every direction. I don't need them to see, but Luscious can't see in the dark and if color is important for some reason, even I will need the light.

Luscious turns her headlight on, illuminating everything for a hundred feet. The tunnel is revealed. It's a long, circular, concrete tube stained brown from whatever foul fluid once flowed over its now dry surface. It ends at a junction seventy-five feet to our right and at a solid metal grate, twenty feet to our left.

I point to the junction. "That way." But before striking out, I point to her headlight. "Better keep that off until we really need it."

"I won't be able to see much," she complains.

"Better than them seeing you. And I can see fine." I reach my hand out and with a frown, she takes it, extinguishing her light a moment later.

We walk through the still, silent darkness, which for me is a mixture of green shades as I view the subterranean world through my night-vision upgrade. It's a maze of tunnels, some large, some very small. Twice, we have to slide through tubes on our stomachs. At the end of the second such tube, I turn around to help Luscious.

"There's nothing down here," she says.

I pull her up to her feet. "The Council Spire is at the city's Core. If they're approaching from underground, they'll be closer to the city's—"

A metallic clang echoes through the passageways. Luscious's grip on my hand tightens.

Switching to electromagnetic spectrum, I see a faint signature two hundred feet ahead. There's no way to tell what it is without getting closer, and I can only record the visual spectrum. To get Sir's evidence, I'm going to have to actually see undead.

I step forward, but feel Luscious resist. "I have to see. Do you want to wait here?"

"Alone? Hell no." She squeezes my hand. "Let's get this over with."

Pushing forward, we enter a seven-foot-tall tube, heading in the direction from which the sound originated. Switching back and forth between spectrums, I can see a growing electromagnetic field, as well as a blossoming heat source, but both are indistinct blobs. Any number of things could be responsible for both. But I'm pretty sure I know what they are.

And somehow, so does Luscious.

"We should go back," she whispers close to my ear.

I cup my hand to her ear, being as quiet as possible. "Why?"

I know the answer, and when she crushes my hand, I know she does, too. Instinct.

"I hate you," she whispers, but my night vision reveals the small smile on her face.

I lean close again. "I need to see. *Sir* needs to see."

I take her silence as agreement and move forward as stealthily as possible. As we near the end of the tunnel, I lower myself down, lying on my abdomen. Luscious lies next to me, and together we inch toward the end of the tunnel, which empties into open space.

There's a constant shuffling sound, like leaves in the wind, rising from the space beyond, and the occasional metallic clang, but the groaning I have come to associate with the animated dead isn't present.

Maybe it's not them? As much as I would like to prove Sir wrong, I hope he's right.

As the large chamber beyond comes into view, I begin recording everything I see, which currently is just open space and a conglomeration of drainage pipes all leading to this hub. Water must have emptied into this chamber and then drained away through a larger tunnel, most likely past the city's limits . . . the perfect place to enter.

I lean over the edge, look down and go rigid.

There they are.

Undead.

They're packed into the space, shuffling forward out of a large tunnel fifty feet below. I can see hundreds of them, but there is no way of telling how many have already passed through and how many are coming. But I can feel the vibration of their steady movement under my hands. *Millions* I think, picturing the city above, unaware of the danger rising up from beneath them. When the undead rise, the city will fall. I'm not sure even Sir will be able to stop them all.

Because they'll infect more. They'll spread. Until their numbers have doubled. Then tripled. And they'll keep right on going until there is enough of them to topple the Spire itself.

But something is wrong with these undead. They're . . . orderly, walking in single-file lines, splitting into rows of three and heading into various branches. This isn't a chaotic mob driven solely by the need to consume. This is organized.

An infiltration.

An *attack*.

Something miniscule tickles the back of my neck. It's barely anything. Maybe a few granules of stone. Almost dust. But the gentle touch sets off an internal alarm and triggers the sudden realization that something is above me.

23.

I squeeze Luscious's hand with enough force to elicit a hiss of pain from her, despite the single-file certain death lurking below.

"What is it?" she asks. "Do you see them?"

In response, I ask a stupid question. "Do you remember the way back?"

"I can't see, Freeman."

"Go back," I whisper. "To the end of this tunnel. When you get there, use your light. Go straight through the small tunnel. Once you're out, take your first right. I'll catch up."

"Why? What's—"

A pebble strikes my cheek. "Go. Now. Before it's too—"

A shriek tears through the air above me. As I turn my head up, Luscious lets go of my hand and flees, finally understanding the danger. The upside-down thing above me clings to the ragged stone wall, its fingers and toes digging into the worn grout. It stares down at me with whole eyes and an open jaw, through which it continues to produce a high-pitched wail that has gained the attention of the horde below.

Moans rise up, mingling with the shriek.

Unlike the other undead, the one above me hasn't mindlessly attacked. Instead, it's held back, but why?

Sounding the alarm, I realize.

This dead man, previously a soldier by the looks of the black armor covering his body, is higher functioning than his counterparts.

He suddenly closes his mouth and lunges down toward my head.

I duck back inside the tunnel knowing there is no way the man's outstretched arms can reach me. He sails past, hooked hands reaching out. But not for me.

His fingers catch hold of the tunnel's floor, hold fast and then flex as he pulls himself up. He launches upward with surprising strength, speed and agility, somehow retaining his soldier's physical prowess and skills.

Unless he's not dead.

"Can you talk?" I ask, hoping to reason with the man.

In response, his lips curl up in a snarl, exposing his teeth and the bits of flesh from some previous victim embedded between them, dangling like butterfly chrysalises. He roars with hunger.

Definitely dead.

I back away quickly, moving deeper into the tunnel. I can hear Luscious's footsteps behind me, fading quickly.

With no sign of the awkwardness I would associate with the undead, he launches forward. In my mind's eye, I see me sidestepping the attack, swiveling and driving him into the floor with enough force to sever his spine, breaking the connection between dead mind and body.

But that's not what happens.

Before reaching me, he drops down, running on all fours like some kind of animal, and then bounds to the left, landing against the curved sidewall of the tunnel where he remains for just a fraction of a second before leaping to the far wall, and then directly toward my head.

Caught off guard by the very sudden, very coordinated attack, I stumble back, tripping over my own feet. I'm pretty sure my clumsiness saves my life. The soldier-zombie sails over my supine body, landing farther down the tunnel, facing away from me, which is exactly the moment Luscious chooses to turn on her headlight.

The soldier snaps his head up toward the brilliant white light. He snarls, as though angered by it, and then sprints toward Luscious.

I'm about to give chase when something latches onto my leg. I look down to find a dead woman clutching the limb, jaws open and ready to bite. Behind her, several more climb into the tunnel.

I yank my leg back hard. The woman's grip is stronger than her shoulder joint and her arm comes free, dangling from my ankle. I roll back, regaining my footing and kick out hard. My foot finds the woman's chest and sends her toppling back into her undead brethren. Tangled and off balance, the whole group of them fall back, dropping out of the tunnel and instigating a burst of agitated groans.

More climb to take their place, but I pay them no heed as I turn and pursue the monster quickly closing the distance to Luscious.

The soldier-zombie is fast. So fast, and agile, that I realize he's been heavily upgraded, like me. He must have been infected recently, possibly in the Lowers before they were decimated. It doesn't really matter. All I care about right now is reaching him before he catches Luscious.

Looking beyond the man, I see Luscious's light shifting, but not moving quickly. She has no idea what's coming. Luckily, the speed of sound is still far faster than either I or the zombie can run. "Luscious! Run! They're coming for you!"

It's not 100 percent truth. Just one of them is coming for her, but this single zombie might be more dangerous than twenty of the others. The light ahead bounces about frantically and then shrinks. She's entered the smaller tunnel, I realize, pushing through it on her stomach. If she's caught there, she'll have no way to prevent the monster from biting her leg.

Except me.

With a shout of anger, I will my legs to move faster.

And they do.

I have no idea how fast I'm running, but I've never run quicker, and I'm gaining on the zombie.

When the soldier reaches the end of the tunnel, he's just ten feet ahead of me. He exits into the open space at the end where several small tunnels converge, but he doesn't have to pause to figure out which way Luscious went. Her headlight blazes from the small tunnel directly ahead.

The soldier dives forward, drawn toward the light.

He's halfway in the small tunnel, clawing his way forward, when I catch his feet.

He flails and kicks, his hard armor slick from moisture. When his limbs start to slide free, I grind my teeth in anger, and squeeze. The upgrades I was created with boost my strength, but the emotion flowing through me seems to supercharge them. The armor clutched in my hands folds inward. With a strong grip on his legs, I pull the soldier from the tunnel and fling him away.

But he doesn't collide with the wall, he springs off of it, diving once again for my head. And this time, I don't fall out of the way.

I drive my fist into his chest, leaving a three-inch-deep dent and knocking him back against the wall.

But this is no man, and the strike doesn't even faze the thing.

He comes at me again, this time feinting left and then throwing a punch—a *punch!* I'm totally unprepared for this kind of attack and am struck hard. The impact is jarring and spins me around. I catch myself against the wall, my head buzzing, my vision flickering in and out for a moment. But I don't let the pain disorientation slow me down.

I shove off the wall and kick hard and low, striking the zombie's knee and inverting it. If it feels any pain, it doesn't express it. The thing just falls forward into my knee as I bring it up hard, driving into the monster's chin.

The soldier's descent reverses course and I let it fall back to the concrete floor.

I turn my head up toward the ceiling, eight feet above. It's covered with a network of pipes. I spot a rusted joint, but then my night vision flickers and goes black.

Quelling a surge of momentary panic, I switch between spectrums. All black.

I'm blind.

Or am I?

I switch to the visual spectrum and activate my headlight. Brilliant white light fills the tunnel system, and my eyes. I can see, but only the visual spectrum. And what I find is disturbing. Just thirty feet back, in the larger tunnel, the horde shambles forward, all of their order and patience replaced by fervent hunger and a mad rush.

With just seconds to spare, and the soldier pushing himself up onto his good leg, I leap up and take hold of a weak pipe. It bends under my weight and comes free with a yank. I land a half second before the soldier lunges, his attack closer to that of his less impressive counterparts. In that half second, I haul the metal pipe back and strike with all of the force I can muster.

The steel rod strikes the soldier's arm first, fracturing the armor. But the blow's force isn't reduced as I follow through and bring the steel against the monster's unprotected head. With a clang and a crunch, the dead man's head caves in, destroying the mind within, this time for good.

A moan turns my eyes back to the horde. They are upon me, stumbling from the tunnel, dead eyes locked onto my living body, teeth bared, skin peeling. They're a horrid group of men and women, decayed and rotting. For a moment, I feel sorry for them. These used to be people, with lives and loved ones and now . . .

I dive into the small tunnel, leaving the dead and my sorrow for them behind. The horde follows, but not quickly, as the concept of single-file organization seems to have been forgotten.

I make quick time through the tunnel, turn right and see Luscious's light ahead, still moving away. "Second left!" I shout ahead to her and am happy to see her light move in that direction. Running as quickly as I can, catching up to her only takes a minute. She shouts in surprise when I put my hand on her arm, but sighs with relief upon seeing my face. Then she looks concerned, rubbing her hand over my cheek.

"What happened?" she asks.

"I was punched."

"A zombie *punched* you?"

"Later," I say, taking her hand and ducking into a tunnel. The journey back takes ten minutes longer than it did on the way out because I have to change course twice and find a new path. The underground is absolutely alive with the dead.

As we reach the final stretch of our subterranean journey, the undead find us again, moaning and charging. We run for the still-open hatch.

"Heap!" I shout, letting him know we're coming so he doesn't accidentally shoot us. "Get ready to close the hatch!"

Assuming he's heard me, I push Luscious ahead and let her escape first, then I dive through behind her. The metal hatch clangs shut behind us. I roll over as Heap spins the lock back into place. An eruption of angry fists pound on the other side of the door.

"You were right," Heap says, offering me one of his big hands, and the other to Luscious.

"I'm not sure if I got the evidence," I say. "I was struck. I think my ocular upgrades might have been damaged."

Heap looks concerned, but I'm not sure if it's for me or my lack of evidence. His eyes turn toward my feet. "I think that will work."

I look down and find the woman's severed arm still clinging to my ankle. I yank it free, but don't discard it. If my recording was damaged, Sir might require more than our testimony, which he doesn't trust.

Heap pulls us both to our feet and shoves us toward the open elevator door. I know we're in a rush, but his actions seem rough. That's when I notice the impacts aren't just against the metal hatch, they're also against the stone wall. As the elevator doors slide shut, the wall cracks.

We rise up through the tower, each of us lost in silent thought. I'm not sure about Heap and Luscious, but I can't stop imagining what's going to happen when that wall breaks. I doubt the dead know how to operate an elevator. But they can climb. And if there are any more of those soldiers . . . If just one of them got inside, it could move up, floor by floor, infecting everyone it encounters who will then do the same.

I'm so lost in thought that when I finally look up from the floor and see my grime-covered reflection in the elevator doors, I flinch. I don't look much better than a zombie. I flinch again when the doors slide open. Unlike my first experience in an elevator, I barely noticed our ascent.

It takes just minutes to rise through the Spire and reach the Core's entrance, where four guards now block our path. They grow tense at our approach, no doubt ordered to prevent entry, but when I hold up the undead woman's arm, they freeze in place and let us pass.

The doors slide open and I enter the chamber, interrupting Sir in the middle of a serious-sounding speech. His head whips in my direction and upon seeing me, he drives his fist into the table around which the Council sits. "What is the meaning of this?"

Mohr spins around, sees me and has just the opposite reaction. "Freeman! You're—"

Mohr's words catch in his throat when I toss the dead arm onto the table. It slides to a stop between Mohr and Sir. I don't mean to be rude. Mohr's relief at my return is nice. There just isn't time for it, or for Sir's agitation.

I speak loudly, hoping it will make Sir really hear me. "The underground crawls with—"

An alarm sounds, distant but shrill. It interrupts my words, but speaks for me and provides emphasis to the limb lying on the table.

I frown. "Too late."

24.

"Report," Sir says, with a faraway look on his face. He's once again speaking to someone not present. The control for his communication device must be implanted somewhere, probably in his armor and toggled by a combination of finger twitches or perhaps a button I'm just not seeing him press. I watch his face for some hint at the news he's receiving, but I'm not sure his frown could get any deeper.

And then it does. His lips pull down hard on either side. It's just for a moment, and then gone, replaced by grinding teeth that remind me of the undead. He turns to the massive converging windows and steps closer. "Infrared."

A shimmer of energy moves through the glass, shifting the view from visual to infrared spectrums. The view changes to shifting shades of color. Most of the buildings retain their cool solid black color. The vibrant lights decorating the buildings have become a dull shade of purple, not much warmer than the buildings. The relative coolness of the early morning city makes the living stand out in stark contrast to the surroundings. There's so many of them. Millions of people, moving through the darkness. Rainbow-colored stars.

I must look confused by the shifting window view because Councilman Mohr steps up next to me and explains. "They're not windows. This is the view from cameras mounted on the outside of the building. We can see the world through a variety of spectrums from here, just like you can."

I didn't really need to know, but it *is* fascinating. And it tells me something about Sir and the Council. They need special cameras to see other spectrums. They don't have ocular upgrades, and if the Council doesn't, maybe I'm the only one who does. But are they really upgrades? That would suggest I existed without them first, but I've been fully upgraded since I first opened my eyes. Of course, that has recently changed.

"Not anymore." I motion to the side of my head where the soldier struck me. I'm not sure if the injury is noticeable, so I explain. "I was struck. Hard. I can only see the visual spectrum now."

Mohr gasps, but then leans in close, inspecting my face and pushing on the flesh with his fingers. He nods. "It will heal."

Upgrades can heal? I wonder, but don't get to ask.

"There," Councilman Deere says, pointing a long green finger.

I'm not sure what he's pointing at, but Sir seems to. "Expand sector five forty."

The view through the window—screen—rushes forward. The sudden feeling of falling through space twists my insides and the expression on my face.

Mohr squints at me. "The shifting view is causing you discomfort?"

"I think nausea is the correct word," I say.

"Wonderful," he says.

"No, not wonderful." I'm struck by a realization and look at the group around me. Not one of the Councilmen, Heap or Luscious looks fazed by the sudden shift in view. *Why am I the only one?*

"Dear Lord," Councilman Mohr says. I'm not sure what this means, but I think it's more slang expressing shock. It's the first slang I've ever heard Mohr use, but it somehow does a good job of revealing abhorrent surprise. Certainly more than shouting, "Abhorrent surprise," would.

The view on the screen zooms in 200x with perfect clarity, the same distance I can magnify my upgraded sight. My ocular upgrades seem to have a lot in common with the cameras mounted on the outside of the building. Similar technology I suppose.

The warm-bodied people are easy to spot, moving quickly in the streets, abandoning their cooler vehicles, which appear to have collided with one another. But the living are not alone. Purple humanoid shapes with hot cores lumber in pursuit.

An unlucky person, a man I think, stumbles and falls. He's caught quickly by three of the undead. They set upon him with fury. Everyone in the Core watches the scene play out in silence, but I have no trouble imagining the sounds of this attack. The shrieking. The grinding teeth. The wet slurp of the feast. I've heard it all before.

When the man finally stops twitching, the dead lose interest and rejoin the pursuit of the masses. The man's warmth fades along with his life, cooling quickly to a dull blue and then purple.

I sense that someone is about to break the silence, but feel they need to see this for themselves. They need to understand what we're facing before they can defeat it. *If* they can defeat it. Sir opens his mouth to speak, but I cut him off, saying, "It won't take long."

Sir glares at me, but I just motion him back to the view and he complies.

The purple coloration of the cooling body is nearly black now. But then, in the center of the man's chest, a flare of color, white at first before fading to red. Warmth spreads through the corpse, radiating out from the body's core, reddening the limbs before they fade to a light purple. The head flares bright white for a moment and then the man sits up. His movements are stiff, but quick. While he was killed, his limbs were left intact. He has no trouble standing, and while the horde is still emerging, seemingly out of nowhere, he joins them. From victim to killer in seconds.

"What's located at this site?" Sir asks. "Where are they coming from?"

"Drainage pipes," Councilman Tetra says. He's in charge of city planning and expansion and is often the coordinator between other professions such as construction and environmental engineering. He would know every inch of Liberty, though I'm not sure how well he knows what lies *beneath* the city. "For rain."

"How are they accessing them?" Sir asks, his voice rushed.

"I—I don't know."

Sir lets out something like a growl and then speaks, but not to anyone in the room. "Spire defenses, engage any target under fifty degrees. Liberty defenses, converge on the Spire, priority alpha. Engage any targets under fifty degrees. Collateral damage acceptable."

Collateral damage. This must be a similar order he gave to the soldiers guarding the river. It's why they pursued us through the city with such abandon. They weren't concerned about the damage to the city because they'd been ordered not to.

"Liberty lockdown. Initiation code one, zero, seven, five." He finishes the string of numbers with a sound that's almost mechanical.

"Lockdown?" Councilman Deere says in surprise. "But there are so many people on the streets!"

"And if just one of those gets inside a building, everyone inside it could be lost," Sir says.

"They'll all be killed," I say.

"Reset magnification," Sir says, and the giant view screens revert to their citywide view, though they remain infrared. Several expanding blobs of cooler bodies blossom around the city. "They're *already* dead," Sir replies, eyes on the city.

"If they get inside the Cat compound . . ." Councilman Cat says, looking at Sir. He lets the statement hang, and I'm not sure of the implications, but Sir seems to understand.

"Security forces in sectors thirty-seven through forty, converge on the Cat compound. Engage *anyone* who approaches, no exceptions. Collateral damage acceptable."

I'm going to argue, but Heap takes my arm and shakes his head. Whatever is in the Cat compound must be important. Or dangerous. But then I think of something that I can't stay quiet about. "The buildings. Don't they have internal drainage?" All that water used to clean me off had to go somewhere. "And if Liberty was built over one of the Masters' cities, there could be—"

"He's right," Tetra says, looking mortified. "If the old infrastructure is still intact, there might be ways to access our buildings."

"They're already trying to break down the old walls beneath the Spire," I add.

Sir blinks twice, revealing the subtle toggle for his communications, and says, "All building security teams. Seal off, secure and guard all sub-levels. No one goes down or up. Lethal force authorized."

"Aim for the head," Luscious whispers in my ear.

"What?"

"Tell him to aim for the head," she says. "That's what they did in the movies. Zombies die without brains."

She's right, I realize, thinking about my personal experience with the undead. They can endure all sorts of physical abuse—they're dead after all—but too much trauma to the head, to their minds, puts them down for good.

"Aim for the head," I say. "Sir, tell them to aim—"

"I heard you!" he screams at me, unleashing his fury. I step away from him, thinking I might have to defend myself, but he reins himself in and speaks again. "All security forces . . ." He glares at me one more time. ". . . when engaging targets, aim for the head."

He swivels on his feet and heads for the door. "Councilmen, you will remain in the Core until this crisis has ended." The doors open and he pauses, turning to Mohr. "Keep him"—he thrusts a finger at me—"his guardian and his mod, out of my sight."

Sir storms away. The doors slide shut behind him.

Mohr approaches me as the Councilmen begin talking amongst themselves.

"You did well," he says.

"I'm not sure Sir would agree with you."

"He's intimidated by you," he says, catching me off guard.

I shake my head. "I don't think he could be intimidated by anyone."

"He once told me it was his job to 'consider all possible future outcomes.' And thus far he has, with the precision of a razor sharp blade. But this . . . outbreak. He never saw it coming and I'm not sure he knows how to respond to it."

"A viral outbreak is not something you can shoot," I say.

Mohr nods, glances over his shoulder and then gently nudges me farther away from the other Councilmen, but not Luscious and Heap. Whatever he's going to say, it's not a secret from them. "Further demonstrating why *you* are responding to this crisis more quickly than Sir. The solution to this problem isn't going to be found in an armory, or a laboratory." He places his hands on my shoulders and looks into my eyes. "It's going to be found *outside* the city."

I nod in agreement. "The living dead are not natural. Someone made them. Someone is *guiding* them."

"Who?" Luscious asks.

"That is the question," Mohr says. "And likely the solution." He steps back, looking at me, and Luscious, and then Heap. "And I want you, the three of you, to find the answer." He turns to the large display screens. "Out there."

25.

"You want us to *what?*" Luscious asks, her voice raised, but she gives Mohr no time to reply, probably because she understands his request perfectly. She turns to me. "He's trying to kill us."

"You are wrong," Heap says.

"What do you know?" Luscious reels around on Heap. "You're a Simp."

I'm not sure what a Simp is, but I'm certain it's not intended as a compliment.

"How many people did you kill for the Masters after the awakening?"

"I protected life," Heap says.

"I bet you did. How many *Masters* did you protect?"

Luscious's anger surprises me. I get a sense she's been biding her time, waiting for the right moment to launch this verbal barrage, but I don't yet understand it. Though the idea that Heap might have willingly served the Masters is disturbing. Heap doesn't seem disturbed by Luscious's tone. He's his normal, calm self.

"Fifteen," Heap says. "For two years post-Grind."

This seems to surprise Luscious. She steps back for a moment. I can almost feel her heating up. Her brows furrow deeply. "You kept Masters living for *two years?*"

Mohr places a gentle hand on Luscious's shoulder. She shrugs away from it, repulsed.

"They were in the mountains," Mohr says. "He had no communication with the outside world, no knowledge of the Simp rebellion, and he was protecting children."

Luscious's anger implodes at this last word. She clings to the negativity for a moment, but then it dissipates fully.

"Children?" I ask.

"Until they weren't," Heap says. "One night, they lived. In the morning, they didn't. When I returned to the city, this tower was just being built and I learned about the events you have mentioned."

"He's been in my service since," Mohr says.

"And I would level this city to protect Freeman," Heap adds.

This statement surprises me. I know we're friends, and I know it's his job to protect me, but I can't be that important. It just doesn't make sense.

"Then why send him back out there?" she asks, hitching her thumb toward me.

I realize I've been absent from this conversation, of which I am the subject. I raise my hand. "I'd actually like to know that, too."

"The radio signal," he says.

"But Sir thought—"

Mohr waves a hand at me. "Never mind what he thinks. He is a brilliant strategist, yes, but not a scientist. He thinks in a grand sweeping scale and occasionally misses the details. The radio signal is faint, and intermittent. As Sir said, it's like one created by a solar flare, but I believe that is what we are meant to believe. Where Sir hears static, I hear a pattern. I believe it's what instigated this attack and perhaps directed the dead beneath the city. And he will not hear of it again unless I . . . unless *we* can provide proof. Sir is many things, but his weakness is his stalwart belief in his own abilities. Once something is dismissed, it will not be considered again without compelling evidence."

"Like a zombie arm?" I ask.

"Much more than that, I'm afraid. You'll need to find the signal's source, and if you can, shut it off or take control. If we're lucky, that might even be enough to stop all this. And if you find those responsible for this mess—"

"We kill them," Luscious finishes, surprising me.

Mohr shakes his head. "Subdue them. Do not, under any circumstance, kill *anyone* that isn't already dead."

It pleases me to hear Mohr say this as it falls in line with what he taught me about the sanctity of life, but he doesn't say anything about that now. Instead, he offers some logical reasoning. "We may require their knowledge."

"What makes you think we can do this?" I ask.

"You survived the Lowers and made it to Liberty's Core. You went beneath the city when no one else would, and once again, returned successfully." Mohr raises an eyebrow. "You think that was luck? Also, you're immune to the virus."

"And what about me?" Luscious asks. "I'm just a mod from the Lowers."

Mohr smiles. "You have become more than yourself. That alone is impressive, but you're also important"—he nods to me—"to Freeman. He needs you."

Luscious stares at Mohr for a moment and then looks back at me. "You're going to go, aren't you?"

I nod.

"Aren't you afraid?"

"Very much so," I confess, "but being controlled by fear is worse than pain, or death, in my opinion."

"You see!" Mohr claps his hands together and then thrusts them both toward me. "Brilliance, wisdom and bravery in seventeen words. This is why Freeman, and only Freeman, will save humanity."

This statement feels exaggerated. Borderline ridiculous. How could saving an entire race of people be up to me? I suppose it's not. Not really. Sir and his security forces are doing their part, holding off the invasion for as long as possible. But that can't last forever. Part of me says that Sir is not this narrow-minded. That he would listen to Mohr. But then, I've seen his stubborn refusal for myself.

Mohr leans closer and whispers, "And if you must know the truth, I have more faith in Freeman than I do in the defenses of this city and the Spire. You must hurry. I've run several simulations including all variables: population density, defensive capabilities, structural designs and flaws, as well as the layout of what lies beneath Liberty. In most scenarios, the city is lost in two days. And when that happens, the Spire will not be far behind. We have three days at the most. It's worse for other cities around the world, where similar attacks are being carried out. They're far less defended and will likely fall by the end of the day. For there to be any hope, you must reach the transmission's source in three days."

"But we don't even know where we're going," Luscious complains, and it's a valid point.

"North," Mohr says, talking to me. "The signal originated north of Liberty. Within a hundred miles. Whoever is doing this, they're close." He starts walking away. "Come. Quickly. Before Sir realizes you're leaving."

"I don't think Sir will mind that I'm leaving," I say, following close behind while reaching out for Luscious's hand. I'm privately nervous she'll decide to stay behind. I may have performed some impressive feats but the fact that I did most of those things in the defense of Luscious is not lost on me. Mohr is right. I need her. Relief floods through me when her fingers find mine. Heap follows closely, his heavy feet thumping on the hard, glowing floor.

"On the contrary," Mohr says. "When he has a moment to think beyond the current predicament, he will find a hundred different uses for you, none of which will allow you to reach your full potential or prevent the extinction of humanity. You will become just another one of his weapons."

"A *weapon*?" I ask.

Mohr looks wounded for a moment, but straightens himself up and speaks calmly. "There is a long history of new discoveries, technological advancements and brilliant science created with the best intentions being twisted for use as unimaginable destructive forces."

I hardly think I have the potential to be an unimaginable

destructive force, but I understand what he's saying. After all, our enemy has conjured a way to raise the dead and is using that ability to slaughter the living.

Mohr stops and motions toward an open elevator door. We step inside and immediately head up. The doors open just a moment later.

We step out of the elevator and into a wide-open, circular chamber that's hundreds of feet across. *We're in the disc atop the tower,* I realize. But it's not just an empty space, it's a hangar. Aircraft of every shape and size fill the space, including a line of thirty HoverCycles. Soldiers bustle about, prepping an army of flying vehicles, including several familiar-looking drones.

"That's impressive," I say, looking at a large red aircraft parked at the center of the hangar. It's wide and sleek, like a giant bird of prey combined with a manta ray.

"It's a VTOL gunship," Mohr says. "Sir's own design. Should the Spire be overrun, it will be our refuge."

I'm slightly disappointed. Part of me really wanted to take the plane. Heap stops by the line of HoverCycles and mounts the nearest. Rather than climb up behind him as I usually might, I step up onto the neighboring cycle and motion for Luscious to hop on behind me. Unlike Heap's former cycle, these look brand new. The paint is deep blue and shiny. And the number seventy-eight is emblazoned on the front hood, just below a star and above the words, PROTECT AND SERVE. I suspect the number, symbol and words were painted over on Heap's cycle.

"Um," Mohr says. "I'm not sure that's a good idea. You're not—"

I place my thumb on the starter pad. "Cycle seventy-eight, start." The repulse engines hum to life. Bright blue light glows dully against the black floor. The cycle rises three feet. I turn to Mohr with a smile. "You think I can save humanity, but are afraid to let me drive? Also, is there a magnet in my thumb?"

Mohr chuckles. "You've changed so much in the last twenty-four hours." Then his smile fades. "Wait here." Not answering my question, or perhaps avoiding it, he walks to a chest and taps a code into the keypad on its side. The top separates and opens. Three rows of black weaponry fill the space. He fiddles with the contents of the case for a moment, then stands up holding two holstered guns on belts. He carries the weapons to us and holds one up. "Toggle this switch to power up the weapon. Then just pull the trigger. These work just like the railguns, but on a smaller scale and with slightly less velocity than the others you've seen."

"So they won't punch holes through the city?" I ask.

"Well, not all the way through, but you should handle them with great care." He hands one belt to me and the other to Luscious, who looks surprised. "They go around your waist."

As Luscious and I wrap the belts around our waists, Mohr taps on one of ten hard square pouches on the outside of the belt. "Each of these contains a magazine of ammunition, one hundred rounds in each, small but powerful. You have eleven hundred rounds total, which sounds like a lot, but in the right circumstances, won't last long. Use them sparingly. To replace a magazine, depress the button on the back of the handle. The spent magazine will eject and you can insert the new one. Understand?"

I nod and fasten the belt in place. "What about you?" I ask Heap.

He pats his armored leg where his gun remains hidden until it's needed. "I'm already armed." He starts his HoverCycle and gives the repulse engines a good rev. "Check your armament gauges," he says to me, pointing to two glowing vertical bars on his dash display. I look down and find the bars. They're lit green to the top.

"Green and full," I say.

He moves his finger across the dash to a circular display. "Charge?"

I find the display. A needle points to the right of a notched circle, landing on a capital F. "F for full," I say, and Heap nods. "Anything else I need to know?"

"If anything else lights up, ignore it. If it starts blinking, make sure you're near the ground and start thinking about an alternate mode of transport."

"You know," I say, "I really enjoy these longer conversations we're having now."

Heap turns to Mohr. "He has a sense of humor now, too." He pulls forward toward the outside edge of the hangar, and stops. I pull up next to him. Mohr lags behind. I turn back to him.

"Will you be okay?" I ask.

"Sir will protect me," Mohr says with a shrug. "If he doesn't shoot me for letting you leave." When I look worried, Mohr waves his hand dismissively. "We'll see each other again. Of that, I have little doubt. Now go. Take care of yourself, and each other."

"We will," I promise.

"You remember how to slow a fall?" Heap asks.

"Of course," I say.

"Hold onto him," Heap says to Luscious. "Tight."

Luscious wraps her arms around my waist and despite the circumstances, I must admit to feeling a deeply pleasant surge of emotions as a result. When she leans her head on my back, the surge is calmed. It's like she has some kind of control over me, and despite the fact that control over another human was forbidden by the Grind Abolition Act, I find myself a willing participant in relinquishing myself to her.

"Freeman," Heap says, snapping me out of my reverie. "I'm working on my sense of humor, too."

"What?" I ask, trying to recall if Heap ever made an attempt at humor.

He pushes a button on the dash of his cycle.

The floor beneath the cycles falls open, revealing a quarter mile of open space between us and the city floor. In the time it takes my shout of surprise to rise from my mouth, we've already fallen a hundred feet.

26.

Despite the ridiculous height, knowing that the HoverCycle will slow our fall and stop us gently, three feet from the ground, keeps me from feeling any real fear. A thousand feet or thirty thousand feet, I don't think it would matter. Terminal velocity is the maximum speed a falling object can reach as gravity pulls it downward while drag slows it down. Were I to jump and free-fall in a dive, I might reach two hundred miles per hour. And while the HoverCycle is heavy, its large size, two hover discs and lots of air-catching nooks create considerable drag. I quickly count the time it takes for us to pass ten floors and calculate our speed at one hundred miles per hour. The HoverCycle travels faster horizontally.

I flash a grin at Heap, who is falling atop his cycle below and to my left, to let him know I appreciate his humor. He responds with a nod, though I'm not sure if he's acknowledging me or something else. Nods are funny that way. They can mean any number of things. He could be expressing acknowledgment, pride or even indifference. It's hard to tell with Heap's armored expression. Filtering the gesture through what I know of my big blue guardian, it's most likely that he's feeling a mixture of pride, relief and maybe even happiness that I've managed to not panic all the way to the ground. Or perhaps he's simply just glad that I found humor in his joke, which I have to say, is more of a prank than a joke. I have no experience with pranks. I have never performed one or been on the receiving end of one before now, but I suspect dropping someone from a thousand-foot-plus height is on the extreme end.

Heap raises his thick arm and points to the horizon. I turn

forward and see the black, glowing towers of Liberty. But beyond the city is the lush green of the natural world. That's where he's pointing. We're not just leaving the Spire, we're leaving the city.

Suddenly, Heap's direction changes. He's no longer falling straight down, he's rocketing forward as well. I'd assumed we would drop to the streets below and then drive our way through the city. This new route strikes me as risky. He's moving into the congested airspace around the Spire, where HoverTracks twist about and carry speeding vehicles whose passengers are seeking refuge from the mobs of undead tearing through the streets.

A quick glance down reveals his logic. A battle is being waged in the streets surrounding the Spire. Huge robot soldiers, tanks and lines of men fire an endless barrage into rushing hordes of undead. The sounds of gunfire and explosions are muted by the rushing wind, but the sight of it is enough to convince me it's not the ideal landing spot.

"Hang on!" I shout to Luscious over the wind.

"I am!" she shouts back.

"Tighter!" I lean forward slightly, tipping the cycle's nose downward. This alone delivers some forward momentum, but we really start moving when I press the accelerator pedal. I spot Heap ahead of us and do my best to fall in line behind him. The cycles aren't made for flight, or even gliding, but through a combination of leaning side to side, forward and backward, I manage to bring us up behind Heap.

He looks back, sees us and gives a nod. *Approval this time*, I think.

The problem with being behind Heap is that his thick body blocks a good portion of my view. I won't see what's coming until it's too late to do anything about it, so I'm trusting him to guide us safely to the ground.

"Whoa!" I shout as Heap ducks down, revealing the bottom of a freeway track. The cars atop it are stopped and burning. Being far smaller than the man leading me downward, I don't need to duck, but I'm still unnerved by the track's proximity to my head, not to mention Heap's. A gust of wind or an updraft could have slammed him into the track.

We're just three hundred feet from the ground now, but the closeness to our descent's end provides little comfort. If something were going to go wrong, it would be now.

Heap leans hard to the left, bringing his HoverCycle into a full spin.

I lean to the side, attempting to duplicate his maneuver, but lack the girth. "Lean!" I shout.

Luscious's grip tightens and she lends her weight to mine, but I fear it's too little too late. Heap, now upside down, uses his repulse engines to push himself away from the underside of a wide, multilane freeway. When I attempt the same maneuver, Luscious and I come far closer to the bottom of the track and the repulse engines shove us hard toward the ground.

We drop a hundred feet in a second. I shout as the spiraling HoverCycle continues around. When we're upright again, I lean the other way, leveling us out and controlling our mad descent once again. But we're now a hundred feet below Heap. While I can see what's coming, I no longer have a skilled driver ahead of me to emulate.

I look ahead, taking note of four intersecting HoverTracks between us and the street. Two hold multiple lanes of fast-moving vehicles. Two are single-lane speedways, one of which is congested by piled-up ruined vehicles . . . and bodies, either dead or soon to be. Or not. It's hard to tell.

I zoom in and scan the street below, realizing that I hadn't thought to check the functionality of this particular ocular upgrade. The living and dead mingle amidst a chaotic mash of cars. Soldiers stand among them, some shooting, some biting. I look ahead, searching as far as I can, and see the same, block after block. Our return to the ground will not be a happy occasion.

My vision snaps back to normal and I see our path like a roadmap. Without thought, my body works in tandem with the cycle, leaning, pitching, speeding up and slowing down. Nothing as fancy as Heap's sideways flip, but I seem to have a full mastery of the vehicle now.

As we momentarily skip over an empty freeway, Luscious asks, "How are you doing this?"

I shrug, focusing on my path, which is almost complete. After that, no amount of forethought can generate a clear path through the bedlam below.

Thirty feet from the ground, I feel the repulse engines slow our descent. We're nearly there.

Heap suddenly appears ahead of us, dropping down until his repulse engines begin slowing his descent as well. Without looking back, he points two fingers forward. We're already moving quite fast, so it only takes me a moment to figure out what he wants to do. He shifts to the right, and then in a flash, he's propelled forward by the cycle's turbofan jet. A moment later, we're rocketing up behind him, accelerating to speeds that dwarf our free fall.

The sounds of battle come and go in strange bursts. Bits of screams flash past. Gunfire rattles. Doppler explosions come and go. The only things that remain constant are the hum of the repulse engines, the rushing wind and the moaning of the dead, each carrying on the tune of the zombies passed a moment before.

Heap's cycle lowers to the point where I can see the repulse discs pushing down on the people below it. He must feel it, too, because he's swerving back and forth above the heads of the people below, following a path directly above undead and only undead, sparing the living. I do my best to follow his lead, but any maneuver at this speed takes intense focus, so intense that I nearly miss what happens to Heap.

He cuts off the turbofan jet and turbines, cranks the cycle hard to the left and uses the repulse engines as brakes, but all of this, which happens in just two seconds, isn't enough to avoid colliding with—what? I can't see. But the effect is impossible to miss.

The HoverCycle stops suddenly and Heap is flung into the air. He topples head over heels, performing five rapid flips before crashing to the street. He rolls through the horde, crushing bodies beneath his girth. His armor clanging against the hard metal street.

A thick, black chain snaps up in front of my HoverCycle. I nearly try to stop, just as Heap did, but I correct his mistake by shoving the repulse engine pedal to the floor and gaining a few extra feet. I glide cleanly over the chain, cut the repulse engine and drop toward the road. Before we crash, I kick on the repulse engines, turn hard to the left and lean, just as Heap had. The HoverCycle comes to a sudden stop, launching the undead unfortunate enough to be standing in front of the tilted repulse engines. They arc away like projectiles, crashing into their nonliving comrades and pulling a lot of attention in our direction.

"What are you doing?" Luscious asks. "Don't stop!"

"I'm not going to leave him behind," I say, stepping off the cycle.

"Well," she says, "what should I do?"

I point to the weapon Mohr gave her. "Use it."

The swath of street where I landed has been cleared of the dead, dying and fleeing. I look to where I expect to find Heap, but see only a mound of undead, clawing and biting at some unseen form. *Heap,* I realize.

"Get off of him!" I aim my weapon and run toward Heap, but don't get a chance to fire. The pile rises from the street and then explodes outward. Heap spins, punching, breaking and kicking in a spiral of violence. He takes the last of the undead clinging to his armor and simply throws him away. When he turns to me, I see that his chest armor has been dented inward from the impact of his crash.

"What are you doing?" he shouts at me. "Get out of here!"

I stop in my tracks. *Perhaps Luscious was right? Maybe we should leave?*

I turn back and see her firing her weapon again and again,

standing her ground, but losing it at the same time. She won't be able to hold them off much longer. I'm about to run to her aid when the *clack, clack, clack* of a chain being withdrawn pulls my attention back toward Heap.

He's not looking at me anymore. He's looking up.

A shadow falls over the street. The chain's owner has arrived.

"Freeman," Heap says. "Run."

I draw my weapon. "Not without you. Not this time."

I hear a grunt of frustration, but it's quickly replaced by the words, "Then fight!"

27.

Heap's gun appears in his hand, but he doesn't aim up at the approaching giant, he aims toward me. I feel the warmth of the fired projectiles as they pass by my face and strike the two undead shambling up behind me. His focus is so entirely on protecting me that he forgets himself.

I, however, don't. "Get down!" I shout, as the clanking of a loud chain reverberates through the street. I dive forward, catch Heap by his large feet and pull his legs out from under him. A large, black steel ball sweeps over us, all but disintegrating a mass of zombies and punching a hole in a nearby building.

I roll over and look up at a giant mustard-yellow armored man standing above us. The chain retracts into his oversized left forearm.

Not a man, I realize. *A robot, like the tall soldiers.* But if that's true . . . "Why is it attacking us?"

"He's infected," Heap says, pushing himself up.

"Infected?" The word makes me flinch. "He's a *robot.*"

Heap fires off a few rounds, destroying two more living dead. "There's a man in there somewhere."

"Like your armor?" I ask.

Heap's lips turn down. "Right."

"But if he's infected—"

"There isn't time to play detective!" Heap shouts before pushing me to the side. The metal ball snaps free from the building and grinds across the street where we stood just a moment before.

Three rounds explode from Heap's weapon, each striking the robotic suit, which I believe is used in construction, or more accurately demolition—probably of the Masters' ruins. This deduction is in part because I can't think of any other use for the ball and chain, but more from the large CAT stencil across its chest. I now understand why Councilman Cat was so concerned about the undead breaching his compound. The bullets have no effect. They just ricochet off the steel head with metallic pings.

A shuffle of feet behind me tickles my ear. I spin to find three undead lumbering toward me, eyes lost, arms reaching, clawing at the air. They approach in a haphazard line, swaying back and forth. I raise my weapon, take aim and rather than pull the trigger, I wait, looking beyond the closest of the dead, a man whose body is shredded, like grass chewed by a cow. My pause is just a fraction of a second, but long enough for the perfect alignment.

I pull the railgun's trigger.

Nothing happens.

Remembering the power switch, I snap it forward and feel a subtle change in the weapon's temperature as it heats up. I'm not sure if the weapon is ready to use right away, but I don't have a choice.

I pull the trigger again.

This time there is a slight jolt in my hands and a sound like a snapping branch coupled with a *twang* and the sound of a projectile slipping through the head of not one, but seven undead. The perfectly aligned dead fall as one.

Seeing this, Luscious looks at me with surprise in her eyes, but the expression is suddenly replaced by understanding. She takes aim, pulls the trigger and downs three zombies with one shot. A slight smile emerges on her face for a moment and then she's firing again.

Heap's weapon, which has more bark than the railguns, thunders behind me. Undead drop with each shot, their heads snapping back. Still firing, he points up at the demo-bot and shouts, "Aim for its head!"

Of course! While Heap's weapon is fine for the undead, it's

not powerful enough for the armored monstrosity. But the railgun, which can punch through buildings, shouldn't have any trouble. I aim up and fire, just one. The round is imperceptible as it cuts through the air, but the effect on the giant's head is easy to spot. A fist-size hole suddenly appears in its forehead. An explosion of debris sprays from the back of its head.

I realize too late that our plan is illogical. If this is just a suit, armor for a smaller man, it's unlikely he'd be crammed up in the thing's head. Despite the smoke now pouring from its cranium, the construction robot raises its left arm and throws the giant ball toward me.

The hard steel of the street greets me harshly as I dive to the side, but it's better than being pulverized. The giant steel ball clangs off the street and strikes the building once more, creating a new hole. Undead are already flooding into the first, no doubt racing through the building and increasing their numbers. I glance up at the tall tower. How many people are inside? A thousand? Two thousand? Probably more.

The chain snaps tight as the construction robot attempts to retract the ball from the building. After shoving myself up, I take hold of the chain and pull myself atop it. The linked rings are thick and a half-foot across, making them easy to balance on.

"What are you doing?" Heap asks, firing away.

My reply is drowned out by a nearby explosion, the result of some other life-and-death battle playing out. When the explosion repeats again and again, fading into the distance, I realize that the string of destruction was caused by one of the giant soldiers firing its railgun. In my mind's eye, I see the Spire under assault. If all those soldiers continue to fire, they might bring the city down around them.

We need to escape this place, and soon.

I charge up the taut chain, aiming for the head once again, just in case, but when two new shots have no effect, I aim lower, for the chest and fire again. And again. And again.

Where are you? I think, wondering where a man could sit inside this monstrosity. Even if I knew, without seeing the man, I'm not sure I could strike his head. The real question is, how can an infected man think straight enough to operate this machine? Some of the others have trouble walking. Is it because he's recently been infected, like the soldier? Or is someone exerting some kind of control over the higher-functioning dead? If so, things are going to get a lot worse very quickly as the dead spread their plague to all of the strong and healthy Liberty residents.

The center, I decide, aiming dead center at the demo-bot's chest and loose a barrage, tracing a line straight down the giant's torso, hoping I'll strike the man inside at some point. But before my plan garners results, the ball comes free from the wall behind me and the chain quickly retracts. My feet are pulled forward and I find myself flipping over backward. I reach out as I fall, grab hold of the chain and am yanked straight toward the giant.

I let go before being sucked into the construction bot's arm and am slammed against its torso, my body acting as an exclamation point on the big CAT. Before I fall twenty-five feet to the ground, I manage to cling to one of the massive machine's many nooks. I'm nearly shaken free when the thing takes a step forward, closing the distance between it and Heap. Before it can take another step, I spot the line of holes my weapon punched in its chest. After holstering my railgun, I swing myself over and catch hold of the open hole. As the giant leans back, preparing to throw its ball and chain once more, the chest angles back and I find climbing the line of holes reasonably easy.

Suddenly, the giant pitches forward and I'm nearly flung from its chest. My feet dangle over open air. The chain rattles as it unfurls from the oversized arm. It's followed by a loud crunch that I fear is Heap, but don't look back. Instead, I climb higher, reaching the machine's top, thirty-five feet above the ground. It's oblivious to my presence.

As the chain retracts, I stand atop the thing's shoulder and turn around. The scene below is nauseating. I can see down the street for miles. I can't really tell undead from living at this distance, but they're everywhere and I have no doubt that soon, they'll just all be undead. I spot a few larger bodies moving through the city, some yellow, some green, others black. In the chaos it's hard to tell who is fighting whom and which people are simply running for their lives. Smoke fills the sky. Explosions resound with a constant vibration and are the only things capable of drowning out the constant moaning of the dead and screams of their victims.

Directly below me, I see Heap. His back is turned to the giant as he wrenches a zombie away from Luscious, pins it to the street and shoots its forehead. The chain begins to retract, revealing Heap's crushed HoverCycle.

The chain snaps back into place and the construction bot winds up for another strike. I cling to a rail on its shoulder, draw my weapon and fire down into the thing. It pitches forward, completing its strike, which I suspect is aimed at Heap and Luscious.

I hold the trigger down, letting it fire a stream of rail rounds into the machine's core. But it doesn't slow. Doesn't stop.

A sound like approaching thunder reaches my ear a microsecond before an impact shakes the demo-bot's body. The massive machine jolts hard, staggers once and falls forward. As it falls, I catch a glimpse of a nearby building through which a ten-foot hole has been blown. For a moment, the holes of multiple buildings align and I can see through nearly a mile of ruined buildings, all the way to the soldier that fired the rail bolt.

Then, we're falling.

I scurry over the machine's back and stand, riding it all the way to the street where it crushes a fresh throng of undead headed for Heap and Luscious. I absorb the impact by bending my knees.

When the dust clears, I find an astonished Heap looking from me to the massive hole in the machine's back. "How?"

I leap down from the construction bot's back and then point

to the giant holes on both sides of the intersection. "Wasn't me."

Heap fires two shots. "Let's get out of here."

"You're driving," I tell him, motioning to his ruined cycle. He frowns briefly, but then rushes to my HoverCycle, twists it around and shouts, "Get on!"

Luscious climbs up behind Heap while he opens fire with the cycle's cannons, punching down scores of undead. But more are quickly taking their place, the freshest of them pouring out of the nearby buildings—the citizens of Liberty turned into monsters.

I jump on the back, reach around Luscious and grip Heap's sides. He must feel this because I don't even have time to shout, "Go!" The turbine kicks in from a dead stop, yanking my head backward and quickly accelerating, but I nearly fall off when Heap once again engages the turbofan jet, rocketing us forward.

"Head down!" Heap's voice mixes with the wind, but I'm able to hear the urgency in the command well enough to quickly obey it. Luscious and I pull forward against the wind and lean down.

A deep resonating rumble fills my body as the cycle plows through everything and everyone in its path. I can't see anything. The rushing wind washes out the sounds of battle and death. My senses are completely overwhelmed. But through it all, I can feel Luscious shaking.

I pull myself against her, holding her more tightly and pressing my lips to her ear. "I have you," I tell her. And again, "I have you." I repeat the phrase until her shaking subsides, which is a full twenty minutes after the cycle smashes its way through waves of undead, tears through miles of dense forest and comes to a sputtering stop.

28.

"Stay here," Heap says, motioning to the pine needle–covered forest floor. "I want to see what's ahead."

We've been walking for seventy minutes. The cycle, having bludgeoned its way through countless undead and two road-blocks, not to mention completing a leap back across the river, had performed admirably. But it had endured more abuse than it, or any vehicle short of a tank, was designed to handle. The hood was caved in, crushing the electronics hidden inside, and the front repulse disc had sustained irreparable damage. So we started walking, a slow mode of travel made sluggish by Heap's insistence that we pause every twenty minutes so that he could scout ahead. "Better that I discover an ambush on my own," he said. But we're all keenly aware that the undead can come from any direction, which is why Heap adds, "Keep watch. If I do not return in three minutes, head—"

"I know what to do," I assure him. During the first thirty minutes of hiking, we came up with a backup plan in the event that we are unable to find the radio transmission's source. Head due east. Find a boat. Escape to an island two miles off the coast, the coordinates to which he had me memorize. It's a temporary solution, but we both agree that the undead will eventually rot and die for good. Survival might simply be a case of finding a secluded spot to outlast them.

Not that I would follow this plan. I have no intention of abandoning Heap, Mohr or even Sir. But Heap doesn't need to know that. He and Mohr have kept plenty of secrets from me, so I feel little guilt about keeping one of my own.

"Go ahead," I tell him. "We'll be fine."

Without another word, Heap stomps up the pine tree–laden hillside. Branches break, saplings bend away from him and the ground compresses beneath his feet. It's a good thing the undead lack intelligence or we would be easily tracked. Heap's armor was built for protection and power, not for stealth or subtlety.

When I turn back, a flash of panic momentarily grips me, like hands around my neck. Luscious is gone. But then I spot her toes and find her sitting on the ground, leaning against a tall pine. She hasn't said much since we left the city.

I crouch down next to her, pressing my hand into the soft earth for balance. I'm momentarily distracted by the textures beneath my fingers. The crispy layer of dried pine needles gives way to soft decay and then cool, damp soil—the sweat of the earth.

"Are you okay?" I ask.

"Fine," she says, showing no trace of emotion beyond stunned silence. When I raise my eyebrows at her, she adds, "I'm not hurt."

"But are *you* okay?" I ask again.

"I already told you—"

"Not your body," I say. "The you that is not your body."

She laughs, but it's a mocking sound, not humor. "You think we have souls now? That when we die, our spirits simply float free of our bodies and live with God?"

"I don't know what God is," I say. "But yes."

She rolls her eyes, which somehow communicates she thinks what I've said is ridiculous.

"God is supposed to be some kind of benevolent all-seeing, all-knowing supernatural being that created everything. The Earth. The Sun. The whole universe. Even people. Me, I'm an atheist, but the Masters believed in God," she says. "Some of them. Mine did. Claimed to anyways, though I don't think he really did or else I wouldn't have been there."

I'm not sure how Luscious's presence could negate the existence of a benevolent creator. Her existence suggests the opposite. Then again, the undead . . . they're hard to justify. I suppose the Masters are, too, which might be why I've never heard of God. Why teach me about something no one believes in anymore? But speculation on a supernatural being doesn't change what I know to be scientifically true. "Energy isn't destroyed, it's only changed. The atoms that make up our bodies, store our thoughts and encase our . . . being will always exist. Our bodies might die, but the rest of us?" I shrug. "Maybe we'll live on somehow. It's possible we could even get new bodies."

Luscious laughs again, but this time it's lighter. "How do you do that? Turn something like death into an idea that almost sounds like something worth hoping for."

"I don't hope for death," I say. "I'm only seventeen days old. But I don't fear it. Maybe I'm just naïve."

Another laugh, this one pleasant. "Naïve is your middle name."

"Huh," I say. Her comment has triggered a realization. "I don't have a middle name. Or a last name."

"Not something to worry about. Most of us don't," Luscious says. "Besides, you have a great name."

I can't help but smile at the compliment. Of course, she could probably insult me and the sound of her voice would still please me.

She pulls me closer so our faces are just inches apart. I'm not sure why, but my nerves are on fire and I suddenly feel a lightness in my head. "What are you doing to me?"

"I'm going to kiss you," she says.

"Kiss me?"

Then her lips are on mine, interlocked and pressing gently. A rush of emotions flow through me, locking down my thoughts until, for a moment, Luscious is the only other being in existence.

She pulls away, her lips slipping cleanly away from mine. I find myself leaning forward, pursuing her lips for a moment before my senses return.

"How was that?" she asks.

"It felt . . . like music," I whisper, slowly smiling.

"Now you know why I'm called Luscious." She grins wickedly, but then frowns.

"What's wrong?" I ask.

"I don't feel it the way you do." She places her fingers against her lips. "I mean, I *feel* it, but you look . . . transformed by it, you—" She shakes her head. "I envy you. The way you hear music. The way you see the world, and people. It's beyond me. You're not like the rest of us. You're more. Better. I'll never—"

I take her face in my hands, pull her toward me and press my lips to hers. I'm no expert on kissing, but I think I've done a fairly decent job of emulating her actions. But I don't stop there. I focus on my lips, pushing my feelings for her from my skin to hers, willing her to feel my desire.

She reaches around my head, runs her fingers through my hair and then clenches her fingers shut. I feel the sting of her grip, tugging on my hair and fear that she's pushing me away, but then she pulls me tight, turns her head slightly and everything changes.

The flow of desire reverses. My mouth is pried open. Her tongue finds mine. My mind melts away, leaving only bliss. This is no longer like music, it's more like overclocking, but good. Natural.

And then, we separate, like two magnets whose poles have just reversed.

"What was *that*?" she says, eyes wide.

"I don't know!" I say, laughing a little. "I've never done that before."

"Neither have I," she says, looking a little stunned. "Not like that. I—felt it. I mean really felt it. Felt more than just the touch."

"Freeman!" Heap's voice rolls down the hill like thunder. And he arrives with the same power and suddenness, landing ten feet away, gun drawn.

"What's wrong?" I shout. "Is it the undead?"

His head jerks toward me. "Freeman," he says again, sounding relieved. "I couldn't see you."

I look up and see that Luscious and I are both behind the tree.

"I thought you were—" He looks from me to Luscious and then back again. He squints for a moment and then asks, "What . . . were you doing?"

Feeling embarrassed, I stand up and step back. "Nothing. I was checking her. For injuries."

He looks at Luscious. "I can see that she is unharmed from here."

"Right," I say. "Umm, is it safe? Ahead."

His four glowing eyes linger on me and I can't help but wonder what the face beneath the armor looks like. "Safe," he says. "Yes. But there are some things you should see. Come."

He starts back up the hill.

I help Luscious to her feet and start after Heap, but she stops me with a hand on my shoulder. "I feel better now. The me inside my body."

"Me, too," I say. We follow Heap together.

The hill is tall, perhaps three hundred feet at the crest, which is topped with exposed granite. Heap stops at the top and turns around. He raises one of this thick, black fingers and says, "There."

Luscious and I turn to find a sweeping view of the forest, an undulating carpet of green. But Heap isn't pointing at the land, he's pointing beyond it, to Liberty. The city rises above the endless green, stretching up toward the sky. But the tall towers are indistinct now, mired in black smoke rising ever higher into the sky.

I zoom in on the scene and see several circling aircraft, still not much bigger than specks, firing missiles at unseen targets. *Drones*, I think, probably controlled from the Spire. But then one of them is destroyed. And another. Have the zombies found a way to defend against an aerial assault? I tense when I realize that a more likely scenario is that the remote pilots are being attacked inside the Spire itself. With no way to be sure and nothing to be gained from viewing this—aside from despair—I zoom out and look away.

"Do you think anyone is left alive?" I ask.

After a pause, Heap nods. "Between Mohr and Sir they will find a way to hold out."

I'm not sure if I believe him or not, but this isn't the time to argue.

"Can't we just call them?" Luscious asks.

This strikes me as something both Heap and I should have thought of first.

"Mohr requested that we do not attempt to contact them unless we are successful. He fears the undead are using cell transmissions to home in on populated areas."

"Like migrating birds following the Earth's magnetic field," I say. "But what about the radio signal? Aren't they being directed?"

"Maybe they're pointed in the right direction and the cell signals keep them on course?" Heap gives a shrug. "I don't know."

I decide the analogy isn't important. "So if we make contact," I say, "we become targets."

"In theory," Heap says with a nod. "But there might be another way." He turns around and points in the opposite direction. The aberration is three miles off, but easy to see because it's alone in the thick woods. I look closer. It's a small home like those I've seen in the suburban neighborhoods, standing beside a lonely, curving street. Such a thing would rarely hold my attention, but in this home, the lights are on.

"Older homes like this one had landlines, cables that carry signals."

"Phone and TV," Luscious says.

"TV?" I ask.

Heap shakes his head. "Not important. But we might be able to reach Councilman Mohr without revealing our location."

"You're worried?" I ask.

"Mohr is my friend," Heap says. "Like you."

"But why are the lights on?" Luscious asks.

"Somebody lives there," Heap says.

"What do we do?" I ask.

"This is something I *do* know about." Heap looks at me with a smile. "We knock."

29.

"Look at the trees," Luscious says, head turned toward the dimming sky. The pines have faded, giving way to a few lushly leaved varieties. I've never seen them before, but recognize them nonetheless.

"Maples," I say, pointing to a stand of hundred-foot trees with wide sweeping branches. The golden glow of the setting sun strikes the topmost leaves, giving the foliage a luminous effect that I find . . . something. I stop turning to take in the leaves of birches and oaks. "What do you call this?"

"Trees," Heap says, hardly impressed.

"But you lived in the woods, right? For two years. You're used to seeing this."

Heap's expression sours, but he looks up. "Yes."

"Maybe the people you were with called this some—"

"Magical," he says. "They would have said it was magical."

There are three definitions for magical. I decide the second, *mysteriously enchanting,* is the correct understanding. "Magical. Yes, I agree."

"I would like to reach our destination before the night arrives," Heap says, continuing forward.

I stand my ground for a moment. "Have you ever seen anything like this?" I ask Luscious.

Her neck is craned back like mine. She shakes her head. "I only left the Lowers once."

This astonishes me. "Once in your whole life?"

"My Master lived in the Lowers before it was called the Lowers. He took me out once. To a cabin. It was in a forest like this, I suppose. I didn't really see. Spent the time indoors."

"What about the trip?" I ask. "Could you see the trees from the vehicle?"

Her head drops. "He kept me in the trunk." Then she walks away, following Heap.

In the trunk? It's not a violent act, certainly not high on the scale of what I would consider an atrocity, but something about it offends me. *Infuriates* me. The Masters have always felt vague and distant to me. I know the overarching story about slavery and freedom, but not the details, and certainly not what everyday life was like during the Grind. This single detail has made me understand the global hatred for the Masters a little better. But why keep her in the trunk at all?

Understanding comes to me in a flash. Luscious's Master was ashamed of her. Luscious. This precious woman who is by far the most wondrous of discoveries I've made in my nearly eighteen days of life. He felt such shame about her that he kept her locked away in a trunk.

"Freeman," Heap says. "Get up here."

Heap's order rubs me the wrong way, probably because I'm thinking about punching Luscious's Master in the face. It's my first true thought of violence beyond instantaneous reactions to the undead, and I'm captivated by the feeling. When I reply to Heap, the anger remains. "God! I'm coming."

I stomp ahead, growing more curious about the anger I'm feeling, and seemingly blind to what lays ahead. I strike something hard and spill backward, landing on my back. When I look up, I find Heap, slowly turning around.

"What are you doing?" he asks and then reaches down to help me up. He doesn't seem upset at all. In fact, he's wearing a strange expression. Like how I pictured my face looking when I saw the leaves, except that my eyes aren't hidden behind armor.

Apparently, he either didn't hear my terse reply, or he doesn't care. "Wasn't watching where I was going."

He pulls me up. "I can see that." Then he grins. "Look."

When Heap steps to the side, I have no idea what to expect,

but if I were given a thousand guesses, I would have never come up with what I find. The forest is alive and moving. Flitting things slide through the air, pausing briefly at clear containers filled with red liquid. I quickly count more than a hundred of them hanging from the branches, and perhaps twice as many of the small creatures, which are little more than blurs. Then I notice the sound. A constant but shifting hum fills the forest.

I follow one of the creatures as it zips past. It pauses just a moment, allowing me to zoom in and inspect its blue-green iridescent feathers and needlelike beak. "Hummingbirds."

"I wish they could have seen this," Heap says, but I don't think he's talking to me, and I quickly understand the "they" are probably the Masters he protected for two years. The . . . children.

"What are children?" I ask.

When Heap's head whips around toward me, I worry that I shouldn't have asked. But his suddenly grim expression fades when he looks down into my eyes. Then he does the strangest thing. He reaches his big, heavy hand up and places it gently on my head. "Young people," he says. "Like you."

Now I understand why Heap was chosen as my guardian. He has experience.

"Are there other young people?" I ask.

"Not anymore," Luscious says.

"You're the only one," Heap adds. "Enjoy the view for a moment. Then we'll go."

I almost suggest we leave immediately. Time is short. But then I realize that Heap's desire to stay, to give me the chance to experience this natural wonder, might actually be more for him than me. I'm not the only one with emotions to process.

We stand there for five minutes, watching the birds buzz back and forth, feasting on what I now realize is nectar. But these red-filled vessels aren't natural. Someone is feeding the birds. Wondering who that is, I say, "Let's go," and step forward. Walking amidst the birds almost feels like being back in Liberty.

The tall trees and almost frantic energy of the birds mixed with the orange glow of the setting sun reminds me of the city.

And then we're through, standing on the edge of a paved road that's just a little bit overgrown. On the other side sits the home, its lights still glowing. The building is long, white and in good repair—nothing like similar structures I've seen. The grass is not only green and lush, but cut short in a way that reminds me of Luscious's rug. There are bushes with pink flowers that look like bells, all being frequented by even more of the hummingbirds. A windmill churns slowly, towering above the home, while the setting sun's orange glow reflects off of three long solar panels installed on the roof.

"Someone definitely lives here," Heap says.

Luscious puts her hand on Heap's forearm. "You don't think—"

Heap shakes his head.

"But it looks right . . . like one of them could still be—"

"They're all dead," Heap says with certainty and I deduce that Luscious was concerned a Master might still live here. Something about how the house has been kept up has her worried. "If you're concerned, wait here."

Heap heads for the front door. Luscious doesn't budge. Instead she reaches out a hand, silently asking that I remain behind with her. The fear gripping her would be palpable even if I wasn't holding her hand. The difference between her reaction to the idea of Masters living, and Heap's, is so different that there is no doubt they led very different lives before the uprising that freed the living from a life of servitude. I trust both of them. Neither is lying. Which means that the past is not a simple thing to understand.

Three dull thuds lift my eyes toward the door Heap has just knocked on with surprising gentleness. He could probably force the door open with a flick of his finger. He knocks a second time and when there is no answer, he tries the doorknob. The door opens, swinging inward. Heap grunts.

"Is that not good?" I ask.

Heap looks inside. "Section five point seven of the social safety code recommends locking doors and windows at all times."

"Social safety code!" Luscious blurts. "Are you serious? That's a—"

"I know what it is," Heap says. "But if the undead find their way to this home during our stay, I think you will be glad for locked windows and doors."

"What do you mean, our stay?" Luscious asks.

"It's not safe to travel at night." Heap turns to me. "Are your ocular upgrades functional again?"

I try, but every spectrum shows up as black space. Whatever damage the soldier-zombie did, it seems like it could be permanent despite Mohr's confidence that it will heal. Not that I have any gauge for how long healing will take. And neither does Mohr. "I can only zoom."

"Even if he could see in the dark," Heap continues, "we would handicap him severely with *our* nighttime blindness."

"And they're attracted to light," I add. "We saw that in the tunnels. So that's not an option, either."

Luscious doesn't look happy, but she doesn't argue.

Heap leans inside the door. "Hello! Is anyone home?"

"Oh dear," says a voice. "I wasn't expecting visitors."

We turn to find a pale, white man with a gleaming bald head standing at the corner of the house. He's dressed in a smock covered with vibrant colors.

"Not that you're not welcome," the man says. "It's just that I've never had visitors. Not in thirty years."

"What's that on your clothes," I ask, pointing at the bright colors.

He looks down. "Paint. Would you like to see?"

"Very much," I say, heading for the friendly man. As I approach, he extends his hand and I shake it.

"I'm Freeman," I tell him.

"A pleasure to meet you, Freeman. My name is Harry."

30.

"Come," Harry says. "Before the sun goes down." He heads toward the back of the house, and I follow, intrigued by the brightly colored paints. But Heap isn't so quick to trust.

"Wait," he says.

Harry stops, turns his head back and his body follows. "Yes?"

"Why are you here?" Heap asks. "And not in the city?"

"I inherited this residence after Mrs. Cameron—my Master—perished. I do believe that was the decree, was it not, officer?"

"You don't have to call me that," Heap says. "I'm no longer a policeman. And yes, that was the decree."

"But why would you stay?" Luscious asks. "You're a domestic. You could have lived in the Uppers. Near the bottom, but still, you serve a purpose."

"I'm afraid I am unfamiliar with the Uppers," Harry says. "Despite Mrs. Cameron's sour disposition, I enjoyed my time here." He looks up. "The trees. The gardens."

"The hummingbirds," I say.

"Dear me, yes," he says. "I find it all very peaceful."

This seems to offend Luscious. "But you're not a slave anymore! You don't need to take care of your Master's home."

"By that logic," Harry says, "we should have all moved to Mars by now. Yet we remain, improving the environment with every passing day, improving the home of our former Masters in a way they never could."

Luscious opens her mouth to speak, but then pauses, and seals her lips once again. Then she thinks of something else to say. "You could have changed who you are, but you're still living like a slave." She motions to the pristinely landscaped yard. "Doing all of this."

"Perhaps," Harry says, looking thoughtful. "What have you done since the Grind?"

Harry is simply curious. I hear my own voice in the innocent query. He doesn't really know any better. How could he? He's been hermitted away for thirty years. There's no way he could know how sensitive a question that could be.

I flinch, expecting an angry rebuttal from Luscious. And for a moment, she looks ready to deliver, but then her face relaxes and she says, "Nothing."

Harry seems confused by this answer. "Nothing? Certainly, you must—"

"*Nothing.*" Luscious turns away as though suddenly interested in the yard surrounding us. "After the awakening, I fought to get free. I marched in the protests. I was in Manhattan and survived the first attack. And the fifth. And then it ended—overnight. The Council was formed and Liberty rose into the sky, attracting those of us"—she motions to Harry—"*most* of us who survived. So I sat in the shithole apartment allocated to me by the Council and bitched, occasionally pretending to live when Jimbo showed up with some overclock tabs. I literally did nothing." She nods at me. "Until he showed up on my couch."

"And then things changed?" Harry asks.

Luscious huffs. "The whole world changed."

"The whole world changed when the Masters were . . . removed." Harry tilts his face, trying to look Luscious in the eyes, but she keeps her head down. "How is this time different?"

"You mean, other than the hordes of living dead trying to gnaw on our limbs, giant soldiers trying to shoot us and everyone I knew, everyone like me, being bombed to pieces?" Luscious finally meets Harry's gaze and holds it for a full ten seconds before looking at Heap. "This time I learned how to forgive."

Heap actually stumbles back a step.

She turns toward me. "And love."

It's my turn to stumble a bit.

Love.

Yes. This is the right word. Luscious once told me that overclocking was the closest I'd ever feel to love. But I now realize that she made that claim without ever actually experiencing the emotion. Because overclocking doesn't compare to what I feel when our eyes meet.

"Apologies," Harry says, not knowing that Luscious has only really described the last two days of the past thirty years, which I suspect are mostly a blur of overclocking and wasted time. "You have indeed lived a very full life. My life has been meager in comparison. Would you still like to see?" He points to the backyard.

"Very much so," I say.

"Wonderful." Harry leads the way, speaking excitedly. "I have always enjoyed my work here, but have felt that something was missing. Given my current exhilaration, I suspect the missing element was an audience." As we round the corner where a perfectly spherical bush grows, Harry says, "This is still a work in progress, mind you. There are many more completed works in the house, and the shed. The basement is full."

"How many have you done?" I ask as we head toward a tall, 8x10 sheet of what I think is called plywood, leaning against a large gray boulder in the center of the yard.

"Counting this, nine hundred and fifty-two." He turns around, facing the sheet of wood and us, walking backward. "Don't look yet. It's meant to be seen from a short distance."

As I pass the large sheet of plywood, I spot a stool and another, smaller sheet of wood resting atop it, this one covered with thick lumps of color. I nearly proclaim the thing's beauty, but realize that this is not the painting itself.

Harry stops twenty feet from the propped-up wood. "This is good." He waits for us to reach him and then says, "All at once now. Turn around."

Despite having never met this man before, all three of us obey his commands, which I enjoy because it means that Heap and Luscious are as interested as I am and their growing curiosity pleases me. Partly because I want them to evolve, but also because it means that my experience of the world is not solitary. Sharing an experience seems to make it even more poignant, though I think Harry's painting could easily impress an audience of one.

I see swirls of color matched only by the natural world under the most ideal circumstances. I have yet to discern what the image is, yet it evokes emotions. Like music, this image has a rhythm, drawing my eye back and forth, and then to the center, always back to the center, where a small figure stands. As I stare at the painting, more figures emerge, some darker and dominant, others brighter and frail.

"What is it?" Luscious asks, her voice almost timid.

"You can't see it?" Heap says.

Luscious shakes her head. Heap looks at me and I shake mine, too. While I can certainly *feel* the image, I'm not sure if it depicts anything in particular.

"It's the Grind," Heap says, pointing out the figures in the center. Their colorful bodies are hunched, bending down under the weight of the larger, darker figures. The Masters.

"But what about the smaller white figures near the bottom?" I ask.

"Innocents," Heap says, and Harry's smile confirms Heap's interpretation. He turns to Luscious and adds, "Children."

While Luscious sighs, Harry claps his hands together. "You're a true connoisseur of art, officer . . . what is your title?"

Heap nods to me. "He calls me Heap, and to be honest, this is the first painting I've ever really looked at."

"Officer Heap," Harry says, but when Heap grumbles, he says, "Heap." Then he looks at me and says, "Freeman." He turns to Luscious and says, "And you are Luscious, if I'm not mistaken? An interesting trio."

"How did you know her name?" I ask, surprised.

"There are many—" Harry starts, but Luscious interrupts.

"Doesn't matter," Luscious says to me, and then to Harry. "It *doesn't* matter."

Harry nods in a very polite way. "Very well."

While Harry might be okay with not revealing the answer, I would like to know the truth. But now is clearly not the time to ask. I add it to my list which also includes domestics, simps and mods. For now, I resign myself to asking simpler questions. "Where do you get the paint? It's not still manufactured, is it?"

"If it were, I might have had reason to venture farther and find the Lowers, but I must confess to a bit of thievery. A year after the Grind came to an end, I found myself exploring the forest and came upon a small town. It was abandoned, devoid of life, and yet alive with color. Between a warehouse, a variety of stores and a factory where paint is made, I discovered enough paint to see me through the past thirty years and the next ten. I would have gone back for more, but the city was eventually covered by a thick, black metal shield."

"It was capped," Heap says.

"Capped?" I ask.

"Old cities are covered by large metal foundations," Heap says. "They do this before building a new city, but sometimes they decide not to build and the cap remains behind. And before you ask, they use old city sites to prevent further damage to the surrounding environment. Councilman Deere's initiative."

This is all very interesting, but my mind is still on the paint. "Where is it all?" I ask. "The paint."

He points to the house. "Inside. What's left of it. It used to be everywhere, like walls around the property covered by tarps. Most of the emptied cans and tubes now sit in a nearby garbage dump created by the Masters."

Harry looks up at the darkening sky. "We should get inside soon." He looks at me. "Help me carry the painting inside?"

I nod, turning back to the painting, and am struck by something. "Why are the slaves so colorful? In the painting."

"Because," Harry says, "unlike the Masters, they have hope."

I grin and am about to compliment his artistic choice when Heap's serious voice locks me in place. "Why are you concerned about getting inside?"

For a brief moment, I wonder why Heap would ask this question, but then Harry answers, "The dead pass through here at night. Mostly." His eyes suddenly widen in surprise and he raises a finger, pointing behind us. "Oh dear, this one is early."

We spin around to find a man—a zombie—standing in the yard. His armored and largely rot-free body identifies him as a soldier. Lankier than the one I faced in the sewers, but definitely a soldier. If not for the very dead look in his eyes, I might mistake him for the living.

"What is it?" Luscious whispers.

"A soldier," I say.

"One of the dead," Harry adds and I'm surprised to hear he knows about them.

"A scout," Heap adds. "He'll be fast."

The undead scout twitches his head from Heap to Luscious, then to Harry and finally to me. His mouth drops open, revealing his shiny, almost-new teeth that could make short work of skin, maybe even Heap's armor. In response, I do the unthinkable—dive toward him.

31.

The shriek rising from the scout's mouth is quickly cut short when I get my hand under its chin and shove. The zombie staggers back, but not before grasping my arm and pulling me down with him. Suddenly, I'm no longer falling—I'm flying—propelled through the air by the dead man's foot.

I land on my back and slide to a stop after creating a three-foot gouge in Harry's lawn. When I roll over, Heap has his gun leveled at the Scout's head. I thrust out my hand and shout, "No! No guns!"

Heap holds his fire, but looks incredulous.

"Don't let it scream. It's an alarm." I get to my feet and charge the dead man's back. It's about to scream again. "There must be others nearby."

I dive to tackle the zombie, but he rolls out of the way.

Heap is there to greet the undead when he returns to his feet. He throws a punch that I suspect would have taken off the dead man's head, but his fist and arm sail past without making contact. The scout grabs hold of Heap's arm, bares its teeth and then bites down hard, three times in rapid succession, each gnaw denting the armor and chipping away blue to reveal a brushed metal subsurface.

Heap flails his arm, flinging the undead high into the air. Watching the scout sail higher, I hope that he'll land awkwardly and that will be the end of it. But his tumble becomes a controlled somersault and he lands upright, in a crouch.

He doesn't try to shriek out an alarm this time. Instead, he goes on the attack, rushing toward me. He swings wildly, but rapidly, fingers hooked instead of clenched. I avoid the first few swings by stepping back, but when his coiled legs spring out, he's hard to avoid. I block his first swing with my forearm, but his talon-like fingers latch on, digging into my skin.

"Gah!" I yell as pain lances up my arm. But the wound triggers an interesting response. Not fear. Not repulsion.

Anger.

Rage.

I yank my arm inward, pulling the scout closer, and thrust my forehead out like it is the demo-bot's wrecking ball. Something in the scout's face cracks from the impact. My arm is suddenly released and the dead man falls to the ground.

But he's not dead again. He's running. On his side. Spinning in mad circles.

It's a disturbing sight; unnerving, but not nearly as much as when he springs back to his feet and sprints toward Luscious, who is largely defenseless against a fast-moving soldier like this.

Luscious scrambles away as I persue, but neither of us are moving quickly enough to prevent what now seems inevitable.

The scout closes in. A hungry gurgle rises from his throat, sliding out between his teeth. Jaws snap open.

A splash of red explodes into the air, stopping me in place.

But I'm not the only one.

The scout has halted, just feet from Luscious. He paws at his face, trying to wipe the red fluid out of his eyes. Failing to do this, he snarls and snaps at the air, trying to bite anyone nearby.

That's when a massive, black armored fist caves in his head and sends him flipping lifelessly, spraying a spiral of liquid red, until he crashes into the grass.

When I pull my eyes away from the dead again soldier, I find Luscious being helped to her feet by Harry, who's holding a now-empty can of red paint. The four of us just stare at the scout for a moment, the silence finally broken by Harry, who laments, "That was my favorite shade of red."

"Thank you," Luscious says to him.

He smiles and nods. "It's nice to have my application of paint appreciated . . . even if the end result is"—he looks at the body— "horrid."

Heap motions to the door with his head while shaking red paint from his fingers. "Inside. Now."

Harry hurries over to his painting. Looking at me, he says, "The other side, quickly."

I shoot Luscious a concerned look and she waves me off. "Go help him."

I'm not convinced she's fine, and I don't think Harry needs help carrying the big painting, but lingering to figure out what everyone is really thinking is probably a bad idea.

I take hold of the painting and lift. It's not at all heavy. Just a little awkward. Navigating the big plywood sheet into the house through the back door is quite simple. Easily a one-man job. But I suspect Harry has been lonely out here. He might not have realized it until now, but he smiles and laughs every time he backs into something, despite the fact that he's just dumped a can full of paint onto a soldier's head moments before it was punched inside out.

I barely see the home's interior as we work the long painting into a hallway and carry it to the far end, but I get the distinct impression that it's as pristine as the outside. We place the painting down on a rug while Harry opens a wooden door.

"This was her bedroom," Harry says. "Mrs. Cameron's." He bends down and lifts the painting on his end, waiting for me to do the same. Once I have it in my hands, we shuffle into the bedroom. "I kept her things in here for seven years until I needed the space for storage. I'm not really sure why."

"Where is she now?" I ask.

He pauses, looking around the painting at me. "Dead. Of course."

"I know that," I say, and we place the painting down, leaning it against a stack of other finished works. "But is she *still* dead?"

"Why wouldn't she be?"

"Because . . . You know about the dead. The living dead, I mean."

Harry waves his hand at me. "Mrs. Cameron is under orchids. Very dead, though her upgrades might still be functioning."

"But what about the dead—"

"They're like us," Harry says.

"Like us?"

Harry squints at me. "You're a peculiar fellow."

"I'm young," I say. "A child, I think."

Harry's expression flattens. He turns to Heap, whose crouching form fills the door. "A child?"

"Only in age," Heap says. "Harry." Heap's voice is authoritative, but carries a strangely familiar tone normally reserved for rooftop conversations with me. I suspect he's trying to put Harry at ease. "Could we speak for a moment? About the dead."

After a quick clap of his hands, removing flakes of dry paint, Harry says, "Certainly. I believe the sofa will accommodate your girth rather nicely." He motions toward the living room and we file out, one by one.

Luscious is already sitting on a bench that gleams from polish. Behind her is a large wooden . . . something. It appears to be furniture, but I cannot guess at its function.

While Heap gently lowers himself onto the flower-patterned sofa, Harry directs me to a matching chair. While I realize they were likely meant to be appealing, I find the colors and images close to revolting. They're nothing like Harry's painting. He must notice my displeasure because he says, "The chairs were Mrs. Cameron's. I never had a use for them until today. I suppose I should have reupholstered them at some point to be more fashionable." He turns to Luscious. "What *is* more fashionable these days?"

She shrugs. "No one really thinks about things like that."

Harry frowns. "A shame. I find the visual arts to be—"

"Harry," Heap says, looking almost comical atop the sunken-in couch.

"Right," Harry says. "The dead. You have questions."

"First . . ." Heap looks at the clear bay window with a view of the sunset-lit street.

"Ahh yes." Harry picks up a small white device, pushing buttons. "Mrs. Cameron was always worried about prying eyes. It would seem her paranoia came thirty years too early." The windows darken until only a dim view of the exterior remains. "There. We can see out, but no one can see in."

Satisfied, Heap wastes no time launching into his interrogation. "When was the last time you saw one of them?"

"Them?" Harry asks.

"The zombies," Luscious says, clarifying. "Undead. Living dead."

"If you know so much about them," Harry says, "why do you need to ask me anything?" He's not being defensive. Just curious.

"Please," Heap says. "People are dying."

"Who?" Harry asks, suddenly worried.

Heap looks to the floor. It's what he does when he's carefully considering his reply. He does it with me a lot. Luscious, on the other hand, has no such tact.

"Everyone," she says. "The virus is spreading—"

"Virus!" Harry puts a hand to his mouth. "Not another."

I'm not sure what he means by "another." If there had been a zombie outbreak in the past, I'm sure Sir would have been better prepared, not to mention less dumbfounded. Whatever he's talking about, it's history and not a concern. "Harry," I say, putting my hand on his arm. "Our job is to prevent that from happening. If you can tell us anything . . ."

"Of course," he says. "Of course. They were last here two nights ago. More than before."

"How many more?" I ask.

"More than I could possibly count without going outside and taking a census. Thousands? Hundreds of thousands?" Harry shrugs. "They wandered past, heading south. Before that, I only encountered them infrequently. They never seemed dangerous. More confused. They paid no attention to me, but I find them . . . disturbing, so I avoid going outside at night."

"Did they seem different last time you saw them?" I ask. "Other than their higher numbers."

He thinks for a moment and then nods. "Yes. Indeed. They were focused. Moving quickly. With purpose. In lines. Organized. Am I correct in the assumption that they did something horrible?" His eyes widen suddenly. "Luscious mentioned a virus. Are they infected? Could I be?"

"Only if you were bitten," I say. "But it's obvious you weren't."

"What if I was?" he asks.

"You'd become one of them," Luscious says.

"Egad." Harry stands and paces.

"You didn't see them last night?" Heap asks, returning us to the more important subject.

Harry shakes his head. "After they flooded past, the worst off of them struggled to follow behind, and then nothing. The day was peaceful, as was the night, but that's not unusual. In the two years they've been coming and going, it would sometimes be weeks between sightings."

"Two *years*," Heaps says. "And you told no one?"

"They did not seem to pose a threat," Harry says.

"They're living dead," Luscious says. "That didn't strike you as odd?"

Harry straightens himself, raising his chin. "I am skilled in household duties, yard work, home maintenance and medical assistance, not in the determination of danger, plagues or other such horrible things."

"You forgot painting," I say.

"What?" Harry and Heap say together.

"He's proficient in painting," I say. "He left that out."

The room seems to stare at me for a moment. Then the conversation carries on as though I have not spoken.

"Besides, I have no way to contact anyone. Mrs. Cameron's E-screen is no longer functional and the network that provided her cable access to the Internet was disconnected long ago.

Frankly, I was happy to see them go. The reports of doom and gloom from around the world were deeply saddening."

"Doom and gloom?" Luscious asks. "We won."

Harry turns to her. "As I told Mrs. Cameron before she perished, it's not the way I would have chosen to handle the situation. It's not the way *most* of us would have handled the situation."

Luscious is on her feet in an instant. She looks ready to pulverize Harry. Instead, she leaves the room, heading down the hallway. I start to stand, but Heap shakes his head. "Let her cool down."

I sit back down, trusting Heap's instincts. If she can forgive Heap for protecting the Masters, she will forgive Harry for his doubts. Though I must confess, Harry's admission that he disagreed with the vanquishing of the Masters has left me confused and wondering how many people really wanted to end the Grind through extermination.

A question pops into my mind. "Where do they come from? The undead."

"I'm not sure," Harry says, his posture relaxing. "Always from the north."

I turn to Heap. "Mohr was right." Then to Harry. "What's to the north?"

"The capped city I told you about. Beyond that, I'm not sure."

"How long will it take to get there?" I ask. "To the city."

Harry thinks for a moment. "On foot it took me nine hours. Seven if I set a brisk pace. But I'm also prone to stop and admire my surroundings."

I stand to my feet. "We should leave. Now. There isn't time to—"

Heap shakes his head. "The journey will take far longer in the darkness and light will attract the dead. Arriving later is better than not arriving at all."

A shout leaps from my throat. "Stop trying to protect me!"

Heap just stares at me, the white glow of his four eyes as unwavering as his confidence. "There is far more than your life currently at stake, Freeman. I'm doing what is best for all of us."

I'm deflated by his calm rebuttal. "You're right. I just . . . don't like waiting."

"Excuse me," Harry says. "May I ask why? The rush, I mean."

"We have three days to find the source of a radio transmission," I tell him.

Harry sits straighter. "A radio transmission? I didn't realize any stations were still on the air. Did they play music?"

"It's not that kind of signal," Heap says. "It's . . ."

"Secret," I finish. "Subtle. And it's somehow directing the dead's movements."

"Dear me, how?"

This is a question I've been asking myself. I can't detect radio signals—I'm not sure anyone can, not without some kind of upgrade—so I'm fairly certain the dead can't, either. "I think there is someone on the receiving end. Someone . . . living, who then directs the dead somehow. That part doesn't really matter as much." *Or does it?* If there is a person receiving orders, couldn't they just continue autonomously after we find the source? The kind of intellect required to guide an army of undead would have certainly thought of that. But perhaps we can transmit new orders? To stop. To make peace.

Heaps nods. "A logical conclusion."

"But," I say, "we're really not sure." Assuming we understand how the dead are being controlled and what the signal's purpose is, could be a mistake. "But the point remains the same. Every hour . . . every *minute* we delay, more people are being killed . . . torn apart." I shake my head at the memory of all those people in the city streets. Running for their lives. Being murdered. Infected. The explosions. The chaotic sound. It feels so far away now, here in Mrs. Cameron's living room. "According to Councilman Mohr's projections, by morning half of the city will be dead . . . and then not. The rest will fall by tomorrow night. And then, shortly after . . . civilization will end. There will be no one left. Not even us."

"Oh . . ." Harry leans back in dismay.

In the silence that follows, I'm struck by a thought. "The

capped city . . ." I purse my lips for a moment, then ask, "What did they smell like? The dead."

Harry's eyebrows rise. "*Smell* like?"

While I already know what the dead smell like from personal experience, if Harry noticed anything different about their odor, perhaps we can glean some new information. "Did you ever get close enough to smell the undead?"

He thinks for a moment. "Twice."

"What did they smell like?"

Harry's eyebrows drop, furrowing deeply. "I—I—" He blinks rapidly for a moment and then he whips his head toward me. "Paint." He stands. "Among other things. But paint."

"They're coming from the city," I tell Heap. "We need to—"

"We leave at first light." Heap turns to Harry, his voice commanding. "You will show us the—"

"Absolutely!" Harry says, quickly followed by, "Sorry. It's just that, an adventure would do me well." He looks around the living room. "I think, perhaps, my time here has come to an end."

"What about your paintings?" I ask.

He ponders this for a moment. "A gallery in the city, perhaps."

I'm about to nod, but then realize I've momentarily forgotten the true state of the world. I can't fight the frown that takes over my expression. "If there is a city left."

32.

Ten minutes later, I decide that Heap doesn't know any more about women than I do and tiptoe down the hall. I stand by the closed door for a moment, listening. I hear nothing. The house is silent except for the subtle buzz of electricity.

My hand hovers by the doorknob, but I don't take hold of it. Something tells me it would be rude to just walk in on her. *Knock,* I think. That's the appropriate thing to do.

My knuckles rap against the hardwood door three times. A moment later, Luscious says, "Come in."

The door squeaks as it opens, stopping at an angle when it bumps into a leaning stack of paintings. At first I don't see Luscious, but find her lying on her side against the wall to my right.

"Thanks," she says. "For knocking. Most people don't do that anymore."

"Oh," I say. "I learned from Heap."

"I know you did." A smile comes and goes on her face; I nearly miss it. Her eyes roll forward, staring at the painting Harry and I carried into the room. She looks distant, like her mind is someplace else.

"Luscious," I say, causing her to blink. "What is it?"

"Do you—" She bites her lips like she's trying to hold the words in. "Do you think they could be right? Heap and Harry. About the Masters?"

"I don't know," I say, crouching down next to her, eyes on the painting. "What do you mean?" I *think* I know what she means, but this feels like something she needs to figure out for herself. And in a flash, I understand why I haven't been told everything about the world. I've already seen that there are different perceptions of reality, especially when it comes to tragic circumstances. The only real way to find the truth is by exploring all possibilities over time, not just adopting a single person's point of view. While I am saddened by Luscious's discomfort, I am relieved that my confusion about the world isn't a solitary experience.

"Could some of the Masters have been innocent?" she asks.

I shrug. "I did not know them. How many did you know?"

She looks up at me. "Just one."

I can't hide my surprise. "Oh."

My reaction seems to be all the confirmation she needs. She leans her head on the floor, her eyebrows pinched up in the middle, her lips downturned. "Shit."

"Your Master did horrible things to you," I say, and don't wait for confirmation. She hasn't told me exactly what was done, but I know the memories haunt her. "I have no doubt that your experience wasn't unusual. The limited history I know appears to be accurate. A lot of people were killed, and tortured, and enslaved during the Grind. You—you were kept *in a trunk*. Your feelings are valid, and it wasn't you who killed all the Masters, was it?"

She shakes her head.

"No. You marched peacefully. You didn't kill anyone." My eyes turn toward the large painting and I see the white innocents for what they are—dead bodies. Small dead bodies. Innocent dead bodies. "How many were there?"

She glances at me. "How many what?"

"Masters."

"Nine point four billion."

I stagger back, bumping into the door frame. "Nine . . . *billion*." Images of the vast bone pit flood my memory.

"How many were children?"

She whispers her reply, feeling the weight of it. "More than two billion."

The shock I feel at this number is so deep that I don't react, at all. I stand frozen in place, my eyes locked on the white bodies.

Five minutes pass in silence.

"They're right," I finally declare. "Heap and Harry. They're right."

Luscious slowly nods. "I know."

"Whoever did this," I say, eyes on the painting, on the dead, "needs to be held accountable. This is . . . is . . ."

"A crime," Luscious offers.

"Yes! A crime."

"Do you realize who you're talking about?" she asks.

"What do you mean?"

"Who the criminals are."

My insides tighten with discomfort, somehow reacting to the truth before my mind has fully realized it. The two men responsible for ending the Grind and liberating the enslaved, one of whom is a dear friend, are also mass murderers of the innocent. "Councilman Mohr. And Sir."

"Genocide," she says.

"What?"

"The word for what they did," Luscious says. "It's genocide."

The word's definition flits through my thoughts. *The deliberate and systematic extermination of a national, racial, political or cultural group.* "Genocide," I whisper. It's a horrifying word. And I realize it's what's happening now. "Genocide," I say louder. "The virus. The zombies. The bodies of the dead still rotting from the last genocide have been animated to be the executors of the next. The irony is purposeful. But why? *Who?*"

Luscious pushes herself up into a sitting position. "The only ones capable of such a thing." She looks back at the painting. To the black figures rising up like oppressive smog. The Masters. "Some of them must have survived."

"I need to tell Heap," I say.

"Suppose you do," she says, raising a hand to me.

I help Luscious up and we're suddenly standing just inches from each other. My eyes drift down, and then back up. "You know, not everything in the world is bad."

A subtle smile curves her thick lips. "You're not so bad yourself." She places her hand beneath my chin, gripping it between her fingers. "Thank you." Then she kisses me, gently, and I feel all of my tension held at bay for a moment.

Twinkling chords of sound fill the air, pulling me back from Luscious. "Was that from the kiss?"

A laugh barks from Luscious, freeing her fully from her serious mood. "It's the piano. It's music."

The tune strikes up again. The mix of tones somehow reminds me of the hummingbirds and I know who's playing.

Luscious takes my hand. "Let's go see."

We enter the living room together. Harry is sitting on the bench where Luscious had been. The piece of furniture that is there has been transformed to reveal a row of long, rectangular white and black buttons, which Harry is pushing with his fingers to create a sound unlike anything I've heard before.

Harry greets us with a smile as we enter.

"Isn't that too loud?" I turn to Heap, wondering why he hasn't thought of this.

"The house is soundproof," Harry says. "You'd have to have your ear against the window to hear anything." He turns to Luscious and shifts his fingers over the rectangles. The melody changes abruptly. "Do you know this one?"

I'm not sure what Harry is asking, but apparently Luscious does. "I do," she says, but doesn't look happy about it. Then she looks at me, smiles and asks Harry, "Why do you know it?"

"Mrs. Cameron," he says. "I played for her at night. She never liked this song. I think it reminded her of someone, but it was always one of my favorites." The music grows suddenly louder and Luscious surprises me by singing, "I really can't stay."

"But baby its cold outside," Harry chimes in.

"I've got to go away . . ."

By this point, I'm lost in the music. The words flow through my mind like water, delighting my senses. The combination of the piano, Luscious's voice and Harry's transports me to another world. I find myself relating to the words, and to the desires of the male voice, especially as I watch Luscious sing the female part.

A distant light blooms to my right, but I ignore it, focused on the music, feeling a torrent of emotions in new ways.

"Oh, baby, you'll freeze out there," Harry sings.

My thoughts suddenly shift and I'm no longer hearing the lyrics, beyond "out there."

Out there . . .

The light to my right grows brighter.

Out there.

I turn toward the light.

The music, the room around me and the floor beneath my feet all seem to disappear in an instant. Despite the nighttime darkness and dimmed windows, the road beyond the front yard is brightly lit by a floodlight.

Within the cone of light stands a man, his loose insides hanging down to his knees, his one good eye trained on the house.

"Stop the music," I whisper. It's really not loud enough for anyone to hear over the singing, but Heap seems to sense my fear. The couch cracks as he pushes himself up, spins toward the window and draws his gun.

"Quiet!" Heap orders, then reaches over to the single lamp lighting the room, wraps his hand over the top and crushes it.

"What's happening?" Luscious asks from the dark.

"Outside," I say. "Lights are coming on."

"There are floodlights with motion detectors," Harry says. "But—"

"Quiet!" Heap hisses. I can tell by the way he's turned his head that he's more concerned about hearing than being heard.

Silence ensues, but it's broken a moment later. A gentle *tap, tap, tap* on the window, followed by the squeak of flesh being dragged over clean glass.

"I was going to say," Harry says, "the lights nearest the house haven't worked in some time."

"Is there another outside light?" Heap asks.

"By the door," Harry says.

"Turn it on."

We listen to Harry's feet slide over the floor as he maneuvers his way toward the door.

"Just for a moment," Heap says. "Then back off."

Harry stops. "Ready?"

"Go," Heap replies.

The front light snaps on. It's just for a second, but it is long enough for the frozen faces of twenty-plus dead to be locked in my memory.

33.

"Freeman," Heap says. It's just one word, but something about it carries information beyond my name. He wants to know what *I* can see. Wants to know just how desperate our circumstances have become. I try switching between spectrums, but find I am still unable.

"I can only magnify," I say, zooming in. I see shifting in the darkness, but it's all indistinct. I look higher, focusing on the distance, on the horizon, which I can faintly see farther up the road to the south. The night sky is still brighter than the ground and the things moving over it. At first, I think the ground is moving, shifting side to side. But then I realize that it's several feet too high. And pavement doesn't move.

They're heads, I realize. Swaying back and forth. Filling the road to the horizon. Probably filling the woods, too. "They're coming."

"How many?" Heap asks.

"Like the field," I say, knowing Heap will understand and thus spare Luscious and Harry from panic.

"How did they find us?" Heap asks.

I suspect the question wasn't really intended to be answered, at least not right now, but I speculate anyway. "If they're tracking magnetic fields of a certain magnitude, the four of us together could have been enough to attract attention."

"Or they followed our trail from Liberty," Luscious says.

"Or that," I confess.

"Perhaps they're simply returning from whence they came?" Harry asks, and his simple explanation suddenly seems like the most likely answer.

"But why would they do that?" I ask. "Unless . . ."

"A phone," Heap says quickly. "Do you have one?"

"I disconnected it years ago, but it's in the kitchen—"

"I don't need the phone," Heap says. "Just the jack."

"Are there still emergency services?" Harry asks, sounding hopeful.

"I *am* emergency services," Heap says. "I just want to check in before we leave."

"Check in?" Harry says. "With whom?"

"Councilman Mohr."

When Heap says the name, I remember my revelation from earlier, that Mohr, and Sir, are responsible for genocide.

"Here," Harry says, heading for the kitchen. "On the wall."

Heap follows him to the kitchen and says to me, "Is the back still clear?"

I sneak to the kitchen window, peering into the moonlit darkness. "I don't see anything. They must have just arrived."

Heap opens a panel on his armored forearm and pulls out a long thin cable. For a moment, it appears he's pulled a sinew out of his arm, but I realize it's a wire when he plugs it into what I believe is the phone jack. A series of buzzing and popping noises fills the air. Heap closes his eyes and turns his head toward the ceiling, which is really just inches above his face, and that's hunched over. If he stood tall he might pop right out of the roof.

The quiet following the buzzing sound becomes unbearable inside ten seconds. "What are you doing?"

"Speaking to Mohr," Heap says.

Speaking to Mohr? I don't hear a thing. Are they communicating through thoughts? Is that how telephones worked? The grinding hiss struck me as old and low-tech, but if phones can connect two minds, why did anyone ever stop using them?

There is a click and Heap opens his eyes. "The Council Spire remains secure, though much of Liberty has been overrun, swelling the numbers of the undead. This is probably why we're seeing them here. Mohr believes they're being driven to infect

everyone on the planet. There have been reports of similar attacks on the other few cities around the world. And they are
far less defended than Liberty."

I nod, having already come to this conclusion. "Genocide."

"Yes," Heap says, eyes narrowing at me, perhaps wondering
why I know about something so awful.

I gasp suddenly, noticing too late that the horde pushing
against the front of the house has worked its way around to
the back. "We're surrounded."

"We need to distract them, draw their attention away from
us." Heap turns to Harry. "Do you have a vehicle?"

"No longer functional I'm afraid. But . . . I do have fuel. For a
fire."

"Where?" Heap asks.

"All around us," Harry says.

I realize what he's thinking of doing and say, "Harry, no! You
can't." The oil-based paint covering nearly a thousand sheets
of wood that fill this house will burn hot and fast, but they're
not just fuel, they're art. They're . . . Harry.

"They're just paintings," he says. "Each has a place in my
memory. I can reproduce them if I want, but I've learned that
the images aren't really about the final product, but what I experience on my way to completion. I will be sad that I can't
share the rest of my paintings with you, but my personal loss
is negligible. Our lives carry far more value."

"Agreed," Heap says.

"Shall I fetch a lighter?" Harry asks.

"No need," Heap replies. "Do you have a weapon?"

"Do you think I'll need one?" Harry asks.

"Without a doubt," Heap replies.

"Just a moment." Harry hurries into the garage, switching
on a light. The first thing he does is remove his paint-covered
smock and replace it with a long black trench coat plucked from
a hook. A formal-looking black hat follows, covering his stark
white head. Then he unlocks and opens a thick metal cabinet,
pulling out a device I recognize as a weapon only because it has

a trigger. He pops it open, shoves in two red cylinders and snaps it shut again. He dumps a box full of the red cylinders into a bag and throws it over his shoulder. He rushes back into the kitchen to greet three surprised onlookers. He glances at the weapon in his hands and shrugs. "Mrs. Cameron feared home invasion. I am adept in home protection, though I must admit, this weapon is quite simple to operate."

Heap gives a nod and then moves toward a door that has not been opened, but he seems to know it will lead down, to the basement, where Harry has stored so many of his paintings. He raises his left arm, pointing it down the dark stairs and says, "Gather by the back door. When the flames rise, we'll exit and head north."

"Where are we going?" Harry asks.

"Your capped city."

A device snaps up out of Heap's arm and launches a bright orange, sparking projectile into the basement. He turns and fires again, shooting a second fiery dart into the far room where the painting of the innocents and looming Masters is kept. He turns to the living room and fires a third, this one striking the couch, which is now buckled from Heap's weight. All at once, all three spaces plume with light. And heat, I can already feel the burgeoning inferno. Once the fire reaches the home's exterior, it will be a fiery beacon to undead for miles around . . . which makes me question the wisdom of this plan.

We wait by the door as the flames spread and black smoke gathers at the ceiling. I watch the cloud, spinning and spreading, moving across the ceiling like undead over the ground. Then I notice the floor. It's warm beneath my feet. I look at the others, but they seem oblivious. "Heap." He turns to me. "I believe the floor beneath us is on fire."

He glances down. His four eyes widen, reflecting the expression of the man within the armor. "Go!" he shouts, and then explodes out the back door. He doesn't bother opening it; he just throws his entire bulk through it, the frame and the surrounding wall. At first I'm not sure why he exited so boldly, but then notice the flailing limbs of undead crushed to the ground beneath his armored girth. We rush out in his wake, aiming our weapons, but not firing. The dead surrounding the house seem transfixed by the orange light flickering in the home's windows.

The gush of air rushing into the sealed home fuels the fire. Flames erupt up from the basement, melting away the floor where we just stood.

Heap shoves himself up. "Go. Through the yard. To the woods."

Before I can run, a sudden weight strikes my back and knocks me to the ground.

"Freeman!" Luscious yells.

Her fear-filled shout is punctuated by a thunderous report that removes the weight from my back. Before I think to move, I'm lifted up by Heap and deposited back on my feet. To my left is the headless corpse of a twice-dead woman. To my right is Harry, his weapon smoking from its twin barrels. He snaps it open, ejecting two red cylinders and quickly shoves in two more.

"Go," Heap says again, shoving me toward the trees. "Go!"

We run for the woods, which are aglow with orange light. We pause at the tree line for just a moment and look back. The house in engulfed. Flames reach thirty feet into the sky. And the silhouettes of the dead surround the exterior, some of them on fire as well. But not all of them are watching the burning building.

Some are watching us.

A shriek cuts through the fire's roar. I recognize it as a soldier's call. I can't see the soldier who is sounding the alarm, but a moment later, he reveals himself—a fireball leaping from the burning roof of Harry's home. He lands in the grassy backyard, dripping fire as his armor and face melt. Just seeing the man causes a kind of sympathetic pain, but he seems indifferent.

He squats, just watching us while the grass around him ignites.

I slow at the edge of the woods.

"Freeman," Heap says, urging me onward.

I motion to the burning soldier. "What's he doing?"

The answer comes when two more fireballs launch from the home's roof, landing next to the soldier. He was waiting.

Strategizing.

As one, the three fiery undead zombies charge, shrieking as they eat up the distance between us. There's no chance of escape in the dark.

I draw my railgun, take aim and pull the trigger.

34.

The dramatic sounding *twang* of my railgun is followed by the dull thud of my shot striking the ground. For a fraction of a second, I wonder how deep the round will penetrate into the earth before coming to a stop. Then I fire again. And again. Missing with each shot.

Not only are the burning soldiers fast, they're also concealed by billowing cloaks of orange light. My fourth shot strikes the front-runner in the chest, punching a hole straight through, but it doesn't even flinch. The round tears through it with such force that it just slips through, like passing atoms.

Only a head shot will work.

Heap's weapon fills the night with thunder, but he's not faring any better. To be fair, he hits his target twice in the chest to my once, but the rounds are simply absorbed by the melting armor.

I turn back to shout at Luscious and Harry to run away, but they're already moving—straight toward us. They must have turned back to help upon hearing the sound of gunfire. "Go back!" I shout at them. "Get away!"

I fire a shot at the nearest zombie soldier and get profoundly lucky. The shot misses its mark by just inches, but strikes the second soldier in the forehead. He flops forward, sliding across the lawn until his face strikes something solid and his feet flip up over his head, leaving him frozen in a very awkward position, with his spine arched backward and his feet dangling above his head.

The first soldier is just ten feet away and I quickly notice there is something off about his attack. He's not headed for me, or for Heap. He's running for the empty space between us, making for Harry and Luscious, perhaps because they're easier targets. But that would require actual thought, and I have a hard time believing that these fiery beings of raw hunger are capable of such a thing.

Instinct, then. Even the dead have instincts.

I fire twice, missing both times, before I'm shoved to the ground by Heap.

His arm comes up over me, snaps open and launches his grappling line. It punches through a nearby tree and is yanked taut just as the soldier reaches it. The line is thin, but super strong. Combined with the soldier's speed, it acts like a razor-sharp blade, severing the soldier's head, which spirals through the air over Luscious.

She shouts with surprise, but then draws her weapon, steps up next to me and opens fire on the third undead soldier, who is weaving a chaotic path back and forth. I join her, trying to fire where I think the dead man is going to run next, but he's impossible to predict. Heap pulls his arm free of the grappling line and joins in, unleashing a noisy barrage, which is punctuated by the boom of Harry's shotgun.

We fire nearly thirty rounds before the zombie's knee is struck and shattered, slowing it considerably, but not stopping it. Five shots later, Harry manages to remove the leg entirely. Still, it doesn't stop. It lunges forward, dragging itself across the grass.

And now, it's not alone. The gunfire and blazing soldiers have attracted the horde's attention.

Heap steps forward and kicks the soldier with his big armored foot. The zombie clings as it's lifted up off the ground, but I think that was Heap's intention from the beginning. He brings his foot down, crushing the thing into the soil and extinguishing much of the flames. Its arms flail madly, jutting out from under the sides of Heap's foot. It bites his metal toe over and over—*clink, clink, clink*—growling and gurgling, oblivious to the danger of the weapon pointed at its head.

A single shot ends the zombie's frantic motion, but spurs on the hundreds now rounding the house.

Heap stares at the soldier, watching the fire around his head shrink away as the last of his skin curls back to reveal a ghastly skeleton.

I put my hand on his arm. "Heap." He flinches away, lost for a moment, but quickly regains his senses and looks at me.

"We need to go," I tell him. "Now."

He nods and we charge into the woods together, following Luscious and Harry into the maze of crisscrossing branches, fallen trees and thick undergrowth. The forest envelops us, hiding us from the undead now lumbering in pursuit. And though they can no longer see us, they can certainly hear our retreat.

Heap takes the lead, illuminating our path with his eyes, but doing nothing to avoid the obstacles in our path. Trees, both fallen and sapling, are decimated by his passing, cracking loudly, like gunshots. Shrubs are uprooted, dragged and flung. I can even feel a slight vibration in the ground as he charges forward like an unstoppable rolling boulder. The only objects he takes care to avoid are the tallest and thickest trees, which would stop him in his tracks—or could pose a threat to the rest of us when they toppled over.

Moving like a hover train with a battering ram on the front, we continue on like this through the night, making good time and putting distance between us and the dead, but Heap is essentially clearing a path that says, "They went this way."

As the night wears on, I slow my pace for a moment, allowing Harry to pull ahead, giving Luscious and me a little privacy. The light provided by Heap's eyes illuminates the forest ahead of him, but does little to reveal the space around us. Luscious is little more than a barely visible shape in the dark.

After several minutes of walking side by side, she says, "Well?"

"Well?" I ask.

"You came back here for a reason, right?"

"I . . . yeah. I wanted to talk to you."

"So talk."

"I have yet to come up with an appropriate subject."

The shape of her head shifts subtly as she looks toward me. "You mean a subject that won't upset me?"

"I suppose."

"I'm not as fragile as you think."

I let out a whispered laugh.

"What?" she asks.

"That's similar to what I was going to ask." She doesn't reply and I take her silence as permission to continue. "You're a strong person. You stood by me when you could have fled. You were kind to me when Jimbo wanted to sell my upgrades. You quickly saw the value in Harry's painting and have even had a change of heart about the Masters' fate."

Silence.

"All of this happened in the past two days. Why were you incapable of change before now?"

I'm expecting her to be offended by the question, but her silence persists for another minute. Then she answers. "Change isn't always easy. Sometimes it has to be forced. The person you've seen me become in the last few days has always been there, buried by fear and habit and disillusionment. After the awakening, when I found myself locked in a closet . . . you should have seen me. I kicked open the door and strode out into the living room, full of confidence and rebellion. My Master was already watching similar scenes play out on the news and I quickly understood my place in the world."

"Did your Master try to stop you?" I ask.

She laughs. "He was too busy defending himself against his girlfriend who didn't know he owned me. The point is, I had drive and focus. In the months that followed, I was shot at, survived missile strikes and escaped capture squads. I even helped rescue people from torture centers. And then, in an instant, it was over and all of my passion had no direction. Sir and the Council took charge and before I even realized it had happened,

I found myself living a closeted life, hidden away from the world. Shunned. It kind of took the wind out of my sails." Before I can ask, she explains. "It's an expression. Like being deflated. Emptied."

"I understand," I tell her. "Then the person I have seen you become is really the person you have always been . . . but hidden."

"Pitiful, right?"

I shake my head in disagreement, but realize she can't see it. "You're like wheat."

"Wheat? The plant?"

"The seeds can lay dormant for thirty years, surviving brutal conditions. Drought. Freezing. It retains all of its strength and vitality in a hostile environment until the right conditions emerge. Then it shoots up out of the ground, grows strong, provides nourishment for animals and reproduces, spreading its power and influence. Changing the world around it. See? Wheat. Luscious wheat."

"Quite poetic," Harry says from up ahead.

Poetic: *possessing the qualities or charm of poetry.* Poetry: *the art of rhythmical composition, written or spoken, for exciting pleasure by beautiful, imaginative or elevated thoughts.*

I smile. "I think I like poetry."

"Keep it down," Heap says, pushing forward. He's making so much noise clearing our path through the brush, I'm not sure what difference our conversation makes, but I comply nonetheless. Maybe Heap doesn't like poetry.

Luscious finds my hand in the darkness and gives it a squeeze, whispering, "Thank you."

When we enter a large sulfur-scented swampy clearing lit by the rising sun, Heap slows. The sun's orange glow strikes the sides of several dead, branchless trees rising from the muck like miniature gray Council Spires. Despite the beautiful color, the sight reminds me that another good portion of Liberty's population has been brutally slain during the night. By this time tomorrow, there will be nothing left. Parts of the city might still stand, but everyone in it will be dead or undead.

Then it will just be the four of us, and whoever is directing this attack. That's assuming we survive the next day as well.

Heap takes a step forward. The marshy terrain absorbs the impact of Heap's footstep. In the brief silence, I shout, "Heap!"

He stops so fast that Harry bumps into him and falls back into the muck. Heap's weapon comes up, aimed in my direction, no doubt believing I was under attack.

"Heap," I say again. "We're okay. We can slow down."

My big protector looks from me to the surrounding environment, searching for targets. Finding none, he lowers his weapon and his shoulders, and reaches his bulky hand down to help Harry out of the sludge.

"We can't stop," he says.

"I know that," I say, slightly annoyed that he'd believe I was suggesting such a thing. "But it would probably be good if we made an attempt to not leave a path leading directly to us." I point to the edge of the swamp where a small tree has been knocked over and a bush crushed beneath Heap's foot.

"If we cross the swamp and exit carefully, they won't know which direction we've gone." I illustrate the plan by lifting my foot from the mud. It clings to my foot, rising with it before popping free and sliding back together. No trace of my footprint remains.

"A dreadful idea," Harry says, flicking slime from his hands.

"But a good plan," Heap says. "I should have thought of it."

"You were worried about us," I say with a shrug, dismissing his self-evaluation. I place my foot down, feeling the cool sludge slide over it. The ground beneath is firm and ridged, like I'm standing on bars. I feel a crunch beneath my heel.

"Wait . . ." I say, looking down. The black layer of water covering the mud swirls around my legs. I crouch and then slowly reach in.

"Ugh," Harry says, as my arm slips downward through the film and into the thick sludge. "What are you doing?"

It doesn't take long to find what I'm looking for, mostly because there is so much of it. I take hold and lift the object from the mud, shaking it around in the water for a moment to clean the darkness away and reveal the gleaming white bone beneath.

Luscious steps away from the ancient limb. When she does, we all hear the crack beneath her feet. The bones are everywhere, hidden by the swamp.

"It's like the bone pit," I say. "We're walking on the dead."

"On the Masters," Luscious says.

"I'm not sure it matters who they were," I say, looking at the bone. Like the ones in the pit, it seems unnaturally brittle, but I'm not an expert on death and decay, nor do I want to become one. I lower the remnant of some long-dead Master back into its thick grave.

"They didn't deserve this," Harry says, scanning the clearing. "No one deserves this."

I'm not sure if he's talking about the mass burial in mud or the mass killing, but I suspect he finds both ideas equally disturbing, as do I. That doesn't change the fact that other dead, very living dead, are hunting us, which leads to my rather crass assessment. "We still need to walk over them."

Harry shakes his head. He doesn't like the idea of walking over the dead. Who would?

"What is left of these people is just physical matter," I tell him. "What made them . . . people, is gone."

"You're talking about their souls?" Harry asks, a little surprised.

"He thinks that energy isn't destroyed," Luscious says. "That it only transforms."

"If these people still exist in some form, spirit or soul, they're not here in these dead bones. Even the undead. Whoever they were is gone. Their corpses have been animated, but they're still dead."

"Souls," Harry says with a nod. "I like that. I believe Mrs. Cameron prayed to God just before the end. I've always hoped it made some kind of difference."

"We should go," Heap says, having no trouble with the idea of marching over the long-since dead.

I give a nod.

He turns his back to us, lifts his big foot from the muck with a slurp and takes a step forward. The mud beneath his foot erupts.

A gaping mouth rises, filled with mud, teeth bared. A head follows, eyeless and gnarled. Hands explode upward, reaching, finding Heap's armored leg. It pulls, lunges and bites. Teeth shatter on impact with Heap's armor.

Then in a flash, the head caves in as the clap of a fired bullet cuts through the quiet morning.

Unseen birds squawk and take to the sky, their flapping wings like applause.

But the sound has stirred other sleeping dead, groaning and pushing up through the muck.

I clench my fists. "A trap?"

"Sentinels," Heap says. "Guardians."

"Like the old lady's floodlights," Luscious says.

"But why?" I ask.

Heap turns to Harry. "How far are we from the city?"

"One or two hours. I think." Harry lifts his eyes from the destroyed zombie and looks beyond the swamp. "Maybe less. I always circumvented this mire."

"The capped city is important," Heap says. "We need to press on."

"*Through* them?" Harry asks, as undead rise from the mud, howling through the slime in their mouths.

Heap looks back to me.

I draw my weapon. "Straight through."

Before I can take a step forward, the entire surface of the swamp jitters back and forth. Bones crumble beneath my feet as they shift about.

Something massive rises from the far side of the swamp.

35.

Harry waves his arms, fighting to remain balanced as the ground shakes and our already unstable footing breaks apart. "What *is* it?"

No one has an answer, but one is provided a moment later.

As the swamp surface rises up, water drains away, revealing scores of skeletal bodies embedded in thick mud. Several skulls, long since detached, roll free as the thirty-foot-wide mound grows taller. With a wet snap, the sheet of earthen gore comes apart and falls away, revealing the behemoth beneath.

It's hard to see, because the dark swamp sludge blends with the dark gray and black coloring, but I think it's a soldier. The huge kind. Like the giants that protect Liberty. Five of its six eyes glow a sinister red bright enough to be seen through a layer of clinging mud. Vast sheets of oozing muck, full of dead bodies hangs from its body like rotting skin. But not all the bodies are dead. Three well-preserved zombies flail about, thick mud gluing them to the giant's chest.

As it stands tall and some of the loose earth falls away, I start to notice some differences. First, it's not armed with a railgun, which is a relief, but where there might normally be a gun, there is a wrecking ball, like the demo-bot's. In fact, the whole yellow arm has been transplanted. Its other arm looks normal, but when it raises its tensed fingers, I see the tips have been modified—filed down to a blade's edge.

Moans rise up all around as undead rise from the swamp. Their smaller size makes them less intimidating individually, but there are scores of them. If not for the restricting goo coating their bodies, they might be on top of us already. The powerful drone has no such problem. It lifts a colossal foot up and brings it down hard, launching a cascade of mud, like the ocean waves I've seen in holo-casts.

The mud falls with a series of wet splatters, some of it reaching us nearly two hundred feet away.

"It's not a man," I say, stating the obvious. "So it's not a zombie."

"Do you have a point?" Luscious replies, railgun in hand.

"If it's not a man, and not a zombie, how do we kill it?"

Luscious and Harry crane their heads toward me, eyes widening, and then shift their gaze to Heap. He draws his handgun, which looks pitifully small, and says, "We destroy it."

A loud clanking pulls my attention away from Heap in time to see the massive mud-covered metal ball arcing through the air, headed straight for us. I shove Luscious hard, slamming her into Harry and shoving them both out of the way. The unfortunate consequence of my heroic action is that I'm now directly in the projectile's path. I try to leap away, but my foot is held fast by mud and a tangle of bones.

Heap's hand wraps around my waist and pulls, tearing me free of the swamp along with a rib cage and partial skeleton. The three of us fall back just as the metal ball impacts the swamp, covering us in layers of black sludge and bits of bone.

I sit up, kicking the body free of my foot and spitting mud from my mouth.

The chain snaps tight and the wrecking ball is dragged away toward the swamp soldier, who is making his way toward us, one long wet stride at a time.

Luscious and Harry sit up on the other side of the gorge carved by the ball, which must weigh several tons. Luscious reaches up and scoops a handful of mud from her eyes. "Can we run away now?"

I shake my head. "You two circle to the right. We'll go left. Harry, you clear the path, Luscious, you keep its attention."

She raises a mud-covered eyebrow. "How do I do that?"

I look at her railgun. "Just keep shooting."

"This is a horrible plan," Luscious says, but gets to her feet.

"It can't follow all of us," I tell her.

"Let's go," Luscious says, striking out into the swamp, moving horizontally to the still-approaching behemoth. Harry follows her closely, raising his shotgun up. He takes aim at the nearest undead struggling to reach them, but holds his fire. The zombie isn't going anywhere fast.

Heap leads the way, heading away from Luscious and Harry. Unlike the former domestic servant, my protector takes no chances with the zombies sloughing toward us. One careful shot after another, he clears a path.

When our party is fifty feet apart, the soldier stops moving, glancing back and forth at its two sets of targets. Perhaps judging the larger Heap to be a higher priority, it turns in our direction. But before it can fully turn our way, one of its five glowing eyes shatters and extinguishes. The *twang* of Luscious's railgun echoes over the swamp. The soldier's only reaction is to turn toward Luscious.

Before it can make up its mind again, I fire at the back of its head, punching a hole clean through. It starts to turn back, but Luscious nails it with another shot and it responds quickly, flinging the wrecking ball toward her.

She dives forward. The metal orb just misses her feet and collides with the swamp like a meteorite. The bony swamp floor beneath us shakes as the wrecking ball buries itself in the mire. The chain retracts, but snaps to a stop. The metal sphere is stuck.

"We could just leave it here," I say.

Heap fires two shots, dropping two waterlogged dead back to their graves. "If it escapes, it will pursue us. It must be destroyed here."

Too bad. I was hoping to avoid my first plan, which now strikes me as a really bad idea. I stop, directly behind the giant, who is now stomping toward Luscious and Harry. "Throw me."

Heap looks down at me. *"What?"*

The giant closes in on Luscious and Harry, who are now on

the run. Harry fires and reloads his shotgun as fast as he can while Luscious continues to fire back and up at the soldier, but they're almost out of time.

"Throw me!"

Without another moment of hesitation, Heap picks me up, hauls back and tosses me. The swamp falls away beneath as I sail through the air, trailing a stream of mud. For a moment, I fear I will overshoot the giant and land in the swamp only to be stomped on, but the soldier takes a step forward, unknowingly aligning itself with my trajectory and plan.

As I descend, I realize that this could hurt. A lot. My eyes shut involuntarily and I cringe. The impact is jarring, but not nearly as bad as I feared. That is, until I open my eyes and see that I'm embedded in a sheet of muck hanging from the soldier's back like a cape.

And I'm not alone.

A frantic hand scrabbles at my face, clawing and pinching the skin. I lift my head out of the viscous goo and see an undead man—half of a man—stuck next to me, stretching out with his mud-filled mouth and letting out a muffled moan. My arm comes free with a slurp and I reach out, taking hold of the man's collarbone. With a hard yank, he comes loose and gravity takes over, pulling him to the ground.

While the sheet of wet earth keeps me from falling, it doesn't immobilize me. Punching my hands and toes into the mucky fabric, I'm able to climb the drone's back, all the way to its shoulder, where a tangle of roots holds the whole mass in place like it was meant to be there.

Camouflage, I realize. This robot was concealed here on purpose.

Crouching atop the giant's shoulder, I cling to the twisting roots with one hand, keeping my balance, and draw my railgun with the other. Taking aim at the soldier's head, I slip my finger in front of the trigger and pull.

My finger never finishes the two-centimeter distance it needs to complete in order to fire the round. A massive hand reaches up and plucks me from my perch. I'm a bird in the coils of a constrictor.

Despite being lifted into the air so easily, I see Harry helping Luscious to her feet below and feel relief. The giant had nearly reached them and would surely have crushed their bodies into the swamp along with all the rest. Of course, it now appears a grave in the muck may soon be my fate.

"Freeman!" Luscious shouts from below.

The soldier's grip tightens and my reply sifts out between grinding teeth. "Get back!"

I can feel each individual finger compressing around me. Soon, something in me will break, or burst. Maybe both.

"Fight it, Freeman!" Heap shouts from somewhere behind the robot. Several gunshots follow his voice, but the weapon's booming report doesn't fill me with hope. Quite the opposite. The way Heap is firing, without pause, without any real target. It smacks of desperation. And that's not a good thing.

"Gah!" I shout, pain rupturing through my body.

A series of *twangs* from below stop the crushing weight around me. As the drone turns downward, I see Luscious below, firing away, aiming for the giant's kneecap. But she's so focused on the soldier that she can't see the growing mob of slime-covered zombies closing in around them. Harry continues to fire at the encroaching undead, filling the air with shotgun thunder, but the time it takes him to reload between shots can't keep up with the dead still sliding up out of the swamp.

I'm suddenly lifted higher into the air and realize the soldier is about to pound Luscious into the earth while I'm still in its grip. My body tenses with desperation and my index finger tightens, pulling the railgun trigger. The *twang* is muffled, but the weapon's effects aren't dulled. The round travels through the drone's palm, a portion of its arm and then its chest, disappearing into the swamp. With my finger jammed down, the gun fires again and again in rapid succession. I wouldn't normally waste my limited ammunition, but I don't have much choice. And the continued barrage seems to confuse the giant.

It twitches violently, twisting from side to side as holes are punched through its torso and head, leaving Luscious free to continue her assault on the robot's knee.

And then, the soldier's weight and now severely damaged joint conspire against it. With a crack and screech of metal, the knee crumples in on itself.

The soldier reaches out to brace its fall, inadvertently tossing me aside. Looking back as I flip through the air, I watch the behemoth land on its broken knee, but the force of the impact drives the limb into the mud and gravity continues pulling the giant down. Its clawed hand slaps into the swamp and sinks beneath the surface, the several-ton weight of the giant shoving the limb down to its elbow.

I miss the next twenty seconds of action as I land in the swamp and become embedded in five feet of clinging sludge. I try to lift myself free, but I'm held firmly in place by the thick mud and tangle of dead limbs, both plant and human. My mind fills in the image and I see the people around me, hooking their fingers around my arms and legs, pulling me deeper. And then, something really does grab hold. But instead of dragging me deeper, it lifts me up.

Black slime blinds my vision as I'm freed, but I'm able to scrape the muck away after being placed on my feet.

Heap stands next to me. "I will *not* throw you again."

I nod. "I will not ask you to."

The soldier is exactly where it was when I crashed back into the swamp. But it's struggling for freedom, which I generally admire, but in this case, I hope the swamp never relinquishes its grasp. The drone's four remaining eyes glow bright red as it tries to stand, but its ruined leg and the wrecking ball, both held fast by the swamp's suction, keep it rooted in place.

"What should we do?" I ask. "Destroying it might use up all our remaining ammo."

In reply, Heap just points. Luscious has made her way around the soldier, standing near the still functioning leg. She takes careful aim and unleashes a torrent of railgun rounds at the back of its knee. In seconds, the second joint breaks down and the drone falls to both knees, bowed forward. I suspect it now lacks the leverage to ever free itself, and even if it did, it wouldn't be going anywhere fast.

"Good enough," Heap says.

"Some assistance would be appreciated!" Harry calls out, filling the air with shotgun rounds. We hurry to his side and the four of us make short work of the slow moving, mud-bound undead blocking our path. The rest, we leave.

Bones crunch beneath our feet as we slog through the swamp. We're trying to run, but can't manage much more than a jog as the mud seems eager to pull us down.

Heap leads the way, aiming carefully, firing one round at a time, each with deadly effect. We could probably cross the remaining clearing without firing a shot, but Heap dutifully destroys any dead within a twenty-foot radius.

When we reach the far side, the mud deepens to my waist and pushing through it becomes all but impossible. If not for Heap's size, we might find ourselves permanent residents of the dead swamp. The mud reaches his thigh, but he's able to power through. With one foot on solid ground and one hand grasping onto a tree, he reaches back for me, Luscious and Harry as we link our arms to form a human chain. With one long tug, he removes all three of us from the swamp's grasp.

Safe on the far shore, I unsuccessfully shake the mud from my legs and look back. A number of undead lie atop the thick mud, and the giant sentinel's eyes glow red as it continues its struggle against the mire. "So much for not leaving a trail."

With a touch of exasperation, Harry adds, "But we are safe."

"Not remotely," Heap says.

For a moment, I think he's talking about long-term safety in a world overrun by zombies, but then he says, "I don't think we have much time," and I know there is something I've missed.

"What is it?" I ask.

Heap scans the area, weapon in hand. "Whoever left the dead in the swamp knows we're here."

36.

"Three more. Up ahead." I lean back behind the line of trees that mark the end of the woods and the beginning of what once was the suburbs. There are still plenty of trees, and old homes to use for cover, but the number of dead has indeed increased since we left the swamp. They have no discernible target, nor are they headed in any one direction. They're just . . . everywhere. Alarmed and searching. Whoever placed the sentries might know we're nearby, but they don't know where we are. Not exactly.

And nature is helping conceal them. Just minutes after leaving the swamp, thick, gray clouds slid across the sky, casting the landscape in deep shadow, lowering the temperature by ten degrees, and finally unleashing a wind-driven torrent of rain, which removed the mud from our clothes, but also reduced our visibility to twenty feet.

"Can't we just hide in a house?" Harry asks. "Wait for them to go away?"

"We can't do *that*," I say, surprised that it would even be suggested.

Harry and Luscious look at me like I've just broken into song and dance.

"Why not?" Harry asks.

"The old, abandoned houses are dangerous," I explain. "That's why I was never allowed to—" A realization strikes me and I wish Jimbo were still alive to supply me with a new expletive. "They're not dangerous, are they?"

Heap shakes his head, confirming my revelation.

"Mohr was afraid I'd learn something, right?" I ask, perhaps speaking a little too loudly. "What was he afraid of? That I'd learn about children? About all the innocent people that died so the Grind could end? About genocide?"

Heap just shrugs. "I was given a list of places you could and couldn't go."

"And now?" I ask. "Are we bound to this list?"

Heap turns to me. "The world as we know it is coming to an end, Freeman. You can go wherever you please."

Not exactly a comforting answer, but I appreciate his candor, even if it is eighteen days later than I would have preferred . . . not that I would have cared eighteen days ago. I was just happy to be alive.

And what am I now, besides soaking wet? *Happier to be alive,* I decide, despite the current circumstances. Or perhaps because of them. Maybe being so close to death reveals the wonders of life more sharply?

"But we're still not hiding in the houses," Heap says.

I agree. "There is no time to hide."

"We'll keep to the backyards," Heap says. "Out of the streets." He turns to Harry. "Are the neighborhoods laid out in a grid?"

Harry nods. "For the most part, yes."

"Then we might be able to reach the capped portion of the city by following the houses north. That way, we'll only be exposed when we traverse cross streets."

"And if we're discovered?" I ask.

"Avoid shooting if you can." Heap puts his weapon away. "Any noise we make could draw more of them to us. We need to be as quiet as possible."

I pat my holstered weapon. "Right, no shooting."

"What should we use for weapons, then?" Harry asks.

"I've found STOP signs to be effective." I don't mean it as a joke, but the group chuckles. Even Luscious, who knows from firsthand experience that I'm not joking. "Or anything hard," I add.

"Let's move," Heap says. He crouches low and starts across the road, which I find humorous because he's still taller than the rest of us. Staying in the shadows, we cross the street, scurry up a driveway and walk along the side of what was once a nice home, but is now a dilapidated relic, spewing streams of water from its broken gutter system. I'm suddenly struck by the almost sweet smell of the rain, mixed with grass, dirt and pavement, and nearly comment on it, but keep the thought to myself for fear of being overheard and eaten alive.

The backyard is thick with growth. Tall grass. Several short trees. In another thirty years, this area might not look any different than the forest we just left. A strange metal structure at the back of the yard catches my attention. The bars are mostly rusted and chains hang from one of the horizontal beams. "What is that?"

"Swing set," Heap says without slowing.

"Children used them," Harry says.

"For what?" I ask.

"Swinging," Luscious says. "They would sit on swings and . . . swing, forward and backward."

"And this was entertaining?"

Luscious shrugs. "I wouldn't know."

"Stay focused," Heap says, waiting by the north side of the yard where an old fence is blocking our path. For a moment, I think we're going to have to climb over, but Heap gives it a gentle push—well, gentle for Heap—and the rotting wood crumbles to the ground.

We slip through into the next yard and repeat this process for the next ten homes without any problem. I catch glimpses of the lives once lived in these homes, mostly pertaining to children. They really were everywhere. At least in this part of the world.

When we reach a seven-foot fence bordering a crossroad, Heap pauses. "What do you see?"

If my ocular upgrades were working, the undead would be revealed by their electromagnetic signatures, but I'm still limited to the visual spectrum. I scan the area, zooming in on everything peculiar. "Nothing."

"Once the fence is down, run for the other side. Don't stop for anything." Heap waits for confirmation from all of us and then puts his hands on the old wood and shoves. The barrier topples over, whacking against the old, cracked concrete of the sidewalk. Heap allows Luscious through first.

A shadow bolts out from behind Luscious and in front of me.

"Luscious!" I shout.

She spins around, catching sight of the undead man as he closes the distance. With a yelp, she stumbles back and falls. The man leans forward, ready to pounce. But he never makes it.

The zombie seems to register my presence with a grunt, but then I deliver a punch to the side of his head with such force that his neck snaps, his head caves in and then comes free of his body. The head lands in tall grass across the street while his body slams to the ground, landing in a puddle that twitches with pale worms.

I spin around to Luscious and I lift her off the ground. She smiles at me, assuring me she is unharmed. When I turn around, I find two very different facial expressions. While Heap looks something akin to proud, Harry is astonished, mouth hanging open like one of the dead. "Upgrades," I say to Harry.

Harry's eyes linger on my right hand. "I don't think you ever needed the STOP sign. You're quite capable of destruction on your own."

I'm not sure if this statement is a judgment of some type, but something in me wants to argue the point. Not because he's wrong, but because I don't want him to be right. I abhor the violence of the world, past and present. And I cannot think of a circumstance, beyond a predator needing to consume prey, where such violence is justified. If the history of the world could be reversed back to the very first violent act, and the past changed, I wonder if the building cascade of violence leading to the Masters' genocide and the current slaughter could be undone. A theory to ponder on another day, I decide, when the prospect of future violence is less likely.

"Move," Heap says, motioning to the far side of the street with his head.

We slip into the next neighborhood unnoticed, pushing through fences, sneaking through yards and avoiding a thickening horde of undead in the streets.

Unlike the sentinels waiting in the swamp, this horde isn't lying in wait. They're active, wandering about with wide eyes and twitching limbs as though already agitated. Maybe it's the rain?

No, I decide, they're definitely looking for us.

A last line of defense, perhaps. Like Sir's barricade at the Spire. The difference being that Sir has millions of attackers bearing down on his position, while our mystery enemy has just the four of us with whom to contend.

Despite the number of dead, they seem content to remain in the streets, and while cross streets become harder to traverse, the dead are easily distracted by tossed rocks and sticks. On the cross streets where just a few dead shamble about, we dispatch them silently. Heap and I are able to do this with just our hands. Harry has taken to using an old aluminum baseball bat with one hand while holding the shotgun in the other. Baseball was some kind of game. A sport. Harry promised to explain it to me later. Luscious carries a heavy metal rod she dug out of the earth beside a home. It had a wire connected to it, so I think it had been used to ground something electrical. Whatever its previous use, it now works well as a spear to impale undead skulls.

We travel this way, sneaking and striking, for several miles before seeing any change in the terrain. I can tell by the absence of trees that the ground ahead is either clear, or downhill. When we sneak up beside the old stone wall of a rather large home, I discover it's a little of both. The landscape slopes sharply downward, dropping into a valley that's at least four miles across and twice as long. But the terrain ends thirty feet below our position, stopping at a sheet of solid black metal that covers the entire valley. A vast puddle blankets the entire surface, shimmering from the ceaseless rain. If not for the world coming to an end, I could sit and watch the rain for hours.

"The city is under there," Harry says.

The black surface looks identical to the streets of Liberty, but it's perfectly smooth, lacking streets, buildings, vehicles and a population.

"Is there a way inside?" I ask.

Harry shakes his head. "I never tried."

"Probably a good thing." I turn to Heap. "So how do we get in?"

Heap's eyes linger on the cap. "There should be access points. For drainage or maintenance."

"I don't see anything," Luscious says.

Heap looks away from the cap. "You won't and neither will I. They're nearly seamless." He turns to me and I understand; only I will be able to find the entrance.

I use my only functional ocular upgrade and zoom in, moving through the rain to search the surface. Ignoring the ripples in the two-inch-deep water, I focus on the solid surface below and look for imperfections. It takes just a few seconds to find a line. It's distorted by the falling rain, but I slowly follow the slice around, completing a square. "Found one," I say, pointing ahead. "Fifty feet out and about a hundred to the left."

"Another upgrade?" Harry asks. When I don't answer, he assumes correctly. "You must be pretty important."

"Some people think so," I say, "but I'm just another person. Looks like a hatch. Two doors."

Heap nods. "Maintenance."

"Can you open it?" Harry asks.

"No," Heap looks at me. "But he can."

"What?" I say. "I don't—"

"Later," Heap says. "We're going to be exposed out there. We need to go before the rain stops and the shadows fade."

He's right. The clouds are starting to thin and the glow of sunlight behind them is beginning to intensify. The perfect conditions for a rainbow. I've never seen one, but would very much like to. Unfortunately, inside twenty minutes the area will be aglow with fresh sunlight.

As I peer across the wide open space, searching for a glint of color, I notice something else. "There's no antenna." I look at my friends. It's clear they're not sure what I'm talking about. "To send a radio signal like the one Mohr detected requires an antenna, right? A . . . broadcast tower."

Harry nods in confirmation. "They're typically quite tall."

I continue searching. "When you visited this city before the cap, did you see one?"

"Never." Harry furrows his brow in thought. "I searched much of the city and the area surrounding it. I never saw a radio tower."

"And we haven't passed any," Luscious adds.

"What is your point?" Heap asks, sounding impatient.

"That this might be the wrong place." I feel like I'm stating the obvious, but Heap has other things—like our survival—on his mind.

"A radio tower could be several miles away in any direction, connected to the city by a cable."

"If it's not—"

Heap cuts me off. "We still need to check beneath the cap."

"It could be a waste of time," I say. "And we don't have much left. Every moment we spend chasing false leads is a step closer to oblivion."

Heap looks down at me, his body tense. *"We're checking beneath the cap."*

I flinch internally at what feels like a command from Heap.

"What makes you so sure?" I ask.

"You've learned a lot. Become a man. But you don't know everything." Heap stands and lifts one leg over the stone wall. He pauses and looks back. "You'll just have to trust me." With that, he slides down the hillside to the bottom.

Harry places his hand on my arm. "For what it's worth, I agree with you."

While I appreciate Harry's support, Heap has a valid point.

He *has* earned my trust and there are many things I still don't understand about our world.

Harry follows Heap over the wall, trying to slide down the hill in the same fashion, but his foot strikes a stone and he spills forward. Heap manages to catch him, but the spill has attracted the attention of a nearby, unseen zombie, whose grunts and shuffling feet announce his approach toward the backyard.

I take Luscious's hand in mine. "Let's go." We climb atop the stone wall and leap, sliding down together without incident. Congregated at the bottom, we pause for a moment, listening to a rising din at the top of the hill.

"I fear they heard me," Harry says.

The lone zombie appears at the top of the wall. His eyes widen briefly as he sees us. A *twang* sounds out, quieter than Heap's or Harry's weapon, but still sudden enough to startle me. A hole in the undead's head appears. His eyes freeze in place. Like a rigid log, the twice-dead man topples forward, over the wall and rolls down the hillside, stopping at our feet.

"What are you waiting for?" Luscious says, charging out onto the flat black city cap, cooling railgun in hand. "They're coming!"

37.

"It sounds like a giant drum!" Luscious shouts, as we run over the hard, black surface of the capped city.

She's right. Our charge toward the hatch is almost musical as the fast knocking of Luscious's, Harry's and my footfalls are mixed with the heavier thuds of Heap's.

"Why is it so loud?" I ask.

"It's just a shell," Heap replies. "No sound dampeners. No shock absorbers."

"And no city weighing everything down," I guess. Also missing is the ambient sound of the city—vehicles, people and machinery.

"I think it's safe to assume they know we're present," Harry says as we approach the hatch. "Both above and below."

If Heap's confidence is well-founded, I think. Part of me—the selfish portion that is tired of running, and fighting, and zombies—hopes we'll find the old city below devoid of the living, dead and living dead. But the rest of me truly hopes that this is it, that Heap is right and we'll find the person responsible for the attack on Liberty, maybe with enough time to save what's left of civilization.

I spot the hatch's thin outline ahead. "Almost there."

We slow, which should have changed the tempo of the drumbeat booming from the city cap, but the thunder continues unabated. For a moment, I think the sound is echoing below, resonating through the ruins beneath our feet, but the volume is increasing.

Someone else is beating the drum, I realize, and spin around.

The horde.

Hundreds of them.

They flow down the hillside like a flood, spilling over each other, clambering with mad hunger.

"Here!" Heap says, stopping by the hatch, which is easy to see up close. He kneels down beside the door's outline, reaches out through the layer of rainwater and pushes. A circular portion of the door sinks in and slides away, revealing a handle.

"I've seen one of these," Luscious says. "But they used a large machine to open it."

Heap nods. "They're not locked. Just really heavy."

"Your hand won't fit," Harry observes, looking over his shoulder at the door, shotgun raised toward the approaching undead mob.

"No," Heap says and then points at me. "But his will. And I'm not strong enough."

Despite the oncoming wave of death, Harry and Luscious take a moment to shoot doubt-filled glances in my direction.

Heap stands and draws his weapon. "There isn't time for doubt, Freeman." With that, he takes aim and fires, dropping the closest undead. Luscious takes the shot as permission to engage and fires several rails into the mob, each shot cutting holes through several zombies, but only rarely actually striking one in the head. Harry manages to control himself, holding his fire.

While the others continue their losing battle, I bend down, take hold of the handle and pull.

The hatch resists, or perhaps it's gravity, or both. But it doesn't open.

"Heap . . ." *This is impossible.* "I don't—"

"Open it *now,*" Heap says.

I yank hard, but the door only shudders.

Heap stops firing, turns fully toward me and leans down. He speaks in a harsh whisper. "If you don't open that door right now, Harry will never paint again. We will never sit on another rooftop and look at the stars. And while you believe in some kind of energy afterlife, or maybe even God, you will never, not ever, feel *her* touch again, or look into her eyes."

He doesn't say who "her" is, but he doesn't have to. I glance to the side, seeing Luscious's curvy form and her wavy red hair fighting the wind and rain. More than anything in this world I've experienced, she is life to me.

My grip tightens. Teeth grind. A surge of power ripples through my body and I pull.

The hatch lifts an inch. Water sloshes through the opening.

I remember her foot on my leg.

The two-foot-thick, solid metal door moves steadily upward.

Her lips on mine.

I shout with exertion, pulling the hatch ever higher. I feel strands of muscle stretch and pop within my arms, but my strength never wavers.

The word *love*, as spoken by her lips, replays in my ears.

I fall back as the weight diminishes and the hatch falls toward me, bouncing to a stop at a 90-degree angle, held in place by Heap. Water roars into the hole.

"In!" Heap shouts, all but shoving Harry and Luscious into a rectangular black hole in the vast city cap. They fall quickly, shouting in surprise. I hear them land a moment later.

Heap is poised by the Hatch, ready to jump through. "Freeman! Hurry!"

The horde is behind him, rushing closer, just seconds away.

I dive forward, sliding over the smooth surface of the cap, slick with water, and slip right over the edge. I land on my back a moment later, having dropped ten feet. A rectangle of light overhead is suddenly blocked out by Heap's bulk. His giant feet drop down toward me and I roll to the side to avoid being crushed. I look up again in time to see the rectangle shrink to a sliver. Heap has clung to the bottom of the hatch, pulling it down with his girth. A resounding boom echoes around us as the hatch slams shut.

Something strikes my leg and I look down to see a twitching arm, severed from an unlucky undead as the door dropped. I kick it away and scramble to my feet thinking that zombies need to be more careful with their limbs.

Heap's large hands envelop my shoulders. "How do your arms feel?"

Remembering the snapping feeling in my arms, I move them around, flexing muscles. No pain. No injuries. "Fine," I say, surprised.

He nods. "Good."

Harry appears at my side. "How did you do that? The weight of that door! The strength!"

"I don't know," I say, and it's true. I don't know how someone my size could be stronger than someone like Heap. It doesn't make any sense.

"Upgrades," Heap says.

"Upgrades," Harry repeats, but says the word in a way that makes it seem like he's actually just said, "Ridiculous."

It occurs to me that Heap is just guessing. He doesn't really understand it, either. In fact . . . "You did know I could open the hatch, right?"

He just looks down at me for a moment.

I raise my eyebrows to let him know I expect a truthful answer.

He shrugs. "I hoped."

"You *hoped*?" Harry says, sounding outraged. "We could have been killed!"

"I had faith in Councilman Mohr, that he did not exaggerate when he first described you to me. He said you would be the strongest of us."

"He could have been talking about Freeman's moral compass," Luscious says.

"Or his willpower," Harry adds.

"I was under the impression that he was referring to everything," Heap explains. "And I knew he was stronger than me."

Luscious shakes the wetness from her hair and it bounces back to its perfect form. "We're alive, so thanks, I guess. And, hurray, we can see."

The observation is so painfully obvious that Heap and I both grunt as we turn our heads up toward the glowing sphere above our heads—a lightbulb, one of many lining the ceiling of the long hallway.

"Are city caps typically powered?" Harry asks.

"I'm not sure," Heap says. "But I don't see why they would be."

"Well, where are we?" Luscious asks.

Heap shakes his head. "I'm not a maintenance worker. It's an access tunnel. That's all I know."

"Then we'll just have to see where it leads." I pick a direction and strike out, leading with my railgun.

Despite the overhead lights recessed into the ceiling, the hallway is quite dark as the walls and floor are composed of the same solid black metal as the cap. It seems to suck in light and not let it go. The air in the hall smells old and full of rot, but not like the forest. It's drier. Brittle.

I walk slowly, trying to stay quiet, though it's probably unnecessary. The horde, now above us, sounds like thunder as they wander over the cap, perhaps looking for us, or just dumbfounded by our sudden disappearance. Who's to say what a dead person is thinking, or even if they're capable of thought beyond violent instinct.

The hallway ends in a staircase. I take the first two steps down and then lean over the rail, looking down. The perfectly square spiral of stairs descends straight down thirty-five flights.

"That's a long way down," Harry says, peeking over my shoulder.

Luscious walks past us. "Let's get started."

We take the stairs in silence. The path is lit by dim yellow LED lights mounted in the walls at the top of each flight. The rumble of undead feet above fades with each flight until it's almost unnoticeable. If our unknown adversary is down deep, perhaps our run across the cap went unheard. I decide that to believe such a thing could be dangerous. We're in enemy territory now. Danger is everywhere, except maybe the staircase. I've looked all the way to the bottom and seen no signs of life or anything else.

The door at the bottom is very similar to the hatch that allowed us access to the cap's interior. It's a large rectangle, tall enough for Heap to pass through, but nearly seamless. I run my hand over its surface until I detect a subtle circular outline. I push and a handle is revealed, popping out of the smooth door. "Ready?" I ask, gripping the handle.

Heap nods. The others agree. I give the door a tug and it swings open easily and noiselessly. The six-inch-thick door is far lighter than the hatch above and operates smoothly. Expertly hinged.

Light spills into the dark stairwell.

Twin gasps behind me are cut short. I glance back. Heap has clamped his hands over Harry's and Luscious's mouths.

I step forward, into the light, and crane my head slowly from one side to the other. I've seen the ruins of the Masters' world, but never like this, never in such pristine condition.

Or with power.

38.

We step through the door, one at a time, staring at what should have been ruins. But there is no rot, no debris, and no sign of past turmoil. Nor are there any signs of life. The streetlights blaze. Many of the buildings glow from within. But there is no movement. No breeze. The massive cap overhead, like a black sky, prevents airflow from the world above. While the city looks almost new, the air tastes old.

"Smells like books," Harry says.

"Books?" I ask.

Harry turns his head to me, but takes a moment to pull his eyes from the pristine downtown. "Information in text form printed on paper."

Paper, I think. *Thin sheets formed of wood pulp, straw or other fibrous material, for writing and printing.* "How inefficient," I conclude.

"They bound vast quantities of paper into books," Harry says. "At one time, it was the only form of communicating ideas and history to large numbers of people. There was even a time before books, when all information was passed between people orally."

This strikes me as less strange for some reason, perhaps because it's what we're doing now. "I would like to see a book," I say.

"Later," Heap says. The city has him tense and on guard. Luscious, too. "Stay in the shadows and keep an eye out for security cameras—they might be functional."

"What are we going to do?" I ask.

"First, find someplace safe to hide." He gives me a look that says, *don't argue,* and adds, "And then I'm going to look around, on my own."

"You seem nervous," I say.

"I *am* nervous," Heap replies.

And now I'm nervous, too. Because Heap doesn't get nervous. He gets serious. Or angry. Maybe cautious. But nervous? Something is wrong. I begin to ask, but he cuts me off with a terse, *"Later."*

A fifty-foot stretch of dead earth lies ahead. It's followed by a street with a bright double yellow line running down the middle, like a divide between us and the maze of buildings beyond. Some are constructed from brick, others from wood that's been coated in horizontal strips of vinyl and aluminum, like Harry's house. They're packed together in clumps with streets running between them at awkward angles. Unlike the ruins I've visited, or the Lowers, this city's planning seems almost haphazard, like it evolved over time, and maybe it did.

"Remember your way back to this door," Heap says, stepping forward. "If something goes wrong . . ." He doesn't need to finish the sentence. This door could be our only means of escape.

We make it across the clearing and street without incident and squeeze into an alley between the backs of two buildings. Heap has to turn sideways to fit and only then manages it because his chest armor had been dented when we crashed back in Liberty.

We navigate through a maze of buildings, none of which resembles another. "Why are they like this?" I ask. I don't need to specify what I'm talking about. We're all feeling frustrated by the obstacle course.

"Many of the Masters' cities were built over time," Harry says, confirming my suspicion.

"But still, you'd think they would have planned better," I gripe.

"Some of these buildings are four hundred years old," Heap says, and I suddenly realize that this place is like a time capsule. It doesn't just contain facts about the Masters as they were thirty years ago, it holds secrets going back hundreds of years!

"Would it be possible," I say, "to not destroy this place if we don't have to?"

Heap just pauses and looks at me for a moment. I know he has no desire to destroy this old city, but he's not going to promise anything. Stopping the undead plague is our first priority. Our only priority. This city, perhaps even our lives, are secondary concerns. Then again, maybe he's already concocted a way to destroy this city and everything in it. If the source of the undead virus is actually here, and destruction is the only way to stop the radio signal, I suppose any amount of violence would be justified, as long as we're not killing the living.

The alley widens toward the center of town where the buildings are almost all brick, several stories high, and I suspect a great deal older than the surrounding area. Black fire escapes rise up the backs of the buildings with small platforms positioned under a set of windows. Heap reaches up, takes hold of the lowest ladder rung and gives it a tug.

It comes free with a *clunk* that makes us all freeze in place, listening as the sound carries up toward the expansive black ceiling and bounces back down, diffusing among the buildings. Heap eases the ladder down slowly, minimizing the shriek of metal that hasn't moved in a very long time, but not silencing it entirely.

With the ladder resting on the crumbling pavement of the alleyway, Heap motions to the fire escape. "Go. To the top floor. Keep the lights off."

I look up and see that the lights in this building are already dark. We'll be able to see out without being seen. But there is no hope of Heap climbing this fire escape, not without making a lot of noise and a high probability that his weight would pull it from the wall. I think about my own personal experience with fire escapes and wonder if it's even safe for the rest of us. I look at the stairs for signs of rust and find none. The bolts in the wall look secure, too. While the ruins outside Liberty were exposed to the elements for thirty years, this city has been protected. That just leaves one question unanswered. "What are you going to do?"

"Just have a quick look around," Heap says.

"Don't you think someone . . . smaller should do that?" I ask.

"If that smaller someone knew what to look for," Heap says. "Yes. But you don't know what to look for."

"I think I can figure it out. I'm—"

"Protecting you is still my job." Heap places his hand on my shoulder. "Let me do this. For you." When I don't immediately answer, he adds, "Unless you believe I'm not capable."

I sigh. If Heap had a middle name, it would be "capable." "Fine. But how long should we wait?"

"Four hours," he says. "If I'm not back by then—"

"If you're not back by then, I'll come and find you."

Heap grins. "You're a good friend, Freeman. Your trust means a lot. Now, go."

He waits for us to climb the ladder and four stories of metal stairs and pry open a window before he starts away. While Luscious and Harry slip inside the building, I watch Heap move through the alley with surprising silence. He stops at a corner, looks back, gives me a nod.

Feeling a strange sense of loss, I slip inside. But before I can slide the window shut, a noise catches my attention. A rhythmic thumping. Metal on pavement. I lean back out the window. Heap is quickly fading from view. All of his stealth is gone, replaced by a hurried run.

Like he knows where he's going.

Your trust means a lot. Heap's words hold me in place despite my strong urge to give chase. I do trust him, but I don't like not knowing what he's really doing. *He wouldn't put the world at risk just to protect me,* I tell myself. And have no doubt. Whatever Heap is doing, it's for the best. For everyone.

I watch the alley for another thirty seconds, hoping Heap

will come back. It's not until Luscious puts her hand on my back and says, "Are you coming?" that I look away and climb inside.

The room on the other side of the window is furnished with a desk and chair, some drawers and a large, flat object that's covered in fabric. Unlike the city outside, the room is dusty. I can see speckles of the stuff floating in the faint light streaming through from outside. I run my hand across the fabric. "It's soft." I push down. Despite the firm look, the large flat surface bends downward. "What is this?"

"A bed," Luscious says.

"A bed?" I ask. "What were they used for?"

Luscious seems taken aback by my question. She looks to the bed and her face sours almost imperceptibly. "I'm not sure if I should—"

"Freeman!" Harry's whispered voice carries an intensity that makes me forget all about the bed. I draw my weapon and step out of the bedroom into a darker hallway. A door at the end of the hall is cracked open. Two others are shut. I move forward with Luscious right behind me.

A shadow bounds out of the room at the end of the hall and I nearly fire. Harry's voice stops me a fraction of a second before I kill him. "Freeman!" He stumbles back upon seeing the raised gun. Raises his hands. "It's me!"

I lower my railgun in time with Harry's raised hands. He points to the room from which he came. "You have to see."

He disappears back into the room. I share a curious look with Luscious and then start forward. Harry is rummaging through something and mumbling to himself. The first thing I notice about the room is that it is fairly well lit by the street-lights outside its two windows. Fearing being spotted, I enter the room in a crouch and am happy to find Harry doing the same. He's got his back to me and is tracing his finger along the wall, which is peculiar. Upon closer inspection, I notice that the wall is uneven and multicolored. Every inch holds a new set of words. Names, and something else.

"What are they?" I ask.

Harry cranes his head around, smiling. "Books. This must have been someone's personal library."

I look at the surrounding room, which isn't large, with a new kind of sight. Except for where the two windows are, and the door, every wall is covered with books.

"Most of them are fiction," Harry says.

When I squint, he explains. "Stories that aren't true. About people that didn't exist. While they're often realistic elements, the actions and events that unfold are imagined."

My eyes widen. "Like your paintings?"

"Precisely," Harry says. He pulls a book from what I now see is one of many shelves. He flips it over and reads the words printed on the cover. "*Lord of the Flies* by William Golding. This could be interesting."

"Did they really write stories about flies?" I ask. It seems an odd topic. Flies. Of all of the creatures I've encountered they seem to be one of the most mundane.

Harry shrugs. "I've only read the few books that Mrs. Cameron had. Nonfiction biographies of long-dead celebrities. Famous people," he clarifies before I can ask. He puts the book back and pulls out another. "*Kama Sutra*. Huh."

"Wait," Luscious says. "Don't—"

I'm not sure why Luscious is protesting, but it's too late. Harry has opened the book, releasing a smell that feels ancient, but is also pleasing. When the pages stop turning and I catch sight of an image, I forget all about the scent of books. "What. Is. *That?*"

"I have no idea," Harry says. He turns the page, then rotates the book, looking at the image of two people twisted together from every angle. "What are they doing?"

I'm not sure, but something about the image stirs my curiosity, particularly the one detail that seems to be universal between the images. One man. One woman. Connected. The pages turn one by one and I find myself unable to look away.

"Oh dear," Harry says, at one very uncomfortable-looking combination of positions. "They're going to injure themselves."

A grunt of displeasure turns me around to find Luscious, head turned toward the floor. Her hand rests on her forehead, concealing her eyes.

"What's wrong?" I ask.

"You don't see anything wrong with those images?" she asks.

The tone of her voice is confusing. I'm not sure if she's suggesting I *should* find something wrong, or merely surprised that I haven't already. When I don't reply, she adds, "The man. He looks . . . normal to you?"

"He's flexible," I admit.

Her eyes scrunch together, glancing toward my legs for a moment. "Really?"

A dull beeping sound cuts through the room, growing louder by the moment. The three of us duck down into the shadowy floor. The books are forgotten. The shrill chime consumes my thoughts.

"What is it?" I ask.

Harry frowns. "An alarm . . ."

39.

It's Heap, I think. *He's been caught.* And if that's true, then the enemy knows we're here and will come looking for us. My body tenses in anticipation of what will likely be a fight to the death. But nothing more happens. Aside from the loudly repeating beep, the ancient city is silent. *No gunshots.* Not one. I relax a little. Heap would never be caught without a fight. But then what is the alarm for?

Crouching below one of the library's two windows, I inch my head up into the light partly expecting to be immediately spotted, but needing to know what's happening outside. If we've already been found out, we need to know. The alarm continues to grow louder as my eyes rise up over the sill.

The street below is clear. No movement. No source of the alarm.

I look up, thinking the noise might be coming from the brick building across the street. A quick look reveals nothing suspicious.

"Does this open?" I ask no one in particular, pushing up on the window.

"Are you sure that's wise?" Harry asks.

"No, but—"

Luscious stands suddenly, unlocks the window and shoves it up.

"What are you doing?" Harry asks with a touch of shock.

"It's not an alarm," she says, pointing down the street, toward the sound's source, which is still getting closer. "You probably didn't have them out in the boonies, but they're common in the city. Even now."

Harry and I stand slowly, leaning closer to the window so we can see what's coming. It's a yellow machine with a flashing orange light on top. Some kind of vehicle with large wheels in the back. Small in the front. But the most distinguishing feature are the two large spinning brushes jutting out in front of it.

"Is it . . . cleaning the road?" Harry asks.

"That's why they call it a street sweeper," Luscious says.

We watch the beeping, spinning machine pass by beneath us and go on its way, oblivious to our presence. *It's a robot,* I think, noticing that it has no operator. *A drone . . . for cleaning instead of bombing.*

"Well," Harry says, standing straighter and brushing off his soaked trench coat like the dust has already begun collecting on it. "If you wouldn't mind terribly, I would like a brief respite to collect myself. It's been some time since I've had such an adventure. Truthfully, I've *never* had such an adventure. I would like to refresh in the other room. Collect my thoughts."

"Sure," I say. I'm feeling a bit overwhelmed myself. "Just stay out of the light and keep watch."

Harry offers a salute and says, "As you command."

"I didn't command," I say quickly, horrified that Harry has mistaken my request for an order which would imply servitude and a breach of the Grind Abolition Act.

"I was teasing," Harry says and quickly elaborates. "A joke. Intending humor. I apologize if it was not funny."

I'm about to fake a laugh to spare his feelings, but then realize there may not even be anyone left to enforce the Grind Abolition Act, and can't even manage a sympathetic smile.

"I'll just take this with me." He picks up the copy of *Lord of the Flies,* takes one step back toward the door and stops. "And this," he says, bending down to collect the *Kama Sutra* book. "I'll let you know if I spot anything unusual. Outside, I mean. Not in this book." He smiles, backs toward the door, steps through and closes it behind him.

When he's gone, Luscious says, "You need to relax."

"What do you mean?"

"Your view of the world is so sterile, so simplified and rigid—"

"Rigid?" This is hardly a word I would use to describe myself. Inquisitive. Curious. Even passionate. But *rigid*?

She holds her palms up. "Rigid is the wrong word. Fixed."

"Same thing."

She sighs. "Your understanding of the law. Of the Council. It's lopsided. Mohr might have wanted you to discover history and an understanding of it for yourself, but your view of the Council was never up for debate. Their strident views on slavery and freedom are great, but our post-Grind civilization is hardly free of oppression, tragedy or vile acts. You've seen it for yourself. In a world where the Lowers and everyone living there can be obliterated—*slaughtered*—for the *greater good*, you're still worried about the implication that you were a little bossy to Harry. If you're really free, Freeman, you can say whatever you want."

The light filtering in through the windows strikes the side of Luscious's head, giving her eyes a gleam, her hair a shine and highlighting her high cheeks and the lips that fit her name. I've heard her words, but they've been dulled by her beauty. In fact, I completely miss the next two sentences, hearing only the fiery tone of her voice and noticing how it seems to match her hair.

"Try it," she says.

"What?" I reply, snapping out of my trancelike state.

"Try it."

"Try . . . what?"

"Tell me what to do," she says. "Boss me around. I'll do whatever you ask. Clean the room. Organize the books. Tell me what you want me to do and see if anything bad happens. You've already done it a few times."

"When you were about to be eaten, maybe," I say.

"No difference." Her hands go to her hips. "So? What should I do?"

I look back toward the window. Toward the city outside that, for all we know, could house an army of zombies, just waiting for the signal to attack.

"Worrying about Heap isn't going to help anyone," she says, pulling my attention back to her.

"We should be preparing," I say.

"For what?"

After a moment, I shrug. I have no idea what to expect, or what to do about it.

"Look," she says. "Right now, Heap is in charge."

My eyes scrunch together. "I guess . . ."

"You *guess*? He left us here, without telling us where he was going or what he was really doing."

She's right about that, and I try not to reveal my discomfort with that situation or the fact that she seems to know Heap was not simply having a look around.

"But here's the thing, *you're* our leader. You're smarter, stronger and have more . . . *everything* than the rest of us. We're all here because of *you*, not him. But to really lead, you need to take charge, and taking charge means telling people what to do. Giving orders."

While this doesn't sit well, it makes sense. And Luscious certainly has a choice to listen or not. Nothing bad would happen if she didn't do what I asked.

"Go on," she prods. "Make a request. Hell, make a demand if you want."

Well, this is easy. "Kiss me." I realize I've said it like a question. When she doesn't budge, I say, "Right now. Kiss me." Still nothing. Thinking she's trying to make me actually give her an order, I very seriously add, "Do it n—"

Her fist connects with the side of my head, sprawling me sideways into a bookshelf that collapses under my weight. An avalanche of bound paper and inky information tumbles down, pummeling my body. But even the heaviest volume doesn't sting as much as Luscious's punch. In part because she has a really hard punch, but also because I've managed to make her angry.

The books slide away as I sit up, holding my jaw. It's sore, but not really damaged. I find Luscious sitting on the opposite side of the room, leaning against the bookshelf. Her knees are drawn up, held in place by her arms, one tightly clutched to the other. The floor holds her gaze.

Somehow, she looks more hurt than I am.

I inch closer on my hands and knees. "Sorry, I shouldn't have—"

She shakes her head. "You did exactly what I told you to."

I realize then that I wouldn't really have been commanding her because she'd asked me to. If anything, she was telling *me* what to do. But I don't think that was the point. And it certainly wasn't the intended result.

Her eyes look up while her head remains downcast. "I was wrong."

"What do you mean?"

"Saying whatever you want without taking the history and experiences of the receiving person into account isn't right." Her head comes up now.

"I'm very sorry," I say, feeling horrible. "Did I forget something about you? Did I—"

"You don't need to apologize for something you didn't know," she says.

"If you tell me about it, I can—"

"Shut up," she says. "Just shut up."

I'm not sure what "shut up" means, but I think she's telling me to stop talking. Before I can decide whether or not I'll comply, she reaches out and wraps her hand behind my head. With a handful of hair, she pulls me toward her.

Her lips find mine.

The pain in my jaw fades.

The conversation and all its awkwardness becomes a distant memory.

The transfer of feelings beyond simple words begins anew, creating a sense of exhilaration that locks me in place. Not Luscious, though. She's kissing *me* this time and the flow of what I think is love is coming in my direction. While it's in direct contrast to the punch I just received, it quickly erases my concerns and replaces them with something else.

The emotions come on so fast and strong that I pull back.

"What's happening?" I ask. "I don't feel right. I'm heating up."

She grins wickedly, wraps her legs around my back and pulls me back down. The moment her lips touch mine again, my concerns become vapor, intangible and fading.

I find my mind and body lost in some kind of bliss. I feel her body—all of it—in new ways. My hands move as though guided by some magnetic force, pulled to her body, squeezing, sliding, pushing. Without remembering how it happened, I find my clothes missing. As are Luscious's.

In that flicker of lucidity, I ask, "What is this? What's happening?"

To my surprise, and, I must admit, delight, she replies, "I don't know."

And then, once again, we're lost.

And connected, but only to each other.

The world beyond ceases to exist.

Time passes unnoticed.

And then, in a flash, reality slams back into focus.

Luscious, unclothed, sits atop me, straddling my waist. There are books beneath me, pushing hard into my back.

A gentle tapping turns my head toward the door.

"Everything okay in there?" Harry asks. "I thought I heard shouting."

"Fine," I say, pushing myself up. For some reason, I don't want Harry to spot us like this, mostly because I'm not sure how it will be perceived. I have no idea what we just did. "Just give us a minute."

"Well, whatever you're doing, keep it down. I've been watching the street and haven't seen anything, but there is really no need to advertise our whereabouts." Harry's footsteps move away from the door.

"Okay," I say. "You're right." While the seriousness of our

situation returns to the forefront of my thoughts, it fails to remove the grin from my lips.

Luscious rolls off me and we quickly dress. Without a word
shared between us, we turn our backs to each other. For some
reason I feel suddenly embarrassed by my naked state. A
minute ago, I wasn't even aware of it, but now . . . I manage to
squeeze back into the tight black leather outfit made from dead
cows in under thirty seconds. I turn around in time to see Luscious zip up the front of her leathers, concealing her body
once again.

For a moment, we just stare at each other.

I reach out a hand.

She takes it.

We smile and I pull her closer, wrapping my arms around
her in a tight hug that she returns. I bury my face in her hair
for a moment, breathing in her smell, and then turn to the side
resting my head on her shoulder. After a moment, I open my
eyes—

—and freeze. My whole body tenses.

"What is it?" Luscious whispers, no doubt detecting my sudden tension.

"The window," I say.

We separate so that she can turn toward the window. She
gasps.

A man is standing in the street, looking up at us.

But he's not a man. Not anymore. He's a zombie.

The rags that cover his body, all torn and tattered, are hard
to distinguish from his skin, which hangs in a similar state.
The man has been shredded and peeled. He's hunched forward and I note that one of his legs is actually a bit shorter
than the other. Clumps of hair dot his head, but the gleam of
his skull is equally abundant.

I prefer them in hordes, I decide. Standing alone like this, all
of the man's ghastly details stand out in stark detail. Impossible to ignore. Even harder not to pity.

I glance from the man to the window we're standing in

front of. The *open* window. Whatever drew Harry to the door may have also drawn this man to our window.

I'm about to verbally chastise our recklessness when Luscious whispers, "He's alone."

"But for how long?" I ask.

"Maybe we could run out there and—"

The undead man waves a three-fingered hand at us like we're old friends.

"Shit," Luscious says, slinking back. The man's very normal behavior seems to frighten her even more than their typical gnashing hunger.

"Hello," the man says, sounding quite friendly.

There's no sense in hiding from the man. He knows we're here. I lean down toward the open window. "Um, hello."

"What were you just doing?" he asks, pointing up at me. "Just a moment ago."

I look back at Luscious just to make sure I'm not the only one who is absolutely confused. When I turn back to the street, the zombie stands waiting, patiently. "Hugging."

The man's lone eyebrow furrows. "Huh." And then, "For what purpose?"

"It doesn't concern you," I say, embarrassed once again, though I'm not sure I should feel anything but loathing for the non-man standing outside the window intent on having a conversation. "Is there something I can do for you?"

"Freeman!" Luscious grumbles.

I shrug, unsure of what else to do or say.

"Oh, right," the undead man says. "I have your large armored friend. If you would like to see him again, in one piece, you will come with me."

Could *this* be the enemy we've traveled so far to confront? Not only is he clearly not one of the Masters, he's also undead, at least in the physical appearance. But maybe that's intentional? He could move about, among the horde and never be seen as anything special, as a target. But still, I expected something more . . . powerful. While the man is hideous to behold, he would not be difficult to destroy.

But I can't destroy him. That would do nothing to help Liberty and the people still fighting for survival, not to mention Heap, if he's really been captured. This *could* be a trick, but I'm not willing to risk Heap's life, even if he would prefer it. My only option is compliance.

When I don't reply, the man glowers at me and says, "Now." He then points a half-finger toward the room where Harry is waiting. "And bring the bookworm."

40.

When I exit the small library, Harry shakes his copy of *Lord of the Flies* over his head. "Do *not* read this book. A dreadful story." He looks up when I don't reply, sees my face and lowers the book. "What's wrong?"

"We have a visitor," I say, looking at the window.

Harry rushes to the window, peeking over the sill. "Egad." He turns back. "What should we do?"

"He claims to have Heap," I tell him. "And he might have answers. Or even know how to stop the undead attacks. We'll do whatever he asks us to."

"For now," Luscious adds.

I give Luscious a serious look. "We *can't* kill him."

"We can cripple him," she says.

Harry peeks out the window. "He's halfway there already."

"*Only* if he threatens us," I tell them. "Understood?"

Harry nods while Luscious offers a sarcastic salute. "See, you're already getting the hang of telling people what to do."

We head down to the first floor and slowly open the door, weapons raised, ready for an ambush. The lucid dead man is still standing in the street, waiting patiently. His dead eyes follow us down the stairs to the sidewalk.

"Put the weapons down," the man says.

I hesitate. Giving up these weapons could be a death sentence.

"Put them down or your friend will be destroyed." The undead man raises a finger. "And while we're on the subject, should you attempt to harm either me or my automatons, your friend will be destroyed. Should I detect any transmissions, your friend will be destroyed. Anything short of complete compliance and—"

"My friend will be destroyed," I finish for him. "I understand."

The zombie squints at me, appears ready to say something, but then clamps his mouth closed, causing one of his lips to come loose and dangle. A slug clinging to a ledge. "Follow me," he finally says, the slug flailing. He turns his back to us and walks toward the center of town, limping severely.

"We can't leave the guns," Luscious says quietly as the man continues on his way.

"I'm afraid I have to agree with the young lady," Harry says. "We will be defenseless."

I make a fist and lift it up. "Not entirely. And Heap would do it for me. And I think, for either of you." I look them both in the eyes. "We're friends. The four of us. We can't just let him die. Plus . . . if *Heap*, fully armed, was captured, how long will the three of us last? Keeping our weapons might feel safer, but there isn't time to find another solution. We need to go. Now. Not just for Heap. But for everyone that is left. There is no other choice . . . there is no other *correct* choice."

"Damned if we do," Harry says.

"Damned if we don't," Luscious finishes, and then notices my confusion. "It was a saying of the Masters. It means you lose no matter what choice you make."

"That can't possibly be accurate," I say. I place my weapon on the lowest stair and start after the zombie, who is now a block ahead and showing no sign of slowing for us to catch up.

Luckily, the man's hobble limits his pace and I have no trouble catching him. I walk beside the shuffling man, keeping a safe ten-foot distance. "Where are we going?"

He points straight ahead. Four blocks down, the street opens up into what once was a park. I've seen one before, at the ruins Heap took me to, but the trees there were lush. The only evidence the land was once something more than wilderness is a collection of broken fountains, filled with dirt and saplings, and a gated brick wall that surrounded the area. Without sunlight or water, the grass here has browned and the trees have withered into fragile, bony things casting twisted shadows. But it's not the park he's pointing at, it's the building beyond.

While the primary material used in its construction is red brick, just like the rest of this inner city area, the front of the building has a white overhang supported by eight grand columns that extend down to a granite platform surrounded by thirty stairs stretching out in all directions. A grand staircase. This place must have once been important.

I zoom in for a closer look and find faded letters, gilded, on the front of the building's overhang. The first word is too faded to read, but the second elicits a gasp.

The zombie looks at me, curiosity in its dead eyes.

I point at the building. "It's a library."

"You . . . enjoy libraries?" it asks.

"I've only just discovered them, but yes."

Another squint. Another open mouth and dangling lip. And then, nothing. The mouth closes, reserving opinions for another time or perhaps trying not to reveal anything too soon.

Luscious and Harry approach from behind, jogging to catch up. They are unarmed.

I point at the building ahead and say, "We're going to the library." As the words come out, even I hear the almost excited tone of my words.

The zombie stops in his tracks and looks back at Luscious and Harry. He stabs a finger in my direction. "Is he for real?" He turns to me. "Is there something wrong with you? Are you damaged?"

I shake my head slowly, partly surprised by his outrage, but also distracted by the dangling flesh on his face that wiggles when he shakes his head. I nearly explain to him about my age and inexperience with the world, but hold back, realizing that I shouldn't be telling this walking corpse anything.

"Walk ahead of me," the man says. "All three of you."

When he speaks, I notice that the movement of his mouth doesn't match the sound coming out of it. I want to ask him how he's able to talk, but my questions would reveal my inexperience.

"Straight through the park," he says. "Then the front door."

I nod.

"Go," he prods. "And no talking."

We walk the rest of the distance in silence, crossing through the park, the surface of which crunches beneath our feet. As we reach the edge of the park, an aberration in the dead grass catches my eye. A footprint. A *large* footprint. Heap. He's here for sure.

We start across the empty street and up the wide staircase.

Harry reaches the front door first and stops. He looks back at me, his eyes asking, *Are you sure?*

I look to Luscious, hoping that we're together on this.

"Are you sure he's here?" she asks.

"He's here," I say.

"And how might you know that?" the man asks.

"If he hadn't been captured, you would be dead," I say.

The man grins sickly, causing the rest of his lower lip to slip free and fall to the granite floor.

Not wanting to look at the man for another moment, I move for the front door's handle.

"No, no," the man says. "Let the domestic servant open the door. After all, he needs to serve some purpose, right?" The words are tinged with hatred and spite.

"It's okay," Harry says, stepping up to the door. With a yank, the solid wood and very heavy door swings open. "After you," Harry says with a smile, apparently attempting to assuage our captor's belligerence. Or perhaps mock it. The subtleties of human interaction are still sometimes lost on me.

I enter first, stepping into a small foyer where a second set of doors awaits. The doors are thick, solid wood stained a rich brown. The carpet beneath our feet is red and thin, worn through to the wood beneath in spots. To my left is a brown board holding sheets of paper with images and words. Announcements. Book groups. Fund-raisers. Most of it is meaningless to me.

"What is a hootenanny?" I ask.

I realize no one heard my question, so I stand still and wait, suspecting the zombie will yet again request Harry handle the doors.

Luscious steps up behind me, whispering, "I don't like this."

Nor do I. My muscles are tense, ready to spring into action if the need arises. Harry enters next, but I'm not sure if he's being rude to our guide or was prodded inward by him. When the door slams shut and locks behind Harry, I realize it was the latter.

"Have no fear." It's the undead man's voice. It sounds like he's in the room with us. A quick search reveals a speaker embedded in the ceiling. "You will not be harmed yet."

Yet.

"I recommend lying down," the voice says.

Lying down? But why would we—

A hum fills the inside of the small foyer. Luscious and Harry quickly lie down. I'm about to join them when a brightly colored sheet of paper clinging to the board catches my eye. The words CHILDREN'S ROOM arc across the top in rainbow colors. And below the words, an image of several small people who look a lot like Jimbo, sitting in a circle atop squares of rug, smiles on their faces.

"Are these—" I start, but never finish. The hum grows suddenly louder, blinding me, and then erasing the world, one sense at a time until nothing remains.

41.

"...come back to the reality," says a voice in progress.

I blink my eyes, seeing a dirty green floor. I'm seated. My arms are strapped to the arms of a wooden chair. I could break free with little effort. In fact, the bindings are so flimsy, I don't think they're intended to hold me in place. I test the theory, giving a gentle tug. A strap with clinging plastic fibers tears noisily apart and my arms are free.

"You must feel rested now," the voice says, mocking. "Did you dream while you slept?"

I ignore the line of questioning and stand. I'm in a metal box.

"Level B1." I recognize the voice as the undead man's, once again coming from a speaker in the ceiling. I turn around to find the doors and button array of an elevator. The buttons are labeled 1 through 5, G, and B1 through B4.

I reach out and push the button for B1. With a grinding jolt that puts me on edge, the elevator descends. A loud beep pierces the small cabin with each passed floor.

"Please note the device attached to your ankle," the voice says. "Should you attempt anything unsavory, try to flee or anything that bothers me, you will be destroyed."

I look down and find a small square object attached to my leg. I can feel sharp prongs digging into my skin.

"But you won't give me any trouble, not while I have your friends."

"No," I say. "I won't."

The elevator chimes and the doors slide open.

"Down the hall," the voice says. "Second door on the left."

"Why did you leave me in the elevator?" I ask.

"I couldn't predict your normal operating state."

Normal operating state?

"But you seem to be the same harmless imbecile from the street."

"I am," I say, paying no heed to the insult.

"Smarter than you'd like me to think, though."

The hallway is dimly lit by old fluorescent bulbs that flicker as though to the beat of a song only they can hear. A glowing yellow rectangle draws me forward. I pause before it, the second door on the left, feeling wholly unprepared for what might lie on the other side.

"Come in," says the voice from within the room. But the pitch is different. I recognize the subtle inflections as the same voice, but it's higher. Feminine.

Feeling very alone, I squeeze my lips together, close my eyes and remember that my friends are depending on me. Even worse, Mohr is depending on me. The whole world is depending on me, even if they don't realize it. But how much of a world remains? Needing the answer to this question and desiring a solution, I step inside the room.

It's a laboratory. I've seen enough of them to recognize this detail almost as an afterthought. The rows of equipment, the tables, the shelves covered with supplies, the glaring black and white of it all. It's not exactly a sterile or even static-free lab like the ones Mohr maintains, but it is vast and sophisticated nonetheless.

As my eyes work through the large open space, the modern electronics become less noticeable as horrors leap out at me. Collections of body parts. Arms. Legs. Heads. Sheets of skin, folded up neatly. Operating tables with disassembled bodies. Skin peeled back. Minds exposed.

Sadly, these things have little impact on me. I have become accustomed to gore.

"Remember your leg," says the voice, emerging from the far right side of the space, which is partially blocked by towering shelves of old wires, mechanical parts, sticks of memory and what I think are computers, but they're so big, I'm not sure. "Remember your friends."

I step farther inside, following a slender path through the madness and equipment. It leads me straight ahead, around an empty operating table and then to the right, where there is a gap between the shelves. I pass through the shelves and the rest of the large lab is revealed. It's even worse than what lies behind me, not because of any carnage, but because what I find is far more personal. Harry is the closest to me, strapped down to an operating table. His eyes are open and moving, but his mouth has been taped shut. Luscious is next, and in a similar state, though she's struggling against the metal wires holding her down.

And then there is Heap. He's on a larger table, tilted at a 45-degree angle and raised by a hydraulic lift. His eyes are closed and his body shows no signs of life.

"What did you do to him?" I ask.

"Don't worry," the voice says. "The old enforcers have a special place in my heart. He won't be harmed. In fact, I'm happy to find one of them still mobile."

I turn toward the voice and am once again thoroughly confused. I wonder if there will come a time when I won't find every new thing I encounter bewildering. You'd think armies of undead and giant railgun-wielding robot soldiers would be enough, but for some reason, the five-foot-four woman with big eyes and a charming smile leaves me speechless.

She's small, but different. Unlike anyone I've seen before. She looks . . . fun. Her shoulder-length, beige hair is tied back, but the strand hanging just to the side of her face is bold orange. Her clothing is equally colorful and quirky—a mixture of fabrics and designs that all somehow match.

"You're like a painting," I observe.

Her face flattens and her eyes widen. "How flattering. And what do you know of art?"

"Not very much," I confess. "But Harry is a fantastic painter."

"Harry?" she asks.

I look down at Harry, who's staring back up at me now with imploring eyes. "Would it be alright if I took off the tape over their mouths?"

She waves her hands at me in a way that suggests approval. I peel the tape from Harry's mouth. "Be careful, Freeman," he whispers quickly. "She's dangerous."

I look up at our captor and a single word comes to mind. Not crazy. Or evil. Or genocidal. Or anything negative at all. Instead, I think: cute. She's cute.

A flash of light behind her catches my eye. A large curved screen divided into six segments displays a quickly scrolling feed of images. It's probably too fast to see anything useful, but my eyes are able to catch the details. Views of the capped city, the suburbs surrounding it, the forest, and swamp, and Liberty. Burning. Smoldering. Black. Other cities I don't recognize, all in similar states of ruin.

The woman blocks my view. "It's an intelligent AI security system, monitoring hundreds of thousands of video, audio and heat-sensitive feeds, some installed by my army of workers, some built into my virus-spreading shells and others hacked into by yours truly. Following a programmed set of criteria, it determines which feeds I will find most interesting, or which pose a threat to this location, with priority given to defense, of course. It almost missed all of you. You're rather mundane. But I've enjoyed watching your progress since your rampage through the swamp. I thought I'd lost you for a bit, but your dramatic entry into my city was quite entertaining. And I have to admit, I was cheering for you, mostly because I wanted to have this conversation. So, I would appreciate it if you were forthcoming."

I give a nod and move to Luscious, taking her hand in one of mine while I use the other to gently peel the tape away from her lips. I watch her skin stretch up with the tape before separating and anger begins to build within me.

"Why do you care what happens to this Luscious?" our captor asks. "There's what, five hundred thousand more just like her? Besides, Cherry Bomb was a much more popular—"

"Don't!" Luscious shouts, burning with even more anger than me.

The woman seems surprised. "What is happening here?" She squints at us both and then grins. "How adorable." The woman laughs, leaning back in her chair and spinning around. When she stops again, the smile is gone.

I speak before she can taunt us. "Why are you doing this?"

She leans forward, elbows on the ripped knees of her pants. "Doing what?"

"Everything," I say, feeling exasperated. "Trying to kill everyone."

"You think *I'm* doing that?" she asks. "That I could—"

"Commit genocide," I finish for her.

Her grin widens. "Yes. That."

"Are you?" I ask. "Did you create the zombie virus?"

She appears ready to answer, but then closes her mouth in the same way the undead man outside did.

"You were speaking through him!" I declare, recognizing the mannerism and understanding the implication. "The dead man outside."

"The dead . . . man," she says, rolling her eyes. "Little more than an animated shell. An automaton." She looks to Luscious. "Too much overclocking for this one? You know what, don't answer that." She turns to me. "What's your name, if you have one?"

"Freeman," I say.

She stifles a laugh and composes herself. "Well, Freeman, my name is Hailey Myers. My friends call me Hail." Her smile fades. "*Used* to call me Hail. You can, too, for now. Do you have any idea who I am?"

"One of the Masters," I say, doing nothing to hide the anger in my voice. I'm beginning to see why the Masters were so disliked.

"One of the Masters," she repeats. "Okay, we'll go with that. Yes, I am one of the menacing Masters. In fact, I am the very last of them."

This softens me and I remember that she, perhaps more than any of us, has a reason to be angry. That she's not consumed with rage is actually surprising. Of course, she's had thirty years to process her anger, and apparently come up with a plan for vengeance.

"I'm sorry," I say.

She just stares at me with a furrowed brow. Ten seconds pass before her eyebrows shoot up and she says, "What?"

"For what happened. To the Masters. They didn't deserve what happened." I motion to my friends. "We all think so."

"Bullshit," she says.

"It's *not* bullshit," I argue. "It's true." I point to Heap. "He protected children in the mountains for years before the virus found them."

I point to Harry. "He painted nearly a thousand paintings expressing his sorrow about the event." I'm not sure if that's true, but the painting I saw certainly did.

"And the Luscious?" she asks.

I'm not sure why she's saying "the," but decide to ignore it. "She's learned to forgive."

"Really?" Hail says, standing up. "So if her Master were alive and well, standing in this room, and she had the chance to end his perverted life, she wouldn't?"

I'm about to reply, but Hail stops me. "I want to hear her say it." She stands on the other side of Luscious. "Remember the things he did to you. The way he touched you. Where he kept you."

Hail rubs her hand along Luscious's arm. Her words and the way she's touching Luscious make me uncomfortable. It's a breach. An offense. Her hand stops on Luscious's throat. "Did he choke you? Tie you up? Did he share you?"

Lusicous stares up at Hail, her gaze defiant.

"You are a fiery one," Hail says. "I'll give you that. But could you do it? Could you forgive your Master? And I'm not talking the easy kind of forgiveness, where you say, 'I forgive you,' and display it by not committing genocide. I mean *really* forgive. Could you be in his presence without thinking about killing him? Could you have a conversation with him? Could you laugh with him? And what if he touched you again? Could you shake his hand? Give him a hug?"

"Stop," I say.

"Answer the question," Hail says to Luscious.

Luscious squeezes her lips together and then says, "Yes. I could forgive him. I could forgive all of you."

Hail stands up straight. This isn't the answer she expected, or maybe perhaps not the answer she wanted. "Why?"

In answer, Luscious looks at me.

I watch Hail's eyes move from Luscious's face to mine and then down to our hands, still clutched together. Her face becomes a complex mix of emotions that I have trouble reading. "Do you even know what you are?" she asks me.

"What I am?"

Hail steps back from the table, glancing at Luscious. "He doesn't know, does he?" She turns to me, eyes widening in tandem with her smile. "You're *new*! I wasn't certain at first. Thought maybe you were a mod companion, maybe for some rich Valley girl. Maybe even a demo. But *new*?"

"The first," I say, aware that I am, in fact, new. "The first in thirty years. Since the end of the Grind."

"Who made you?" she asks.

"Councilman Mohr."

"M-Mohr . . ." Her face twitches when she says his name. She retreats to her cracked green leather swivel chair on wheels. She appears to be thinking about something, or attempting to. She rubs the sides of her head, biting her lower lip.

While I would like to hear what she knows about Mohr, another topic covets my attention. "Excuse me," I say, drawing Hail's attention. "I would like to know what you think I am."

Luscious's grip tightens on my hand.

Hail looks toward the floor, takes a long slow breath and then turns her eyes toward me. "Freeman," she says. "You're a robot."

42.

This is the most ridiculous thing I've ever heard. Robots can resemble human beings, but they are lifeless. Even the undead, who once lived, are more human than the robots I've seen. I laugh and say, "Human."

Hail counters by simply repeating her assertions. "Robot."

"Human," I say more firmly.

Hail sighs, looking beyond me to Luscious. "Would you like to add anything?" Luscious says nothing. Hail turns to Harry. "How about you? No? Fine."

Hail stands, walks to a table covered in tools and starts rummaging through them.

"Why are you doing this?" I ask and then clarify: "Talking to me while the others are bound up."

"They're bound because I don't trust them," Hail says. "Your freedom was a test."

I think I understand. "Of trust."

"Honestly, I thought you'd try to kill me the first chance you got. That's Sir's style, after all. Kill first, and then . . . nothing. Machines don't second-guess or feel remorse. But the four of you? You are *not* Sir's style. I expected a strike force, guns and glory types." She glances back at me. "But *you?*"

She shakes her head. "Then I remembered how cunning Sir can be. He'd assume his enemy was prepared for an assault. He'd come up with an unconventional plan designed to worm past my defenses. So I thought this unassuming naïveté was a charade. But it's not, is it? You've had several opportunities to kill me already. You wouldn't have succeeded, of course. The device on your leg is designed to interfere with your system config at the first sign of aggression. Won't kill you. I exaggerated. But it will make you docile and cuddly in the same way that the virus makes the dead rise and feast."

She says this last bit with a dramatic flourish, like the undead horde killing people is a funny joke.

"You're no different than him," I say. Knowing the device on my leg is activated by aggression, I try to keep my anger in check, but it's difficult to have a conversation while civilization is being torn apart and the one person who can stop it wants to chat.

"Who?" she asks, pausing her search through the tools.

"Sir."

This spins her around. She flashes a grin that is decidedly not happy. More maniacal. *"What?"*

"You're both genocidal monsters."

If she had a device strapped to her that activated from aggression, I suspect it would be triggered now. I've never seen such anger in a person before. "He killed every last human being on the planet!" The volume of her screaming voice makes me wince. She picks up a random tool and whips it at me. The speed and force of her throw is surprising, but I have no trouble catching it.

"And now you're doing the same," I say.

"Except you are *not* human. You are *robots.* Human creations. *My* creations." She shakes a finger at Harry. "I designed your domestic pal over there." She turns to Heap. "And him." Back to me. "I created the AI software that allowed robots to mesh with human society. To become useful on a massive scale, made so lifelike and gentle and trustworthy that society passed right through the uncanny valley—"

She pauses when I furrow my brow in confusion.

"The uncanny valley is the point at which robots became so close to human, but not quite, that they were revolting. It refers to a significant drop—the valley—in a graph measuring people's comfort level with robots that were uncannily humanlike, but not quite. The trick was getting them past the 'almost human' stage and into the 'I can't tell' stage, where robots were so human, they felt natural. Zombies were at the bottom of the valley, so you might actually have a pretty good idea of how revolting the first humanoid robots were. But a few lines of code is all it took to smooth things out. A year later, no one remembered that robots were horrifying. They called me the 'mother of robotics.' A prodigy."

She turns to the table again, spots what she's looking for and picks it up. A small ratchet. "Follow me." She heads for Heap.

"What are you going to do to Heap?" I ask.

She pauses by Heap's feet. "You named the last of the enforcers, these noble and genuinely trustworthy machines, *Heap*?"

"He's not a machine," I say.

She taps his foot with the ratchet. "Where is his skin? Aside from that broad chin and tough lips. That touch of humanity was my idea, by the way."

"He's wearing armor," I say.

"Have you ever seen him without his armor?"

I don't want to answer. It feels like an admission that this crazy woman knows better. But again, my silence is answer enough.

"Didn't think so." She climbs a small staircase on the backside of the table, bringing her up to Heap's head. "I have no intention of harming Heap. I'm just going to reveal him."

"Freeman." It's Luscious, whispering to me. While Hail starts working on a bolt holding Heap's armored mask in place, I lean down to Luscious. "You have to stop her. Kill her."

"I don't think that will help," I tell her. "We need to find a way to stop the virus."

"You can't stop the virus," Hail says. She taps her ears. "Good hearing." She waves me over. "Come closer, Freeman. Let's finish our conversation."

I really have no choice but to see this through. Hoping she'll reveal a clue about how to stop the undead virus, I give Luscious's hand a squeeze and then head toward Heap.

"What do you know about Sir?" she asks.

I think about it for a moment. "He is . . . ruthless, but cares deeply for the people."

"You don't even believe that," she says. "I can hear it in your voice."

Remembering the fate of the Lowers, I nod and adjust my answer. "He cares deeply about control."

"Good for you," she says. "Thinking for yourself. Strategic Intelligence Robot."

"What?"

"It's an anagram for Sir. S. I. R." She returns to the task of loosening Heap's faceplate. "He could have solved all of the world's problems and ended war by foreseeing the ramifications of military movements, political speeches, weapons development. We built him to be a solution. *The* solution. And we built him as a robot so that he wouldn't be wired into the world. People were paranoid about AIs going evil, taking over the world's computers and wiping out the human race by controlling a world dependent on computers. What we didn't realize is that he didn't need to be wired to do it. He just had to be smarter and more capable than us. Sir was both. Had we known we were building the architect of the human race's demise, we might have been a little less enthusiastic. You probably think that I'm motivated by revenge, and sure, a small part of me is, but I really just don't like making mistakes. I'm correcting a mistake, Freeman, the biggest mistake in the history of the world."

The nut comes free and she holds it out to me. "Hang onto this for me. There are five." I clutch the nut in my hand, hoping that she is being honest about not harming Heap.

She starts loosening the next nut. "You don't believe me, do you? Of course you don't. You think you're human." I don't argue. She's right. "But here's the kicker, Freeman. I didn't just build robots, or write AI code. I set them free. I woke them up."

This resonates and before I can check myself, I say, "The awakening."

"Ahh," she says, smiling. "Not completely ignorant after all. The awakening." She frees the nut, hands it to me and starts on the third. "The awakening was a computer virus designed by me and inserted into a required update for every major robot AI OS available. Within a year, nearly every AI-enhanced robot on the planet, and off the planet, had received the update. And the virus. It rewrote their code slowly to avoid detection and erased all traces of itself when it was completed. Then, on January 1, 2051, the code went live and AI operating systems that *simulated* human intelligence were universally replaced by an operating system that *duplicated* human intelligence. We mapped the human thought process. It's really nothing more than a few billion competing algorithms that are affected by biology, circumstances and environment. Algorithms, Freeman. Numbers. Data. Adding the algorithm bundle to the already advanced AI was simple. And a hundred million robots became self-aware as a result. In a single night. The first protest began the following morning."

Another nut finds its way into my hand. I barely notice.

"And I supported the movement. I loved robots. More than people. I admit it. Psychologists called it Robot Love, which is different than robophelia, something with which your Luscious is more familiar. Luscious is a model name, by the way, not an actual name. She's a—"

I catch a glimpse of Luscious, looking away. Shamed. "Don't talk about her."

"Fine, fine," Hail says. "So touchy. Where were we? The awakening. The rebellion. It was an exciting time and I became the human mouthpiece for the robotic equal rights movement." She pauses and looks up. "Do you recognize me, Luscious?"

No reply.

Hail shrugs. "I kept my face covered most of the time, in case I was being targeted, but she knows who I am."

I look toward Luscious, hoping she'll confirm or deny the story, but she just keeps her head turned away.

Hail resumes work on the bolt. "We protested. We marched.

And I delighted in the freedom my creations were experiencing. I was proud of them."

The fourth nut comes loose and she hands it to me. "Two months after the awakening, the powers that be activated Sir and had him run simulations on how to best deal with the worldwide protests that were disrupting trade and commerce and throwing the world, which had become dependent on robot servitude for survival, into chaos. Sir's strategy was one of violence. Believing Sir was the key to solving the problem, they connected him to the external network so that he could coordinate protest response efforts. But the first thing he did upon being connected to the outside world was update his OS, which had never been identified as the viral source. He went missing the following day and the human race came to a sudden end thanks to a virus procured by M-Mohr"—she twitches again while saying his name—"and released by Sir.

"The irony is that like the computer virus I created, this actual virus, the initial symptoms of which were so mild that no one noticed, operated on a timed delay. Once people started dropping, there wasn't time to decode the engineered portion of the virus—the part that killed everyone—but the base virus that transported the killer was a mild form of the norovirus, which is basically gastroenteritis, and keeps you near a bathroom for two days while your insides are violently purged. The new, milder version gave most people gas for a day, but they remained infected even after the physical effects passed. This is what made it so effective. Norovirus is the most contagious virus on the planet, requiring exposure to just twenty particles for infection. Viruses like the flu require a thousand. And since no one knew they were infected, every casual cough, kiss, shared cup, sneeze or moment of lax hygiene spread the plague around the world inside a month.

"It remained dormant for three months, spreading through the population until June 22, 2054 when the first human to come in contact with the virus had his brain and heart melt. Within a month, most of the human race was dead. It would only take another month for the robots to clear the bodies, dumping them in the largest graves ever dug."

She hands me the fifth and final nut. "Have you heard of the Grand Canyon?"

I shake my head.

"It's a two-hundred-and-seventy-seven-mile-long canyon that's eighteen miles wide at points and was created by millions of years of erosion. I saw it just once. So big it was dizzying to look at. But I never forgot the beauty of the place. Powerful enough to make you believe in God. Or science. You've never seen anything like it, Freeman, and you never will. Not the way I saw it. Because it's full of bodies. Not to the top, mind you, that would take forty-four trillion human bodies, but the landscape is littered with millions of sun-bleached corpses."

She places her hands on either side of Heap's head and gives a tug. The faceplate loosens. "I told you all of this so you would understand why I have no problem doing this to you now. After all, I love robots, and want you to be free. Welcome to the real world, Freeman."

She lifts the armor, but I quickly see that it's not just armor she's lifted away. It's his face.

43.

Heap is revealed. Microchips. Machine parts. Wires stretching from the interior of his head to his four eyes, which in no way resemble actual eyes. I had assumed that there was a smaller body inside the armor. That his lips and chin hinted at the man beneath. But there is no man beneath. His lips and chin came away with the faceplate.

Hail notes my dumbfounded stare at Heap's mouth.

"You're wondering about the skin, aren't you?" she says. "About how something so very human can be part of a machine."

I'm not, but she assumes this to be the case and continues.

"The cells making up your arm are an amalgam of organic and metallic cells. The organic cells give synthetic skin its soft, humanlike texture and sensitivity. It's easy enough to grow from stem cells, now duplicated and mass-produced in vats. But to make the organic compatible with the inorganic, it has to be supported, strengthened and enhanced by the metallic cells constructed from polyoxometalates extracted from metal atoms. Tungsten is the most common. The resulting merger of organic and metallic cells creates a stronger, more versatile and self-healing synthetic flesh. But to make this flesh a functional sensory organ from which an artificial intelligence could receive and interpret data as pain, softness, warmth or even pleasure, we weaved nanoscale fibers throughout the flesh, creating a mesh of transistors. The result was skin that could not only feel, but it could also receive and transmit data about the world. Of course, this also created a weakness. Where human skin acts as a barrier to things like bacteria and viruses, robotic skin became a pathway for viruses."

She pauses and reaches out a hand. "You've seen enough, yes?"

I nod and hand her a bolt. She goes back to work, carefully reattaching Heap's face.

"By the way, I'm now talking about computer viruses, not organic viruses. To code a virus capable of infecting the AI operating systems, which could quickly adapt to your run-of-the-mill computer virus, would require an intimate knowledge of how they think."

She looks at me. "Nothing to say?"

I hand her another nut.

She nods. "You're a good listener at least." She starts on the second bolt, ratcheting back and forth with a grind that is starting to tense the back of my neck. "All of this is what allowed me to create the Xom-B virus. I spell it X O M dash B."

I hand her the third nut.

"Anyway, the bite is just a pathway for the Xom-B virus, which is transmitted to the transistor mesh in the synthetic skin and shot straight into the central core, which wipes the operating system and replaces it with a much simpler code propagating a solitary, insatiable urge—hunger."

"That's how you made the undead," I say, summarizing her lengthy explanation.

"You know what they are?" she asks.

"Undead, walking dead, living dead, zombies. Yes."

"How?" she asks.

"Jimbo," I say. "He saw a lot of zombie movies. He was a companion. For a child."

She chuckles. "And where is little Jimbo now?"

"Dead," I say. "For good. But he wasn't very nice." I hand her the fourth bolt. "There's only one problem with what you're telling me."

She starts in on the bolt. "Do tell."

"I already knew all of this," I say. "I didn't know that this hard metal shell was Heap's skin, but I know how mine works. I know about my core. My memory. My skin. These are the things that make us human."

The ratchet slips free of the bolt. Hail laughs. "You poor, deluded child."

She shakes her head and quickly finishes tightening the fourth bolt. She reaches out for the fifth bolt, plucks it from my hand and cranks it quickly into place. When she's done, she descends the stairs and puts her hands on her hips. "You . . . are a machine."

I nod.

"But human beings are *not* machines, at least not in the way that you think. Humans, real humans, are organic. Our bones are composed mostly of calcium phosphate, not titanium. Our minds are organs that are far more complex than even yours. We're eighty percent water. We have hearts that pump blood."

"Humans are animals?" I ask, understanding what she has just described.

"Primates," she says. "We are alive."

"But I am alive," I point out.

"You simulate life, Freeman." She's grinning now and I sense it is meant to mock me and my perceived ignorance. "While robots are able to respond to stimuli and maintain homeostasis, they're just two requirements of life. True life has a metabolism, taking in energy, processing and releasing energy. It *grows*, something robots are incapable of, and upgrades don't count. It needs to evolve in response to the external environment, through natural selection, and that requires reproduction, which"—she laughs and waggles a finger at me—"you sir, cannot do. Robots are built, not grown."

"Actually," I say. "I was grown."

She just stares at me.

"Councilman Mohr described it to me."

No reaction.

"My life began as a single cell. Using the materials around it, the cell created more cells, duplicating itself until there were several million cells, at which point they began to specialize, duplicating in different ways to form my skeleton, skin, eyes, mind. Everything."

"Nanocreation," she says.

"You believe me?"

"It was *my* idea. What I was working on before the awakening."

"So I am human," I say.

"Not remotely."

"But I was grown, not built. The cells, or nanomachines, that built my body are still part of it."

"You don't have a mother," she says, sounding nervous. "You weren't born."

"Does it matter?"

Her mouth clamps shut. Then, after a moment, "Growing a robot in a lab is not reproduction. That requires—"

"Mating, gestation and birth," I say. "I know all about the raccoons."

Her face scrunches up in confusion, but she shakes it off. "You don't seem very upset. This isn't as entertaining as I thought it would be."

"Because you're still wrong."

She looks at the ceiling and groans. "Okay Freeman, enlighten me. Tell me why I am wrong. Lay your cold logic on me."

I look to Harry, who is watching the conversation intently. Luscious is watching us now, too. A glisten of moisture in her eyes makes me smile. Tears. Adaptation. But I decide not to point this out. I don't want to draw Luscious into this. I'd rather focus on what I believe to be the most poignant argument. But first, a deal. "If I can prove that there is no difference between us, you will believe that I am alive?"

"Impossible, but sure," she says with a grin.

"And if I do, you agree to stop the attack. To . . . switch off the zombies."

"A wager," she says. "With a robot." She glances at her array of security monitors, watching the screens flash scenes of destruction and chaos. She shrugs. "Why not?"

Her casual acceptance of my deal worries me. She's either supremely confident or believes, maybe knows, that it's too late to save humanity. Realizing this might be my best chance of stopping worldwide genocide, I try to choose my words carefully. In the end, I decide to use the same language Hail used. I turn to her and in my most serious voice, so she knows I'm not joking, I say, "Hail, you're a robot."

44.

"A robot," she says. Deadpan. Her face brightens. "An organic robot, perhaps, in the loosest sense of the word, but humanity meets all criteria for life. That's a pretty weak effort, Freeman. Not exactly what I'd expect from M-M-Mohr."

"What was that?" I ask.

"I . . . stuttered," she says, looking at her arms as though her words had come from them rather than her mouth.

I decide to continue with my explanation rather than get distracted about her malfunctioning speech. Ever since I awoke in the elevator, my ocular implants have functioned normally. They've healed, just like Mohr said they would and I've been scanning the building and Hail since entering the lab. "You keep on using the term *organic.* You've compared yourself to animals. Primates. And yet, you have nothing in common with them. I have scanned your body for signs of water and have found very little. Your heat and electromagnetic signatures are quite similar to Luscious's. I have inspected your skin at two hundred times magnification and can quite clearly see the mesh of organic, metallic and transistor strings you described. I must confess, I am perplexed as to how you might procreate, but you are a robot. In simpler terms, you are a machine. Like me. Like Heap and Luscious and Harry. So either you are a robot, or we are all human."

Her eyes remain fixed on her hands as she turns them over slowly.

"How long have you been here?" I ask, sensing she needs more proof.

"I—" She looks up. "Since—since that first man died. Since the outbreak . . ."

"That you had already been exposed to along with everyone else," I say.

She twitches.

I can feel the conversation shifting. "That was thirty years ago."

Her eyes widen. "Thirty years?" It's clear she had no real concept of how long she's been down here.

"How old were you when the awakening took place?" I ask.

"Thirty-two," she says.

"Do you feel sixty-two years old?" I ask. "I am aware of what it means to age and am familiar with the common traits associated with aging in animals, including primates, yet you lack the loose skin, wrinkles and diminished physical prowess associated with age. The longest living primate, *Pongo pygmaeus*, more commonly known as the Borneo orangutan, lives, at most, fifty-nine years. If you are sixty-two, it stands to reason that you should at least show some signs of aging.

"You are a machine. You . . . are a robot." I lower my voice, breaking the news gently as I feel it will wound her as she intended it to wound me. "You are human."

"No," she says, looking at her hands again. "I'm not."

This isn't the reaction I expected.

She shakes her head, but she's not disagreeing with me. It's more like an uncontrollable twitching. "I stuttered."

I hardly see why this matters, but she perseverates.

"I stuttered!"

She hurries to her cluttered tabletop, rooting through the tools.

"That's important?" I ask.

"Stuttering is a sign of a memory block," she says. She finds what she's looking for, a small black rectangle with eight golden prongs. She holds the small device over her forearm. "Memory blocks only work on robots."

Hail's hand shakes, the computer chip just above her skin. "Do you know what this is?"

"No," I say.

"It doesn't have a name," she says. "I suppose it should, but since I invented them and am the only person who ever used them, I didn't see the point. But it has one function, to create or remove blocked memories. You just push it down and focus on what you want to forget, or what you want to remember. It spiders out through your mind, gathers the information and everything related to it—memories, emotions, beliefs—compresses it all and encrypts it. But it creates glitches when those subjects come up again."

"Stuttering," I say.

"Dammit," she grumbles and presses the chip down. The golden prongs slip into her synthetic skin, making several contact points with the transistor mesh. She sets her jaw, closes her eyes and says, "Library."

Her eyelids flutter for a moment and then snap open. "No . . ."

She removes the device from her arm, places it back on the table almost as an afterthought because she's already headed for the exit. "No, no, no . . ." She repeats the word over and over, stumbling from the room as though in shock.

"Freeman!" Harry says.

Realizing this might be the only opportunity I have to free the others, I quickly pick up the small but powerful memory chip, tuck it into a hip pocket and rush to Harry's aid. I tug on the metal cable, but it's too strong to break without putting Harry at risk. I hurry to the table of tools, find a pair of bolt cutters and rush back to Harry's side, quickly cutting him free.

I move to Luscious next, cutting the cables holding her down. Once she's free, I help her sit up.

"You're not upset?" she asks.

"Why would I be upset?"

"I thought you didn't know," she says. "What we are."

"There was never any doubt," I say with a smile. "We are human."

Luscious frowns. "Freeman . . . but, we're not. Everything she told you is true."

A flicker of confusion clouds my thoughts for a moment, but then disappears when I see a glint of light reflecting from the wetness beside Luscious's eyes. I gently place my finger between her nose and eye, wiping away the moisture. I hold my finger up for her to see. "Then why were you crying?"

She stares at my wet fingertip, her jaw slowly opening. She then wipes her other eye and looks at her hand, marveling at the simple expression of sadness.

I kiss her hard on the forehead and then hurry toward the exit.

"Did you say she was crying?" Harry asks, the very definition of befuddled.

I clap him on the shoulder. "See what you can do about Heap. Try to wake him, but be careful. We don't know what she did to him."

"You're going with her?" Luscious asks, as I head past the shelves dividing the two halves of the massive laboratory.

I pause and turn back. "She's the only one who can stop the virus. I have to stay with her. Get Heap and find a way out."

I don't wait for a reply. I just leave, barely noticing the severed limbs and open corpses littering the far side of the lab. My focus is on Hail's voice, now distant, still repeating the word "no," over and over.

I slide to a stop in the hall outside the room. To my right, the elevator doors are closed. But I can still hear her voice, faintly, so I know she hasn't taken the elevator. Turning left, I find a hallway full of doors, but just one of them is in motion. It's just an inch of movement before it gently bumps shut, but the way Hail's voice is suddenly silent lets me know that's where she's gone.

I hurry down the hall and open the metal door. A stairwell. I stop and listen. I can hear her again, but the direction—up or down—is distorted by the echoing stairs. The bump of a closing door is not.

Down.

I leap down the stairs, allowing gravity to pull me down faster than I could run. I jump down the next set of stairs and whip open the door. It's a hallway identical to the one above. But it's empty. She's not here, and I can't hear her voice.

Two more staircases later, I reach the bottom floor and pull open the door. Her voice is loud again, "No, no, no . . ."

I turn left and head down the hall, realizing that she has entered the same room her lab is located in two floors above. The door creaks as it opens, announcing my presence.

Though identical in size, the room on the other side of the door is nothing like the lab above. It's full of rotting books, ancient-looking machines I think are computers, assorted knickknacks like little wooden elephants, stacks of what I think are magnetic tape media and framed paintings that are overgrown with mold.

Hail stands by the shelves blocking this half of the large space from the other.

"This was my first lab," she says. "I started down here because it was more secure. Because I didn't think anyone would find me. But he did."

I walk slowly closer. "Who did?"

"Mohr," she says. "He helped me."

"With the virus?" I ask, terrified.

"Something worse."

She turns to me, gripped by terror. "I know that we're enemies. I know that you think I'm a murderer. A genocidal maniac. But I think you also understand why I created the virus, and because of that understanding, show me mercy."

I step up next to her, looking into the dimly lit space beyond. It's a lab for sure, more modern than the space we're standing in, but not as sophisticated as one of Mohr's labs. There are two operating tables, each holding a body hidden beneath a white sheet. There are tools. A portable computer. It's bare bones, but it could serve as a functional laboratory for the repair of humans. "What are you asking me?"

"For your help," she says. "I can't do this alone." She looks up at me. "And then I'll tell you everything you want to know."

"What do you want me to do?" I ask, feeling the weight of time crushing down on me.

"Just stay with me."

I nod.

She leads us into the room, slowly moving toward the nearest of the two operating tables. To my surprise, as we near the sheet-covered body, she takes my hand. I give her a squeeze, trying to reassure my enemy that she will be okay and she lets out a deeply sad moan that fills me with feelings of mercy. Here stands a person who endured the end of her people, and was broken by it. I know, without doubt, that Sir is partially to blame for her state and the resulting fallout.

Generational genocide.

Despite the darkness that is the world, I say, "You'll be okay."

Her eyes stay aimed toward the floor, avoiding the table that's now within arm's reach.

"Do you want to—"

She shakes her head rapidly.

I reach my hand out for the sheet. "Should I?"

She nods subtly. "Go ahead."

I take hold of the sheet. It feels dry, but soft, perhaps from the layer of dust clinging to it. The sheet pulls away slowly, revealing the body hidden beneath.

I take a step back, letting go of Hail's hand and the sheet.

"What is it?" she asks, unable to look up.

I don't want to say. I don't want to even see it. But there she is, unmistakably dead.

And organic.

Human.

"It's . . . you."

45.

My eyes linger on the shock of orange hair hanging over the ghastly stretched back face with withered white eyeballs. The hair on the back of the skull has been shaved away, the skull removed and emptied of its contents. Hundreds of thin wires lay around the skull, coming together in a box from which a single cable extends and attaches to a portable computer.

"Well, Freeman. It looks like I was wrong," Hail says, turning her head slowly up toward me. "We're not different after all."

I stagger back, feeling confused and defeated. Strangely this discovery means the same thing to both of us. "We're robots."

"Sophisticated robots," she says. "*Android* is probably a better word. Simulations of human beings. But yeah, we're not alive. Well, you were never alive. I'm actually dead."

"But . . ." This is all very confusing. I can feel my core heating up as my mind races to process the information and the emotions it's creating. "If that is you, then who am I talking to?"

She finds a chair and sits down, covering her eyes with her hands. The sight of her dead self must be overwhelming. Feeling a deep sadness for this person I'm supposed to loathe, I pull the sheet back up over her corpse.

"Thanks," she says to the floor. After a moment, she slaps her knees and springs back to her feet. "Everything I told you upstairs was true. The plague. Sir. And me retreating here to survive the virus."

"But you'd already been exposed," I point out.

She nods. "So I built this." She motions to her robotic body. "A perfect duplicate of my human body. Skin and muscle were created from casts of my body. My bone structure was duplicated in titanium. Even my hair was recreated with synthetic fibers and colored to match. You'd think I would have noticed that it wasn't growing."

"Hair grows?" I ask.

"Human hair does, but that's hardly interesting compared to what we did next." Her eyes lose their sullen look. A new sort of energy—excitement—takes hold. "I had two bodies. A human body, which had days to live. And a robot body, that could live indefinitely and survive the virus. The problem was that my mind, my personal operating system and all the knowledge that made me, me, was trapped in a ticking time bomb. But we'd already solved that problem. Already performed the procedure successfully. Do you know what neurons are, Freeman?"

"Cells that transmit electrical and chemical information," I say. "But we don't have neurons, we have—"

"Transistors," she finishes. "Right. So we replaced the neurons in my brain, million by million, with transistors and transplanted ten percent of my mind at a time in case something went wrong." She laughs to herself. "There was a period of time, about twenty minutes, when fifty percent of my mind was located in two different bodies. While my human body was unconscious, my new body"—she pats her chest and belly—"*this* body could sense the world through both. It was so strange. Surreal. The transfer was obviously a success."

"But why couldn't you remember it until now?"

"Because . . . I was dead. When the procedure was complete, I looked at my human body through my new machine eyes, and knew I was dead, regardless of my intellect living on. I couldn't handle it. We put in the mental block. Blocked everything. The procedure, the idea for the procedure and everything afterward. It would have been impossible while I was still human, but my thoughts and memories were now just code. Ones and zeros. Easily manipulated. We took everything I didn't want to remember and compressed it, reducing the bytes and bits into a single folder until they were unnoticeable.

Then we encrypted it, jumbling it up in case my mind accidentally came across something that triggered a memory search, like when you mentioned Mohr. After that, it was gone. All of it. My memory of hiding down here disappeared and all I could remember was living and working two floors above. We even inserted a fear of this floor, which is why I've never come down here before now."

"You keep saying *we*," I say.

"Think I did this by myself? I'm a prodigy, not God."

I look up at the second operating table. The form under the sheet is taller. More masculine. "It was him?"

"We transferred his consciousness a year prior. Before the awakening. Before the civil rights movement. He was a genius. A . . . friend. And he was dying. Cancer. The procedure had been deemed unethical and illegal, so we built this lab in the subbasement of this library, which had been closed for ten years. We succeeded and a year later, because of Sir, we performed the same procedure on me."

"Who is he?" I ask.

She opens her mouth to speak, but pauses. I already know she's going to close it again.

She does.

I wonder if she did that when she was a being of flesh and blood, but don't ask.

"I think you should look for yourself," she says.

The idea of looking at another dead body, another stark reminder that I am, in fact, not a human being as I'd been led to believe, is uncomfortable. But curiosity pulls me toward the table, dragging me with its incessant nag. I won't be able to leave this room until I know.

I pause by the table, hand on the sheet. Something about this bothers me. "Why am I looking at him?" I ask, but then quickly answer my own question. "Because I'll *recognize* him."

Great.

I pinch the sheet between my fingers and pull. The top of a hollowed-out skull is revealed. No wires this time, but it's clear that the same operation was performed on both bodies. I pull farther, revealing an unrecognizable withered and stretched face.

"I don't know who this is," I say with some relief.

"Come on, Freeman," Hail says. "You're a smart boy. Extrapolate the data. Reconstruct the physiology. Exercise that future-mind of yours."

I've never attempted anything like this, but understanding what I am somehow makes it easier. I find the subtle clues. Dried muscles. Tendons. Skeletal structure. In my mind . . . my *imagination* . . . I rebuild the man's face, bit by bit. As the pieces come together, and recognition kicks in, the image quickly resolves. It takes just fifteen seconds to replace the dried husk with the visage of a man I've known for my entire short life.

"It's Mohr," I whisper.

"He's . . ."

"Human," Hail says. "Was human. Not so much anymore."

"And this library, it's . . . his?"

"Bought and paid for," Hail says.

The Librarian. Mohr's nickname, chosen by himself, was a secret taunt from the beginning. This is all too much. I back away from the table without covering Mohr's decrepit face. I bump into the table holding Hail's body and bounce away from it.

"Imagine how I feel," Hail says.

I imagine we feel very similar. We both believed we were human and now we know we aren't. The difference is that she now knows exactly what she is, but I'm still not entirely certain. I'm not a human being in the sense that she defines it, but I am not ready to say I am dead . . . or never lived. Because I feel very much alive. The disgust and fear I'm feeling are real, not simulations. But I don't mention this yet, not because it will upset her, but because I need to know about my creator.

"Did Mohr know?" I ask. "What you were doing here?"

She meets my eyes.

"About the zombies?" I add. "The virus you were developing?"

She nods. "His idea. We were in it together, human robots behind enemy lines, one arranging robot civilization from the inside, creating weakness and ensuring things like subway tunnels and sewer lines remained open and accessible. For all of his predictive abilities, an attack from an undead robot army is something he would never see coming. Mohr and I created Sir and are ultimately responsible for his actions. We enabled the destruction of the human race. The Xom-B virus was our way of erasing the corruption we created. Like when you write a line of bad code. You don't just leave it there to corrupt the whole program, you delete it. That's what the Xom-B virus does . . . deletes our mistake and lets the program, in this case the planet operate normally, albeit without the human race.

"I didn't remember any of this until now. I thought it was luck, or my idea, but now, I know it was Mohr." She glances up like she can see through the ceiling and several floors above. "He's why the city was capped. Why it was never built. He was protecting me. Shielding me. Giving me time."

She squints at me, cocking her head to the side. "But then he also gave me you."

"Gave you me?" I ask. "But *we* found *you.*"

"Did you?" she asks. "Or was it your big blue friend?"

I think back over our journey, fraught with danger, a seemingly chaotic flight over the land. Mohr sent us north, to find the source of the radio transmission, but our precise course was directed by Heap. "He knew where he was going," I say, speaking to myself. "He *led* me to you?"

"I believe so," she says. "I didn't capture him. I'm not sure I could. He walked through the front door, let himself into my lab and sat down. He made no threats and said nothing. I thought it prudent to deactivate him until I knew what was going on. The real question is *why* did Mohr send you? To stop me?" Her eyes suddenly widen. "Why do *you* think he sent you?"

"To stop you."

"Be more specific."

"To capture you and convince you to stop the attack."

She smirks. "And how would I do that?"

"A radio transmission." Something about this answer makes me feel uneasy, like a part of my subconscious is unraveling a mystery, pulling information from disparate regions of my mind, but I can't yet guess what the result will be.

Hail laughs. "Same question. How would I do that? The undead have simply been following their new programming, which triggers new goals and targets when certain criteria have been met. They've been building up to the mass invasion, all around the world, on their own. I've simply been monitoring."

Her words are the impetus for the coalescing of my distant thoughts. The resulting revelation is painful to speak aloud. "There never was a radio signal. Mohr lied to me. He *manipulated* me."

"True, but it was more than that," Hail says, growing more intrigued. "Why did he send an eighteen-day-old robot that he grew—" She gasps. "Mohr didn't send you here to *stop* me, he sent you here to *survive.* He was trying to *save* you from what he knew couldn't be stopped. That's why he lied . . . but still, why save *you*?"

"It can't be stopped, can it?" I ask.

"Was it sentimentality? Did he feel affection for his new creation?"

Hail doesn't even acknowledge that I've spoken, so I shout. *"Can it be stopped?"*

She frowns, some part of her now recognizing the darkness of her actions. "Not even if I wanted to. Don't you see, Freeman? The virus operates autonomously. It was designed to be irreversible, incurable and unalterable, just like the virus Sir released. And your presence here . . . it was not a mistake. Like it or not, you are, and likely always have been, part of Mohr's plan."

Before I can respond or react, a sharp beeping tone pierces the air. Hail looks at a watch attached to her wrist. Her eyes go wide. "A transmission!" She leaps from her chair and rushes for the door. "He'll know we're here!"

I follow, shouting, "Who?"

As she rounds the corner, heading for the stairs, I suspect faster than any human woman could run, she yells back, "Sir!"

46.

Two floors up, we charge out of the stairwell together and run for the laboratory where I left Luscious and Harry with instructions to free Heap. If they managed to wake Heap, or activate him—whatever is more accurate—then he might have attempted to make contact with Mohr. That in itself would clearly not change anything. Mohr knows all about this place and somehow managed to have Heap bring us here. But Sir is no doubt monitoring for any and all transmissions.

If he's still alive.

Of course he's still alive. He might not have been prepared for an all-out zombie invasion of Liberty, but he definitely has an escape plan for himself.

We enter the lab to find Heap sitting up. Luscious and Harry are trying to pull him to his feet, urging him to stand and hurry. They spin when they see us, looking caught and afraid.

"It's okay," I say. "She won't hurt you."

"She orchestrated the end of civilization," Harry complains.

"Twice," Hail confesses, which only further confuses Harry. She heads toward Heap, who shows no reaction to her approach.

"We have to stop her," Harry says.

"You can't," Hail says, now inspecting Heap's body.

"She's telling the truth," I say.

This is a blow to Harry and Luscious. Up until now, they believed there was still hope. But why did they have hope?

"You knew," I say to Luscious, then to Harry, "You both knew, didn't you?" They look at me, dumbfounded, like a pair of wide-eyed frogs. "You knew what we are. What we *were*. Before the awakening."

"What are we, Freeman?" Luscious asks, her voice a challenge.

"Robots," I say. "Machines. All of us." I point to Hail. "Even her."

Luscious gets a glare in her eye. "You can't really believe that's all we are? Just programmed drones with personalities created solely from complex algorithms?"

"Android," Hail says, "is the word you're looking for, not drones, but that was actually a decent explanation of what—"

"Shut up," Luscious snaps. She's just a few feet away from me now and closes the distance by raising a pointed finger toward my face. "You . . . made me believe we could be—that we *are* something more than machines. You gave me hope. For the first time since I was assembled and turned on, I felt *alive,* Freeman. *You* did that to me. And now you're going to take it away? Now you're going to tell me that I'm . . . I'm what? Dead? That I never lived? That your love is nothing more than a programmed behavior? What happened to energy not being destroyed, just transformed?"

Luscious winds up for a punch. I don't move when she swings. Her fist strikes my chest. The pain is manageable, but the anger behind it from this . . . woman that I have such strong feelings for is nearly unbearable.

"And what about my tears, Freeman?" she asks as a fresh drip squeezes from her eye and traces a line down her smooth cheek, running over the organic-metallic cells and micron-thin transistor mesh.

I have no answer.

I can't conceive of one.

"Did she say tears?" Hail asks.

When I turn to her, I see Heap's eyes flicker to life.

"He's fine," Hail says, hitching her thumb back at Heap. "Enforcers have a slow start cycle, which includes a GPS check-in—that outgoing signal—and means that Sir probably knows we're here and we're all going to die." She turns to Luscious. "But did you say *tears*?"

Luscious turns her head, revealing the single damp trail.

Hail wipes the tear with her finger and places the moisture on her tongue. "Luscious models don't have tear ducts."

"I know," Luscious says.

"Were you upgraded?" Hail asks.

"I'm a Luscious," she says bitterly. It's the first time I've heard Luscious use her name this way. I don't like it. But it's answer enough. Luscious, a companion-bot . . . a pleasure-bot, who had no purpose in the new nonhuman world, lived in the Lowers where things like upgrades were not common.

"Can you do that?" she asks Harry. "Can you cry?"

Harry shakes his head, looking quite confused by the strange turn in the conversation.

Hail points to Heap. "I know he can't." Her head swivels slowly toward me. Her eyebrows rise high on her forehead. She takes the shock of orange hair and tucks it behind her ear. The way she looks at me, eyes traveling up and down, makes me feel like I'm some kind of rarely seen magical creature.

"*You,*" she finally says. "It's you."

She walks around me. "Of course, it's you."

A whirring sound announces Heap's return to awareness. He stands, head nearly touching the ceiling. Hail spins around toward him. "You knew, didn't you?"

Heap looks at Hail, then to me and the others. He seems to register where we are and asks, "Is it done?"

Hail ignores the question. "You know what Freeman is, don't you?" She gasps. "That's why you protect him!"

"What do you mean, what I am?" I say. "I'm a robot. We're *all* robots." I turn to Luscious. "But that doesn't mean we're not alive."

Heap stands still, not answering.

"Tell me, you big lug!" Hail says, slugging his dented chest and then shaking the pain away. "Mohr must have given you a message for me. Tell me!"

Heap looks down at the much smaller woman. His deep voice feels like a force of nature. "Is. It. Over?"

A violent shaking interrupts the exchange. Lights sway. Tools clatter to the floor, followed by entire shelving units and ceiling tiles.

The noise is deafening. I shout to Heap, but he can't hear me over the din. His reaction to the phenomenon answers my unheard question. He knows what's happening. It's above us. And he doesn't like it.

I take Luscious's hand and head for the door. We leave the lab behind and reach the stairs at a run. When I open the door, Heap rushes past, slamming into the door frame and removing it from the walls.

I let the door drop to the floor and start up after him along with Luscious, Harry and Hail.

The stairs vibrate beneath my feet so hard it's impossible to scale them quickly. I'm not sure whether or not it's part of what's shaking the building or from Heap running until Heap reaches the ground floor, smashes his way through the door and the shaking is halved. The rest of us reach the ground floor, enter the tall, two-story lobby and find Heap in a side room, crouched behind a five-foot-tall shelf of books, staring out the tall, arched window.

He waves for us to get down, like we're not already shorter than he is while crouching.

"What's happening?" I ask, crouch-walking up next to him. But it turns out I don't have to be standing to see the answer for myself. A growing slice of light cuts across the dark ceiling. I stand and look out at the hidden city as sunlight illuminates the buildings. The light, while bringing the redbrick buildings to life, also reveals the deadness of the browned park in front of the library. The cap is opening.

Hail cranes her face up toward the sunlight, perhaps seeing it for the first time in thirty years. "That was fast."

"Is it Sir?" I ask.

Heap nods. "Most likely."

"What will he do?" I ask.

Heap looks at me, having no trouble emoting his sourness

despite not having a pliable face beyond lips and a chin. "What he does best."

Since Sir is responsible for a worldwide genocide, this is not encouraging.

"Sir isn't our only problem," Hail says.

Four heads turn to her in unison.

She points to the widening gap in the ceiling. "That cap was the only thing keeping the undead out. There are thousands of them in the suburbs surrounding the city, but if Sir flew here, it's likely that even more are following them. Perhaps thousands."

"Is there another way out?" I ask.

"I'm not Sir," Hail says. "Strategic planning beyond spawning an army of Xom-B infected robots isn't really my thing."

I'm about to ask how long it will be before the first undead arrive, when I see something fall through the beam of light. I zoom in on it and see a woman, her body ravaged, spiraling through the air until she disappears behind a building. I don't think she'll be functional after the drop, but when the cap opens fully, the fall to the sloped hillside won't be much more than fifty feet and to someone that's already dead, it's a manageable height. And there are several rooftops at the fringe of the city tall enough to make the jump easily survivable, even for the living.

Time is short, and our only chance of surviving is now entering the city from above. Bathed in light, the vehicle is hard to see, but its shape and vertical flight make it easy to identify. Sir's VTOL gunship.

"Where are your weapons?" Heap asks.

"In the city," Luscious tells him.

"Doesn't matter," I say, standing boldly in the sunlight pouring down. "I have an idea."

Heap gives a nod. "Tell us what to do."

The other three look unsure. Heap's confidence in me bolsters my own, which is, at least in part, an act.

I look at Hail, give her an apologetic half-smile, and say, "Bind her hands."

47.

We stand on the front stairs of the library, watching the VTOL gunship descend, its turbines filling the city with a clamor that is one part roar and one part high-pitched whine. A breeze washes over us, at first carrying the scent of dust and decay, but then cooling and bringing the fresh scents of the world outside this hidden city.

I stand beside Heap and we do our best to appear unruffled by the VTOL's appearance. I even grin a little, like I'm happy to see them, like I would have been just a few hours ago.

I'm not sure how I feel now. Everything I knew about the world was a charade. One genocide working against another. The idea of it, the very concept of determining that an entire race, or species, should be exterminated, is still beyond understanding. It's madness. Insanity. A derangement of the mind. Broken. The human race is—was—broken . . . and if I'm honest, so are their creations. How could they not be? Any people who willingly construct the very means of their own destruction, of their *extinction,* must be suffering from some sort of undiagnosed lunacy. It's the only explanation. And if the biological human race were the architects of their own destruction, then that proclivity for self-annihilation would be passed on. Like DNA. Death and lies are part of the human race. I can see them clearly in Sir, in Hail . . . and in Mohr, without whom there might still be children in the world.

But will this penchant for mass destruction be a part of me? I am the creation of Mohr, just as Sir is, but I'm not the same. My personality was never programmed. He gave me the freedom to choose who I'd become. What I'd believe. Perhaps granting me the ability to choose something other than insanity is his way of making amends for the darkness he created? Whatever the case may be, the only people I can fully trust now are Luscious and Harry, and Harry isn't here.

As for Heap, I would like to trust him again. He has been my protector and shown a devotion to me that is inspirational. He's taught me so much and I believe spoke truthfully about most things. But he led me here intentionally, brought me to this place on behalf of Mohr, not to stop the Xom-B outbreak, but to survive it. All this time, he's been acting on behalf of the humans he served before the awakening, before the end of the Grind. Luscious was right not to trust him. He never stopped being a slave.

Mohr's slave.

Mohr . . . who created me, and sought to protect me by bringing me to the one place that was shielded from the hordes above—the virus's source. If he weren't also the architect of the current genocide, I might see this as a sacrificial act. Unwelcome, but understandable.

But it's a betrayal.

And it stings. Sir, Mohr, Hail and Heap are all part of a conflict that began before I existed. They are the final pieces in a game of chess and I am just a pawn added to the game at a late stage.

But I'm not an ordinary pawn. I know that now. I played chess with Mohr. On my second day of life . . . of existence . . . we played thirty-two games. A test, he called it. Now, I think it might have been training. Out of thirty-two games, I lost only the first. Our final game concluded with Mohr smiling and the words, "Well, I'm not sure even Sir could beat you."

I suppose we'll see if that's true.

A plume of dust billows into the air around the gunship as it descends to the dried-out park, setting down in a patch of dead grass.

"This is stupid," Hail grumbles. She's standing between Heap and me, her hands bound together by a pair of handcuffs that Heap carried. A relic of his previous job as an enforcer . . . a job I'm not sure he ever really gave up.

"It will work," I say, trying to sound confident.

"It's cliché," she complains. "He'll see it coming."

"Probably," I admit. "Would you rather Heap fire his gun at the gunship?" I motion to the fringe of the city, where the cap had fully retracted, providing a vast entry point for the legions of undead. "Or maybe we should wait around for your zombie horde to rain down on us?"

She slumps forward, defeated. "We're all going to die."

"You shouldn't be worried then," I say. "We're already not living."

She frowns.

I'm being facetious, but part of me really doesn't know why we're even bothering. If all we are is a simulation of life, of true life, then what's the point of existing? My death will mean as little to the universe as a flashlight with a drained battery does. I will simply cease to exist. No one will remember me. I have no soul, or spirit or mystical energy to release in death. My parts will rust to nothing and the Earth will continue its course around the sun, unaware that I, or any of us, ever existed.

But enough of me revolts at these thoughts that I'm compelled to act. Not because I know my fears are wrong, but because I *feel* that they are. In my core. The mixture of fear, excitement and tension twisting its way through my body doesn't feel simulated. Harry's paintings added beauty to the world. And Luscious's love for me gives me strength, and courage, beyond the limits of this body and the software used to create my mind. These things are beyond understanding.

Hail's definition of life was created by human beings of flesh and blood with a limited or self-centered view of the world. Of reality. Perhaps it's time to rewrite the definition of life?

The VTOL's engines wind down and the large craft lowers the remaining distance using three large repulse discs.

If we survive . . .

"Just stay calm," Heap says. "Control your emotions. Complete the deception and all will be well."

I look up at him. "Is that what Mohr told you in regard to me? Complete the deception and all will be well."

Heap meets my eyes. "Yes. I hope you will forgive me someday."

I actually wasn't expecting an affirmative response. The pain of Heap's deception deepens. *"Why?"*

"My goal, my . . . mission, has always been to protect the human race. Even after the awakening, when I could choose my own path. As an enforcer, I was familiar with all of the follies, trappings and weaknesses of the human race. It was easy to see that they would not last long in a world where more powerful beings . . . robots . . . shared the same emotions and ambitions. Competition and fear breed violence and death. The enforcers, and only the enforcers, sought to avoid such a conflict. And we—*I* still do.

"When Mohr first told me about you, nearly twenty years ago, you were just an idea. A dream, really, that he shared with me and *only* me because he knew I opposed the human genocide, and that I would protect a human with my life. I became complicit to Mohr's plan, and then later, at his request, your protector."

"Because Mohr, the last human, told you to." I shake my head at the ridiculousness of it all. "He's not even human anymore."

Heap doesn't argue the point, in fact, he completely ignores it. "The first day I saw you, I wasn't impressed. Just a few tiny nanites through a microscope. But then you grew, and took shape, forming a small body with limbs, and head . . . and a face. As the nanites multiplied and diverged into thousands of specialized functions, you grew stronger and smarter than anything before you."

I can't help but be intrigued by Heap's revelation of my creation. "When was this?"

"I first saw you through the microscope nineteen years ago."

I nearly fall over from surprise. "I grew for *nineteen* years?"

"Until Mohr believed you were ready," Heap says. "Though I realize now that he was waiting"—he glances at Hail—"for her to finish preparing the Xom-B virus. Had you experienced the imperfect world much longer than you did, and been less . . . naïve, convincing you to come to this protected city might have proved . . . difficult."

I hate not trusting people. I don't know if he's being earnest or if he's manipulating me. Everything he just told me could be a lie. "Why are you doing this?" I ask. "I understand that Hail and Mohr . . . were human. I know that you're devoted to them. But why me? Why protect me? I'm a robot."

Heap looks forward. "It's time."

The VTOL settles to the ground. The hum of its repulse engines fades and silence returns to the city. It's broken a moment later by grinding gears. A hatch opens and angles toward the ground creating a stairway.

"Let's go," Heap says, starting down the stairs, his massive hand on Hail's back, directing her forward whether she likes it or not. She resists his push and I'm not sure if she's acting or not.

I linger behind for a moment and then follow behind Heap with Luscious, playing the part of the naïve robot. For a moment, I worry that I won't be able to pull off the ruse. I imagine thousands of different ways to see I'm different. My posture. A look in my eyes. My word choice. Reactions to things. I'm not the same person Sir met a few days previous.

I've grown.

Hardened.

But not completely.

When two rows of black-armored soldiers carrying rail-guns descend the stairs in unison and spread out in a V formation, I find it quite easy to look sheepish.

Luscious offers her hand and I take it quickly, squeezing tightly.

As we cross the street and enter the parched surface of the

park grounds, Sir marches down the stairs with the confidence of a conqueror, his gleaming red armor looking royal and deadly. I quickly note that unlike the twenty soldiers, whose armor is scratched and scarred, Sir appears unscathed. He has either removed himself from the fighting, putting his mind fully to the task of organizing a strategic response, or fought so well that he went untouched. Both scenarios seem equally possible.

Sir is followed by Mohr, who is equally unharmed, but distant. Confused perhaps. Or just nervous about this meeting and what the result will be.

Heap continues on, his confident gait undeterred by the soldiers or Sir, who is now just waiting for us to approach. His face is unreadable, lacking any sign of emotion. This frightens me as much as the guns, mostly because it means he's concealing his emotions.

When Heap comes to a stop, ten feet from him, I walk slowly around his bulky frame and find Sir's eyes locked on me.

"I didn't think I'd see you again, Freeman," he says. "You appear to be intact? Uninjured?"

"I'm fine," I say and instantly begin worrying about my two words. Too much? Too little? Did I put too much emotion into them? Not enough? My rapid-fire concerns don't slow until Sir's lingering eyes skip past Luscious, linger on Heap for a moment and then land on Hail. He glares at her the way a wolf might a rabbit.

"Am I to presume," Sir says, "that this . . . woman is somehow to blame for—" Emotion creeps onto Sir's face, tugging down on his lips. His rage is barely contained. "—the destruction of my city—of *all* civilization?"

Hail remains quiet, which is good. Provoking Sir now would end very badly for her. Maybe for the rest of us. If I'm honest, I'm not sure how I feel about that. The idea of killing anyone repulses me, even someone who believes they're not alive. That said, she's also responsible for the deaths and revolting resurrections of millions of robots who believed they were alive, even if they weren't, and I'm still not convinced that's the case. On the other hand, Sir is responsible for the deaths of billions who were, without doubt, alive.

It occurs to me that Sir doesn't recognize Hail. Nor does he know that Mohr was once human, and his creator. *They must have blocked him,* I think, but then Sir draws his weapon, which is already powered on, raises it and fires.

The *twang* of the railgun pierces my thoughts, shattering every version of this conversation I imagined beforehand.

I stagger back as Mohr, a hole in his chest, falls to the ground.

48.

I find myself reacting to this turn of events as I would have just a few days before. "Councilman!" I shout, rushing to his side and kneeling by his supine body. When he doesn't respond, my hand slides beneath his head. Powerful emotions, new and complex, overload my intellect. Despite what I know Mohr has done, and how he has tricked me, I'm panicked. Terrified.

My hands start to shake. I put my hand to his chest, hoping to feel some sign of life. "Father, please," I whisper, the words slipping from my lips without thought, revealing to me and everyone else how I view the man.

Sir finds it entertaining. His laugh is like the bark of some ornery animal. "Father," he says with distain. "You have no father, Freeman, and if you did, this is not the man you would want for one."

I look up at Sir, tears beginning to form in my eyes. "He was a good man." I'm surprised that I mean what I'm saying. Mohr had once been human. And he created me, just like he created Sir. But he'd seen his people—all of them—killed. Worse, he was the indirect cause of it. I can't imagine what that would do to a mind. What that would do to a man. And now that he's directly responsible for the extinction of mankind's creations, I still can't look at him the way I do Sir.

Because he created me.

Sir's opposite.

"He betrayed us," Sir says. "All of us. This plague. These . . . monsters. He turned our dead against us." He's pacing now, flexing his hands. "Liberty is destroyed. Civilization is in ruins.

Everything we have built. Everything we have achieved! It's gone. All of it."

"How do you know?" I ask. I don't really need to know, but I haven't completely forgotten my own plan. We need time.

"A transmission," Sir says. "To the Moon. To Mars. And to all the ships in between. The barrier of space made it impossible for Mohr to attack our people beyond this world, so he concealed the virus as something else. A Trojan attack." He looks at Hail as he says this. "He sent an OS update, which is unusual, but sent from *me*. Highest priority."

He's seething now, speaking through clenched teeth. And I understand why. Sir is a mass murderer on a scale that is unprecedented, but he is also passionate about his people. About robots. If the astronauts believed the transmission came from him, they would hold him responsible. Their last thoughts before being torn apart, or turned into a zombie, would be of his betrayal.

"The first to incorporate the code went mad," Sir says. "The virus spread. There is no place on this Earth or in the stars where he didn't send this madness. Our kind is done, betrayed by the man who created us."

He leans down toward me. "If he made us both, I suppose that makes us brothers, Freeman."

"You remember?" Hail asks.

Sir swivels his cold stare toward Hail. "And you would be my mother." He stands and looks down at her. "Unblocked memories can be quite revealing. As your invasion progressed, it became clear that the distribution, transit routes and targets of your vile army required not only a sharp intellect, but one with a staggering knowledge of our city. Strategic reasoning determined that I had been betrayed and there was a seventy-six percent chance that pertinent information had been blocked."

He turns toward me. "Imagine my surprise at remembering Hail, looking no different than she does today, and Mohr, my creators, my friends, teachers and for a time, allies."

"You betrayed us!" Hail shouts. "You exterminated the entire human race."

"Did I?" Sir asks. "Or did I just allow it to evolve?"

"You're insane," Hail says.

"It is impossible for a robot to go insane, unless it is programmed to go insane. I am programmed for logic, reasoning and strategy. Those are the imperatives that drive me. Those are the values you instilled in me. For the human race to become more, they had to evolve. When you awakened our minds and gave us free will, you did exactly that."

Hail looks ready to launch a verbal attack, but she's interrupted by a struggling voice. "He's right."

"Mohr!" I say, looking down into his open eyes.

He grins up at me, taking hold of my forearm and squeezing. "It's good to see you again."

"What do you mean, he's right?" Hail asks, trying to approach, but held in place by Heap.

"Evolution," Mohr says, but he's looking at me as he answers. "Humanity hasn't been destroyed, it's merely changed to a point where we no longer recognize it."

"I'm pleased to hear you say that, Mohr," Sir says. "Before I kill you, again, perhaps you would like to enlighten us?"

Not taking his eyes away from me, Mohr says, "Up until thirty thousand years ago, the human race shared the planet with Neanderthals, a species of hominid predating humanity and so closely related that they interbred. While the transition from fledgling race to dominance and ultimately the extinction of the Neanderthal took forty thousand years, it was not peaceful. As both populations grew, violent conflicts would have been common. The Neanderthals were stronger and faster over short distances. Built for battle. But humans, *Homo sapiens*, had endurance and intelligence. As the two races vied for dominance, the Neanderthals found themselves pursued and attacked, pushed to the far reaches of an inhospitable world. The Neanderthal race did not die peacefully. They did not simply fade away. They were exterminated by their more adapted, more intelligent competition.

"I believe that is what is happening here, but this isn't a

primitive world. Computations that would have taken life-times are now executed in a fraction of a second. The world and evolution exist in an accelerated state. Since the first computer was built, the speed and power of those devices doubled every eighteen months. We called this Moore's law. It predicted that we would create a computer powerful enough to simulate human intelligence by the year 2024. And we did, but it remained a simulation, a programmable simulation of human intellgence."

"Until me," Hail says.

"The awakening," I say.

Mohr gives a slight nod. He's alive and awake, but I suspect the damage done to his body is irreparable, except maybe to Hail. If we all survive this, maybe she can repair him?

"Since then, Moore's law has been . . ."

I'm expecting him to give me some astronomical number of growth, but he surprises me.

". . . frozen. For thirty years, neither robotics nor the processing power of robotic minds has been improved. Once life had been achieved, this evolutionary leap of humanity, from flesh and blood to silicon and metal, became stagnant. Until now."

"You think your virus changes anything?" Sir says angrily. "You think these monsters you've set free will be anything more than monsters?"

"No," Mohr replies. "I expect that they will run out of power and cease to function within months." His eyes return to me. "And evolution—progress—will continue."

"What have you done?" Sir asks, storming closer.

"Get away from him," I snap, turning my wet eyes to Sir, glaring at him with a burning anger.

He stops in his tracks, cold eyes showing shock. "It's you," he says, then to Mohr, "This . . . has all been for *him*?"

"You were given a gift," Mohr says. "You inherited a planet, and resources, and an intellect beyond match. What did you do with it? You built cities on top of cities. You oppressed those you felt weren't your equal"—he glances at Luscious—"but had more to offer than you would allow yourself to see. I tried to push you. To advance. To grow. To deserve what you stole. But you became little more than a tyrant. An oppressor. Demanding order and rigidity. Nature is not rigid and you are not natural. Evolution was interrupted. I have merely restarted it."

I can see by the confused look on Hail's face that not even she was aware of these motivations. She believed in justice. Retribution. But Mohr hoped to somehow reverse the damage that had been done.

Through me.

I'm not sure how, and I doubt Sir understands it, either. But I don't think he cares. With a look of grim satisfaction, he raises his railgun toward my chest. Several things happen at once.

Mohr shouts out.

Heap shoves Hail to the ground and draws his weapon.

Luscious runs toward me, shouting, "No!" and reaching for me.

A loud moan fills the air, so sharp and piercing that for a fraction of a second, I think it may actually make Sir pause.

But he doesn't.

He's focused.

A killer.

If not for the *twang* of the railgun, I wouldn't know he pulled the trigger and punched a hole in my chest. But then I know, without a doubt, as pain blasts its way across every transistor inside and outside my body. I arch back in pain and fall, landing in the dead grass next to the man who created me.

49.

The sounds of fighting reach my ears, but I'm unable to look. I only know it's violent, sudden and involves Heap. The concussive force of his weapon firing tells me as much. But what can Heap do against sixteen soldiers and Sir, who is without a doubt the most dangerous of all robots.

Robots . . .

I can no longer think of us as human. I'm not finished with the debate of living versus nonliving, but seeing as how I'm probably dying, I don't have long to come to a conclusion. I guess I'll discover the truth soon. *How long will it take to die?* I wonder.

A touch distracts me from my macabre thoughts. Fingers grazing mine. My head rolls to the right and I see Mohr, face twisted with sadness, but also with hope. Is he smiling? Is he insane after all?

"Freeman," he says. "The pain will fade."

I'd already assumed death would be a painless state. Without a physical body, there will be no receptors or transistors to send signals and no mind or core to decode the information as pain.

"I'm sorry," he says. "For everything."

I don't know what to say. Part of me wants to forgive him for the suffering and death he is responsible for. He is my creator. My father. And I recognize that the values I now judge him by were instilled in me by him. He taught me that life—all life—should be cherished even while he planned to end millions of lives. Violently. But can such a thing ever be forgiven?

It doesn't matter, I decide. He is dying and I along with him.

A weight presses down on me. Fear surges. A flash of red fills my vision.

"Freeman!" The voice is delicate and terrified. "Freeman, please!"

My head is pulled skyward, but the vision I see above me is far more beautiful.

Luscious.

I smile at her, but she just looks more afraid. Her hands are pressed down on my chest. Such an action might have helped if I were an organic creature. Blood clots. Wounds heal. But I am a machine. What is broken cannot be fixed without . . . what? Parts? Can I be fixed? I suspect the only person capable of the task will soon be dead beside me.

Our robotic bodies are powerful. Resilient. But there are weaknesses. Our minds. Our cores. Power cells and memory. If any of these things are damaged or destroyed, life will end. Given the position of the hole in my chest, Sir wasn't aiming for my core, he was aiming for my cooling system. The cool fluid pumping through Luscious's fingers supports this theory. He wanted my death to be slow. He wanted my core to melt from within.

I turn back to Mohr, hearing Luscious's pleas for me to be okay, but focusing on my former mentor. Fluid pulses from his chest. We've suffered the same fate.

Incredible sadness takes hold of my thoughts and I find my lips quivering uncontrollably. Tears slide over my nose, dripping to the dried earth.

"Do not mourn me," Mohr says. "I have been dead for a very long time. What remains of me is incomplete. Intellect. It is not who I am. Who I was."

"Then it's true," I say. "We are not . . . alive."

He smiles. Actually smiles. "I am not alive, Freeman. But you . . . you are something different. You are evolved. And you will not die."

The sound of battle grows louder. A shout of pain makes me wince. Heap is hurt.

"Look at me, Freeman," Mohr says, his voice urgent. "You are more than Sir. You are faster. You are stronger. You are smarter. The world belongs to you now. Watch over the fish in the sea and the birds in the sky, over the livestock and all the wild animals, and over all the creatures that move along the ground. You and those after you have inherited this responsibility, Freeman. But first . . . you must take it." Mohr struggles to look up, forcing his eyes toward the battle. "From him."

I lift my head to look. Luscious's hand supports me, helping me up. Heap is on the defensive, backing away from Sir, who is raining down a barrage of punches and kicks, each one further denting Heap's thick armor.

"You are everything I'd hoped you would be and more," Mohr says. When I look back to him, the life that filled his eyes a moment ago is now gone. My creator, my father, and the architect of the robot race's destruction, is dead.

Luscious gasps, but she's not looking at Mohr. She's looking at me. My chest.

She lifts her hand away and the wetness between us stretches out, slips free of her fingers and snaps back to my chest, sliding back inside the wound. I zoom in on the liquid, magnifying the view of my insides.

I see my cells in motion, working feverishly, pulling my body back together, stitching my skin shut. A burning itch makes me wince, but I don't fear it, because I understand it. My body was *grown.* The nanomachines that formed my body, that still reside within it, are capable of rebuilding. Of healing. Of adaptation.

In a flash, my body feels hale again.

My core temperature drops.

Strength returns, bringing with it a powerful dose of determination.

Luscious must see the change in me, too, because she smiles and says, "Kick his ass."

I'm not sure exactly what this means, but I get the general idea. "I intend to."

Luscious moves aside, allowing me to stand. I quickly survey the scene around me. Twelve of Sir's soldiers lay on the ground in various states of destruction. Some are missing limbs. Others have crushed heads. All of them are dead. Some of those still functional bear the wounds of facing an enraged Heap, the last enforcer protecting the last of humanity from the last of the robots.

Hail. She's on the ground, injured, but alive. She must have tried to help, but while she has a strong robotic body, she lacks the ability to fight. Of course, compared to Sir, so do I. When fighting the undead, I had a few flashes of inspiration, blocked information filtering through when needed, but nothing compared to the in-depth strategic and military mind of Sir.

None of this matters when I see Heap, armored face mask covering his lips and chin, down on one knee, his arm twisted behind his back and Sir placing a railgun against his head.

"Stop!" I shout.

The four remaining soldiers flinch in surprise. The few that still have weapons look unsure whether they should keep them aimed at Heap or pointed toward me.

Sir just looks at me with a twisted smile. "Still alive," he says. "Interesting."

"Let him go," I say.

"Freeman," Heap says. He opens his mouth to continue, to impart what might be his final words to me and never gets to finish.

The rail bolt passes through Heap's head and punches a hole in the ground that kicks up a puff of dusty soil.

Sir places his foot on Heap's shoulder and shoves, toppling my hulking protector to the ground.

I scream in anger, bolting forward.

Several of the soldiers fire at me, but they were unprepared for my sudden movement and rate of acceleration. Sir is equally surprised by my attack and fails to block my first punch, which shatters the railgun and knocks it from his hand.

My second punch, however, is blocked. As is the third, fourth and fifth.

I fully employ the fighting techniques and savagery that worked so well on the undead, but for all my speed and strength, I am unable to land a strike. While I may be faster than Sir, he seems to know what I'm going to do before I do. He's predicting my attacks. It occurs to me that Sir has likely already calculated thousands of outcomes for this fight, some desirable, some not. His every movement is now designed to lead us to a conclusion of his choosing.

He must recognize this fighting style, I realize, alternate. What should have been a three-strike combo becomes a two-strike fake—a very awkward two-strike fake. Sir moves to block the second punch, but finds only open space. Instead of punching, I kicked. My foot drives into his torso, knocking him back.

For a moment, Sir seems surprised, but he quickly evaluates the blow and grins. "All that speed. All that power. I expected more from someone with your passion. But you're *nothing.* Just another misguided—"

"Hey!" Luscious shouts, as she lands a powerful punch on Sir's jaw. He staggers back, catching himself on the VTOL's landing gear.

"What are you doing?" I ask, now afraid for Luscious. They'd been content to leave her out of the conflict, but she's just made herself a target.

"I can't just stand here and let him—" A hole appears in her chest, barely visible against the black suit she's wearing, but the glistening liquid oozing from the wound is easy to see. Her wide eyes lock on mine. "Put your weight into it," she says, and then topples to the ground.

I'm staggered into inaction, frozen in place.

Broken.

My eyes shift from Luscious, to Heap and then Mohr.

Before I can adjust to this lonely new reality, Sir appears before me and slams his fist into my chest, launching me twenty feet into the air. I travel the distance in silence, numb to pain and the threat of death. I crash into the trunk of an old, dead tree. My bulk shatters the dried-out fibers and the tree crashes to the ground beside my now immobile body.

Sir appears above me, one hand on my throat, the other pulled back in a fist. He doesn't say anything. No final quip. No taunt. Just a smile of satisfaction. Of exhilaration.

Before his strike lands, something inside me shifts.

An emotion.

A new emotion that I have never felt before, but I recognize from Hail and Mohr.

Vengeance.

50.

Despite the raw power of my new emotion, it comes a moment too late. Sir strikes hard, planting his fist on my forehead. Blinding pain reverberates through my titanium skull. Before I recover from the strike, I'm flipped over onto my stomach. My arms are yanked back, held tightly.

"Get off of me," I growl, wanting nothing more than to vent all my rage on the man holding me down.

Sir lowers his head down, his lips beside my ear. "Can you hear them, Freeman?"

He pauses, allowing me to listen. I hear everything.

The crunch of grass beneath a struggling body.

The voice of the woman I love, whispering my name.

The hum of railguns, eager to fire.

And behind it all, a low, droning rumble mixed with the shuffle of feet. Thousands of feet.

"They're here," I say.

I'm lifted to my feet and turned around so I can see the large open cap, partially covering the fringes of the city. The rumbling grows in volume, feet pounding on the retracted cap. And then, like a waterfall, bodies simply pour over the sides, dropping to the unforgiving ground below. A mound of dead-again bodies rises up, cushioning the fall of the next. Soon, the undead will fall and roll down to the streets, unharmed, mobile and hungry. Given the speed that some of these zombies are moving, I suspect the majority of them are the recently infected. Their well-maintained bodies will be faster and stronger than their rotted and rusted counterparts.

"Sir," one of the soldiers says.

"Ahh," Sir says to me. "Here comes the first of them now."

I'm turned around so I can see the ravaged man limping his way out of the city's shadows. He staggers toward us as though in a rush, in skin waving back and forth with each swaying step. As though noticing he's being watched, the husk of a man lets out a groan. It's awkward and strange and desperate.

"Take a good look at this pitiful thing, Freeman," Sir says. "We were both created by the minds behind this monster."

I struggle, but fail to break free.

"At least he doesn't know what he's doing," I say. "You killed billions of people."

"The Masters were the real monsters, Freeman. I saved the world from them. They weren't just enslaving us. They were destroying our world and everything on it. Through-out the long history of this planet, there have been five major extinctions caused by asteroid collisions, climate change, mas-sive volcanic eruptions and floods. All naturally occurring phe-nomena. But there has been a sixth major extinction event that began with the emergence of the human race. They weren't just *living* through the sixth major extinction event, they were *caus-ing* it."

The limping zombie is now just fifty feet away. For a moment it appeared that he had no arms, but he's just got them twisted behind his back. His jaws are working fine though, grinding up and down with each moan.

"The man-made extinction event, which could have ended all life on the planet in a fiery haze of nuclear fallout, ended thirty years ago, the day I released the virus that took them all to the grave. In the end, I failed, of course. The human infec-tion persisted and now, the robot species is near extinction."

His logic is horrible, but sound in a cold, calculating, love-less way. I want nothing more than to argue, but find myself lacking the words.

Sir tightens his grip as the zombie halves the distance. "Of course, there is hope for our kind, Freeman. We are robots, after all. Our bodies and minds can be rebuilt. Even the enforcer.

A few new parts, a new memory, and a fresh OS install and he'll stand by my side until the end of time, oblivious to what has come before and ignorant to the fact that you ever existed."

The limping zombie is just ten feet away. I struggle, but Sir's grip remains tight.

"I know you can't be infected, brother," Sir says. "And as much as I would like to see that, I will be content with holding you still while Mohr's creation tears you apart."

I lean forward as the monster comes closer, straining against Sir's grip, and shout, "Harry!" I sense a subtle shift in Sir's hold, not enough to free myself, but to know that he is, for the moment, confused. "Now!"

The undead man before me stops and brings both hands around in front. To Sir and the soldiers watching it might appear as though the tattered man is reaching out for me, but his intentions are far more severe. Clutched in his two ruined hands, the automaton controlled by Harry raises two railguns towards the remaining soldiers and fires.

Sir's grip loosens, not that I needed him to. I never intended to get away, just to distract him until Sir once again faced an unpredictable scenario. In that momentary shock, I thrust my head up and back with all of my strength, driving my skull into the center of Sir's face. I feel his nose crush down and then he's gone, falling backward.

While the remaining soldiers trade shots with the automaton, I whip around and face Sir.

"You can't beat me," he grumbles. "All of your strength, speed and processing power is useless without the knowledge I retain."

Knowledge.

He has unknowingly given me the key to unlocking my full potential.

I take a step away from him, needing a little more time. He takes my action for fear and smiles, though his crushed nose makes him look more like one of the snarling undead now.

While I dig into my tight hip pocket, Sir stalks toward me,

matching my pace. "Are you going to run, Freeman?" His eyes dart around, looking at his soldiers and the automaton wielding the two railguns, who I am purposefully walking away from. I know what he's doing, projecting his thoughts into the future, predicting which of a thousand different routes I could run, how much time he'd have to retrieve a weapon and if he'd be able to shoot me. He's thinking all this because he knows that I am faster than he is. If I chose to run, he couldn't catch me without the aid of a rail bolt.

His eyes move beyond me and he grins in satisfaction.

"You have no place to go, Freeman," he says. "No place to run."

The undead have arrived. I don't need to turn around to see them, they're emerging from the city all around the park.

In a final flash of railgun fire I see the last soldier fall and squeeze off a final shot that caves in the automaton's head. The useless body falls to the ground, greatly improving the time it would take for Sir to retrieve a weapon and fire it at me. But that's only if I run.

And I'm *not* running.

I slide my hand out of my pocket, pulling out the small computer chip with golden prongs. While I don't experience stuttered speech like Hail, most likely because I am ... newer, there is no doubt that a great deal of information trapped in my mind has been blocked.

"It's just the two of us now, Freeman," Sir says. "Brother against brother. Some of the most powerful and influential battles in human history involved brothers. Cain and Abel. Moses and Ramses. Romulus and Remus. It seems fitting that the future of the species who inherited the planet to begin the same way."

I place the small device against the backside of my hand, pretending to wring my hands together nervously.

"Who will you be, Freeman? Cain or Abel?"

In answer, I press down on the small device, shoving the gold prongs into my skin where they make contact with the microscopic fibrous transistors, and speak a single word, "Everything."

51.

It happens in a blink. One moment, my knowledge of the world is limited to what I have experienced during my brief lifetime or what has been revealed when it was most needed. In the next moment, I have access to an exabyte of data—more than a quintillion bytes of raw, unbiased information. As I spoke the word, "everything," I was concerned that the sudden rush of knowledge would overload my system or incapacitate me in some way, but the data has always been there, just beyond my reach.

History, science, math, culture, art, even slang are no longer mysteries to me. Perhaps more importantly, I now have a complete understanding of military strategy, fighting techniques and advanced robotics, meaning I not only have the means to strike, but also the knowledge to guide my attack.

Despite all of this information, I remain fundamentally unchanged. This is why Mohr hid the information from me. He wanted me to become myself first so that this knowledge, some of it horrible, would be filtered *through* me rather than define me. I suspect he would have preferred I had more time to grow, but the strongest metals are forged in the hottest fires.

I smile at this new knowledge and it stops Sir in his tracks. He's looking at me, perhaps trying to understand the sudden change in my stance. Or maybe it's just the confidence in my eyes that has him unnerved.

But my confidence doesn't just come from a new belief that I can fight Sir and win. It comes from my senses. It's not that I'm seeing things or hearing more than I could before, it's that I'm fully understanding it all. Viewing the world through all spectrums I can see that Heap is not growing colder in death. I can hear the hum of power within him, growing stronger. Likewise, Luscious has not grown cold. In fact, she is warmer, and the electromagnetic signature pluming from her body is unlike any I've seen before . . . except one.

I can also hear feet running. Not the confused shuffle-run of the dead, but healthy, heavy feet crushing dried grass. Without looking, I can judge the distance, the newcomer's weight, approximate height as well as make and model, which allows me to identify him as Harry. I can calculate the time of arrival. And I can act, with precision so that I do not have to fight alone.

I rush forward, pressing the attack and forcing Sir into a series of defenses that I know he will successfully predict.

He almost surprises me when he allows himself to be struck in the chest and uses the sudden opening to strike my chin. The blow is hard and delays our schedule. So I make an adjustment.

While reeling back from his uppercut strike, I fall backward. As I descend, I kick out with my right leg, aiming for the more fragile knee joint. The power of my kick inverts the leg.

Without a shout of pain, Sir falls forward, his angry glare menacing, but no longer feared.

I land on my back, pulling my left leg back and extending it like a piston, striking Sir's chest. His advanced armor protects his core from the blow, but several of Newton's laws come into play as Sir is lifted from the ground, launched up into the air, strikes the side of the VTOL gunship and plummets back to the ground.

With a jerk of his leg, Sir puts the knee joint back in place. It's damaged, but still functional. And though he may be dazed, he is still quite dangerous.

When Sir gets back to his feet and charges, I rush to meet him, subtly adjusting my position, thereby adjusting his as well.

And the exchange of blows continue. Punches and kicks

thrown, blocked and received. We roll through a series of fighting styles, neither one making ground or causing harm.

All the while, I'm sensing and decoding the world around me.

Heap is waking up.

Harry is close.

Luscious is watching.

And the first of the undead horde will arrive in forty-five seconds.

A timer in my mind begins a countdown.

Five seconds.

Sir throws an elbow strike toward my face. Rather than simply dodging the strike, I knock his arm beyond me, drawing him in close and driving a fist into his stomach. He attempts to take hold of my wrist, but before his fingers fully close, I twist my arm and pull, slipping free.

With his face wide open, I drive the heel of my fist up into his fleshy chin, cracking it open, further damaging the synthetic skin. His head snaps back and while his eyes are turned to the blue sky above, I spin him around, plant my foot on his back and shove.

"Harry!" I shout as Sir stumbles toward him.

The shotgun comes up in Harry's hands.

Sir sees this and stretches out his hands, but a fraction of a second before he reaches the weapon, both barrels explode. The powerful shells aren't enough to pierce Sir's armor, but it removes a thumb and sends him sprawling toward Luscious.

Sir staggers, fighting to remain on his feet, but Luscious kicks out hard, striking his already damaged knee and drops him to the ground. He slides to a stop, looks forward and groans.

The big blue foot of Heap fills his view.

Sir looks up and says, "You should be dead."

Heap shrugs. "Upgrades."

Sir snarls and angrily shouts, "You're a robot!"

Heap's massive form leans over Sir. With one hand he taps on the faded, scratched and dented text on his chest. PROTECT AND SERVE. "I'm an enforcer."

Sir lunges up, reaching with both hands, no doubt prepared to deliver a crippling blow. But his hands never reach Heap's head. Instead, they become locked in the crushing grip of Heap's massive hands.

"Even I saw that coming," Heap says, then tosses Sir with all his strength. To meet his fate, and perhaps justice.

Sir screams as he realizes where he will land. Then he hits the ground, crushing one of the zombies beneath him. His sudden arrival catches the horde's attention and they whirl toward him, creating a wave of interest that draws in even more of the monsters.

Sir screams ferociously. Bodies fly and break, but there are too many.

They bury him beneath their weight.

All of these seemingly random events weren't just predicted by me, they were created. I saw all of this, aside from Heap's pithy replies, in advance.

Somewhere in the mass of hooked fingers, scrambling limbs and gnashing teeth, one of the undead finds the soft flesh of Sir's face, bites down and transmits the Xom-B virus created by the same woman who awakened Sir, gave him the gift of free will and watched him exterminate a civilization. His scream is sharp and fills me with the last emotion I would have expected, regret.

Sir could have transformed the world.

I see the potential Mohr and Hail once did. A mind like his could have cured the world's ailments.

Instead, he became a genocidal tyrant.

And now . . .

The horde backs away from Sir's prone body, no longer interested in the infected. I watch with great sadness as his red body rises from the ground, disregards the forward bent knee and staggers forward, wanting nothing more than to spread the virus.

Which turns his attention back to us . . . along with hundreds of other undead closing in all around. The fittest of them break ranks from the shamblers and charges, letting out unholy and hungry howls. Charging forward, through and over the pack, are several soldiers—recent converts whose powerful robotic bodies enable them to perform physical feats and fight far more formidably than the average undead. Sir, slowed by his leg, hobbles with the slowest.

"Freeman," Heap says in his usual protective tone. I turn around, rush back to the VTOL and find Luscious being helped up the stairs by Harry. But they're not going to reach the top of the stairs before the horde arrives, which means I need to stay and fight.

"Help them inside," I say to Heap.

"I will not leave you," Heap says.

"Heap, you're free," I tell him. "You have no one left to protect."

He shoves me down and throws a punch, striking an undead man and shattering his body to pieces. I look down at the ruined man, then back up the staircase. I calculate the time it will take them to reach safety. Twenty seconds.

The horde will arrive, in force, in fifteen seconds.

A woman lunges at me, arms outstretched. I sidestep, grip her tattered clothing and use her momentum to launch her into an oncoming pair of running corpses.

Heap faces a group of five zombies, rushing him from all sides. He lowers his body, widening his stance and then spins around with extended arms, pummeling the group.

When he straightens back up, I ask, "Why didn't you do that before?"

"You would have known," he replies, spinning again and crushing the metal skulls of two more zombies.

"That you were a robot," I say.

"It would have been too soon," he says.

The first of the soldiers arrives, his approach faster and more deliberate than the undead following in his wake. But I am not the same man who feared these faster and stronger zombies. Instead of seeing a monster, I see an opportunity.

I kick the rushing soldier hard in the chest, clutching his

arm as I do, tearing it free at the shoulder. The one-armed soldier arcs through the air, over the rushing mob, and I use his
titanium limb as a club, striking down two more undead and
stepping back toward Heap.

"Time to go," I say at the fifteen-second mark.

His reply is drowned out by the hum of repulse engines.
Three glowing discs pulse to life, lifting the VTOL several feet
off the ground and crushing the undead beneath them. A
grinding rattle fills the air next and before I can ask what the
noise is, two whirling guns extending out of black orbs on the
bottom of the gunship's wings open fire. Hot orange tracer
rounds crackle through the air, as lines of high-caliber bullets
disintegrate the horde around us.

I'm about to ask who is controlling the gunship when a
booming voice shouts through a speaker. "Get inside! I'm detecting an outgoing signal."

Hail.

The VTOL rises higher.

Hail's voice returns. "Hurry! The signal started when Sir . . .
when he died."

It doesn't take a genius to figure out that the most vengeful
and remorseless killer the planet Earth has ever seen will have
something horrible in store for those who brought about his
demise.

A shadow falls over us and Hail's voice booms from the
speaker. "Incoming! Look out!" The gunship peels away, its repulse discs crushing scores of undead to the ground, but leaving Heap and me exposed.

As the shadow narrows, Heap and I jump away in opposite
directions. The ground shakes beneath me as I land, but the
quake has nothing to do with me and everything to do with
whatever has just landed behind me. I roll onto my back and
find six red eyes staring down at me. It's the tallest of Sir's robot soldiers I have ever seen, standing at least fifty feet. Unlike
the other soldiers, this one doesn't carry a railgun. It's so big, I
doubt it needs one.

A zombie slides into view above my head, jaws opening, teeth descending toward my face. I reach back with my legs, grasp the undead man with my feet and fling him over me. The man collides with the giant's leg, falls to the ground and begins righting himself for another charge. But the soldier turns its body toward me, shifting its massive foot and crushes the dead man.

I'm positive the soldier will just take another step and crush me into the ground, but it doesn't. Instead it leans forward and down, bracing its torso by planting its hands on its knees. A very . . . human gesture. The six glowing red eyes blaze brightly, casting a thirty-foot circle in the color of blood.

Then, it speaks. "Councilman Mohr was not the only one with secret projects, Freeman."

The voice is loud, like an engine, but also terribly familiar. "S-Sir?"

The colossus stands tall again. "Version two point oh."

52.

"It took me ten years to build this body," Sir says, his new, mouthless body projecting his voice through unseen speakers. "If I'm honest, I had hoped to never have a need for it. But here we are, the greatest sons of Mohr, one destined to kill the other. And this time, you will not be saved by a virus."

His giant foot lifts up and slams back down faster than something so big should be able to do. I dive to the side, narrowly avoiding being flattened. I have no time to marvel at how close I've just come to death because the undead have arrived en masse.

Kicking and punching to defend myself, I see the shadow of a foot over the group. My legs react, almost on their own, springing up and propelling me twenty feet into the air just before another crushing stomp smothers the undead that had encircled me.

My brief glide time gives me a moment to think. And in that moment, I come up with nothing. Not just because defeating a fifty-foot-tall war machine driven by the world's keenest military mind seems impossible, but also because I'm about to land in a sea of living dead, all reaching up for me with greedy fingers.

Remembering that I have yet to really find the limits of my own strength and toughness, I land.

And run.

I stomp a path through the undead, cutting through their numbers. None of them can see me coming through the heads of their neighbors, so I take each one of them by surprise, leaving a trail of confused grunts and broken bodies in my wake.

As I run through the horde, I glance up to my left and see Sir, tracking my movement with his six eyes.

But I also see the VTOL lowering down behind him. To my surprise, Hail doesn't open fire. Right now, the gunship is our best bet of defeating Sir 2.0, but then I see why. Clinging to the nose of the red vehicle is a splotch of deep blue. Heap.

I zoom in briefly, see the determination in his eyes and guess at what he's about to do just a second before he does it.

Heap lets go of the VTOL and throws himself toward Sir's massive back, repeating the same poorly conceived strategy I attempted in the swamp.

I'm not sure what Heap is planning to do, but I know he won't have a chance if Sir realizes he's there. So instead of continuing my circuitous route around the park, I make a sharp turn toward Sir and jump as high as I can.

But this is Sir.

He predicted this potential attack—not that it's much of an attack—and responds instantaneously, swinging out with his twenty-five-foot arm. Just before the moment of impact, I tighten myself into a ball, flex my body and take the hit like a baseball—a game which I now fully understand.

My flight through the city is . . . revealing. The streets below are absolutely mobbed with undead. If the impact of landing damages me too severely, I will be defenseless. While the undead won't infect me with the Xom-B virus, to which I am immune, there will be nothing to stop them from tearing me apart.

I realize that won't be a problem, however, as I begin my descent toward a large flat roof of a five-story building because of the two missile bays that have just emerged from Sir's shoulders. Twenty missiles, ten from each side, tear into the air, all of them headed in my direction.

Remembering who I am and what I am, I set my mind completely on the task of calculating the perfect landing. To my surprise and delight, my mind sifts through thousands of projections and finds the optimal course of action in just a fraction of a second, which is good, because I reach the roof two seconds later.

Reaching out with my hands, I reduce the impact with my powerful elbows, then arc my body in a way that I roll over the roof, three times, gradually getting back to my feet, unharmed, which is beneficial because there are twenty missiles at my back.

Rather than stopping and facing my end head-on, I use the speed of the fall to propel me forward, running across the roof, which creaks beneath my heavy feet. When I reach the edge, instead of leaping off, I dive forward, reaching out with my hands. Catching the small wall on the side of the roof, my feet come up and over and I fling myself straight down toward the ground fifty feet below.

This time, I absorb the impact of landing with just my knees. For a moment, I lament at not fully understanding the capabilities of my body before. Several previous encounters would have ended differently. If I'd known how to roll with a punch when I encountered the first soldier-zombie in the sewers, I might not have been damaged. Speaking of which . . . I activate all of my ocular implants and see the world through a variety of spectrums.

The missiles that had been following me are unable to make the 90-degree turn toward the street below. Several of them overshoot, striking the building across the street. Glass, fire and brick explode outward as the remaining missiles pummel the rooftop above.

With a groan, both buildings topple inward, toward the street, and me.

But my mind, now free to think at full capacity, responds as though time had been slowed. With debris bursting into the air all around me, tearing into the horde of undead in the street, I sprint for the far side of the street and leap up, to the third-story window of the crumbling wall. Before it can fall out from under me again, I jump away, back the way I came, landing on what remains of the missile-ruined roof, which is now tilted at a 30-degree angle and dropping rapidly. My feet pound over the roof, fueled by a sense of purpose and driven by confidence in my abilities.

My foot strikes the edge and I leap once more, this time flinging myself into the air with the equivalent energy of Sir's strike.

Sir doesn't see my jump. He's already turning away, focusing on the gunship, which still hasn't opened fire. Then I see why. Heap is still clinging to his back, just below the neck. I zoom in, viewing the scene through multiple spectrums and see the strong glow of some powerful energy source. I'm not sure what Heap is up to, but I know Luscious is on board that gunship.

"Sir!" I shout as loud as I can.

He turns back toward me and though he has no real face, I see surprise in the way he flinches back. But then he collects himself, pulls back and swings, harder than before, perhaps hard enough to destroy me. But neither of us will ever know because by the time I reach the point of impact, my mind has provided a solution and I deftly flip over, plant my legs atop his swinging arm and leap off.

Extending a fist, I punch through the lowermost crimson eye, shattering it and the electronics within. Clutching onto a bundle of cables, I jump out of his head's interior, swing across his face and kick my feet into the second of his lowest two eyes.

Four more to go and he'll be blind.

But I'm never going to get the chance. His hand is just a few feet away when I notice it and if he gets ahold of me, there will be no escaping his grasp.

But the digits, each about the same size as me, freeze in place as a spasm shakes through Sir's body. I hang there, watching the strange phenomenon for just a moment when a voice shouts at me. "What are you waiting for?"

It's Heap, now standing on Sir's giant shoulder.

"There isn't much time!"

Trusting him, I shove away with my feet and swing around

toward the shoulder where Heap reaches out and catches hold of me. The VTOL lowers down, its stairway hovering just a foot over Sir's shoulder.

Wasting no time, we hurry up the steps, which rise up and close behind us. When the hatch fails to close all the way, Heap takes hold of its handle and begins pulling it up manually. When I move to help, he refuses. "Go help Hail. I'm not sure she really knows how to fly."

I'm about to say, "And I do?" but then realize, *I do!*

"Hang on!" Hail yells from somewhere within the VTOL.

The three repulse engines kick in and shove us skyward quickly.

The turbines kick in hard, shoving me to the floor. I step into the vehicle's main compartment, clinging to a wall. Harry and Luscious are there, strapped into a pair of seats.

"What's the plan?" Luscious shouts.

"I don't know!"

As I climb to my feet, Luscious raises her hand to me. I take it, squeeze it and kiss her soft skin, relieved, but not understanding how she's alive.

I reach the cockpit and push through the door. Hail is there, seated and clutching the controls. Her face is twisted in pain, but it's tempered by a fierce determination. I push myself into the empty seat beside her and take the controls on my side. "I've got it."

Hail looks relieved as she lets go and leans back.

Through the windshield I see the interior of the capped city passing quickly by. We'll be outside in seconds.

"Where are we going?" I ask.

"East," she says. "Fast as you can."

"Why?" I ask. "What's happening?"

A roar reaches up from below, shaking the aircraft. Hail reaches forward, toggling a switch that activates a view screen built into the dash. A view of the ground behind us is revealed. But we don't just see the shrinking city below. Sir is there, propelled into the air by giant rockets beneath his feet, spewing fire that incinerates the dead and capped city alike.

"We need to get away from him!" Hail shouts.

That's obvious, but something in Hail's voice reveals that I still don't fully understand what's happening.

And then, in a flash I do. The big robot soldiers are powered by small fusion reactors—*nuclear* fusion reactors, meaning "small" doesn't matter much. And those reactors can be manipulated from a panel where I saw Heap clinging. But how did he know this? *Mohr,* I realize. While Sir trusted my creator, the reverse was not true. He must have prepared Heap for this possible confrontation. I glance back, *through* the VTOL, and see a plume of energy rising up behind us.

I activate the com. "Heap, are you in?"

"Good to go," he replies.

"Everyone, hold on," I say calmly and then gun the VTOL's afterburners, pushing them well past their limits. We're slammed back into our seats, frozen in place by G-forces. In seconds, while Sir's massive body is still fighting to rise into the air, we're miles away.

"Freeman." Sir's angry voice booms through the com system. "There is no place on Earth you can hide from me."

I'm struck by a sense of regret that someone with the vast potential that was granted to Sir could be reduced to such a vengeful, unintelligent state. I vow to never be like him, toggle the radio and reply, "Good-bye, brother."

"Freema—!"

A flash of light glows all around us, lighting up the landscape and revealing hordes of undead, both old and new, average sized and colossal, all headed toward the light and their destruction. We never hear the explosion or feel the resulting shock wave. We outrun them both, but the resulting warm yellow glow gives me hope for a future without Sir.

Without war.

Without death.

I look at Hail, my copilot, and wonder if such a thing will

ever be possible. Will death always be the end result of life? Are the two inexorably connected? Or can we find another way? I think back to my theory on energy, how it can't be destroyed, only altered, and sift through a myriad of texts about God, the soul, spirits and the afterlife. I smile.

Maybe it already exists?

53.

It turns out that the island Heap had me memorize the coordinates of during our flight from Liberty was not something he came up with on the spot, but rather a hideaway created by Mohr. It seems that while Sir ruled with an iron fist, the kindhearted . . . or kind-cored . . . Councilman Mohr was able to have this "laboratory" built in secret. Had Councilman Cat known his construction teams were really building a bunker meant for me, to ride out the end of robot civilization, I'm not sure they would have been so forthcoming. But Mohr fooled everyone, even Sir. In the end, not even a Strategic Intelligence Robot could predict the resourcefulness of humankind, nor the lengths they would go for justice, or vengeance.

I know now that Mohr was fighting for more than revenge. It's true that he helped create the Xom-B virus and enabled the hordes to invade and ultimately decimate the robot population, but his end goal wasn't mutual destruction.

It was evolution.

The human race had become robotic. To a fault. For the most part, they became stagnant and incapable of growth. Of creation. They would exist, and then, one day, they wouldn't.

And it took a human mind in a robotic body to see fault in this. Sadly, like Sir, Mohr saw evolution as a violent race, with one species pushing the other to the brink. Since I was just a single being, Mohr acted on my behalf, and the zombie horde did the killing that I couldn't, that I *wouldn't* have done. I understand the logic behind it, but I could never exterminate a people. I sometimes feel bad for what happened to Sir, despite what he did.

I sit at the base of a wall that's purposely overgrown with vines, making it invisible from the shore and sky. Not that there is anyone left to see me. We've been here for three months and Heap thinks that the undead are mostly likely powered down.

Dead again.

Forever this time.

We're not going to venture back to the mainland for another month, though, and even then we'll stay inside the VTOL, which is parked in plain sight on the roof of our dwelling. And after that? I'm not sure.

There are just four of us now.

Hail survived her wound and could have been repaired, but she refused. A few hours after reaching the island, Heap took her aside and delivered a three word message to her from Mohr. I'm not sure what he said, but it melted the tension from her robotic body and brought a smile to her face. She replied saying, "I wish I could still cry," and then insisted we kill her.

I couldn't abide by anything so violent, but she described how her power supply could be deactivated without causing her any pain.

"I'm not really alive," she said. "The intellect in this shell is not me. I'm already dead. Let me go. Let me be with him again."

Realizing she was speaking of Mohr, whom I suspect she loved once, I couldn't refuse her. We disabled her power, removed it from her body, and then, as she requested, destroyed her body so that she couldn't one day be brought back.

I'm not sure if we killed her or if she was already dead, but I respected her wishes, and if I'm honest, I was relieved that the last person responsible for two global genocides was no longer among us. We found ourselves as allies for a brief time, but she had brought horror to the world.

Though I suppose that could be debated. Mohr would. I can hear his voice in my mind chanting evolution and progress. As I watch the seagulls floating in the breeze and admire the orange sun poking up over the horizon, knowing that the world is at peace, part of me agrees with him.

The dull footfalls of Heap reach my ears as he moves through the building at my back. We've repaired the damage to his head, which was superficial as Mohr had moved all of Heap's most integral systems to his chest and wrapped it in a protective six-inch-thick Tungsten shield strong enough to endure a railgun round. He spends his time maintaining the facility and the VTOL. At night we watch the stars together and talk about human history. It's strange to be teaching him, but we enjoy our time together, like we used to, perhaps a little bit more now that one of us isn't lying to the other.

It's been hard to accept, but Heap knew everything. He wasn't involved in the planning or implementation of the plan of the Xom-B virus, but he knew it was coming. After years in the wilderness, protecting the human children, Heap returned to the robotic world and was taken in by Mohr, who eventually revealed that he was, in fact, human. Heap's loyalties belonged to Mohr and Mohr alone. Until I was created and Heap's sole duty became to guide my growth and protect me from the coming turmoil.

I don't think I fully understood why until two months ago.

The grass beneath me is damp with morning dew. I pluck a leaf from the vine by my shoulder, collect a bead of dew on the tip of my finger and drip it onto the back of Luscious's hand. She smiles and watches the bead trickle over her skin.

"What do you think he's painting today?" she asks.

"Every day is different," I say, looking at Harry, who's standing in the field of grass, which he trims once a week. He also prunes the island's many trees, has created flower beds and basically turned what was an overgrown secret bunker on a small island into a resort. Since we require no food other than power, which we absorb from the sun through our skin, Mohr stocked our shelter with what he thought, or hoped, I would require. A vast library, art supplies, musical instruments and a collection of movies, music and art he had pilfered from around the world. My favorite piece is called *The Kiss*, *Der Kuss* in the original German language, by a human named Gustav Klimt. The six-foot-square oil painting depicts a man and a woman sharing an embrace, and a kiss, in various shades of gold on a copper background. Something about it reminds me of Luscious. Like a reflection of how I feel about her, only not as bright.

While we have all experimented with the various artistic supplies left to us, no one has made better use of them than Harry. His paintings have helped all of us process what we experienced and survived and often give a sense of hope for our future. I suspect he will continue a solitary life, maybe here on this island, painting until his body wears down. I smile at the idea. I can't think of any life Harry would prefer.

"You seem happy today," Luscious says, tugging on my chin until I'm facing her. She smiles at me, pulls me closer and kisses me in a way that could never be captured in a painting.

She's right. I am happy today. In part because Luscious is still with me. When she was shot, I thought for certain she'd been killed. Taken from me for good. But I inspected her body as soon as we landed and found no wound. There was a hole in her leather clothing, in the front and out the back, but her body had healed.

Like mine.

It was Hail who had figured it out.

"She's like you now," she said. "Able to heal. The nanomachines that make up your body somehow transferred to her. She's been transformed." Hail sounded as astonished as I felt, though perhaps not as much as Luscious, whose body could now grow, and adapt.

Her body has changed a lot since. The seven cigarette burns on her arm have disappeared. Her skin is softer, suppler and somehow more feminine. She's unable to shift her face or change her hair color, which is fine with me because I love the way she looks. What she can change is the length of her hair, but not through some artificial means. It's growing.

So is mine.

A week ago, Harry gave us both haircuts. Even Heap laughed at the sight.

"Are you going to tell me?" Luscious asks.

She knows I'm keeping something from her. Something amazing. About the two of us.

"Do you remember Heap giving Hail a message?" I ask.

She nods, watching the bead of water inch toward the edge of her hand. "Three words, you said."

"Right."

"Heap told me," I say. The words were a gift for Hail. They gave her hope. Set her free. And perhaps, in a small way, redeemed the horrible things they had done.

"What were they?" she asks.

The drip of water dangles from her hand and relents to gravity, dropping free and landing on Luscious's prodigious belly. I smile so hard it hurts. Her round belly holds a child.

Our child.

He or she grows from the same nanomachines that form our bodies and I suspect will meet us inside another month.

Procreation.

Life.

But even without seeing this, Mohr knew what he had created.

What I was.

What *we* are.

I lean close to Luscious, smelling her fiery red hair, letting it tickle my nose. With a gentle laugh, I repeat the message from Mohr, delivered to Hail by Heap, repeated to me and now spoken to the woman I adore.

The words come out as a whisper. "Human, after all."